# FILE UNDER FEAR

## Geraldine Wall

Books in this series:

*For the countless people who now and in the past have suffered violence from those close to them and for the ones who have helped them break free. Small steps – giant leaps.*

# 2

# Secrets

# 1

Anna thrashed against the rope feeling her nails shred on the tiny ledge of rock. A centimetre of one trembling foot was connected with the wall and the other was kicking blindly against air. It didn't help that Steve and Ellis were convulsed beneath her.

'Don't you dare!' she gasped, 'Don't you dare, either of you!'

'Too late, Mum,' Ellis called up winking at Steve, 'Already gone viral!'

'Not funny! None of this is funny,' she spat at them, 'Get me off this bloody wall now!' She saw a face above her look incredulous and then felt the rope gently slacken so she released the hold and let herself be lowered like a stack of sandbags to the ground. She pulled at the buckles and straps furiously until Steve stepped forward.

'Can I help?' Expertly, he released her.

She strode out of the gym towards the pool. To her astonishment she felt tears prick her eyes and she dodged into the toilets for some privacy. Sitting in the cubicle she reviewed the ridiculous triviality of the incident which had made her so angry and upset. It should have been funny - it was funny to Ellis and Steve. She had been in no danger. Why on earth would she be so affected by it? Something about being constrained by the harness, being expected to do more than she could. She glanced at her watch and quickly got up, left the cubicle and rubbed her eyes, peering at herself in the washbasin mirror. She stuck out her tongue at the owly reflection.

Harry was serenely and slowly swimming laps. His long white body lay inertly in the water, only his feet splashing as his arms lazily windmilled. In the next lane Anna could see Joan's bobbing pink cap as she patiently kept pace with him in a sedate breast-stroke. In about two minutes dozens of assorted children would be leaping in and Harry had to be got out. Anna slipped her shoes and socks off and nodded to the pool attendant, making her way towards the shallow end which Harry was approaching. She crouched down and smiled at him as he lifted his head to breathe. It still made her heart expand to see the answering recognition and pleasure in his face. He reached the edge and put out a cold, wet hand to take hers. Joan joined them. 'Time to come out?'

Together they coaxed Harry across to the steps and then out and Anna led him through the shower, dodging the water herself, and into the attendants' cubicle which they had been given permission to use. Joan had disappeared to get changed. Anna had the towels waiting and rubbed Harry's torso and legs vigorously, bringing back the blood to the skin as he attempted to dry his face and hair. She grinned up at him, her weird mood gone, and gently dried the nest of auburn curls around his penis and even more gently the shaft and head. He did not respond. Did she want him to?

They met the others in the cafeteria. Joan's face was shiny red, her short grey hair clinging to her skull but Steve and Ellis, lounging in their oversized chairs, might have had a stroll in the park rather than a struggle up a fifty-foot wall on the second most difficult route. 'Good swim?' Steve asked Harry, pushing a plate of shortbread towards him. Harry looked perplexed but took a piece as his glance slid off Steve back to Anna. She took one, too. Steve still forgot sometimes about direct questions.

'Anybody'd think you'd actually done some exercise,' Ellis said watching her take it in in two huge bites, 'I don't think being lowered down a wall from about the height of our kitchen ceiling qualifies, does it? Totally OTT – or rather,' he grinned, 'de trop.' Ellis' obsession with words had entered a new phase since starting Year 7 and learning French. Anna knew that Steve was watching her reaction, wondering if she had really been mad with them and if she had been whether she still was. Ellis was giving her a chance to get over the bad-tempered moment.

She laughed, spitting crumbs, trying to look mischievous. 'Next time, I'm going to take you both to my yoga class and film you falling over trying to do Kak Asana - the Crow. Two can play the ordeal by exercise game, you know.' She allowed a flicker of a glance at Steve and saw his expression relax with relief. If she couldn't explain her reaction to herself how could she to him?

Joan had sucked down her hot chocolate and regarded Anna fondly. 'So what's next in the sleuthing pipeline? How about you finding me a long-lost millionaire, now conveniently deceased, who left me all his money?'

'Oh, I've done that,' said Anna, 'but I knew you were far too high-minded to accept so I donated it to a charity for all geriatric eccentrics.'

Joan licked her spoon. 'Lucky George.'

'How dare you,' Anna laughed, 'my father is quite deranged, not merely eccentric.' She wrinkled her nose. 'Actually, I've been given a job that's a bit different. I'm not sure whether to be pleased or not.'

'It's a vote of confidence,' Steve said. 'They're a very wealthy family and Ted's big buddies with the older Mr Draycott – Chamber of Commerce or something.'

'Mm. I suppose. Not very challenging, though, to do a family history, is it? Why me? I'm just a librarian cum probate researcher.'

'You don't see the standard of English that the others have,' Steve said, smiling at her, 'it's not just the researching, it's the writing Ted wants you for. You should be pleased. It could be very interesting. It's not everyone gets that close to the mighty Draycott empire. Play your cards right you could have a lifetime's supply of Drake – the drink to fly by.' Anna grimaced.

Ellis stuffed his paper napkin into his cup. 'Did mum tell you what Pops did last weekend?' They were all too relaxed to even nod or shake their heads. 'Mum and dad and Pops and me were over at Steve's to watch the Chelsea/Liverpool game on Sky sports and Alice woke up. Pops said he would go and settle her and next thing he was out in the back garden with her telling her the names of the constellations. She's only four!'

'He did that with you,' Anna remembered, smiling, 'and Faye.'

'And when I said, "Pops she's just a baby" he said, "She's already seen the sun and the moon. It's never too early to greet the stars."'

Harry reared up and looked from one to the other of them, suddenly agitated. 'Where's George?' So it was time to go.

Outside, they split up. Ellis climbed into Steve's Yeti slinging his bag into the back on top of a pile of ropes and tackle. They would spend the afternoon climbing the Roaches in Staffordshire with Steve's club. Anna watched them leave feeling, as usual, both pleased and sad. Steve was good for Ellis, that much was obvious. He had come into their lives just when Harry was fading out and Ellis needed adult male company but it should have been his father teaching him about rock holds and topography. Harry would have loved to do that. Pointless thinking. Harry was tugging at the locked car door in frustration so she moved quickly across to their old VW. Joan had left already waving cheerfully and promising, 'Next week!'

On the short drive home Harry was silent but she could sense his tension. She turned on some music, a Mozart concerto which was already loaded, but he reached over and switched it off. She had not replaced George in his world, she was an addition. He needed both of them and that was good because she had to work, had to leave him, and George needed some time to himself, too. It *was* good. So much better than how it was just over a year ago when Harry had broken her arm and kicked her to the ground out of terror of her. Now, sometimes the only way she could leave him would be to bring George to sit with him. Otherwise if he saw her starting to drive off he would become so distressed that she would have to return to calm him. The first time it happened she had driven on thinking that he would forget her the moment she was out of sight but in her rear-view mirror she had been horrified to see him flailing and stumbling behind her down the street among the traffic. She hadn't tried that again. As they waited for the lights to change she put her hand over his and smiled at him. He looked at her warmly but his hand under hers was trembling. A loud toot from the car behind made her jump and she lurched forward.

George was in his shed with Ashok brewing up a pot of tea. A battered old tin of biscuits sat beside mugs black with tannin. Bobble was on George's cardigan on the desk, huge paws crossed, completely oblivious. Harry's long body sank down into the battered armchair and within seconds he was asleep, exhausted by his swim.

'We're almost ready to launch!' George announced. 'We've added it to the website and got the first hundred copies ready to stick in envelopes.' He picked up a slim book. The cover showed a door ajar with light coming in executed in a soft focus blue-grey and lemon under the single word, *More* in white. Anna thought the reference was too obscure but George and Ashok had agreed on it. 'More than is dreamed of in your philosophy.' She would never have guessed it, but then, she was not a poet.

'Looks good. Lunch in about an hour?'

It was only when she was sitting at the big square kitchen table making a shopping list that she remembered Alice. She leaped up and pounded the stairs calling for Faye who was the designated baby-sitter. The house was very quiet. Quickly she knocked on Faye's door and not waiting for an answer opened it. If anything happened to Alice Steve would never forgive her and she would never forgive herself. Three solemn pairs of eyes stared at her. One pair was ringed with red and blue glitter. It was an uncanny effect. Like a tot on a child abuse poster decorated with tinsel. Faye was poised with a brush and some purple powder to render Alice even more bizarre and disturbing. The third pair of eyes belonged to Tasha. 'It's all right, Mrs Ames,' she said, 'She wants us to. We're practising because she's going to be a fairy at the nursery. They're having a fairies and elves event. Mum said.'

Anna had a lot of time for Tasha's mum, Michelle. She had been in a horrible relationship with their father but had pulled herself away using her training as a psychiatric nurse to earn enough to keep Tasha and her younger sister and herself and now was also volunteering at a refugee centre. She always seemed to know what was going on everywhere which was certainly more than Anna could boast. 'When is it?'

'Tuesday,' Faye said, 'I'm making her a really cool fairy outfit, aren't I, Lisha?' Faye and Alice gazed at each other in mutual adoration. Alice's wispy blondness and almost translucent skin contrasted strongly with Faye's vibrant caramel and cream colouring. This infatuation had been a big surprise for Anna who hadn't suspected that Faye had a maternal fibre in her being. It had never emerged in her dealings with her little brother, that was sure.

'Great. I'll get lunch on in a bit. It's only grilled cheese and fruit but you will stay won't you Tasha?'

'Is it all right if Nicola comes over, too? Mum's at the Centre today. I know she's old enough to look after herself but –'

'Of course. That will be great. The more the merrier.'

In the kitchen Anna booted up the laptop and opened her home page. Ted had only given her the assignment on Friday and she'd had no time to do any research but Steve's comments had intrigued her. Once she found the right website she started to read. It seemed that the company which made their globally known soft drink, Drake, marketed in lurid orange and green, had always been based in Birmingham. The drink had been the brain-child of Stanley Draycott back in 1873. At that time it had been promoted as a health drink and had become popular in temperance circles and then Stanley's grandson, Edwin, had secured a contract with the War Office to supply the WRVS trolleys and wagons as an alternative to tea and cocoa in the Second World War. Good business move. Its current ISP was to replace electrolites after exercising. She knew, because she had looked, that the ingredients list on the bottle promised nothing but glucose energy and added vitamins but the packaging was sleek and contemporary and the bottle design funky. She had no problem with it. Draycotts employed hundreds if not thousands of workers on reputedly fair wages. There was an archivist, she noted, and a small museum so it should be easy and may even be interesting. Not. She sighed and closed the lid.

She couldn't help remembering her first solo case as a proper probate researcher the previous winter. It had been challenging and the outcome dramatic. Briony Clark! What a tangle of shock and horror that case had turned out to be. Researching a wealthy family's history and writing all that up didn't seem all that thrilling in comparison. But it was work and she should be grateful. In between Briony's case and this assignment she had covered a variety of searches from the straightforward to the bizarre and Ted seemed to allow her a grudging respect now which had not been reflected in a pay rise, she thought with some irritation. She got up from the table and started preparing lunch.

Ted regarded her anxiously. 'Have you got something else? Something a bit -'

Anna glanced down at her fleece and cords. 'I'm only in the office today, Ted. I'll scrub up for Mr Draycott.' He didn't look reassured. 'Can you tell me more? Is it just history he wants or the living family too and is it just immediate family or extended?' Ted rocked on the sides of his feet, his arms folded across his chest. It was his thinking posture and it reminded her of a sturdy tugboat at anchor in a high wind.

'Not sure.' Anna waited. 'I think there's a hidden agenda to be honest.'

'Really?' This was a bit more like it. Ted went behind his desk and sat down to root through a heap of papers. He liked things written down on pieces of paper.

He pulled out a scruffy scrap and looked at Anna sternly. 'Why do you think I chose you?' She opened her mouth to reply but he continued. 'You've shown you can keep a secret.' Anna closed her mouth and did not ask how he knew that. 'I've known Gerald Draycott for a good few years and quite honestly I don't believe for one moment he's interested in the company's family history. They've got an archivist, they could have asked her to do it. He asked for someone intelligent and discreet. Well, one out of two isn't bad.' He grinned at her and checked the scrap of paper. 'I made a note of a name he mentioned three times. I don't think he realised he'd done it. It was his younger daughter, Kimi. There's something about her that's bothering him and I think he wants a bit of sleuthing done on the quiet.'

'But why not just ask for that outright? He knows you well enough to ask for confidentiality.'

'He's a businessman, well, a civil engineer by vocation but he had to take on the family business - he was the only one in line - and he's not the type to shirk his responsibility. He's not a man to delve into motivations including his own. I think that something's bugging him about the family and he doesn't want to admit it, perhaps even to himself.' They were silent for a while but Anna's interest in the job deepened. 'I tried to get a feel for what he wanted, you know, the stuff you asked about, and he seemed quite clear that he wants it to be a study of the current family, not really a history at all. And he's not interested in aunts and cousins and all that. It seems to be that he wants you to get to know his own immediate family.'

Anna felt deflated. 'He wants me to be a spy.'

Ted sighed and looked unhappy. 'I can see you would think that but it's just not the impression I get. I can't put my finger on it. He didn't seem angry or scheming. I think he only asked me because we've known each other so long and he knows I'm not a blabber. He seemed sad and a bit worried.' Ted stood up again. 'I asked him if he suspected anything wrong going on and he immediately denied that. Anyway,' Ted's voice had resumed its normal buoyant tone, 'You like a bit of intrigue, don't you?' Anna looked steadily out of the window and when Ted laughed she made for the door.

Steve was in his office perched on a stool in front of six screens. 'Look at this, Anna,' he said, glancing back at her, 'follow the red dot.' Anna followed the red dot as it stuttered along a satellite-sourced road map wishing the coffee machine in the staff canteen wasn't the only option. 'It's a mobile phone. We've got a trace on it.'

'Isn't that illegal for us to do?'

'Oh, yes,' Steve said happily.

'Then?'

'I'm researching it for a surveillance company contracted to the Home Office. They want to track various people of interest.'

'But surely the people of interest could just leave the phones somewhere or switch them and be untraceable for that time?'

'This works with any phone. The system doesn't need numbers or physical bugs – it hones in on the coding itself. It's all about being ahead of the game. These people are the kind that don't go anywhere without phones and the HO are trying to get the top telecommunication companies on board before someone comes up with blocking technology.'

'But didn't the 9/11 bombers by-pass all that hi-tech stuff by using phone boxes?' began Anna, but she saw Steve's eyes slide past her and noticed the screen go blank. Suzy had come in. There was a second's pause and then she added, 'So Faye and Tasha have got the fairy event all in hand as far as Alice goes.'

Steve smiled easily including both women. 'Should I worry?'

Anna turned to Suzy. 'It's the nursery version of tarts and vicars, they're having a fairies and elves event.'

Suzy groaned. 'Even four year olds have more fun than I do.' Anna laughed and started to leave. 'Please, please say you'll come out with me for lunch, I'm going stir crazy with all these census records. Steve, tell me there's a quicker way to find this aged but still breathing contact before I die of boredom.'

'I'll come by your desk in half an hour?' promised Anna and left smiling, more than ready for a dose of Suzy's company.

At her desk she scrolled through emails just to look busy. She wanted time to think. Ted was right, she did like the idea of getting her teeth into a mystery but she didn't like his none too subtle hints that he had known about her activities in Briony Clark's case. She didn't want him to feel he could push her into dodgy projects by a hint of blackmail. But was it a dodgy job? It could be. Why wouldn't Draycott be up-front with Ted about what he wanted her to find out? Ted's vague psychological explanation sounded woolly and contrived. What would be her position if she found out one of the family was up to no good, maybe even sabotaging the company for some reason? Would Ted expect her to be Draycott's tittle-tattle? Was he setting up the boundaries for her by suggesting that he knew a lot more about what she had done than he had ever admitted? After all, it would have been a sacking offence, no doubt about it, for all that it was in a good cause. Or, was she being over-sensitive, was it just good-humoured teasing that Ted had been indulging in? She didn't know and she couldn't ask. She decided she would just take the job and see where it went. She could always call a halt and ask for a replacement if things got too uncomfortable. She wasn't actually chained to the desk after all. She wasn't Harts' or Ted's slave.

There was still sunshine mottling the front of the house when she got home and one of the upstairs windows was wide open. She stood for a moment on the drive inhaling the smell of damp earth and noticing the first deep blue blooms on the clematis climbing over the shallow arch of the front door. Spring. There was a faint sound of the piano and when she let herself in, a burst of laughter. A good home-coming. One to savour and remember. She pushed the approaching gloomy thoughts away, hung up her coat and went into the sitting room to see who was home.

'Mum, listen to this!' It was Faye at the piano and Ellis at the controls of a sophisticated-looking piece of recording kit. To say the resulting jingle was atonal would be crediting it with a style, Anna thought, wincing.

'That's really horrible, sweetheart,' she said putting her hands over her ears. 'What on earth are you doing and where did you get that, Ellis?'

'Our sound technician lent it,' Faye answered for him, 'I've got to make a soundtrack to edit in to my telly commercial.'

'Oh, right. You mean for the Meerkat Mugger Head Hugger.' Anna had caught up with events. Faye had produced a stuffed toy meerkat mounted on earmuffs as part of her Business Studies A level. The idea was that it cut out extraneous sound so the person wearing it could hear an ipod or similar device better. It was a grotesque looking thing with its silently screaming mouth and huge beady black eyes to say nothing of the massive talons that gripped its wearers' ears but its fantasy-horror appearance had proved slightly commercial, at least among the other sixth-formers. That was to say that Faye had sold a dozen to her friends before her interest in actually making the thing waned. Anna had forgotten that there was this additional element of marketing. Ellis was pushing buttons and the horrible sound was repeated with added distortion. Both of them roared with laughter. 'So how will this help?'

'It's the before,' said Faye and then sensing Anna's bewilderment, 'of the before and after.' Faye's chocolate eyes glittered with creative zeal. 'I've done the storyboard and we'll film it next Tuesday – I can even bring the camcorder home if I need to. I want to get a shot of Pops looking daft with the claws on wrong. It's going to be a montage with lots of jump cuts, you know, fast edits.'

'So where does the before and after and that horrible noise come in?'

Faye pulled up her chestnut topknot even higher. 'The first few seconds will be this noise with people wearing the thing in all wrong ways and looking freaked and then there'll be a cut to someone wearing it right and looking ecstatic, like chilled, and a bit of quiet stuff you know like whale noises or whatever.'

'They could be cross-legged on a cushion meditating,' Ellis added eagerly. 'I can do that.'

'You're not the target demographic,' Faye said curtly. 'Have you got any whale noises, Mum?'

'Gregorian chant?'

'No, you're all right. I'll see what I can find to download.'

Ellis followed Anna into the kitchen and perched on one of the miss-matched chairs. Immediately Bobble leaped up and licked his face with passion. 'Not at the table, Ellis, even if we're not eating. You've got to train him.' She glanced at the funny-looking ragged animal guzzling Ellis and wished she had noticed the size of his paws before Ellis had fallen in love with him at Diane's animal sanctuary. She had a horrible feeling that in a few months Bobble would account for a sizeable drain on their grocery budget. Anna opened the fridge door and stared. She pulled out packages and tubs and put them on the worktop and then added to them from the cupboards.

'Great! Lasagne.' Ellis was a sweet-natured kid but this was pushing it even for him. Anna gave him the grater and a lump of cheese and a breadboard. She began to wash the spinach. All the signs were there that he wanted to talk and probably to ask a favour.

'So how're things? No, wash your hands. You've just been slobbered on.'

Ellis swilled Bobble off. 'Well, you know we should all be keeping fit and all that?' Anna's thoughts ranged over what he was going to ask for. Indoor cycle machine, treadmill, body-building gear, a school trip to climb Mount Kilamanjiro? No chance, mate, sorry. The dull weight of their financial problems dumped itself heavily back on her heart. 'I was thinking about playing tennis now it's spring. You know, maybe I could be good like dad was, sorry, is.' They both let the tactful correction lie. 'I'd rather do that than footie. I like it but I'm crap at it really. I want to be good at something and you can play it all year. The kit doesn't cost too much – I can get whites anywhere cheap and I've got a decent racquet already.'

Anna turned to smile at him from the sink. 'You want to be good at something apart from being top at almost everything in your class?' He didn't look any more cheerful.

'I'm getting a bit of geek stuff. You know, name-calling and things.' Anna stopped washing the spinach and sat down at the table.

'Not from your friends?'

'No. And I know it's just stupid. But I'd still like to have something that isn't brainy, you know? I might get to be a good climber if Steve will keep taking me but I can only do that when he lets me go with them and I want something of my own, like I can do at a club and get lessons.' For a moment he grated thoughtfully. 'Would that cost a lot?'

Anna and her dad never talked about money in front of the children except to say that they now needed to be careful and there wouldn't be luxuries. Faye made her own pocket money working at the Thai restaurant and getting good tips but of course Ellis was too young. He had tried to get a paper round but those jobs were like gold in this neighbourhood. She hated that he had to think about what things would cost but pleased, too, that he wasn't bratty about his needs.

'I don't know, love. Shall we find out? You could google a few local clubs when you've finished that and just see what's involved. I think your dad would be pleased to see you taking an interest. There's cycling as well, he loved that.' As soon as the words were out of her mouth she regretted them.

A month ago, on the first really fine weekend of the year, dizzy with the sunshine, she had pulled her sturdy old bike out of the garden shed together with Ellis' scuffed machine. They had wheeled them on to the overgrown lawn and got busy with the foot pump and the oil can. Just as they were searching for their helmets among a heap of boxes, Harry had appeared. His amber and green eyes, the eyes she had fallen in love with a quarter of a century ago, Ellis's eyes, were bright with anticipation. 'Get my car!' he had demanded, 'Get it for me, please! I don't know where it is.' They knew where it was. It was in George's shed hidden under a carpet. Then he had pulled Anna's hand, beseeching her pitifully, begging her to look for his bike. 'Maybe another day?' Anna had suggested hopefully, weakly. 'No,' Harry had almost shouted, 'Now. I want my – I want it now.' It was awful. Then Ellis had saved the day as so many times before. 'Mine's got a puncture,' he had lied. 'I'm going to take Bobble for a walk in the park and see if there are any rabbits. Will you come, Dad?'

So Anna had put the bikes away and there they had stayed. No-one wanted a repetition of what had happened before Harry's bike had been hidden. He still had the scars on his forearms and knees from the accident that could have killed him if the driver had not been so vigilant. The truth was his finely tuned muscular co-ordination had gone. He could still swim and he could walk and they would make the most of that. The latest MRI scans had shown the inevitable creep of darkness, the hideous ragged edges of a brain dissolving.

Anna shook herself and watched as Ellis finished grating the parmesan. 'Sorry, Ell, I wasn't thinking.' She brought the drained spinach from the sink and sat down with the greased dish ready to assemble the layers. 'Thanks for that.' She pulled the board towards her. 'Why don't you have a look now so we get some info.'

George appeared. 'Ah, lasagne. Good.' Anna smiled. 'I was wondering if I could ask Diane to come over on Friday for dinner. I'll cook. I've found a recipe on the internet using urban foraged products – it looks great.' Ellis dramatized a gagging gesture.

'Where on earth are you going to find that stuff? And don't say in the urban.'

'We're going with a group from the eco-centre to the woods that go along the railway line. There's all sorts of stuff they say.' He had come back to life after meeting Diane, Anna thought happily. His back had straightened and he did up all the buttons on his cardigan. And, of course, the death of Lena had put an end to the spell that wicked witch had cast on him. My bloody mother. Anna closed that door in her mind as so many times before.

'I bet there is. Dad, be careful for goodness sake.'

George picked up the empty feta wrapping and the pasta box and waved them. 'No need for all this – when we have woods and fields and hedgerows packed with glorious local goodies!'

Anna laid the final layer of pasta sheets and tipped the parmesan mixed with mozzarella over it. 'Just as long as we can test it on Bobble first.' Ellis's wail of protest started the dog barking. 'Where's Harry?'

'He fell asleep in front of Flog It,' Ellis volunteered and then hesitated. 'He sleeps a lot now, doesn't he?' George and Anna were silent, quietly laying the table around Ellis's laptop, neither knowing what to say. 'But he seems ok. You know, he seems happier. Don't you think?' Anna smiled at him and checked the oven. It was true. The anxiety, the fretfulness and wandering off had stopped almost entirely. But along with that was deeper withdrawal, another step away. She made herself think about the tennis club and decided to do her own research as well. But Ellis had not finished his train of thought.

'He won't have to go somewhere, will he?' His foxy, clever face was raised to hers, one eyebrow matted with Bobble's saliva. 'We can look after him can't we?' George and Anna glanced at each other and stopped what they were doing to sit down at the table.

'We can look after him for a long time to come, we think,' said Anna honestly. 'Pops is here and now there's Diane sometimes and Joan.'

'And Steve,' put in George. 'Having him and Alice living nearby helps too.' Ellis nodded but still seemed troubled.

'Has someone said something?'

'Melissa at school said her gran got what dad's got and left the gas on and got a bus to Leeds wearing only her panties and they had to put her in a home.'

'Maybe both Melissa's parents work and her gran was living on her own and that was the best thing they could do for her. Some of the homes are great and she might be happy and safe there but your dad hasn't got quite the same form of dementia and there's lots of us around to keep an eye on him and keep him company so we're lucky.'

What a positive and reassuring little speech, thought Anna glumly. Yes, things were working ok so far but the truth was that it was George who was the key person. If her dad hadn't given up his house to live with them and be Harry's prime carer so she could work then what would have happened? And none of them, not even his consultant, knew what course the Pick's disease which was driving Harry away would take and whether they would be able to manage him for the few years he had left. But that didn't bear thinking about. She got up. 'Try not to worry Ell, your dad's not going anywhere if we can help it.'

## 3

Mr Draycott was both smaller and older than Anna had imagined the head of a global brand to be. She was obviously brainwashed by suave actors in tv dramas. Late sixties, maybe? Quietly dressed and tidy rather than stylish but his suit wasn't quite right. It looked a little too big for him. Ted had been at his most genial, even patting Anna on the shoulder as he introduced her. Mr Draycott must be paying handsomely for whatever it was that he hoped would be done. Perhaps she should think about lobbying for a rise? She became aware that her new client was eyeing her closely and tried to concentrate her mind. Lucky that Suzy had persuaded her to snap up the very smart 'day dress' from the discounted rack at M&S obeying her friend's instruction *not* to choose the default black one but a mid-blue that, she was told, complemented her dark hair and olive skin. The only problem was that to satisfy sartorial demands she should suck in her stomach to be flattered by the fitted shape and that was altogether too much like work.

'I've mentioned to the family that you'll be talking to everyone, getting to know them,' he said, answering one of her questions before it was asked. 'I told them that you're working up a piece for a series of articles that's being put together on family businesses. It's a Forbes initiative, the American magazine, but I don't want their researchers coming nosing around. I want Harts to do it and I think you'll be just the job.'

'I don't know anything about business,' Anna said, ignoring Ted's cough.

'No, that doesn't matter. It's more about the dynamics of how a family functions together, you know, how we all keep from murdering each other!' Mr Draycott was keeping the tone light. 'There's a lot of bad press about families falling out when big money is involved but it doesn't have to be that way and Forbes decided to – er – try to find out the magic ingredients in successful enterprises. Of course the Forbes connection is strictly off-record to the general public.' Anna studied the sharp focus of Mr Draycott's grey eyes and decided that she didn't believe a word of it. Ted hadn't mentioned this and she suspected that this was Gerald Draycott firming up a credible cover story. After all, once he had what he wanted, whatever that was, he could always say that Forbes had pulled the series.

'Right,' she said, 'when shall I start?'

Draycott relaxed and checked his phone diary. 'There's a get-together on Wednesday at my house. It's Charlotte's twins' birthday. My older daughter Charlotte. My wife Frances likes to have it at our house and everyone will be there – you know, royal command!' He pulled an envelope from his inner jacket pocket and unfolded two sheets of paper to show Anna. 'This is our family chart so you'll know who's who and then there's the addresses and phone numbers so you can make contact to suit yourself. Just don't wave them around. We're all ex-directory to keep the nutters at bay.' Anna was getting the distinct impression that the family of the head of Draycott Enterprises would do as he told them. Or, possibly as Frances Draycott, the matriarch, told them. She took the information and shook Mr Draycott's hand again as he rose to go. Ted indicated with a minute twitch of an eyebrow that she should leave and she slipped out.

She and Steve walked briskly along the canal towpath that skirted Harts' offices and into Brindley Place through Centenary Square past the stylish new library and on into the central Birmingham shopping area. When Alice had finally come out of the rehabilitation unit Steve had moved to a house near Anna's family for the excellent primary schools which both Faye and Ellis had attended. She would be starting at the Infant School in September. That, like Mr Draycott's story, was the official line. In this case it was true but by no means the whole truth.

Today she was helping him shop for clothes for Alice. Like Bobble she was growing far faster than expected and Steve was bewildered by the variety of clothes available for little girls. Last time they had taken her with them but she had wanted everything she saw and wept piteously and then furiously when she couldn't have it all. It had ended in a full blown tantrum with Alice lying on the floor screaming and drumming her fists. They had both been totally wrung out by the experience and decided that this time they would buy a selection and take back what she didn't like. The car crash that had taken Steve's sister and her husband from their little girl and put her in and out of intensive care for nearly twelve months had had another, unpredicted outcome. Alice was spoilt rotten. Steve knew it and knew he had to bring her back to a normal childhood where she couldn't have everything the minute she wanted it but it would be a hard road. Added to the very natural indulgence that he had shown her while she was so ill was Alice's own nature which was feisty and uncompromising. While Steve was pleased that his niece's appalling early experiences had not left her fearful and withdrawn, he found this imperious little being quite difficult to handle. She reminded Anna of Faye at that age and she sympathised. It was not a chore. Being with Steve was a joy that she held tightly and silently within herself.

When she got home after work she found Harry in the living room staring at a muted television screen. She sat down by him and took his hand. 'Ok?' He opened his other hand and offered it to her. Five pebbles, pieces of pea gravel from the drive, sat there. 'What's this?' she smiled.

'It's so I won't forget.' He withdrew his other hand from hers and picked up one piece. 'That's you, and,' picking up another, 'that's George and these are -'

'Faye and Ellis,' she prompted.

'Yes.' He stopped, looking at the remaining piece.

'Who's that?' Anna put her arm lightly round his shoulder and stroked the coppery brown hair. It still moved her that she could touch him like this when for so long he had not allowed it, believing her to be someone she was not. He seemed sad.

'I don't know,' he said. She felt her heart lurch as she remembered standing near to Steve, making comments on the clothes but also feeling the heat from his body, smelling the spice from his hair.

She picked up the piece and put it with the others. 'It's you, Harry,' she said softly, 'it's you. It's our family. Look we're all together.' Then he turned and smiled at her. Tears pricked at her eyes and she dropped her head to his shoulder, to that familiar hollow where it fitted. By the time she could bear to raise her head again he had fallen asleep and the stones had slipped from his hand.

Anna had tried to imagine a multi-millionaire's house set in the Warwickshire countryside and had swung between bijou castle and modern monstrosity with gold lions guarding the entrance. In fact, the Draycott Senior house was a low-rise, pleasantly sprawling red-brick manor house with discreet additions and beautifully landscaped gardens. The house sat beneath a mound with a dew-pond to one side and converted barns and stables nestling behind it. The old stable-yard was cobbled for cars which could be parked well out of sight of the road. The only sign of their considerable wealth was the high perimeter wall built of old brick and the costly wrought iron gates with their security equipment.

'Made not far from here,' Gerald Draycott told her, waving at them as he met her at the door. 'Feckenham.'

'They're beautiful,' said Anna wondering if she should slip off her shoes on the parquet flooring in the hall. She decided against it. She was more nervous than she wanted to be. Did the family really buy that Forbes story? Had they been told something else? She would say as little as possible and see what emerged.

Two blond boys burst out of the room to her right and grabbed Mr Draycott. 'Gramps! Come on now! We're starting!' She followed the little group into a large room pleasantly edged with low windows and a massive inglenook fireplace. The room was fashionably furnished in muted earth-tones splashed with cream and white accessories and there were landscapes in oils on the walls, each with its own brass light. It was pleasing but it was generic. Anna had expected portraits and memorabilia since this family could be called a dynasty but this looked like any comfortably-off family's room imported straight from a designer's mood board. It was only half a step away from a classy country hotel.

The twins had pushed their grandfather to a heap of gifts loaded on to a large upholstered footstool in front of the fireplace. 'Start now!' one of them ordered.

Gerald laughed but turned to indicate Anna. 'Where are your manners? We have a guest.'

The boys stared at her with considerable hostility. 'Who are you?' the one on the left asked. 'Have you brought us presents?' the one on the right added. It had crossed Anna's mind for one second to bring them presents but she had firmly rejected that as being both unprofessional and unaffordable.

A plump woman jumped out of the depths of a sofa and grabbed them. 'Don't be rude, darlings.' She smiled at Anna. 'This is a business colleague of Grandpa's and she didn't know it was your birthday so of course she hasn't brought you presents. It's not been headline news you know!' Well-handled, Anna thought. She stepped forward and smiled at the boys.

'I'm Anna. Happy birthday to both of you and I'd love to see you unwrap your gifts if that's ok?' She was instantly forgotten. The simple routine of Mr Draycott handing out the packages one by one and then waiting for each to be opened before moving on gave her a few minutes to take in the people in the room. The plump woman was presumably the older daughter Charlotte and the ruddy-faced blond man beside her on the sofa was probably her husband, William. He raised a silent hand to Anna and she warmed to him. He wasn't arrogantly handsome, she decided, he was twinkly handsome. Dear me, she thought, get a grip.

On the sofa opposite and on Anna's left was an older woman who had nodded to her when she came into the room. This woman was far cooler in demeanour than her daughter and son-in-law. Her white hair was cut immaculately in a chin-length bob and tiny lapis globes hung from her ears in perfect symmetry below the severe horizontal of hair. Her face was set in lines which indicated such tight control that there were small tucks either side of her mouth and her pale blue eyes flickered constantly checking the people in the room. After the third gift was opened she spoke.

'Where is Kimi?' she said. Was Anna imagining it or was there a moment of tension in the room? Draycott broke it quickly.

'Be here soon. She phoned to say they'd be a little late. Problem with one of the horses.' Again, Anna had the distinct impression that this was a fabrication for all its reasonableness. 'She said not to wait.'

'I would have thought that she would have made an effort for the twins.'

'Don't fuss, Ma,' said Charlotte the peace-maker, 'it really doesn't matter. They'll be here soon.'

'And where did Richard and his wife disappear to?' Frances Draycott continued. 'They were here a minute ago.' His wife? What an odd way to refer to a daughter-in-law Anna thought. She pictured the family tree in her mind. Richard, the son, the oldest of the three siblings was the heir to the CEO post at Draycott Enterprises, she assumed. She imagined him as a younger version of his father. A fight had broken out between the boys. One had got the latest ipad and the other a G5 phone. Each wanted what the other had. Charlotte tried to reason with them and Draycott stood helplessly watching. The gifts had been from him. Both gifts, Anna felt, were entirely unsuitable for boys who couldn't be more than six years old. She watched with an unsympathetic eye as the boys whined and yelled. There would be tears soon to add to the tantrums. Their father made no effort to intervene but watched benevolently as though they were some-one else's problem. Anna's visceral admiration of him slipped a notch.

'Stop that right now,' said a new voice and Anna turned to see a tall, angular man stride into the room. 'You're acting like spoilt brats.' Even Draycott seemed to fade back a little. 'Here, give them to me. Neither of you is having either of them.'

Quickly, Anna glanced at William to see the effect this intervention was having. Surely he or Charlotte should be doing the disciplining of their children? William looked uncomfortable but not offended. Charlotte seemed almost relieved. The boys, instead of wailing and protesting, sat down quietly and stared at the floor.

'I wondered where you'd gone,' said Frances, 'you should have been here.'

'Sorry Mother. I just needed to make a call.' He sat down in a leather wing-back chair after placing the gadgets on a side table. Anna was astonished to see that neither child tried to argue its case for getting its own birthday present back. Everyone seemed subdued and almost ashamed. So this was Richard. Impressive and a bit scary. Where Charlotte was all yielding curves her brother was sharp lines and angles.

Draycott stepped forward. 'Right!' he said cheerily, 'just one more each and then we'll get some of that amazing cake I happened to notice in the kitchen.' The boys rallied slightly and expressed themselves politely grateful for identical grass-surfing boards.

'Afsoon!' Richard called, 'we're ready for the cake.' Already, before Anna had arrived, a sideboard had been set with a small stack of plates, a silver server, cake forks and napkins. Surely the boys would have a party with other children far less formal than this? Anna made a note to ask Charlotte or William about that later. And then everything was wiped from her mind.

Into the room, her face lit from beneath by candles, came the most beautiful woman Anna had ever seen. Her oval face was turned to pale gold by the candlelight and when she looked up her eyes were the eyes of an oriental queen. Anna found she was holding her breath in amazement. This woman's perfectly modelled face could have appeared in the silk paintings of a mogul princely court. Her hair, black and thick, was brushed back from her face and caught in a simple knot but nothing could have been more elegant. Well blow me down, Anna thought, I hadn't expected this.

Afsoon walked carefully across the room and placed the cake on the sideboard. Her expression was solemn and this gave the simple act an almost religious significance. There was an immediate stampede and the spell was broken. Anna was alone, it seemed, in finding this woman extraordinary. She was as out of place among the Draycott clan as an orchid among daisies.

'Janice?' Frances called sharply, 'the tea!' Then a young woman appeared in the doorway with a tray and in a moment it was all cake-cutting and distributing and tea-cups being passed round and the boys, their mouths bulging, throwing balls of wrapping paper at each other. Taking her own cup and saucer Anna kept an eye on Afsoon. Why hadn't Janice, the maid, also brought in the cake? It was almost as though Afsoon was being placed in the same relation to the family. Over-analysing, Anna chided herself. Wait and see.

After placing the cake Afsoon had walked away from the group to stand by one of the deep windows and was looking out of it up the drive. Anna noted that her figure and her movements were as graceful as her face was beautiful. She was wearing slim black trousers and low heels with a grey sweater that Anna found oddly familiar. It had a distinctive embroidered motif on the breast pocket. Had she seen it in the copy of Vogue which she had glanced through at her dentist last week or maybe it had been worn by a television celebrity? She put down her cup and saucer and walked over to her.

'Hi, I'm Anna Ames. I'm working on a project for Mr Draycott Senior.' Let's see what they've been told, Anna thought. Afsoon turned politely from the window and took Anna's offered hand.

'I'm Richard's wife.' Her voice was low and accented. Anna noted that the woman defined herself in relation to her husband and not by her own name as her mother-in-law had also done and felt hot indignation rising. Her hand was cool and soft but quickly withdrawn.

'Afsoon? Such a beautiful name.'

'I'm Iranian.' The woman turned again to look down the drive. 'Excuse me, Kimi has arrived with Rhea. I must let them in.' Why must you, Anna wondered, is it because you're glad to see them or because this family treats you like a servant? The indignation wasn't going away. Then Draycott was by her side.

'Come and meet my younger daughter and my grand-daughter,' he said taking Anna's elbow, a gesture she particularly disliked.   He seemed anxious for them to meet since he had not introduced any other member of the family and so she eased herself free and went into the hall.

A woman wearing grubby jeans and a flannel shirt was kicking her wellington boots off on the parquet.  A young teenager lolled against the wall watching her mother dully.  She was dressed in deepest black, her eyes ringed with kohl and her face whitened, with talc at a guess.  This was a look Anna was familiar with.  Some of Faye's friends adopted the Goth fashion – usually the more affluent ones – so it was not a surprise.  Kimi was.  If Anna had met her on the street she would have assumed that Kimi didn't have two pennies to rub together.  Her clothes were not simply rather informal for this gathering, they were worn and not especially clean.  Her hair was a mess of dishwater blonde springs crudely pushed back into a band probably hours ago and now almost entirely unconstrained.  Her face was broad and spare and had a weather-beaten ruddiness but the eyes were clear grey and as focussed as her father's.

Draycott stepped up to her immediately, ignoring the girl who must be Rhea, and folded her in his arms.  It was the first sign of physical affection Anna had seen him give but then, she had not been present when the others had arrived.  This might be his normal greeting.  Kimi bore it without complaint but without reciprocating.  Draycott introduced Anna.   Kimi glanced at her with minimal interest.  Rhea ignored her completely.

'Kimi!' came Frances' sharp voice from the sitting room, 'Is that you?  Come and tell me why you're so late.  You've missed everything.'  Kimi made a small attempt to tidy her hair and padded in followed at a distance by Rhea trailing black lace.  William was playing with the boys so Anna was able to sit down beside Charlotte, by far the warmest of the bunch from what she could see.

'Your boys seem very excited by their presents,' she smiled, hoping this was an innocuous but not vacuous remark.

'Oh yes.  Well, children are, aren't they?  Presents are never quite as good when you're grown up.'  Her phone beeped and she glanced at it and then put it to one side.

'I'm working on a project for your father.'

Charlotte laughed.   'Oh yes, the happy family project William calls it!  The thing for Forbes?'  So that was the story they'd been given, too.  'I think you'll find we're a very ordinary bunch – you'll have a job to find anything interesting to say.'

'You all work for the family firm, do you?'

'Sort of. Richard's the main one, of course. He's dad's heir apparent, you know, but William's in personnel and Kimi sort of oversees the accounts people. She's very clever. I'm hopeless with figures.'

'What about you and your sister-in-law?'

Charlotte laughed again, this time incredulously. 'Oh I just run round after the boys – I'd hate to be involved in the business and Afsoon, well,' she hesitated, 'I don't think Richard wants her involved.'

'She's his brood mare, that's what she's for.' Anna turned to look up at the speaker. It was Kimi. 'And his dress-up party doll to impress all the suits at corporate do's.'

'Don't be catty, Kimi, Anna will think we're awful.' So it was an alliance. The sisters seemingly had little affection for Richard's flawless wife.

It was time for her to go and Draycott went off to get her coat. Anna looked across the room to where Afsoon was speaking quietly to Rhea. With a shock of recognition she remembered where she had seen that sweater on sale. It was her local supermarket. Not even a high-end supermarket, just a discount store which also sold clothes. Why on earth would the elegant and beautiful wife of the wannabe CEO of Draycott Enterprises be wearing a cheap supermarket sweater?

## 4

At home Anna sat at the kitchen table and worried over the family budget. The spread sheet seemed implacable. Faye now had a short list of universities which had offered her a conditional place. They had told her that it was her choice but she would also need to be told that if it was away from Birmingham, if she couldn't live at home, then she would need to take the full student loan and work, too. Perhaps they could find a way to give her more independence so that it would be more attractive for her to stay. On the other hand, if she did leave they could do the fiscally sensible thing and downsize their house and release some capital, a possibility that Anna hated even considering. Every time she came home her heart lurched a little with that thought. Luckily, George's offer to teach Faye to drive had meant they hadn't had to find the money for lessons. It had turned out surprisingly well and he had reported that Faye was a sensible and cautious driver as long as she played by the rules and switched off her phone. She probably knew that if she wrecked her grandfather's old Peugeot there wouldn't be another one.

The big unknown was Harry. If he needed nursing care then they might have to sell the house to pay for it. They had no savings now (they had been gobbled up by a new roof and boiler) and there was only her salary from Harts and George's pension together with some small government benefits. She and Harry hadn't worried too much about money with her university librarian's wage and Harry's Head of Department pay but two years ago everything had drastically changed. The rainy day had happened, as so often it does, before it had been saved for.

George came in with Harry, each carrying a couple of hessian bags. 'There was some British stewing beef on special offer,' George announced, 'so I'm making a pie. Will it bother you, love, if I bash around with some flour on this end of the table?' He turned. 'Cup of tea, Harry?' Anna turned, too. Harry was at the cluttered dresser emptying his pockets. He solemnly unloaded three packets of sweets, a toy bone and a pack of hair slides. Anna and her father looked at each other silently.

'Um, Harry.' George moved across the kitchen and looked at the row of objects. 'Where did you get these, son?'

Harry looked surprised. 'At the food place. The shop.'

'I just don't remember paying for them.' George's white wisps of beard were quivering slightly with embarrassment. He looked at Anna helplessly.

'Don't worry, Dad, I'll check the bill and pop in to Customer Services if they're not on it. No big deal.' Harry walked calmly out and they heard the dull noise of the television in the living room start up. 'It doesn't matter. Work your magic with the pastry. Here, I'll move up a bit.'

'I didn't see him do it. I'm going to have to be much more careful.' He put on his favourite pinafore with a canal boat on the front and got out the big yellow bowl and a rolling pin much dented from having been used to knock in tacks when the hammer couldn't be found. Within minutes the savoury smell of meat simmering with herbs and onion on the hob was filling the kitchen and making Anna's stomach growl.

'So have you had any feedback from your regulars about the new magazine?'

He brightened. 'Pretty positive so far especially for Ashok's one about the ghats and the spirits swirling in the mist.' He kneaded vigorously. 'I got a submission for the next issue from Myra, you know she went back to the Cayman Islands now she's retired, well, she wrote one about duppies. She sent it in an email. It's really good.'

Anna folded her arms and smiled. 'Duppies?'

George slapped the dough down on the floured table and waved the rolling pin. 'Yes! They're sort of the spirits of the dead but this is the thing, they look just like them, I mean, you would think it was that person standing there.' He regarded Anna seriously. 'You can't see through them or anything. But when you see the duppie you know that person's died.'

'How would you know the difference?'

'What?'

'How would you know that it's the duppie and not the real person? How do I know you're not a duppie, come to that?'

'Oh. It's a sort of context thing. You would know that the real person wasn't on the island. In the old days before it was all off-shore banking and property developers the local men were brilliant navigators and fishermen and they would go off on quite long journeys sometimes away for weeks across the Caribbean. Obviously there was no way of letting people at home know if there had been an accident - there could even be a hurricane which would wipe out the whole boat but families might now know. You would know they had died if you saw their duppie hanging around in the mangrove or somewhere waiting for you. It would be a terrible shock.' He considered for a moment. 'I don't think the duppies speak, I'll have to check.' George had cut out his circle for the lid and now began to make a series of abstract shapes out of the leftover pastry to stick on top. He glanced at Anna. 'I'm pretty sure they don't make beef and onion pies.'

'Dad,' Anna said, going back to her laptop, 'you need to put the oven on.'

By the time the pie was turning golden brown Anna had researched the three tennis clubs within feasible reach. The nearest one had the highest fees but it also had free places for youngsters showing promise. She had read that there was a dearth of good young tennis players coming through because of the cost of clubs so this was obviously their response to that. Ellis knew how to play and they thought he was pretty good but she had no idea whether he was good enough. If he went for one of these places and didn't get it, would he be even more disappointed since they certainly couldn't afford the full fees? Her phone jingled. It was Steve.

'How did it go?' She didn't seem to be getting any kind of immunity to his voice. In fact, it was becoming more thrilling. She cleared her throat.

'It was quite interesting. All sorts of weird vibes and little tensions.'

'Normal family then?'

She laughed. 'Yup. The daughter-in-law is Iranian – absolutely breath-taking looks.'

'So what's the plan?'

'Tomorrow the intimidating heir apparent is taking me on a swift tour of the factory and offices and then handing me over to the archivist. I don't want to get too bogged down in that. Then I'll see if either William or Kimi has got a few minutes for me – they both work there. I'll just be touching base as they say. The in-depth interviews will have to be arranged to suit their schedules.'

'Any clearer idea of what this is all about?' It was so disconcerting that his voice had the same Derbyshire vowels as Harry. It set up a strange resonance in her.

'Well, they've obviously bought the Forbes story but I get the impression they don't care all that much. They seemed rather distant with each other I thought, except for the sisters perhaps. The mother might be a bit of a tartar.' There was a pause. George was in the hall yelling up the stairs for Ellis and Faye and soon they would all be here. 'Steve?'

'Mm?'

There was nothing she could say. 'Was Alice ok with you taking the other clothes back?'

Steve laughed. 'I didn't ask. I just tucked the ones she didn't try on at once away and they will disappear as if by magic.'

'Good plan. Look, I'll try to stop in at work tomorrow and maybe we can have a coffee and catch up?'

'I'd really like that.'

And that was how things went on between them and there was no way it could be any different. She loved Harry, she had always loved him and even if he was disappearing slowly she was not going to turn away and abandon him. Steve knew that. But it was hard.

George's pies were always welcome. Anna wondered if it was his cavalier way with pastry that made it crumbly and delicious and the meat was so tender it gave itself up in shreds at the first bite. There was silence as they all paid homage with their mouths full.

'How's the video ad going?' Anna asked Faye.

'You can't believe how totally childish Boz is being! All he had to do was sit on a bloody bean bag and look chilled.'

'Isn't that what he does most of the time?'

'Exactly!' Faye contemplated talking through the tasty mound on her fork and then decided to finish the moan instead. 'I only had the camcorder for an hour and he didn't turn up for ages and when he did he just kept giggling like a complete tool the minute I started to film.'

'Can you get someone else?'

'I'll do it,' said Ellis. Bobble barked urgently.

'If you keep feeding that dog under the table he'll have to be put out while we eat,' Anna said. Ellis rolled his eyes.

'No, I want it cool and sophisticated. I can't get someone else because I've already got some shots of him but not enough.' Faye scooped the remaining pie into her mouth. 'Tash has finished filming hers and she's editing it – I could just slap him.'

Harry looked sternly at his daughter. 'If you do, you'll have to pick up litter in the corridors.' It was rare these days for him to make any comment on a conversation and Faye smiled at him and pushed back her plate.

'Ok, then,' she said easily, 'I won't slap him, Dad, or not too hard anyway. Anything for afters?'

The factory and bottling plant had been moved from the original Victorian inner city location and was now the main feature of an industrial park on the outskirts of Solihull. There was also a huge garage to house the company lorries and a separate canteen and recreation area for the staff. To one side of the complex was an extensive car park for the work force and behind that some football pitches which might or might not be part of the Draycott domain. Behind the lorry depot was what seemed to be a social club and car park. Anna drove round to the front of the main building to a visitor bay and turned off the engine. The factory was no more pretentious than Gerald and Frances' family home. She guessed it was a 1950's construction with a modest lobby entrance and no concession to vegetation of any sort. Whatever else they may be, the family did not seem preoccupied with image.

She had expected to have to wait a little for Richard Draycott to see her despite the fact that she was exactly on time for the meeting. It seemed like the kind of thing he would do. But in fact he arrived ahead of her in the lobby and swept her back up into the executive lift he had just vacated. Did he not want her to introduce herself to the receptionist or was he simply efficient in time-keeping? He made no small talk and in a few minutes she was inside his office and being invited to sit down. The office was large but spare and utilitarian. There were framed portraits on the walls of a succession of men. They looked a stolid lot.

'You work for Harts Heir Hunters don't you?' Anna had been expecting she would be asking the questions, but fair enough.

'Yes.'

'I don't understand why my father has hired you. The archivist or a local journalist could have written a profile of us.' Anna briefly considered admitting that she had been puzzled by the same thing but then remembered Ted.

'It may be because your father and the owner of Harts are friends. Through the Chamber of Commerce, I believe.' Richard nodded but the tension hadn't lessened.

'But your usual work is to find people, isn't it? Missing relatives and so forth?'

'Yes.' Anna felt a little more was needed. 'Perhaps your father felt we would be more discreet. We're used to working with confidential material. A journalist might be looking for sensational angles and be less easy to control.'

Richard laughed grimly and for the first time Anna felt him relax slightly. 'You may be right at that. So you suspect skeletons in the cupboard?'

'Most families have them, certainly mine does,' Anna replied easily, 'but no, I have no reason to think that about your family, of course.'

Richard suddenly stood up and walked over to her chair. He was more muscular than she had previously noticed and she felt he was standing a little too close. 'You have to tell me if Kimi, if my sister, confides in you,' he said, and his voice was on the edge of harshness. 'If she tells you who Rhea's father is. I have a right to know.'

Anna could not stand up because he was too close but she straightened her back and dropped her gaze from his face to the window. 'Our contract is with your father,' she said calmly. 'My report will be going to him. What he does with my research and the subsequent article for Forbes will be his decision.' Richard stared at her for a moment and then strode to the door.

'I'll get William to show you round,' he said, 'I have more important things to do.'

Richard's PA took Anna down several corridors and two flights of stairs until she saw the sign for Human Resources above a swing door. On the other side was a large room with a receptionist and administrative workers and through that were several office doors. Anna noted with interest that Head of Human Resources was printed on a different door from the one which simply stated William Grant and on which the PA now knocked. So what was his role?

He opened the door himself rather than calling them to come in and immediately Anna noticed a slightly pungent but not unpleasant smell. The room was full of stuff. Plants sat on every surface and seemed to jostle with each other for space to overflow or stretch up. On a rug in front of the desk was an ancient golden Labrador, now creamy white, steamily contributing to the aroma. It flapped its tail and smiled without expending too much effort. But the most attractive features of the room were the paintings. On every wall were large canvases done in bold abstract shapes and earth colours and the unmistakeable dotting technique of Aboriginal art.

'Come in, come in,' William said warmly, 'I'll clear a seat.' He swept a pile of files on to the floor and pushed forward a swivel chair. 'I was trying to get a handle on these old files, you know pre-digitisation. We still have people even from the 1980's and their details need to be uploaded.'

Surely an administrator could do that, thought Anna, and in any case the job was over twenty years old. 'These paintings are magnificent,' she said, 'are you a collector of Australian art?'

William seemed delighted at her interest. 'No, I've done these. But obviously massively inspired by the Gija artists, people like Queenie McKenzie and Henry Wambiny. I went out to Turkey Creek in the Kimberley in the early '90's and it was a real privilege to meet those guys. I suppose they're dead now, but the art goes on.' He stared at the artwork. 'Obviously my stuff is just a pastiche, well, an homage I suppose. I know a few words of that wonderful artistic language but I've still got to learn the grammar – maybe I'll never manage it. I'm too hopelessly western. I do have some originals at home where security is better. I don't think anyone would pinch these!'

'I think they're beautiful,' Anna said, genuinely admiring them. 'Did you train as an artist?'

'Oh, no!' William seemed astonished that she should think so. 'I was in the army until six years ago and then Charlie wanted to come home and settle. We did move a lot and she got tired of it. Needed a good school for the boys, too. She doesn't want them to board, you see, she wants them to be day-boys.' There seemed to be no resentment or bitterness about his giving up his own career to be part of Charlotte's family concern.

'Was that hard for you?' He looked puzzled. 'Giving up the army?' A complicated emotion passed through his features. What was it? Then the bland good humour was back in place.

'Oh, I joined the local over-the-hill rugby team. That way I can get beaten up and covered with mud as a hobby instead of a job.'

He stood up. 'Anyway, I'm neglecting my duties. Richard asked me to show you round since he's busy.'

Along more corridors and down another floor they came to the doors to the factory floor. William handed Anna a pair of ear defenders. She put them on. The first section was not too bad – it was where huge vats did gurgling things to secret ingredients and it had very few staff. But when they went through the next set of swing doors to the bottling plant the noise hit Anna's nerves like a blow. She adjusted the head piece and decided not to even attempt a conversation. They didn't linger and within minutes they were outside in the yard where a fork-lift truck was shuffling crates on to a lorry which was backed up to a loading bay.

Anna laughed and took off her defenders. 'My goodness, I'm glad we didn't hang about there! How do they stand it? The people working on those lines?'

Well, their protection is actually of a higher standard than these and they can connect them to music or the radio so it's not quite so bad.'

The day had become fine and they were dazzled by sharp lemon light. Anna looked around, squinting. They walked across the concrete yard and into the lorry depot. Anna was relieved that at least William set a reasonable pace since all that she had seen or been allowed to see so far was of very little interest to her. There were three trucks in their bays. One was being worked on by a mechanic, one was being loaded and one was idle. At the far end was a flatbed with a shipping container on it printed with the Maersk logo.

'The lorries usually get loaded in the evening and they're out on the road by around 6.00 a.m. As well as UK deliveries we have a frequent container run to Felixstowe or Bristol – the international business is looking up where domestic sales are dipping a bit, actually. There's not much for you to see at the moment.'

Nevertheless, instead of turning back William walked into the huge garage and knocked on an office door. It was snatched open by a young man wearing a quilted jacket and tight jeans. His hair was gelled back in a yellow swathe and cut very short at the sides. He stared at William for a moment and then glanced at Anna. Another much older and shabbier man was lounging in a beaten up chair by the desk. 'Hi Dook, this is Anna Ames,' William said, 'My dad's hired her for a pet project of his. I'm just showing her round.'

This message was processed in silence. Well, thought Anna, he conveyed quite a bit in that simple statement but what was this young man being warned about?

'You want a coffee? There's nae milk.' Dook indicated a grimy kettle without a smile. What was that accent? Scouse? No, it was Geordie with something else mixed in.

'We'll get something in the canteen,' William said.

As they walked back across the yard Anna wondered why on earth she had been taken across to the depot. No family members worked there, it would be clear to an infant what its function was and so the only reason might be that rather than showing it all to her, she was being shown to Dook. She pondered the young man's appearance. It was his face, or rather the expression on it, which intrigued her. He was certainly good-looking in that his features were regular and youthful and his hair fashionably cut but his eyes, blue-grey and slightly prominent, were vacant, rather like the eyes of male models in glossy supplement advertisements. He missed being truly handsome, she mused, not so much because of anything lacking in his features but rather because of something missing in his personality. She decided to press a little.

'Dook seems young to be depot manager?'

William was dismissive. 'Mm. He's not as young as he looks and it's a straightforward enough job. You just have to be organised with the paperwork and crack down a bit on the drivers if it's needed.'

'So he used to be a driver?'

William pushed open the door to the staff canteen on the other side of the entrance lobby. 'No. He's ex-army. We were in Afghanistan together and when he got discharged he asked me for a job. The old manager was fiddling the stock in transit and I knew Dook was good on logistics because he'd been in charge of that in his unit. So.' Made sense. They went along the line in the canteen and Anna selected coffee and a wedge of lemon drizzle cake. The canteen was not full and it was easy to find a table away from the others. Anna noticed that the woman at the till, like several of the bottling plant workers, smiled easily at William and seemed pleased to see him.

'Do you mind if I ask you a very direct question?' Anna said when they were seated.

''Course not. Fire away.'

'What do you actually do here?'

William threw back his head and roared with laughter. 'Bloody good question. I often ask myself the same thing.' Anna grinned and waited. 'My official title is something like Human Resources Consultant. Daft, of course. It's because I was an officer in the army. The only transferrable skill, and that's in theory, is that you're supposed to be good at getting the best out of the troops. In this case, the workers.' He twisted his lips. 'I certainly don't count myself as one of those.' For a moment Anna thought this remark was class snobbery but then realised from his expression that it was self-deprecatory.

'And do you? Get the best out of the workers?'

He sipped at his black coffee and looked out of the window to the yard. 'I don't know. To be honest I'm more like an agony aunt. It's been a surprise to me, and I wouldn't tell this to anyone, but people do come to me when they have problems. I don't mean pay or promotion or union stuff, HR does all that, I mean they seem to find me easy to talk to about personal stuff. Astonishing.'

Anna studied his profile. He had a pleasant, ruddy face, the face of a farmer or, in fact, what he had been, a soldier on active service. His wavy hair did its own thing within the bounds of a conventional cut. But unlike Dook his eyes were warm, responsive, ready to engage. There was a fully sensate person behind them. His mouth, full and rather flat-lipped, seemed to be congenitally curved into a smile. Yes, she could imagine that this man, who had authority because of his family connection but no real power, would be easy to confide in. Added to his pleasant, non-confrontational style was his gently self-mocking manner guaranteed to put people at ease. Not what she would have expected in a military man but then, what did she know? 'I suppose they realize by now that I can keep a secret, too. That's important.' His permanent smile drooped a little. 'It's just amazing what some people have to deal with. I've become rather close to some of them, oddly enough.'

'And then you have your lovely family.'

William looked startled and then recovered. 'Oh, Charlie and the boys. Oh, yes.'

'And your art, which I really would very much like to see.'

'Oh yes,' William said again, 'we must arrange that. It's not often people are interested.' He paused and swirled the dregs of his coffee. 'Have you talked to Kimi yet?'

'No.' She studied his face.

'You should go out to the farm - the stables. She's different there.' He had turned to Anna and seemed to be trying to decide something.

'Different?'

'More,' he frowned, 'more relaxed, I suppose.'

'She and Charlotte seem to get on well.' Again he looked surprised. 'From the little I saw at the boys' party.'

He picked up his mug and pushed back his chair. 'Mm,' he said, reaching over to pick up her mug and plate, 'possibly.' It was so clearly evasive that Anna almost laughed but it was also quite obviously the end of that particular line of questioning. 'I'll take you down to the archivist. She's a bit of a dragon and she's none too pleased about you doing a thing on the family so I shouldn't hang about there if I were you. Have an excuse ready.' He grinned. 'Or better still, time a phone call to yourself for about four and half minutes from when I open the door. You don't even have to do that. Just pretend the thing is on vibrate and grab it and do a bit of acting.'

'Military tactics?' Anna laughed.

'Yes. Definitely hostile enemy territory!'

The archivist was clearly put out by Anna's presence but not foolish enough to be rude and Anna asked a few questions about the firm's history so that the woman could show her expertise. It's always irritating to believe yourself side-lined and Anna felt for her and did not fake a phone call. She decided to take William's advice and not attempt to see Kimi at work. It was time to go back into Birmingham and her heart bucked as she remembered that she and Steve would be meeting for a chat – just the two of them - so rare these days.

When Steve had bought a house near her family's and installed himself and Alice she had thought they would have many opportunities to be together, innocently, of course. And they were often together but very rarely alone. She could easily manufacture scenarios where this could happen but what would be the point? To say nothing of how unfair to Steve it would be assuming that he was interested in her in that way. Well, assuming he was *still* interested in her in that way. They never talked of their own relationship now. Harry had taken to Steve, enjoying male company of his own age which he now otherwise missed, and it would seem like a double betrayal of the man.

## 5

Anna turned into her own drive feeling irritable and upset. Steve had been, as he always was, calm and amiable. Unknown to most of the others at Harts he had a sideline doing research for the Home Office and sometimes even the NCA. They had picked up on him when he was completing his doctorate in applied physics at Cambridge and when Alice's illness meant he needed a flexible work commitment Ted had offered him that and agreed to let him use the office for his government work so he had given up his lectureship at Aston. In return, state-of-the-art computer tracking systems had been installed which could also be used for probate work. He hadn't wanted to go into theoretical research in any case and was intrigued and challenged by the technological aspects of surveillance. He was, of course, extremely useful to the probate researchers at Harts and was officially their IT guru. Ted cut him a lot of slack knowing his value.

Listening to him chat away and give no intimation that their relationship was anything other than that of friendly colleagues made her crazy. His crystal blue eyes, sparkling with health and intelligence, did not hold hers for a second longer than normal. His curving fall of hair, as full of promise as a freshly turned spade of earth could not be touched, could not under any circumstances be stroked. Sometimes she wanted to scream.

She got out of the car feeling defeated. It was Friday night, poetry night, and that would usually have soothed her but tonight with the sun still shining and everything bursting from the soil in a silent frenzy she felt more like attacking a punch bag.

George and Diane were chirruping in the kitchen like a couple of nesting birds and with a sinking heart she remembered this would be the meal foraged from the disgusting loam which lined the railway tracks. But it was always good to see Diane, she and Joan being her surrogate mothers and so very much nicer than her real mother as it had turned out. She sat down at the kitchen table and rifled through the mail. A postcard from Len, her half-brother, from Hebdon Bridge. She waved it at George and read it aloud. He had been overcharged for his B&B and Ken, their keyboard player, was driving him mad. Situation normal – Len loved a good moan. George remembered he'd left the printer on and rushed out to the shed to check on it and Diane came over to Anna and put an arm round her shoulders.

'Don't worry,' she whispered, 'It's all from Aldi. I made him throw that embankment stuff away.'

'Thank God and thank you!'

Diane's winter apple face put its soft cheek against hers. It was all Anna could do not to sob up a snotty storm like Alice when she couldn't have what she wanted. 'What's the matter, dear?'

'Just tired. I'll go up and have a shower. Where's Harry?'

'In the living room. He's having a good day. He told me that the jet plane is becoming unstable and may bring another ice age. Seemed quite cheery about it. Been watching a documentary. Still likes his geography.'

Anna rose and went out into the hall. She was just hanging up her jacket when she heard the piano but this time it was definitely not Faye. She padded silently into the living room and looked towards the garden end. Harry was sitting on the piano stool playing rippling arpeggios. It had been months since he had shown any interest in the instrument and she felt her spirits rise. She crept closer and he turned and saw her.

'Listen,' he ordered gently. And then he began to play one of their favourite songs. He glanced back at her. 'Come on.' Then he started to sing, 'I don't want to set the world on fire – ' she joined in - 'I just want to start a flame in your heart.' The Inkspots. It was all he could remember and he kept playing it over and over. After a while she stopped singing, kissed him lightly on the top of his head and went upstairs.

'Mum! Is that you?'

She pushed open the door to Ellis's bedroom and took a step back. It was the socks, it must be. Or maybe the trainers. Ellis's friend Mike's room smelt just the same his mum had told her. Faye's room, for all that it was heaped with clothes and bags and other clutter, never smelled like this.     'Could you open a window, sweetheart? It's a bit ripe in here.'

'I know. I love it. The odour of sanity!'

'Very amusing. What are you doing?' Two 2-litre soft drink bottles filled with water were tied with garden twine to either end of a broom handle. Ellis had the stick across his shoulders like a yoke and then bent his knees and lifted it above his head, his skinny arms trembling until he let it down.

'Weight training. If I do this for a week I can add another bottle each side and build up. It's to get me all toned up for tennis.' He was red-faced and determined and Anna regarded him with due solemnity.

'That should do it.' She remembered her research. 'There's a club near here that will take people your age free if they're good enough. But, you'd have to try another one if you don't get in the programme because it's a bit pricey. Is that ok?'

Ellis did a couple more lifts and put the pole down carefully. He stood with his hands on his narrow hips, sweating and breathing hard in the approved manner. 'I know. Hawthorn Road. I've put in for it. I've got a trial next Thursday. They even let you borrow club racquets if you make it. As well as lessons.'

She restrained herself from grabbing him and kissing his flushed face all over. He was such a brave kid and now he had decided on this course he would stick at it until he succeeded or there was no hope. So much like his dad. Now he was eleven hugs were strictly rationed and she missed them. She missed the sweaty pungent limbs and sticky hands and the smacking kisses he had given her when he was a child. Nowadays no-one kissed her. She pushed the thought away.

'Great. Good for you. Let me know if you need a lift over or for me to come with you.'

Ellis thought for a moment. 'Yes,' he said, 'that would show family commitment wouldn't it?' He grinned and the word-lover was back. 'It would be apropos, n'est ce pas?'

'Freak!' Faye shouted from the landing and crashed her bedroom door shut. In seconds Lordi was shaking off the plaster and Anna got her own work-out getting Faye to put a sock in it.

After dinner Anna found she was just too restless to sit quietly and listen to poetry with the others in George's shed. Ashok had arrived with a couple of young men he had met at the temple and invited along. They were first year medical students from Bangalore and one of them was of sufficient interest for Faye's eyes to brighten. That meant that with Diane there would be eight people and a shortage of seats so George didn't protest when she said she needed a walk.

After going a few yards down the street she realised she needed to get further away and turned back to the car. On the back seat was the folder with contact and address details of the Draycott family members and she flushed with annoyance at herself for being so careless with the information. The car could have been broken into or even stolen. She had been in so much turmoil after seeing Steve that she could have breached confidentiality. She had to focus, she had to be more careful. It wasn't that the information was top secret so much as that it was not made known. Mail, she knew, went to a PO Box and was ferried to family members by Gerald Draycott's PA. Phones were all encrypted and each house had discreet state-of-the-art security. It was not their style to have flashy protection, they seemed to prefer the camouflage of being unremarkable.

Glancing through the papers to check they were all there, Anna noticed that the intriguing Kimi was the most rural. Why not? It was still light and would be for an hour or so. She checked the village location on her Great Britain Atlas and saw that Kimi's farm lay beside a famously pretty stretch of the Grand Union canal. As nice a place as any for an evening stroll and if she pressed on she could be there in half an hour.

The sky was beginning to turn turquoise and the rolls of evening clouds were darkening in their centres as Anna stopped in a pub car park by a brick and stone bridge over the canal. Already the laughter was volleying out from a group of drinkers huddled round a canopied table, flopped dogs at their feet. There were steps down to the tow-path and she walked quickly in the direction of Kimi's land. It should start less than half a mile along on her right hand side. The warmth of the evening had brought out some cyclists on the path calling to each other along the glittering water and walkers who murmured greetings. She pulled her hands out of her pockets to get a better swinging pace and felt her spirits rise. The fullness of the fresh green in the hedges, the wide sweep of the sky and the muted splashing from moorhens were just what she needed. What was it Harry used to say? We must have beauty. Yes. It was the end of a very long winter and spring was really here.

Every now and then she glanced to her right and checked the field boundaries marked by hedges and tractor trails. When the trees were dense she made guesses. After a while the bank to her right, which had been cut off from the path by a deep ditch running parallel to it, became a solid earth bridge leading to a gate. She turned off the path and walked the few metres up the rise. The gate was padlocked and had a 'Private – No Trespassing' notice. Clearly not a public right of way so she could go no further. Anna wondered about the horses Kimi kept. Were they valuable or was it some kind of refuge for neglected beasts such as Diane ran? Either way she supposed they would not want strangers tramping about, especially ones who may be up to no good. She climbed as high as she could up the rungs of the gate wishing yet again that she had been blessed with a few more inches and peered across the rolling fields.

There did seem to be some kind of building in the far distance but it was in a hollow and only chimney stacks could be seen. Nearer, the roof of an old caravan pushed into the wooded corner of a field was partly visible behind some kind of fencing but no signs of life. Standard farm fare. A couple of fields away and on the far side of the copse Anna could see some animals grazing which might well be horses. Or cows? Surely she could tell the difference even at this distance. She squinted at them. No. Then she realised that it wasn't the distance that was confusing her, it was the light. Habitually she turned her head to look at the sky and saw that not only had the sun gone but the red sky that followed it was now a dull pewter. She glanced at her watch and climbed down to return to the path. It had really been a wasted journey but she had enjoyed it. Being out of the city, away even from her family, much as she loved them, and most of all away from Steve. Having Steve so near and yet so impossibly inaccessible set up a tension in her life that she was going to have to find some way of controlling or enrol in Primal Scream classes.

The path was deserted and she picked up her pace looking around for walkers but seeing no-one in the gloom. She began to feel slightly anxious. It was stupid to be out this late on her own in an unfamiliar place. To reassure herself she glanced over her shoulder and her heart started to thump. A man was walking behind her, maybe forty metres away, his features indistinct. She tried to remember how far she had walked from the pub and saw that the way the canal turned she would be out of sight of anyone at that end for at least another quarter mile if not more. No houses could be seen anywhere and the light was draining away by the second. It would be foolish to run and in any case he would almost certainly be able to out-run her. She felt in her pocket for her phone and almost sobbed. It was in her bag locked in the car. She hadn't planned to be out so long or to have gone so far. Stupid, stupid.

She kept up her pace but took some deep breaths. He was probably just some innocent guy coming to meet friends at the pub after a busy week. Just because it was a man did not mean he was a threat. Breathe. She felt her keys and without taking them out of her pocket threaded them through her fingers so that the points stuck out between her knuckles. Lucky her old car had a pointed key not a modern stub and there was the Yale from the front door. The back door was hopeless and the others were too small to be any use. That gave her two sharp points to jab at a face. Breathe. She could hear now the crunch of his feet on the gravel of the path behind her and willed herself not to look round. In a moment or so he would pass her, maybe call out a brief greeting to reassure her or maybe not, men didn't know what to do for the best these days did they? Breathe. Then he would be past her and it would all be over and she would never, never make such a stupid mistake again. The trees were now a continuous black silhouette but there was perhaps a glimmer of orange light behind them? Not breaking her stride she moved slightly to the left of the path so that he could easily overtake her. Now she could hear his breathing and her heart was banging fast.

On the few occasions in her life that Anna had contemplated being attacked by a stranger and had idly thought how she might defend herself, she had always pictured the attack coming from the front. Face on. She would scream loudly and chop him under the nose as hard as she could with the side of her right hand so blinding him with tears and pain and simultaneously jerk up her knee to his groin.

But it was not like that. The first thing she felt was her throat being crushed by an arm across it and then a blow to her back had her on her knees. In a second her arms were shoved painfully up behind her and she was pushed full length, face down in the dirt. The arm across her throat was released and a huge hand was across her face, bearing down so hard on her mouth that biting was impossible. Now he was straddling her back pinning her arms down with his knees and with his freed hand he was pulling at her jeans. He was grunting with the effort of keeping her writhing body under control while he tried to get access but no word was spoken. Her knees were grinding into the grit of the path and his fingers dug into her face.

Now she knew she was going to be raped she fought mentally to be calm to minimise the damage to her body. She would try afterwards to see him, when he was at his most vulnerable –just a glimpse of his face and she would never forget. Perhaps she could bite him for the DNA but no, there would be plenty of evidence of DNA without that. She forced herself to drag in a breath through her nose and picked up the smell of cigarettes and manure on his fingers. Maybe engine oil, too. Farm worker? From Kimi's farm? He was scrabbling now to undo her leather belt, the buckle trapped under her. He had lifted his weight enough to get his hand beneath her waist to pull on the strap and she bucked and twisted as much as she could and then she felt the shocking punch of his fist to her head. 'Bitch! Keep still!' The blow exploded her thoughts and pain howled into the void with a ringing like a fire bell.

And then he was gone. She was lying face down on the path and she was alone. Lights appeared and there was someone calling, 'Are you ok? Can you talk?' She raised her head and saw, like an old friend, the half hoop of a shining bicycle wheel and on the path beside her someone in a helmet was kneeling with a water bottle in a hand. 'Here, drink this.'

They held her up between them as she limped towards the pub trying not to sob. No, she hadn't seen his face, no, she would not be able to recognise him from his clothes. It had all been so quick. That's what they all say, but it was true. It had been so quick. She began to shake and one ran ahead so that when they reached the laughter and good-humoured shouting of the pub a quiet room had been made ready and she was helped into it. Tea was brought and first-aid given. She was cleaned up as far as possible and advised not to drive. She kept thanking them but all she wanted was to get into her car and get away as fast as she could and finally, promising to make a call to the police, that's what she did. It had been just one and a half hours since she had left home. Afterwards she had no memory of the drive back.

She crept painfully into the hall and listened. Thank God. No sounds. From the kitchen she could see the light on in George's shed and she hastily scribbled a note to say she had decided to have an early night. Climbing the stairs she had to haul on the bannister to make her stiff legs and aching back work. She would be all right once she could get into the bathroom and close and lock the door. She made herself detour to pick up her dressing gown and then, panting with relief, she closed the bathroom door behind her. Gently she eased off her shoes and socks. The knees on her jeans had been shredded by the stones on the path and she bundled them up to take back to her own room. Groaning, she pulled her jacket and then her T shirt over her head. Finally she stepped out of her panties and bra and put everything apart from the jeans into the laundry basket.

She stood up carefully and examined herself all over. Her knees had been stuck to the denim with blood but the scratches weren't deep and the stones had been eased out by the kind people at the pub. She looked in the long mirror turning her body slowly. Livid red patches showed all over her flesh where his hands and knees had forced her down. There would be serious bruising tomorrow but all that could be hidden by clothes.

The punch to her head had left her with a faint ringing in her ears and she lightly touched the place and then winced. Very sore. But nothing visible and no blood it seemed. Then she looked at her face and tried to brush away the dirt around her mouth and cheeks. She couldn't. So those bruises would need an explanation. Bruises positioned in a very distinctive pattern with four deep purple circles in a parabola on one side of her mouth and one, larger circle on the other. For one mad moment she considered making more bruises so that the hand print wouldn't be so obvious but immediately ditched that idea.

She couldn't let them know what had happened. It was too shocking, too stupid, too embarrassing and shameful and too horrifying. What would she have done if she had been raped? She had always assumed that she would instantly report it and go through the trauma of a trial, of course she would, no question. Perhaps she wasn't as brave as she had thought.

She ran a deep bath and sloshed lavender oil in and then slowly, aching in too many places, lowered herself into the water.

## 6

Usually Saturday mornings were fairly quiet but on this one everyone was in the kitchen when Anna, fully dressed in her most comfortable sweater and leggings, came down. George was reading the paper and crunching toast and Faye and Ellis were managing to slurp cereal and text at the same time. Harry was laying out a line of blueberries punctuated by a raspberry at intervals on the table.

'Woah!' Ellis said and everyone turned to look. Anna had decided that to try to cover the now black bruises with make-up would look worse so she smiled and cheerfully popped two pieces of toast in the machine. Thank goodness there was still half a pot of coffee to go at. 'Mum, what happened?'

'Have you been in a fight?' asked Faye, thrilled at the possibility. 'What about? What does the other guy look like, ha ha?'

'Very funny,' said Anna cheerily, 'and I'd like to live up to your lurid fantasies but what happened is very mundane I'm afraid. Just let me get some coffee.' She walked to the table and sat down without groaning only by exerting every fibre of self-control. 'You know I went out for a walk last night?' They nodded. 'It was a really lovely sunset, you know. You should have had a break from the poetry to look at it.'

'Mum!'

'Right. Well, I drove for a little way down to the canal by Edgbaston and strolled along next to the narrow boats and there were some volunteers cutting back the hedges so I watched them for a bit and then asked if I could help. They needed some more weight to get a shrub disentangled from some barbed wire.'

'They must have been thrilled when you volunteered.'

'Thanks Ellis and less of it. They could clearly see I was fit and strong despite my petite and slender frame.' She grinned and a spasm of pain shot up her jaw. Did she have a loose tooth?

'Anyway, I gave it a really good yank just when the others had seen it had come free and I tumbled over on my back but the pruned stumps of the branches smacked me in the face.'

'Anyone get it on their phone?'

Anna pretended hauteur. 'No, and thanks for the concern from my nearest and dearest, no-one. These were *adults* not horrible teenagers.' The toaster popped but she realised that she would be unable to chew anything hard. She pulled cornflakes over to her and tried to lift the packet. No good. Too sore. At least she had her coffee.

'Mum, can I go with Mike and his dad to the game this morning? It's an away at Balsall Heath.'

She nodded and then stopped. It made her head surge with pain. 'Where are you off to so early Faye?'

'Tasha's mum says can we go to the Centre today because they're having a jumble sale and they need help. Should be a laugh.'

'Good. Great. Dad? Are you off on a jolly with Diane?' Saturday and Sunday were his official days off from looking after Harry and she fiercely protected them for him.

George had retrieved her toast and was loading it with butter and marmalade. 'What are your plans?'

'I'll take Harry to the Sports Centre as usual –' She stopped. Joan would be there and there would be no disguising her badly bruised body if she had to get into a swim suit.

George put his toast down untasted. 'Joan phoned. She's got a very bad cold and can't come. But I can.'

'No need, Dad, we'll be fine.' She smiled at Harry. 'Shall I get your swimming stuff?' Harry stared at her for the first time. He had eaten his berries one by one and seemed unaware of the previous conversation.

'You've got dirt on your face,' he said.

'No, sweetheart. I just had a little accident. Let's go and swim some laps, shall we?'

Harry stood up. 'I have to go to the upstairs. Don't want another little accident.' Had he made a joke? Was that the ghost of a smile? Anna beamed at him just in case.

George stopped playing with the toast and gently prevented her from getting up to follow Harry. 'OK Annie-get-your-gun, now we're alone. What really happened?' She stared at the grain on the table. He had used her pet name from when she was a child and in a rush she remembered the countless times that her only parent had consoled her and mopped up her tears. 'You can hardly move without pain, can you? And those bruises have a pattern and it's one I've seen before.'

'Have you? When?'

'Never mind. Just tell me, please.'

So she told him and he sat with his head bowed for some time in silence. 'Do you need to see a doctor?'

'No Dad,' she said quietly, 'I think I'm past the danger of concussion and that blow was the only serious damage – I'll heal.'

'Do you want me to call the police?'

'No. I've thought about it. I couldn't give them any identifying description because he made sure I always had my back to him and he ran off before the cyclists could see him. It was dark, too. There would be endless questions and reports but none of it would be any use.' George nodded slowly.

'I'm sorry to say I think you're right. It would be pointless.' He stood up. 'I'll make another pot of coffee. Could you manage to swallow some cornflakes if I pour some warm milk on them?' She almost sobbed with gratitude. An absent-minded dreamer he may be but when she needed him her dad knew exactly what to do. While she was sucking gratefully at the sweet mush he stood staring out of the window. 'You may find that you get a bit shaky later,' he said. 'I'll take Harry swimming today and you pop along back to bed for a bit. I could do with chasing the moths out of my natty swimwear.' Anna felt like crying with relief.

'Did you remember to darn the elbows?'

'Cheeky madam. Get up those stairs and don't worry about lunch because I'll take Harry over to pick up Diane and look at the new arrivals, he'd like that, and then we'll all go and check on Joan with some bacon sarnies from the caff.'

'Dad, I shouldn't let you, but thank you. And I've got the number of one of the cyclists – I'll give him a ring to thank him when I wake up.'

George scrabbled in his beard. 'Everywhere there are angels,' he said. 'What kind of a world would it be if there weren't? Get some rest.' She didn't even protest as he started to clear the table and again she needed to haul on the bannisters to get up the stairs but this time, she would sleep.


Surprisingly, it was Afsoon who was the first to answer Anna's group email requesting visits with the Draycott family. Perhaps she had to the least to occupy her time.

Richard Draycott's house was very different from his parents' and much grander. To get to it Anna had first to negotiate the security system and then make her way along a curving single track drive until, behind a plantation of cypresses and Scots pine, the house presented itself in a self-congratulatory way. It was squarely built of pale stone deeply stained and elaborately porticoed with four windows on either side. Round the roof was a parapet with knobby pineapples set into the corners. A small Palladian mansion, in fact. No flowers were visible anywhere but a rather streaky classical statue stood on its pedestal in a pool of dark green water between the trees and the gravel sweep to the front door. There must be garages and outhouses and so on at the back. It was built to impress and perhaps for that reason failed to do so. In the baking heat and searing light of an Italian hillside it might have looked splendid but here, in damp England, it had more than a suggestion of a monument littered Victorian graveyard. No other cars were visible.

Anna's old VW crunched its way up to the colonnaded front and stopped and she peered in the rear-view mirror to check her appearance. The short curly hair had taken a bit of getting used to after the mad-Cleopatra look that had crept upon her and so upset Harry but now she quite liked it. It had been days since the incident by the canal and the facial bruises had faded past yellow to the point where she could now cover them with make-up. She had not told Steve and wasn't sure why except that she still felt ashamed about the foolish risk she had taken. Yes, of course women *should* be able to walk anywhere alone at night but that utopia was a long way off. She had, for once, dressed carefully in a dark tailored dress and jacket – the funeral and job-interview outfit jollied up with red patent heels and bulky red beads.

She almost expected a butler but Afsoon opened the door herself and immediately Anna felt ridiculously over-dressed. Afsoon was wearing washed out denims and a mist grey T shirt and looked stunning. Anna followed her through to the kitchen where the taller woman indicated two large wicker basket chairs by the French window. 'Do you mind being in the kitchen?' she asked gravely. 'The other rooms are so gloomy at this time of day.' Of course Anna didn't although it would have been interesting to see something of the rest of the house. Maybe she could ask later. As before she noted that Afsoon wore no make-up and her hair was twisted into the same simple knot and yet her beauty continued to mesmerise. It was not just the huge dark eyes or the regularity of her features and the creamy smoothness of her skin, it was the way her head balanced elegantly on her delicate neck and the straight-backed grace with which she moved like a dancer.

As she made coffee Anna glanced around. The kitchen was large and functional although not modern; Anna guessed that the last update would have been around 1990. She was at a loss for how to find some neutral way of starting a conversation since Afsoon had said nothing for several minutes. Set on a low table in a corner was an elegant chased silver jug with six small glasses, intricately engraved, around it. The tray itself was silver inlaid with copper and brass. From the shape of the jug she would have thought it was for coffee if she hadn't seen one very similar in Steve's house. 'What beautiful tea things,' she said, 'are they Iranian?' Afsoon turned to her quickly, her face alight with pleasure. She was even more dazzling when she smiled and Anna couldn't help a moment of awe.

'Most people don't notice or think they are for coffee. I bought them in London but they are from Fez in Morocco. They are antique.'

'Ah, that explains it. I have a friend who has a similar set although not so exquisite and he got his in Marrakesh.'

Afsoon carefully set a tray with cafetiere and delicate cups and saucers down on a low table and seated herself. 'Has your friend ever been to Iran?'

Anna so desperately wanted to talk about Steve that her first instinct was to cut the line of conversation off but why? It would be such a pleasure, and useful too, to build rapport with this woman. 'Yes! He said once that Isfahan was one of the most beautiful cities he had ever seen.' Afsoon's deep brown eyes gazed attentively into hers. 'He's a climber,' Anna went on, 'he goes to countries where he can climb but he loves Islamic art and architecture.' Afsoon took a small sip of coffee and then nodded at Anna to continue. 'He brings back rugs and all sorts of things but not really expensive ones.' She remembered the glowing splash of colour that had hung on the wall of his flat before Alice had come to live with him and he needed a family house. Her eyes had rested on it as he had held her in his arms. She wrenched her thoughts back to the present. 'He does have a silk prayer mat which is one of his most prized possessions.'

'This man is your lover?' Afsoon said neutrally.

Anna froze. Had she revealed something? Had she been too engaged, too bright-eyed talking about him? 'No, no! He's a just a friend, well, and a neighbour now. No, he's a work colleague.' She was beginning to gabble and forced herself to stop. 'I'm married.'

Afsoon looked away. 'Yes, there are many beautiful artefacts which people in the West love to own. It's why I came to London.'

Anna was profoundly grateful to her for moving the conversation away from herself and even giving her permission to open a line of enquiry. Afsoon was insightful but considerate, too, she decided. Or possibly she just had good manners. 'Really?'

'Yes, I came as an intern to Sothebys to see how the great auction houses work here. It was nearly two years ago. My degree was in Middle Eastern antiquities and I wanted to set up an auction house in Tehran. You will remember there was the looting of the museum in Babylon by the Americans and others during the war in Iraq. People are interested in retrieving their heritage from the West much as the ex-patriot Russians and Chinese are doing.' She stopped and peered out of the window at the flowerless borders and dark hedges. Her expression was tense like a small child wondering if it was safe to cross the road.

'But you stayed here?'

'I met Richard. He had come for an art sale. The late Lord Breedon's collection.'

'And he saw you and fell in love!' Anna exclaimed before she could stop herself. How could any man not fall in love with this queen of a woman? Afsoon sighed, leaned back in the deep chair and crossed her long legs.

'Well,' she replied, smiling in a way Anna couldn't label, 'Richard likes to own beautiful things, too.' She let a couple of beats pass and then added, 'So the Modiglianis were irresistible.'

'So you chose to give up your own plans?' Anna thought about the two encounters she had had with Richard and badly wanted to ask if it had been worth it but that was impossible.

Afsoon put together the coffee things on the tray and stood up looking at Anna very directly. 'Sometimes life takes a different direction from the one you have planned, don't you find? Sometimes choice is an illusion.' She turned and walked across the room to place the tray next to the sink.

Anna knew that no more could be said on this topic, Afsoon had clearly closed down, but she wanted to keep some kind of conversation going so she asked about the Modiglianis and whether she could see them. 'I'm afraid not. They are not in the house. Richard keeps all the valuable art in vaults in London if they are not being loaned to museums somewhere. His pleasure is in owning them, not in looking at them.' Again there was that mysterious expression. She sat down next to Anna.

'So there's a lot of interest in art in this family.'

'What do you mean?'

'Well, William and his Aborigine art and now Richard and his post-impressionists.'

Afsoon looked genuinely puzzled. 'William? You mean Charlotte's husband?'

'Yes. He told me he has some original work at home and he has an office full of his own paintings inspired by that genre.'

'Does he?' Afsoon seemed mildly astonished. 'I didn't know. He is such a military and rugby football man I had not considered he might have an interest in such things.' She was silent for a moment and then asked Anna, 'Have you seen Kimi yet?'

'No, she's away at a conference at the moment and then has the auditors in so she said that it would have to be next Saturday afternoon. It's the only time she has free.' Why was everyone so interested in Kimi? 'Do you see much of her?'

Afsoon dropped her eyes to her hands. 'No. I don't. I think she does not have time for women friends. Sometimes Rhea comes. I have a little dog, a Llasa, Beulah, and Rhea likes to comb him. They were temple dogs, you know, but here people cut their hair and make them ugly.' She sounded sad.

'It must be hard for you so far from home. Do you go back often?'

Afsoon stood up and folded her arms. Anna noticed the platinum and solitaire diamond engagement ring and the wide platinum wedding band designed to fit to it. Cheap clothes maybe, but very expensive jewellery. 'No. I don't go back. Why would I when there is all this.' She was retreating without moving a muscle and Anna wondered why. Did she feel she had revealed too much or was she simply bored by Anna's attempts at friendliness? Did she feel that Anna had no right to ask about her feelings being, as she was, merely an employee of her father-in-law? For whatever reason Anna had no option but to leave as composedly as she could. The moment had passed to ask for a tour of the house but now Anna felt sure it would not have been granted. Afsoon had kept her conversation and her visitor within carefully patrolled limits.

As she drove away Anna tried to process what she had learned from this visit about Gerald Draycott's family. Afsoon, his regal daughter-in-law and potential mother of his son's heir, was lonely. That was obvious. Also, the marriage with Richard seemed unlikely to have been a love match on her side given the coolness with which Afsoon had described it. Richard himself was hardly over-affectionate from what she had seen at the twins' party. But, there was nothing unusual about a wealthy and powerful man choosing a trophy wife. Perhaps it was Afsoon's motivation in marrying him that was more mysterious. In London and Tehran she must have moved in a sophisticated world where many rich men would have found her attractive and had far more cosmopolitan glamour and social excitement to offer. The Draycotts were certainly wealthy and established but their life-styles seemed curiously drab.

## 7

Charlotte had invited Anna to lunch which meant that her outfit could kill two birds with one stone. She found herself looking forward to seeing yet another Draycott house and finding out more about the family. There was a voyeuristic pleasure in seeing how the rich live and slightly despising it which she disliked in herself. Perhaps this was what sold celebrity gossip magazines – the smug schadenfreude of witnessing the suffering of the gods. When she saw that Charlotte and William's house was a large modern building within clear sight of the road she was unsurprised. There seemed to be little mystery about them. To get to it Anna drove through an exclusive suburb of substantial 1930's houses each set in its own shrubbed and lawned domain and loosely clustered around a church opposite a gastro pub and dress agency.

The house was full of light from huge contemporary windows and inside the furniture was an eclectic mix of minimalist modern and older pieces. Clearly Charlotte was not a woman to be dictated to by interior designers. The living room, into which she showed Anna, was forgiving of dropped coats and there was a messy pile of magazines. Such a contrast from the restricted and controlled atmosphere at Richard's Palladian mini-mansion. Anna almost kicked off her shoes but remembered that this was not a social visit. Three large sofas were arranged in an open box formation which would be perfect for chatting groups. Anna glanced round the room expecting to see the pieces of Aborigine art which William had mentioned and which the large plain walls would happily accommodate but they were not there. Instead there were a couple of forgettable generic abstracts. Charlotte came in with trays. Even more informal, then, than Anna had expected.

'Sorry I've not had time to knock up anything special,' Charlotte said breathlessly, 'the committee meeting went on far too long, the chair is so feeble. I think a meeting should run to time and people should be lashed along to keep to the matters in hand!' Her laughter mitigated the critical words and Anna smiled too. Charlotte fished a phone out of her pocket and placed it on the coffee table by her side. 'Now then, fire away!' She picked up her sandwich.

Anna decided to try to modify this business-like approach. She would not get at what ever there was to be got at by a straight question and answer session. 'Actually, I saw William in his office last week and he mentioned he had some original Aborigine art here at home. I suppose it's too valuable to be on show in the main rooms?'

Charlotte laughed merrily and stabbed a cherry tomato. 'Oh no. I just can't stand those daubs. Poor old Willie, he likes to think he can dabble himself and of course that stuff is easy to copy.' Anna's warm feelings towards Charlotte cooled abruptly.

'I thought they were pretty powerful, I mean, William's paintings.'

'I hope you told him that, poor pet, he would have been thrilled.' The phone did a jig on the smooth surface of table. Charlotte leaned forward, chewing, and studied it briefly. Then she pecked the reject button.

'I was wondering how you two met, if that's not too personal a question.'

'It was a hoot! Real knight in shining armour stuff.'

'Really?'

'I'd just finished uni in Bath and some girlfriends and I decided we would have a jaunt to celebrate. We were all a bit sporty so we thought we'd do a spot of para-sailing up in the Lake District – friend of a friend had opened a centre – you know.' The phone jiggled. 'Oh, do you mind, I have to take this, won't be a mo.' Anna hated this form of rudeness but was hardly in a position to protest. She finished her sandwich and rose to take the tray into the kitchen while Charlotte gave instructions to someone.

It was another large light room fashionably equipped with streamlined units and appliances. On one wall was an extensive cluster of family photos, block mounted, and Anna was impressed by the skill they revealed. Instead of the ordinary grinning and posed snapshots she had framed of her own family, these captured spontaneous moments with almost lyrical lighting and cropping. They were tender, affectionate and skilful.

'Sorry!' Charlotte called from the living room and Anna returned. 'I had to take that, it was the fund-raising committee for widows and families of fallen soldiers. I've promised to organise a silent auction for them.' She chuckled happily. 'Never a dull moment.' Anna sat down and assumed a listening pose. 'What was I saying? Oh yes, Sir William the White Knight! Well, to cut a long story short the place wasn't as well-supervised as it should have been and one of my pals got into trouble. She landed badly well away from any road and broke her leg in two places. The centre called in the Search and Rescue lot – you know, the one Wills joined for a while, but this was ages before. Well, down from the sky came *my* little Willie on a rope! Turned out that the army and the RAF were doing some joint exercises.' Charlotte laughed again, the story clearly often repeated in her circle. 'Scooped up poor old Krista and they rose together into the jolly helicopter like a scene from a Hollywood blockbuster. We dashed for our cars and met her at the hospital and Willie was still there so of course I fell at his feet. So dashing.'

'And you became an army wife?'

Charlotte brushed crumbs from her bust. 'Yes. Fun for a few years travelling around and all that but when the twins were about to come into view I said enough's enough. So dad found him a job in the family firm and here we are.'

'Was William ok with that?'

Charlotte looked hard at her. 'Why wouldn't he be? Not everyone gets such a cushy number surely?'

'But does he miss the life do you think?' Anna knew she was pressing on the edge of a socially acceptable level of curiosity but she hoped it would yield something.

Charlotte's mouth drooped and she looked, for the first time, less than comfortable. 'It was the right time to leave. Things were happening. It wasn't the right place for him any more.' Anna thought of the dates. If the twins were six then she was looking back to a time when fighting was going on in Afghanistan. Was that the reason?

'What was his job in the army?' And that turned out to be one question too far.

'How can this possibly have anything to do with what my father is asking you to write?' Charlotte demanded. 'You want to know how this family has kept this company going for so long, don't you? Well, we keep our heads down and mind our own business.' Anna had no doubt that the meetings she ran went like clockwork. The affable, merry Charlotte was the public face of a woman of steel - or concrete. They both stood up.

'Sorry, but just one more thing,' said Anna, amused and not at all intimidated. 'Do you have much to do with the business or is it just Richard and Kimi, and William, of course?'

Charlotte relaxed slightly. 'I keep track. We all have shares, of course, and one likes to know how they are doing. Dad is about to step back and Richard will take over and that will be the best thing for the firm. We don't need sentiment in these challenging times.'

'How do you mean?'

'I don't want to say any more. Not to just anyone.' The insult was so clearly intentional that again Anna had an impulse to giggle rather than be offended. 'I must get on.' So, thanking her for lunch, Anna left.

Instead of driving home she turned towards the city centre and the offices of Harts. She needed to do some research and the archivist at Draycott's could not be involved. As she drove she mused sadly on how Charlotte had turned a professional rescue of her friend into a comical incident. Her referring to her husband as 'my little Willie' was an absurd and crass joke but one which rolled so easily off her tongue that it must be much used. What had William done or not done for his wife to show such ill-disguised contempt? She remembered the scene at the twins' birthday party when Richard had disciplined them and William had been ignored and had not seemed even to take offence. She had liked the big self-deprecating man she had met at the factory and couldn't make sense of it. But then, she had liked Charlotte, too, before today.

Steve was perched in his usual position before a bank of screens. He was glad to see her. 'To what do I owe this honour?' he asked. 'I thought you'd be hobnobbing with the county set.'

'A bit of sleuthing, please. But I don't know if you'll be able to do it.' She seated herself on a swivel chair next to his.

'How rude. You know I can do anything.' He grinned at her and she had to laugh.

'I mean, I don't know whether you'll be allowed. I want to look at the service record of one of the Draycott family. Well, family in-law. It's William Grant. He left about six years ago from this regiment.' Anna passed Steve a piece of paper. He began to type.

'What do you want to find?'

'Anything really. Reason for discharge mostly and about his time in Afghanistan.'

'Unless it was a dishonourable discharge, very rare for an officer, I don't think we'll find much but I'll look.'

Anna pushed her chair back a little, ostensibly so as not to crowd him but really so that she could sneak glimpses of him unobserved. She was behaving like a schoolgirl with a crush. Only a few months ago it was Harry she missed and longed for – Harry's touch that she wanted and that she couldn't have. Now, ironically, when Harry was easy with her, it was Steve who was beyond reach for very different reasons who dominated her head. 'Well, the regiment definitely did some tours in Afghanistan but I can't find any more detail. Just a minute, let me try something else.' He tapped again and peered at the screen. 'It seems that he did two patrols on the first tour and after that didn't leave Camp Bastion. Um, wait, yes, when the regiment returned he resigned his commission. He'd been made up to Major so that's unusual. Something does seem to have happened out there or immediately after he returned but it's hard to see what.'

'His wife got pregnant and wanted him out, they both said that. Maybe that was it.'

'Um.' Steve gazed at his hands with an expression Anna had come to understand.

'You're thinking something. What is it? Can you find out more through your other work, you know?' She lifted her eyebrows at him hopefully.

'That would be completely unethical and unprofessional and you didn't ask me to do it.'

'Right.'

'No, what I'm thinking is that one of the guys I climb with was in that regiment at about the right time. I could dig a bit, maybe? I'm not seeing him for a while, not until the trip to Norway, and this isn't the sort of thing you can email about.'

'Well, I'm grateful for anything.' Anna allowed herself to lay her hand lightly on his forearm. 'Got time to go out for a cuppa?'

'Believe me, I'd love to but I can't. You're well out of it at the moment. Ted's taken on a really complicated probate search and we're all conscripted. It's interesting but full of knots. Millions of legacy involved.' Disappointed, she got up to leave but Steve stood up too. 'Are you ok? You look a bit stressed.' And amazingly he had his arms round her in a soft hug. He was warm and safe and gentle and her knees almost buckled beneath her. 'Take care of yourself, love.' She stumbled away to find a toilet cubicle, the only place she could be alone, and let the moment sink in.

Faye's concentration was impressive. Her eyes were fixed like lasers on the fingers of her left hand spread out on a piece of kitchen towel. Her right hand was making careful strokes with livid green varnish. Ellis was opposite, equally absorbed in the Lawn Tennis Association rule book. At the end of the table Anna was also focussed, in her case on remembering to double the Madeira cake quantities so that the mixture would fill the large heart-shaped cake tin she had hired for Len's birthday surprise. Poor sod. Hopefully it would make up just a little for the countless birthdays their feckless mother had blown off. She knew from past disappointments that doubling or halving recipes too often led to disaster if any interruptions broke the flow.

'Mum?' Faye spread out her hands and studied the emerald green nails. The Centre people were having an Irish event and since green suited Faye's chestnut colouring she had willingly agreed to dress up in a hastily put together leprechaun outfit.

'Mm.'

'Tash and me're really worried about Nicola.'

'Mm.' Had she put three or four tablespoons of caster sugar in?

'She's being weird.' Faye slid the brush back into its bottle and snapped, 'Mum!'

'Just let me finish – '

'This is really important! Mum, can you listen?' Anna gave up and sat down. Faye was impossible to ignore. 'You know she's only fifteen? I mean that's just a kid but she's acting like a slag.'

'Faye! I'm sure she's not and that's not a good way to talk about -'

Ellis looked up. 'She is, Mum. You should see her when she's not in her school uniform.'

'Michelle wouldn't let her go round like that.' Anna glanced at the recipe trying to remember where she had stopped adding ingredients. 'Tash always dresses in jeans and sports tops.'

Faye groaned and arched her back. 'That's what I'm saying. Nicola isn't like Tash. She's getting out of control and her mum doesn't know. She keeps special clothes and make-up for when she gets away from the house and changes in shop toilets.'

Anna started to pay attention. 'Why? Is it just the clothes or is something else going on?' Nicola had always been the feisty one of the two sisters.

'There's some older guys that hang round the Centre – I don't know, I suppose maybe in their twenties, you know, like old old and she tags along with them a lot. She wears a lot of make-up and she acts flirty, you know? I don't think she knows what she's doing.'

Anna thought. 'But surely Michelle notices?'

'Nic doesn't meet them at the Centre, there's a club down the road and she hangs round there.' Faye tipped her chair back and tugged up her topknot. 'Me and Tash told her she's being an idiot but she doesn't listen.'

'Do you want me to talk to Michelle?' Anna's heart sank but if the situation was reversed she'd certainly want to know.

'Yeah. Great, I was hoping you'd say that. Can you lend me £10 until I get paid? Is your purse in this bag?' And within seconds the transfer had been made. Faster than online banking Anna thought wryly. She stood up and tried desperately to remember where on earth she had been in the recipe. She rubbed the mixture between her fingers and decided that the sugar had been added. She could always adjust the taste by an extra thick layer of icing.

'How's it going?' she asked Ellis when the beaters had stopped. 'All set for tomorrow?' Then Bobble appeared at the open back door, tail waving ecstatically, with a limp rat in his mouth and that was the end of that conversation. She'd phone Michelle later.

## 8

It was at the Hawthorn Road tennis club that she got the call from Gerald Draycott. He asked her if she had seen Kimi yet and she explained the situation and said she would be going to the farm in a couple of days. Ellis was out on court knocking around balls with the other young hopefuls. For a second she was distracted by watching him as his long thin limbs bent and straightened, whirled and dropped and the thick clumps of coppery hair flopped around his face. Harry must have looked like this, must have been full of hope and determination. Now he was more and more like an old man. He had begun to shuffle a little, to stoop. Bloody fucking unfair Anna thought for the millionth time. Why him when he had so much life still to live? But then she heard Harry's voice when he had first been diagnosed saying calmly, 'Why *not* me?' Even when he was staring oblivion in the face he had been rational and brave.

'After you've seen her I'd like us to meet,' Gerald was saying and she dragged her attention back to the conversation. 'You'll have met everyone then? To talk to a little I mean.'

'I haven't had a conversation with Mrs Draycott, I mean Frances, your wife.'

Gerald's laugh was dry rather than warm. 'Oh she's been keeping track, don't worry. Have you got a meeting booked?'

'Yes, on Tuesday we're meeting for coffee. She'll be in town and of course it works well for me.' The youngsters were being put into pairs to play and Anna leaned forward to wave at Ellis and give him a thumbs up. He pretended he hadn't noticed.

'Can you see me Monday afternoon?' There was a pause. 'Not at the factory or at my house. I keep a flat in the city centre near St Paul's Square. I'll email the address. About 4.00?' Anna agreed and lowered the phone. There was something in his voice that intrigued her. He sounded as though he had something to say and that it would be something confidential.

Ellis smashed a difficult high lob and got the point. She noticed the officials huddled at one end pointing to him. After a couple of games new partners were assigned and they played on. Ellis managed to get in one ace serve but then was wrong-footed on a passing shot from a blonde girl. Again the partners changed. This time Ellis was with a bigger, tougher-looking kid who glowered at him. She saw Ellis pull himself up and start to dance on the balls of his feet gently passing the racket from one hand to the next as he waited for the serve. She smiled. He was enjoying himself. His return skimmed the net and a puff of chalk announced a perfectly judged spin. Whether this club took him or another, their boy had talent and, more to the point, was having fun. Her phone pinged. It was George who had just arrived with Harry. She got up and slid past the other parents so that she could meet them at the back and watch the rest of the trials with them. The Draycotts were forgotten.

Saturday turned out to be a perfect spring day. The Warwickshire hedgerows were foaming with new leaf and the ditches and banks were piled with rich green dashed with pink and yellow and white. It was all she could do to keep her eyes on the road and off the sky where torn white tissues of cloud rushed silently across the sparkling blue. Cumulus fractus, she said out loud for the pleasure of it. The earth clapping its hands and shouting for joy. She hadn't forgotten the canal-side incident but its impact had faded. It had been frightening at the time but no real harm had been done. She pushed the memory away. Steve had invited Harry round to watch a Liverpool/Villa game so Anna hadn't had to break into George's time off. He and Diane were up to something – they were getting more and more like mischievous kids these days. No doubt all would be revealed eventually.

She made her way as slowly as she dared down the single-track lane to Kimi's farm. It seemed a shame to dull the day with yet another cold Draycott interview. Ahead she could see a gateway half-hidden in the hedge and drew in for a lungful of air. The wind whipped her hair about as she got out of the car and she raised her face to the sun. A woman's voice was calling. Anna went to the gate and looked across the field. Kimi was there on one end of a long rope calling rhythmically to a horse that was circling her at the other end. In her right hand was a coaching whip but she was only pointing with it. The horse, gleaming with sweat, was politely bounding around its allotted path as slowly as Kimi was asking. It looked like a rocking horse on wheels the action was so restrained and disciplined, the knees raised high and the neck arched, the lifted black tail so long it was catching in the grass. Both woman and animal were totally engrossed. After a couple more circuits Kimi lowered the whip and relaxed the rope and the horse immediately stopped and raised its head looking straight at Anna, ears pricked.

Kimi turned and saw her and gestured towards the house. Anna waved and got back in the car.

There was no security on the gate so she drove straight into the farmyard. Kimi was leading the horse up a narrow path from the field and Anna parked well away in a corner.

'Come and meet him!' Kimi called.

'He's gorgeous!'

'Yes, he's a beauty. Jesse. Do you know Morgan horses?' Anna shook her head and tentatively reached out for the steaming neck. There were flecks of foam on the glossy brown chest and buttocks. Anna thought of how she felt in a tricky yoga pose. Doing things very slowly could be quite a work-out. 'They're quite different from racing stock. Look at the arch on his neck. Perfect for dressage – well, perfect for everything really. It's an American breed. I bought Jesse from a stud in Connecticut.'

'He looks like the horses you see in old paintings of kings and princes – they always have very pretty long manes and tails. The horses I mean. Well, sometimes the riders do, too.'

Kimi smiled and laid her face against the horse's cheek until he nudged her. 'Well, some people think they are an old English breed that we kind of lost track of.' She turned and shouted, 'Kevin!' From the stable yard behind the farmyard a man emerged and walked stolidly towards them. Anna stiffened. No, he was too short. He took the horse's halter without a word and turned back to where he had come from. 'Can you walk him a bit? We've only just finished.' Kevin raised a hand in acknowledgement without turning. Kimi watched them go. 'Look at the muscles in those hind quarters,' she said admiringly and then turned to catch Anna grinning. Kimi laughed too. 'I think we know to which rear end I refer-' And, unexpectedly, they were almost friends. Anna couldn't imagine having the same joke with any of the other Draycott women.

'So Kevin helps here?' They were making their way across the yard to the back door of the farmhouse.

'Yeah. He came with the farm, actually. But I kept him on when I saw how good he is with horses – they really like him and he seems to know what to do by instinct. He lives here actually. He's got a caravan down towards the canal and he's rigged up a generator he told me so he can watch the football. There's a dog guards it. I've never seen it, dogs and horses don't mix in my opinion.'

The kitchen was large and functional. It was also cluttered and barely clean. There were pictures of horses on the walls and one of Rhea with her mother. Kimi did not go to the kettle, she went to the cupboard full of wine bottles and poured them both a glass of red without asking.

'Do you show the horses?'

'Yup. We're going to an American Saddle-bred Show in Moreton Morrell at the Agricultural College next month. He's going into the three-gait and I've got another, just a colt, going in for the One in Hand. We do all right. I don't keep all the stuff in here, the trophies and rosettes and all that, they're in a cupboard. It's what Richard would do – you know, look at me, aren't I something special.' This was said without any special rancour and Anna sensed that this was a habitual sisterly tone.

Anna leaned back in her chair and took a deep drink. This felt good. She really must go and see Michelle and have a girly chat. 'He is rather commanding, isn't he?'

'Asshole.'

'Do you and Afsoon see much of each other?' Anna was remembering the interest that Afsoon had shown in Kimi both at the boys' party and in the conversation in her house.

Kimi snorted. 'No. Why would I? I can't think of one single thing I would say to her or her to me.'

'She just seems a bit lonely.' Was she pushing it?

Kimi looked bored. 'That's what happens when you marry someone for their money.' She took another drink and then re-filled her glass. It was three o'clock in the afternoon. Anna covered her own with her hand. 'Driving.'

'So,' Kimi cupped her chin in both hands, 'what's your story?' Anna was so unused to any of the Draycotts expressing the slightest interest in her that she was taken aback for a moment. Kimi was thirty-one, Anna knew that from the notes, but her fresh complexion and blown-about long wild hair made her look much younger. Rhea was thirteen. She was much more interested in Kimi's story than in telling her own.

'What do you want to know?' Kimi raised her eyebrows in a 'duh' expression Faye might have used. 'Oh, well, married, two children, daft father, dafter dog.'

Kimi smiled and looked away from Anna, staring out of the window over the yard. 'What does my father really want?' She raised her glass to her lips. '*He's* not daft and he's after something.' Anna smiled back and said nothing. 'Is he doing a King Lear?'

'I'm sorry?'

'You know, which of my offspring loves me most so I can leave it all to that one.'

'That plan came to a rather sticky end, didn't it? I mean for the father. Well, for everyone really.' Anna traced her finger round the rim of her empty glass and took a gamble. 'Actually from what I've seen it's pretty clear that you're his favourite one.' Kimi's smile abruptly closed down and she emptied her glass. There was the click of a latch and Rhea came in. Today, instead of the black lace and Emo make-up she was wearing what appeared to be a gold bridesmaid's dress which had been drawn on with thick felt tip. It was fairly filthy. Kimi tensed and beamed at her.

'Darling.'

Rhea opened the fridge and stared gloomily inside. 'Why is there never anything to eat?' Kimi leaped up and pulled plastic containers from one of the shelves.

'Here. Linda made these up for you. Look. Do you want one now? I can stick it in the microwave.'

Rhea looked at the container resentfully. 'Has it got red stuff in it?' Kimi peeled back the lid.

'No, look, it's all white. It's just pasta and cheese.' She pleaded with Rhea, 'Let me heat it up for you, Precious, you've had nothing all day.' Rhea groaned and looked at Anna.

'Who's she?'

'She's working for Gramps. We're just chatting.' Kimi pulled out a chair. 'Why don't you come and join us and eat something?'

Rhea sat down still staring at Anna. 'I've seen you before,' she said.

Anna and Kimi glanced at each other. 'Well, yes,' Anna said gently. 'I was at your cousins' birthday party the other day.'

'Not then,' Rhea said dismissively. 'At the club. The tennis club.' To place this eccentric girl in the context of a suburban sports club was a stretch.

'Really?'

'You were with a boy. He was trying out.'

Kimi visibly relaxed. 'Oh right. Yes, Rhea's good at tennis – she hates team sports – but then so do I. Gramps signed her up at the club a couple of years ago and they're saying she could really compete.'

Rhea got up from the table as though too weary to move. It was hard to imagine her leaping around smashing aces. 'I'm going upstairs. I don't want to be disturbed.' Kimi helplessly showed her the food again and then put it back in the fridge. Rhea made her way out touching furniture on the way as if she couldn't trust herself to stay upright. Spoiled? Depressed? Or just teenage angst?

'I have a teenage girl,' Anna said.

'Nightmare,' Kimi agreed and re-filled her glass.

'Do you see much of her father?' Anna asked casually. It would, after all, in a normal world be a normal question. She wasn't asking for Richard, she was being nosy on her own account. Kimi's reaction was unexpected. She burst out laughing so violently that she choked on her wine and had to mop herself up with a grubby tea-towel. 'Not a good question?'

'I think it's time you went.' Kimi wasn't angry, in fact, she was still chuckling. She waved her wine glass at Anna. 'You're going to have to do much better than that, Vera, if you want to hear the skeletons rattling, and I have to get the colt in from the field.'

So Anna went. But at the car Kimi touched her arm. 'If you ever want to, you know, just have a chat, just hang out without dad's agenda, you know where I am.' Anna was touched.

'I might see you at the tennis club?'

'Yes.' Kimi pushed back her tangle of coir-coloured hair. 'I'll look out for you.'

Anna spent most of Monday getting time to pass by doing background research at Harts. It was appalling how much damage the various Middle-Eastern wars of recent years had done to art and artefacts. The museum at Kabul was smashed by a gang of illiterate Taliban and the giant buddhas at Bamiyan blown to smithereens. What had Afsoon's plan been? To encourage rich buyers to bid for treasures taken overseas and bring them home to Iran, Iraq, Afghanistan, or had she wanted to hunt them down – perhaps catalogue lost and stolen pieces. She would have had her work cut out. But now, what a waste, she was just vegetating it appeared in a dark and gloomy house cut off from everything. It was easy to see why Richard wanted her but why did she want him? Anna remembered the cheap sweater and wondered if maybe Richard kept his desirable wife on a very limited budget so he could control her movements and access. It was an old trick. But why would she put up with it? She didn't seem to be a woman without spirit.

There were pages and pages on Morgan horses and American Saddle-breds and Anna built up quite a file. She had the feeling of entering a world hitherto unknown to her and it intrigued her. The more she read and looked at photographs the more she could see how Kimi might find this a wonderful relief from the rest of her life – her rather leaden family and her role at work where it would have been hard for her to make friends both because of her status and because of her financial over-sight role. She toyed with the idea of asking Kimi if she could go to the show with her. Maybe wait a while. Would it be a relief to get away from her father, too? Remembering Gerald's eager embrace of his daughter Anna didn't want to think too much about that.

None of the family was on Facebook or Twitter which was hardly surprising. They sensibly didn't court publicity or exposure. Anna wondered idly what they were worth financially. What would it feel like not to have to worry about money? Maybe they just had different worries about money. How to hold on to it, where to safely invest and all that. Did Richard fear that Afsoon did only want his money as Kimi had cattily said, and was William's self-respect quietly crumbling under the weight of his wife's fortune?

Steve sat down quietly beside her. 'All right?'

'Yes, just background stuff.' She glanced at him. 'You?'

'I wanted to just have a word. About Harry. Is that ok?' Immediately she was alert and attentive.

'Of course. What?'

'Have you noticed him being a bit – er – emotional?' Steve was clearly struggling.

'What do you mean?' Anna was scanning her memory furiously but nothing popped up.

'You know we were watching the game on Saturday and it was a good one. Lots of goals and shouting and excitement so, you know, there was a bit of leaping up and down and yelling from our side.' Steve looked down at his hands and rubbed them against each other. Anna waited. 'Well, it was a draw until the final moment and then the other side scored and Ellis and I groaned and I think Ellis kicked a ball of paper in the air in frustration.'

'Yes?'

'Well, Harry just lost it. He started swearing, I mean, words I've never heard him use before. He kept punching the back of the sofa over and over and then he burst into tears.'

Anna was astonished and upset. 'Oh Steve. What did Ellis do?'

'He was shocked. We all were. Alice was there as well and her eyes were like saucers and then she burst out crying.' Steve looked up sensing Anna's own distress. 'He quickly calmed down. I just patted his shoulder and said everything was ok and Ellis was great – he went and made us tea and brought in biscuits. After about five minutes it was as though it hadn't happened. Harry was humming, *You'll never walk alone.*'

'What about Alice?'

'Oh, she's fine. She forgot it all pretty quickly too but I noticed she kept her distance from Harry after that.'

Anna sat very still. 'I've been married to Harry for twenty-three years and I've never heard him say more than 'damn'. I hope to God this isn't another phase starting. I'm so sorry Steve.'

'I worried about telling you but I know this sort of thing can happen with Picks. It may be worth mentioning it to his consultant. On the other hand, it may just have been so much emotion that he couldn't cope appropriately like he would have done before.' Steve stared gloomily out of the window.

'No, you were right to say. I'll check on Ellis. Actually, I might have a bit of a family get-together after Harry's gone to sleep tonight and just let them know it would be a good idea to watch the levels of excitement.' Suddenly Anna grinned despite herself. 'Not usually a problem in our house these days!'

But, this was worrying. Generally since his illness Harry had been rather flat emotionally and it was painful to know that Ellis had witnessed this outburst. Of course, there had been others, one in particular seared in her own memory. She so much wanted him to remember his father as he had been but the more things like this happened, inevitably, being as young as he was, these memories might supersede the others.

## 9

Anna walked from the office to the address that Gerald Draycott had given her on St. Paul's Square. The dainty eighteenth century church at the centre of the square was perched sedately among swathes of daffodils and freshly mown grass. It smelled like the country and yet it was less than half a mile from the city centre. An Italian restaurant festooned with ivy chattered with clientele revelling in the open windows and soft air. The RBSA announced its next exhibition in a huge gaily-coloured poster and the old coaching inn had thrown wide its doors. A yellow mongrel made purposefully for its own business meeting along the bricked pavement as she turned into a courtyard and buzzed at the apartment number given her. She was keeping herself in neutral trying not to speculate on what she had heard and observed. Gerald didn't keep her waiting. Within two minutes he was opening his own door and greeting her.

The rooms were spacious with high ceilings and deep windows and one glance round the living area confirmed that this, at last, was where the Draycott dynasty had its home. Gerald led her from one curio or portrait of a family group to another describing and explaining with obvious delight. The walls were lined with mahogany book shelves and every surface of furniture was crammed. She pointed at a beautifully polished sextant and asked about it.

'Ah, that's my great-uncle Sidney's. The one who got away!' He was flushed and animated. He looked so much like a conventional businessman in his mid-grey suit that his boyish expression seemed almost incongruous. This effect was heightened by the fact that his collar was at least one size too big. Anna was surprised that Frances would let that pass.

'How do you mean?'

'Well, after the founder, you know, that chap there I showed you, Stanley, no-one really wanted to run the company to be honest.'

'Why not?'

'Oh, don't get me wrong, they wanted the income from it but they didn't want to turn up every day and run the thing. It's not exactly rocket science – it's a fizzy drink.' He rubbed his cheek as though checking if it needed shaving. 'Stanley's son, the first Gerald, trained as a mining engineer and was actually on the ship to

Australia when the old man died and he had to come home. His son, Edwin, went into the Merchant Navy. Unusual for a person in his position to join that and not the Royal Navy but he persuaded his old man that there may be trading opportunities. I don't think he liked the elitist stuff in the RN. Well, he had ten good years and made it to Master of a two-funnel steamer, beautiful ship, when Gerald dropped off the perch and poor old Edwin had to come home and sit in an office. But, by that time his younger brother Sidney had got the bug and so he passed the sextant on to him. I actually met him as an old man, Sidney, he was quite a character – spent his whole life at sea and never married.'

Anna sat on the arm of an overstuffed sofa without feeling she needed to ask permission. Gerald had never been intimidating in the way Richard was but in this place he was relaxed and expansive. 'What about you? Did you feel the same?'

'Oh me. Yes. I suppose I did. I just knew that was my fate because I was my old man's only child. Not even a girl champing at the bit to take over which would have suited me fine. I must have inherited the engineering gene but with me it was water. Big projects, big results. I was just fascinated by dam building. I remember my dad taking me to see Elan valley in Wales when I was just a kid and it amazed me that all that water could be held back and then used so productively. Elan was a real break-through for Birmingham, you know. Before that we just had these four little rivers coming in and most people in the centre got their water from artesian wells. But the way it was expanding something had to be done.'

'I never knew that, about the artesian wells,' Anna said, making a mental note to tell George and Ellis. And, of course, Harry. She mustn't forget Harry.

'Oh yes, there were wells all over.'

They had been chatting so easily that it was only when Gerald stopped and stared at the floor that Anna remembered he had asked to see her and obviously wanted to tell her something. She doubted it was about Birmingham's water supply.

'I'm sorry, I'm being rude. Do you want a drink?' Anna shook her head and they sat down in opposite armchairs. 'You've seen Kimi? What did you think?' Anna hesitated. She didn't feel that her brief was to gossip about her impressions of members of his family but what exactly was her brief?

'We talked about her horses.' That was true and neutral.

'She's an amazing girl, well, woman. She was brilliant at school you know? She could have read anything at university but she decided on maths and physics. Much brainier than the others. I was so proud of her. And she wasn't interested in Oxbridge – said she'd been around the establishment all her life, a bit like Edwin, I suppose – she wanted to go where the ground-breaking work was happening and of course she was snapped up right away. She was planning ahead, too. Would have done graduate work in the USA.' He stopped and sighed.

'What happened?'

'The very last thing I would have anticipated. The very last. She hadn't even had a boyfriend at school and she went to a mixed one so not for lack of lads. She went away happy as Larry and then stopped phoning or emailing and then when she came home at Christmas she brought all her stuff and said she wasn't going back. That's all. We couldn't understand it. She was so sad, so depressed. I wanted to get counselling for her but Frances said it was just a sulk because she wasn't used to not being the resident genius. I never bought that line. And then, of course, we realised what was going on.' He paused.

'Rhea.'

'Yes. She was pregnant. By the time we noticed she was six months gone. She never told us in as many words and she's never to this day said who the father was. I've always felt very sad that she didn't feel she could confide in me.'

'But surely,' Anna put in gently, 'nowadays that isn't the end of the world, is it? I mean she had a supportive family around her and no money worries. She could have gone back to her studies? Birmingham is a great university and she could have paid for excellent child-care.'

Gerald looked so distressed it was as though it had only just happened. 'You're not saying anything I didn't say to her. Frances was off but then, she would be. But I told her that – I said I'd support her in every way. She just wouldn't do it. Then she decided to get this accountancy degree quickly, did it in two years, and the minute she'd got that she started work at the company and asked me for the money to buy the farm for her horses. Of course I gave it her. That was all she wanted and that's how it's been for the last thirteen years. It's like her brain has just been switched off. I mean, I come from a long line of men who had to give up their career dreams to run the firm but the irony is that she didn't have to and yet that's what she's done. Why? I don't know.' He stared unhappily at the floor.

This was all quite interesting but Anna couldn't think what it had to do with her. 'She seems fairly happy,' she said lamely to end the silence.

Gerald looked at her quickly and with pleasure. 'Do you think so? I hope she is.' Anna decided that this time she would not be the one to break the silence. There must be more than this. Gerald got up and opened a cupboard. He took out a whisky bottle and two glasses looking at her enquiringly. She shook her head. He poured a measure into one glass and sat down with it.

'Funny,' he said. 'In a way we're already talking about what I wanted to see you about. Broken dreams. Well, lost paradises more like.' He sat up and leaned forward looking intently at Anna. 'What I'm about to tell you is only known to three people in the world. Maybe only two. And then I'm going to ask you to do something and that will only be known to me and you. There's nothing dodgy about it but you would have to keep all this information secret. From everyone.' His grey eyes almost glittered with intensity. She noticed that the hand that gripped the whisky glass had whitened around the knuckles. He went on, giving her a chance to think, 'I've been keeping tabs on you in a quiet way. You can't run a company as big as Drakes without having spies. I know you weren't pushed around by Richard and I know you're not a gossip. And I think you're inclined to like Kimi. I gave you the opportunity to say some judgmental things about her but you didn't take it. You don't have to like her to do what I'll ask but it would help.'

'Gerald,' she began, 'I'm sorry but I'm not prepared to search for stuff she might not want known.'

He seemed puzzled and then barked a short laugh. 'Oh, I get your drift. No, I'm not going to ask you to find Rhea's father. I can see you might think that was what I was driving at.' He sighed again. 'It's not Rhea's father I want you to find, Anna. ' She sat in silence. 'Can I trust you?'

'You can trust me not to betray any confidence but I can't promise to do what you will ask until I know what it is.'

'Fair enough.' He had come to a decision and seemed eager to go on. 'I'm going to tell you a story. I'll make it as brief as I can. When I was a young civil engineer fresh out of university a friend of my dad's introduced me to Frances. She was from the same background, she was nice-looking and seemed pleasant. It was just the next step. So we got married. It was never a love match and we quickly realised that a fair amount of 'never-minding' as my mum would have said would be the order of things. I don't suppose I was a young maiden's dream. Anyway, in due course two children arrived, Richard and Charlotte. By that time I was beginning to get work on bigger projects and the biggest yet was a dam to be built in the Wanapitei River basin. North-east Ontario. It was a terrific opportunity and I leaped at it. Frances would stay behind with the children who were just about to go away to school and do her society stuff and I would be out in the wilds building a dam. To be honest, it suited both of us.'

He got up and re-charged his glass. When he sat down the expression on his face was much softer. Anna felt he had almost forgotten she was there. 'God, it was a beautiful place. Wild as you like and ridge after ridge of mountains covered with evergreens. Deer, you know, and bear and sometimes at night you would hear wolves. I bloody loved it. We had proper apartments in the nearest town which was still fifteen miles away, but the best times were in the temporary wooden huts the company put up at the dam site itself. You just can't imagine the night sky, for a kid from the big city it was like a magic show. Some nights I hardly slept watching the constellations drift across and counting the shooting stars. I was never tired. It was like the whole time I was there I was running on adrenalin. There were engineers and workmen from all over the world. In the evenings at the camp we'd build a fire outside and sit around and talk and there was usually someone with a guitar. It was like, well, pioneer life. I went home on leave every three months or so but only because I was expected to. I didn't ever want it to end.' Again he stopped and glanced at Anna. 'I am trusting you now,' he said.

'You can.'

'One morning, very early, I was up before the others and I'd gone down to the river, the one we would dam. I just wanted to look at it all. It was one of those mornings where the light seems to be coming out of the ground, dazzling you. As I turned to start to walk back a movement in the trees on the mountain slope above the camp caught my eye. I could hardly make it out the light was so bright but then suddenly, silently, a woman on a horse came riding down and out of the woods. She was riding bare-back with her legs hanging either side of the horse and her hair blowing up around her head and streaming back as the wind coming down the valley caught it and tumbled it. They stopped just short of the camp and then saw me and she neck-reined the animal so that they were coming towards me. I hadn't even seen her face before I was in love with her. It was like something from a fairy-tale, a myth. It was magic.' Anna waited, not wanting to ask anything, letting him tell the story in his own way. 'I made her breakfast and we talked and it was all easily explained of course. She was staying at a wild-life refuge on the other side of the mountain while she worked. Her work was with us. She was the archaeologist from McGill University the government had sent to check our excavations that were about to start. You know, they do that whenever there's a big dig of any kind. In her case she would be looking for native tribal artefacts. She was half-French and half-Cree herself. She'd just ridden over to have a look and would be starting work properly the next day. She'd borrowed her horse from the ranch.'

Anna sat quietly. Gerald had stopped talking and she listened to the small sounds of the square – a car revving up to take the hill, indistinct voices and laughter from the street and the distant drone of the city. She felt privileged and wary.

'We became lovers. She was experienced, I wasn't, apart from Frances of course but this was unlike anything I had felt before. Sorry. I was completely besotted with her, would have followed her to the ends of the earth, but there was always something a little aloof about how she treated me. You think when you are head over heels in love with someone that they will feel the same way but of course they often don't. It went on for months. I had forgotten Frances and the children even, so when she said she was coming out for a visit it felt totally unreal. I tried to put her off but she was determined. Had she sensed something? I don't know. By this time Cora knew all about me and my family and everything. I wanted her to. I had some mad idea that I might divorce Frances and marry her. I wanted her to know I had money and could offer her a good life. When she told me she was pregnant with my child I was overjoyed.' Gerald suddenly jumped up from his chair as though he could no longer bear to be inactive while his feelings were so tumultuous. He began to pace about the room. Anna watched him. How had the young British engineer appeared to Cora, she wondered.

'Frances came out. I told Cora I would tell my wife everything and marry her but she ordered me not to. She wasn't much of a talker and she didn't give any explanation. The first night Frances was there, in the apartment in town, Cora turned up. You could see by then that she was pregnant. I had no idea what to do but she took charge. She told Frances about the baby and then she said she wanted us to have it. She wanted it to be brought up in England and we would provide for it. There was a man in Toronto who she loved, it turned out, and she would lose him if she went back with another man's baby.'

'You must have been devastated.'

'Shocked, devastated, astonished, bereft. What words are there?' Gerald stood looking out of the window with his back to her until he collected himself.

'What did Frances say?'

'Nothing. She listened, asked when the baby was due, which was another two months, and then went to bed locking the door after her. She showed no anger, no jealousy, she was like a machine. I couldn't believe it. I couldn't believe any of it. I tried to reason with Cora, tell her how much I loved her but it was like nothing to her, it was like I was speaking a different language. From that evening on she had nothing to do with me except for one time which was when she brought Kimi to us. She had our baby eventually with a local midwife.'

'And Frances – what happened?'

'I didn't sleep of course. Frances came into the kitchen the next morning looking as cool and collected as ever. She was wearing make-up and was fully dressed, even in tights I remember. She said to me these words. "I will take your bastard home and pretend it's mine on one condition. You will sign over the business to me and I will take all major executive decisions. No-one will know about this because I will not be humiliated. Do you understand?" I can't even remember if I said yes or nodded. It just happened. She stayed on for a couple of months until the birth, told people back home that was why she had come out to be with me and we took Kimi home with us.' A few months later my dad had to retire because of ill health and my days as an engineer and a husband for that matter were over.' He dropped his head and was silent for a moment. 'Do you know what the name Kimi means in Cree? Secret. It means secret. Frances doesn't know that of course.'

Anna was speechless. Draycott stopped pacing and faced her. 'There is only one reason I am telling you all this,' he said, 'and it's because after thirty-two years things have changed.' Anna stared at him realising that another bombshell was about to be dropped. 'I'm ill. I have pancreatic cancer. I just thought I had an acid stomach, maybe an ulcer, kept self-medicating and then, of course, when I went for a check-up it was too late. The tumour is too large and diffuse to operate on. They offered me chemo and radiotherapy but I made them tell me the truth and there's no point – it's gone on too long. In a month or so I will be dead.' Her brain reeled but he was not wanting comfort, or at least not any kind of conventional comfort. As huge as that statement was, she sensed it was only the prelude to another. 'I told Frances and she said that when I died she would take revenge on me betraying her by not only cutting Kimi off but making sure she had nothing – no job, no home, no horses, nothing. She would tell her that she had been the illegitimate offspring of a casual affair. Frances can be very vindictive and I just can't bear the thought of what she would say and do to hurt Kimi. The others wouldn't stick up for her either – I'm sure you've noticed how selfish they both are.'

Suddenly the whole thing made sense. Anna knew why he had hired her and what the job really was.

'Of course I hadn't expected this, I had expected Frances to in some way regard her as one of the family after such a long time, but still a part of me must have been concerned. I have put away as much as I can for her here and there out of funds I've accrued on my own account but it's not much. In any case she wouldn't starve, she's good at what she does but- ' He stopped.

'She would be alone.'

Gerald nodded. 'Alone and hearing lies about me – lies about how she was conceived and how I feel about her and her mother.'

'You want me to find her mother.'

Gerald seemed relieved that she was alongside his thinking. 'Yes.'

'Then I will do everything I can to trace her.'

'No-one must know. Frances is not just vindictive. She could be dangerous.'

'I understand. I really do.' Gerald was with her in a second, his arms trembling around her. She stepped back.

'Just one thing, Gerald, one thing I have to say.'

'Yes?'

'About eighteen months ago my own mother came back into my life. She left when I was a toddler and my father and I heard nothing from her for all that time.'

'How wonderful for you,' Gerald said warmly.

'No, I'm sorry to say it wasn't.' Anna felt tears rush to her eyes and breathed deeply until she was back in control. 'She died shortly afterwards and we were never reconciled. It was extremely hurtful and to be honest I'm nowhere near over it. I just want you to be aware that things may not turn out as you imagine even if I can find her.'

'I understand. But I want you to go ahead anyway.' Gerald held her shoulders in a fatherly way. 'You see it's all I can do for her. For my love child.'

Outside in the early evening cool a group of young office workers were toiling up the hill eating chips. There was already dew on the grass of the churchyard and restaurants were cheerful with strings of lights and bursts of music. She phoned George and checked in. No wonder Gerald had not wanted a local journalist. Everything made sense now and she had some serious work to do as well as preserving the Forbes story fiction. And yet, as she strode up Newhall Street it was Gerald's expression that stayed in her mind, the look of a man who had only ever been free and in love and fully alive for one summer long ago and had shared that glorious time with her. Now he was dying. Now she knew why the suit and shirt collar were loose. She must find Cora as soon as was humanly possible and hope for the best.

## 10

When she let herself into the house it was quiet. She popped her head round the door and saw no-one was in the living room and then took a few steps down the hall into the kitchen. Through the window above the sink the sky was striated with orange and purple in such brilliant tones that she was transfixed for a moment but then her gaze dropped and she saw the blue jug crammed with daffodils and set in the centre of the table. George bustled in from outside humming to himself and scanning a slim sheaf of papers. When he noticed her he started and ridiculously put the papers behind his back.

'Dad?'

'I didn't think anyone was here. Do you want a cup of tea? Dinner? Of course you do. I've put some aside in the fridge, it will only take a moment to heat up – just sit yourself down, you must be starving. Are you?' He had rolled the papers as he spoke and thrust them into the side pocket of his baggy old jeans.

'What were you reading?' More secrets? It was unlike her dad who was normally as transparent as clingfilm. His white hair was standing up on end in a kind of Smurf coif and he had clearly been chewing the right side of his moustache. These were signs of high excitement or extreme agitation. Her curiosity deepened. 'Dad?'

'Mind your own beeswax,' he shot back at her. 'I'm over 21.' He pottered about setting the timer and laying the table and she sank down gratefully on to her favourite chair. She rested her chin on her hands.

'Dad, did you know that Birmingham used to get water from artesian wells?'

Immediately he was engaged. This was just the kind of information he liked. 'No,' he said, pulling a plate down off the dresser, 'but that explains something I've always wondered about but never followed up. You know we used to take people on local history walks in the old centre when I belonged to that group? There's a Well Street in Digbeth.' He peered into the microwave and stayed bent waiting for the beep. 'There's quite a few places called Holywell, too. There's one out by Rubery. People would go to be cured and there's a theory about that. That well is very rich in iron so it would work wonders on people who were anaemic, wouldn't it? It would seem like a miracle cure.' As he chatted on Anna thought of the strained and deadened family scenarios of the Draycotts. Frances and Gerald in a horrific grid-lock and Richard and Afsoon barely knowing who each other was and then Charlotte and her dismissive ridiculing of her little Willie. All her life, Anna had heard the sound of her father's voice welcoming her, cheering her up, telling her a million fascinating titbits, comforting her. How lucky she was. She sprang up from her chair and hugged him just as he was sliding the quiche on to her plate. For a moment it quivered on the edge and then settled back safely. 'Close thing!'

'I do love you, Dad,' Anna couldn't stop herself saying. He put the food down in front of her.

'Well, I love you, too,' he said matter-of-factly, 'what's brought all this on?'

'Oh nothing. Just that every now and then you get a glimpse into other people's lives and some of them are a bit chilling.'

'Yes.' He sat down opposite her and rubbed his beard. 'Have you had a word with Michelle yet? Faye said you were going to.'

'No, why?' The quiche was warm round the edges and stone-cold in the middle but she was starving.

'Little Nicola was here today – just called round looking for her sister. She might need a bit of attention paid her.' He pushed his glasses up his nose.

'Oh?' Anna cut another large mouthful and loaded it with salad.

'She's got that wild lost look that dogs have when they haven't got an owner or a doggy tribe, you know? Loose and frightened, tail between her legs - running fast everywhere.'

Anna felt guilty. She had forgotten about Faye's request. 'I'll phone her the minute I finish this,' she said. 'Thanks for reminding me, Dad.'

An hour later Anna stood at the bar in The Greyhound waiting for their drinks to be brought. Michelle had been about to leave the Centre when she'd phoned and was more than happy to have a break and a chat to catch up as Anna had put it. Now she was wondering just how she was going to broach the subject of Nicola. For the first time she realised that she was in essence going to tell Michelle that her daughter needed looking after better. Not a good task. Not a good idea. What had she been thinking of to agree to it?

She tried to think of an occasion where Michelle might have given her the heads-up on Faye's behaviour so she could link it with that but couldn't think of one. Michelle had still been out at 8.30. How usual was that? She sighed and picked up the drinks.

'Anna!' It was Suzy from Harts. Always good company but maybe not the person she most wanted to see just now. But Michelle welcomed Suzy and her friend to join them and Anna guiltily thought she would just shelve the Nicola problem until another time.

Half an hour later Suzy and Rob were making their excuses and leaving. Anna couldn't blame them. Michelle had one harrowing tale after another of her refugee clients and she seemed unaware of the effect this was having on the others or the inappropriateness of the desperate narratives. Anna realised that if not stopped she would just keep going all evening so she interrupted her.

'Actually, Michelle, I wanted to talk to you about someone.'

Michelle seemed to wake up out of a dream. For the first time she looked Anna properly in the face. 'What? I mean, who? One of your clients?'

'No.' Anna hesitated but had to go on. 'It's Nicola, your daughter.'

'I know who my daughter is,' Michelle snapped. Bad start.

'I'm so sorry to seem as though I'm interfering, Michelle, but it's just that Faye is really worried about her.' She decided not to mention that Tash was worried, too. It wouldn't help for Michelle to think that her older daughter had gone to a friend's mother for help rather than her own.

'Why?' Michelle was now looking frankly hostile.

'Well, apparently she's mixing with some men who are much older. She changes her clothes and puts on make-up to meet them.'

'Crap. I've never seen her do that.'

'Well, she does, I'm afraid.'

Michelle stood up. 'According to your saintly daughter who if I remember correctly was going to run off to Russia with a chap she'd only just met! Kettle, pot, black, rearrange this well-known phrase, Anna. And mind your own bloody business while you're at it!' She swept out.

Anna got her things together wearily. That went well. Suddenly she felt very tired and wished she'd brought the car instead of walking but it was only half a mile home. Tomorrow was Len's birthday party and she would see Steve. Tonight she would get the cake out of the freezer and put it somewhere out of reach of Bobble to de-frost. She would try to have a word with Faye about how she'd riled Tash's mother in case there was any come-back. Tomorrow was her appointment with Frances which, with her new secrets, she now dreaded as a potential minefield, and the search for Cora would begin.

But the day was not finished. As she trudged down the street towards the railway station where she would turn for home, she saw ahead of her Nicola herself. The girl was alone and staggering slightly. Anna quickened her pace and caught up with her.

'Nicola! Hi.' The girl looked at her under drawn eyebrows. 'It's Mrs Ames, Anna.'

'Oh, fuck,' said Nicola resentfully. She looked drunk.

'Do you want to come back with me?' If she did then maybe they could have a talk or maybe at least she could sober up a bit. On the other hand might it shock Michelle into attention if she saw her daughter in this state?

'No. Can't. Got to get home.' Nicola set off at a diagonal across the road without checking for traffic. Anna followed her at a distance. The girl was a sitting duck for any passing driver with bad intentions. Finally Nicola turned into her own drive and Anna watched as she fumbled with her key and then went inside. Then she turned away and walked thoughtfully home. She hadn't taken Faye and Tash all that seriously. There was always a drama going on in the girls' lives and Anna had respected Michelle for her commitment and sense of responsibility. But now she had seen Nicola for herself it was clear that something was very wrong. Michelle seemed blinded to her own family's needs in her devotion to the desperate situation of others. It wouldn't be the first time that people invested in a cause of some kind ignored the plight of people under their own nose. But what could she do herself? The only thing she could think of was to try to talk to Nicola when she came to visit with her sister – when she was not under the influence of something – when she was her normal fifteen-year-old self. How odd, Anna reflected, that there were now two rather troubled teenage girls in her life. Thank goodness for Ellis. She smiled. He had been so thrilled to get into the tennis club programme. The water bottles were getting a thorough work-out.

The interview with Frances was a huge effort as she had feared it would be. They met in the lobby of a rather grand city hotel and drank Italian coffee from tiny cups. Frances was wearing muted shades of pearl and aqua and looked like what she was – a wealthy and powerful woman. She barely took any notice of Anna's carefully prepared questions but instead uttered a series of set-piece statements concerning the solidity of the family, the work ethic upon which the firm was built and the importance of privacy and living modestly when the family was as prestigious as they were.

'It's vulgar to be showy,' she said. 'Draycotts never have been. We pay our taxes and live in reasonable comfort but we don't put ourselves about.' Nevertheless, three times in the hour they were interrupted by rather obsequious men who whispered in Frances' ear. Twice her phone beeped and she read the messages. Anna wondered whether her own interview had been arranged at a time either when Frances wanted to do more important things or when she wanted Anna to think she did.

When Frances indicated that it was time for her to go she stood up and said pleasantly, 'I met your younger daughter on Saturday. Her horses are magnificent.'

Frances seemed to tuck in the corners of her mouth more firmly. 'Yes,' she agreed. 'Kimi adores them. So important to have a little hobby, isn't it? Especially when there is no man in your life.' She paused and it seemed to Anna with her new knowledge that a chilling tone of satisfaction underlay her next remark. 'Poor Kimi. One wonders what will become of her.'

Len didn't know about the party but had been invited to dinner which was a frequent enough event not to be remarkable. He had come back from the Yorkshire tour on crutches having missed his footing late at night on a steep curb so Anna had gone to pick him up. She asked about the venues but, tactfully, not about the audience turn-out. Len belonged to a band which lurked around the edge of being professional which meant that sometimes they got paid but more often they begged for a chance to play at pubs and festivals, fetes and shindigs of all kinds. The focal point of this jaunt had been to play at the green funeral of a friend of the lead guitar who had succumbed to a poisonous brew of home-made stimulants. It had been a death generally felt to be appropriately dashing and the band were gratified to be playing him out. Len was full of it and regaled

Anna for some time with the discomforts and triumphs of the trip. Anna smiled at the stream of anecdotes, pleased that his life now held more than shopping for food bargains, and tried to ignore the pungent miasma that arose from his sweaty bulk. After a while he fell silent and as they turned into Anna's road he said without any particular emotion as though he had just remembered, which perhaps he had, 'It's my birthday today.'

Immediately a surge of anger swept through Anna and her hands clenched on the steering wheel. Their bloody selfish mother. Len could be a maestro of self-pity but even he had simply not expected anyone to remember or care. 'Really?' she said neutrally.

Primed by Anna and alerted by Ellis watching from the living room they were all there when the front door opened to shout, 'Happy birthday, Len!' He paused mid hobble and stared up at them dumbly. They got him inside and sat him at the kitchen table in front of a pile of gifts and cards. Anna nodded at Faye and Ellis who had forgotten about Len's birthday at breakfast but had been told on pain of being eternally grounded to come up with something wrapped in time for Len's arrival. 'Open them!' Faye ordered. 'Go on.'

Len's large hands fumbled with the wrappings until George said tactfully, 'You're allowed to tear the paper when it's your birthday, son.' He had given Len a CD of James Galway and Anna had found two collarless tunic shirts from an Asian shop on the Soho Road, one black and one dark red. The assistant had had to go right to the back of the shop to find the only two XXL size so it was a relief that they weren't pink. Ellis had given him his own MP3 player which had been superseded by a newer one at Christmas. The kid didn't have much money of his own so it made sense. Faye had made an inspired choice. Len had gone on tour, as he grandly put it, with a beaten up old sports bag that needed an exfoliating scrub. She'd been to the charity shops on the High Street and found a very smart black pull-along bag with multiple zipped compartments which made Len's mouth go round with pleasure.

Finally he spoke. 'I'm sorry I haven't got you anything,' he said gruffly. 'I'll bring you something back next time.' Anna was so enraged she had to go to the pantry and get the cake. She couldn't trust herself to speak. As she lit the candles with her back turned to the table she heard her father gently explaining that the idea of birthdays was for people to show their affection with gifts and that it was a one-way transaction. All that he needed to do was enjoy them. She had iced the cake with the usual message to Len and arranged candles round the edge. Len was thirty-eight and that seemed a tad too many to light. She turned and brought the flaming cake to the table smiling at Len's pink face while everyone burst into song.

He was transported with delight. 'I seen them do this on the telly,' he said. 'I never thought it would happen to me.' Then he got up and hugged everyone in turn. Anna noticed Faye trying to make a break for it and flashed her a Medusa glare. Yes, he was smelly and yes, he could be a pain, so what? As she had pointed out to Faye on so many previous occasions, none of us are sweetness and light 24-7, herself most definitely included.

Harry was staring at the cake which still had its candles lit. Anna watched him carefully. Was this too much for him? As birthdays go it had hardly been a riot so far and was unlikely to get much more charged but he seemed anxious. She went to him and touched his arm. 'Ok, sweetheart?' As he turned his head to look at her the light from the candles danced in the green-gold depths of his irises. She thought of how Afsoon had looked in the candle-light from the twins' cake. No wonder women had protested about the invention of harsh electric light.

'Who is that man?' he said, his glance flickering to Len and back to her again.

Of course, Len had only come into their lives in the last few months well after Harry's memory had started to disintegrate. She must remember to remind him every now and then. 'It's my half-brother, Len,' she said quietly. 'The brother I never knew I had until not long ago.'

Harry's face sagged. 'I want my brother,' he said like a child. 'Why isn't my brother here?' Anna put her arm around his waist, she couldn't reach his shoulder when he was standing. How could she tell him he didn't have a brother? Was there any point? At times like these maybe they should just create a comfortable fantasy world in which Harry's non-existent brother had just stepped out to get some milk. He would have forgotten anyway in five minutes. She laid her head briefly against his chest more for her own comfort than for his. Then she felt his torso shift away from her.

'So sorry we're late,' Steve said, 'Alice couldn't decide what to wear.'

'Here he is!' Harry said happily. 'My brother.'

Anna didn't know whether Steve heard or not. A tide of emotion swept through her. She grabbed Alice and smacked a kiss on her excited face and lifted her up for Len to hug and then everyone was demanding that Len blow out the candles and make a wish. George cut generous slices.

'Ok, all of you, grab a piece of cake and buzz off into the living room. Len, why don't you use one of our cables and show everyone the photos you took of the gigs on the television? I know you've got your camera with you.' Faye rolled her eyes and Ellis made a drowning mime but they knew they had to go along with it at least until dinner.

Anna couldn't wait for them to be gone. She went to the fridge and got out a large tub of pre-prepared chilli, Len's favourite, and stuck it in the microwave. Then she pulled down from the shelf their largest pan and filled it with boiling water from the kettle before it went on the hob for the spaghetti. Next, it was back to the fridge for the guacamole and hummus and then to the cupboard for corn chips. But she couldn't quite make it to the table-laying. She burst out of the back door and stood, sobbing, in the garden. What was going on with her? Why was she being ambushed by such storms of emotion? Len was pleased, everyone was behaving themselves – it was just what she wanted. And yet, deep inside her head she felt a faint creaking as if her brain was tethered too tight and the cable was beginning to fracture.

'All right?' It was Steve. Of course it was. 'Have I upset you in some way?'

Anna hastily dried her face. 'No, no, of course not. I'm just so angry with my mother, my *dead* mother even, that Len has never had a proper birthday.'

'Well, you've given him one now,' Steve said smiling. 'I'm glad it's not me. You seem to have been ignoring me lately.' Anna's head swam. Ignoring him? Thoughts of him ran constantly through her mind like an underground river. So much so, that she had to force herself not to be always contacting him. Perhaps she had gone too far the other way. Who knew what was ok and what wasn't any more? She decided to be honest.

'I'm finding it difficult Steve. This. Between you and me.'

'What do you mean?' His eyes were suddenly guarded. 'What are you saying?'

Anna turned to face him fully and folded her arms tightly across her chest. Almost immediately Steve unconsciously mirrored her action so that someone watching from a distance might have thought they were having a row. 'I want you. I want you all the time. I try not to think about you but then I dream about you and that's worse because-' She stopped, unable to tell him how in her dreams there were no restraints, no guilty self-censoring with the result that some nights she woke gasping and wet with abandon.

'I know why dreams are worse, Anna,' Steve said quietly. 'You don't have to explain.'

The blossom from the cherry tree whirled across them as a breeze lifted the heavy branches and distantly they could hear the sound of a bird piping and the children down the street calling to each other. They looked silently into each other's eyes. What could be said? Could they think about how long Harry would still be around? How many years it would be until he died? No. Literally unthinkable. Could they think about an affair? Then both of them would be betraying Harry whom they loved and who loved them. The glorious virile Harry, full of vitality and fun who had been struck down through no fault of his own, the victim of a grotesque genetic fault. Harry who thought Steve was his brother. What joy could there be in that?

Finally Steve stepped towards Anna and cupped her face in two warm hands. 'Shall we go in, love? I'll give you a hand with dinner.'

# 11

It was 2.13 in the morning when Anna's mobile rang. She moaned and then jerked upright. It was Faye. 'What? Are you all right?'

'Yes, I'm all right.' Anna dropped back on her pillow marshalling expletives. 'It's Nicola, Mum. We're frightened - they're taking her away. Can you come now?'

'Now?'

'Mum, please, there's no-one else. We don't know what to do.' It had been many years since Anna had heard that frightened quiver in Faye's voice. She swung her legs round and jumped out of bed.

'I'm on my way. Tell me exactly where you are.'

It was just as well the streets were deserted as Anna raced down them, hurling the car round corners. She pulled up, as instructed, outside an all-night convenience shop and leaped out of the car. The girls, Faye and Tash, were with her in a second. They must have been cowering round the corner of the building watching for her. They all piled in and Faye gave her instructions. Slowly this time, not wanting to attract attention, they crawled down a side street and turned to the left. There were no houses here, only small factories, shut up for the night or semi-derelict, and very few street lights. 'We worked out they came here because there aren't any cameras,' Faye whispered to Anna. Anna's mind was racing. How could she get Nicola away from a gang of grown men without putting the girls, let alone herself, into serious jeopardy? Should she phone the police, but tell them what? In any case they may take a while to respond and it would be too late.

There they were. A car was parked with its headlights on and a group of men were moving about as though playing a game. They were darting in and out of the circle it seemed but then Anna realised that wasn't it, they were pushing someone. The car was getting very close and she dared not go too slowly and arouse suspicion. She decided to go round the block and try to work out a plan. 'She's there!' Faye whispered hoarsely, 'they've got her. Mum!'

'We have to think,' Anna whispered back, 'let me just turn the corner.'

'Mum, we can't leave her!'

'I'm not leaving her, Faye, but we have to make a plan so we don't -' Anna stopped talking because as she had turned the corner she had seen something. Surely not. She must be mistaken.

'Mrs Ames! We have to go back!' Tash's frantic voice from the back seat broke through her astonishment.

Anna quickly turned another corner and stopped. 'This is what we'll do.' She had remembered a teacher in a tough school telling her once that doing something that would surprise was a good way of stopping dangerous behaviour when reasoning or even threats would be useless. 'Girls, you need to back me up, ok? I'm going to try to distract them and you get Nicola in the car. Don't argue, don't beg, don't say anything. Just grab her as fast as you can and get her in the back of the car. Tash, sit on her to keep her in if you need to. Don't take any notice of anything I say or do, ok? Faye can you drive us?' Faye nodded, her eyes huge. 'Right. As soon as I see you're ready I'll jump in the passenger side, ok? This is going to happen in seconds, right? If something goes wrong then Faye, you and Tash need to drive away and get the police as fast as you can.'

Anna got out of the glove compartment the powerful car torch and put it on her lap. She drove on round another corner and they were back on the side street where the car still stood, its lights dipped. Now the men were whooping and looking down at something in the middle of their circle. Anna revved up and drove at full speed to the group. She slammed on the brakes yards from the men and shouted at the girls, 'Now!' They all jumped out together.

'Police!' She yelled, 'Stay where you are and don't move!' She flashed the torch from one startled face to another so they could not see her clearly. Faye and Tash were through the circle but having a hard time lifting Nicola from the floor. Quickly she shouted again, 'You're all under arrest!' keeping the torchlight jumping and leaping herself round the circle to keep them confused. Now the girls had Nicola on her feet and were stumbling towards the car. Anna yelled as loud as she could, 'Over here! They're over here!' That did it. The men scattered, the car roared into life and in seconds the street was clear. Then she was in the passenger seat and Faye was speeding off herself. 'No, Faye,' she gasped, 'slow down. They've gone. Just slow down and stop.' She reached over and child-locked all the doors. Nicola and Tash were both sobbing in the back.

In the kitchen at home Anna made tea and gave each frightened girl a mug of it. Nicola was shaking badly, her teeth chattering, and Tash wasn't much better. Faye sipped her mug and stared into space. Anna had not asked any questions on the journey back but she knew she had to now.

'Nicola, you need to talk to us. No-one's angry with you. Just tell us what happened.' Nicola shook her head. Anna couldn't help feeling sorry for her. Make-up all over her face and her hair tangled from squirming in the filthy street she was a pitiful sight. For all her bravado she was just a child. 'Sweetheart, you must tell us. We love you. We want to help. Just tell us what happened.'

Again Nicola shook her head. She looked terrified. Faye got the picture first. 'Did they threaten you if you told anyone?' Nicola stared at her and then nodded. There was silence. Anna's heart sank. This could mean that something similar had happened before. There hadn't been time to threaten her before the gang was broken up tonight.

'Come upstairs,' she said, 'and I'll run you a bath. Faye, can you lend her some pyjamas? Tash, what about your mum? Will she be worrying you're still out?'

'No. She trusts us,' said Tash bleakly.

'Ok, can you text your mum and say that you're both here? Don't wake her – we can talk properly tomorrow. Come on Nicola.'

In the bathroom the girl sat silently on the stool while Anna turned on taps and added bath oil. This was no time for showers. She had observed Nicola's clothing in the mayhem of the girls getting her into the car and the leggings she wore, while dirty and dusty, had not been pulled down or torn. They had been in time. This time. There was no evidence to destroy but there was a very scared kid needing comfort. 'Would you like me to stay?' Nicola nodded. Another sign that there had not been a rape that night. Slowly, the girl pulled off her clothes and Anna saw with relief that her pink panties were unmarked.

The same could not be said for her body. As Nicola stepped into the bath Anna couldn't prevent herself from gasping in shock. Fortunately Nicola didn't notice. She was in a house that she had known since she was a toddler, a safe house where the only trouble she had ever encountered was when she had tracked mud in to the kitchen and Faye's grand-dad had made her mop it up. She wasn't thinking about what Faye's mum might see.

How long ago had it been that Anna had been in this same bathroom looking at marks on her own body from rough male hands? Less than a month. And now this frightened girl. What was happening in her world? She felt another strand of that steel hawser strain to snapping point.

When the girls were all in bed, Tash and Nicola in Faye's double and Faye herself heroically suffering the fold-out, a sure indicator of how shaken she was, Anna went back down to the kitchen and started up her laptop. There was no way she would sleep. After two hours of searching and note-taking she closed the lid and put the kettle on. She sat at the table remembering the countless times she had seen Nicola wind up her law-abiding sister, her dark eyes sparkling with the mischief of a child who knows itself to be safe. There was no way now that innocent sparkle would come back.

By the time George pottered in in his dressing gown, hair on end, at 7.00 o'clock that morning Anna had decided what to do. There was no choice. She showered and dressed and went round to Michelle's house. It was a work day but she knew that Michelle wouldn't have to go in until later because she had a flexitime arrangement and didn't usually leave the house until 9.30, working later in the evening. 'Trusting' the girls to look after themselves, Anna thought bitterly. If her husband hadn't been such a dick there might have been someone there to help.

Michelle was still in her dressing gown and her face closed up as she saw who was at the door. 'Let me in,' Anna said without apology. 'We need to talk.'

'I can't.'

'Yes, you can.' Anna pushed past her and went into the living room.

'Just a minute!' Michelle was outraged. 'Who the hell do you think you are?'

'Michelle, please listen. This is really serious. It's about Nicola.'

'Oh, that again. Why can't you mind your own business?'

'Because if I had then she would have been gang-raped last night.'

Michelle sagged on to the sofa. 'What?' So Anna told her what had happened. Michelle stared into space still half unwilling to believe what she was hearing. 'Why didn't she come to me? I mean Tash, why did she call you?'

'I don't know.' Anna waited a moment. 'That isn't really what's important here. This could just have easily have happened to Faye. Don't make it about sides, Michelle, please, it's too serious for that.' For the first time Anna saw that Michelle had taken in what she had been telling her.

'Is she hurt?' Michelle looked at Anna wildly. 'Are you sure they didn't get her?'

Anna took a deep breath. 'Not this time.'

'What?'

'I have to tell you something else. It's horrible but I have to. Are you ready?' In reply Michelle covered her mouth with her hands and almost imperceptibly nodded. 'When she was getting into the bath I saw marks on her body.' Michelle moaned. Anna hesitated. 'Round her groin there were bruises. Some were old, yellow, but some were still quite fresh. Not from last night but I would say maybe 48 hours ago. I think she may have been forced to have sex on a regular basis.'

'No! I can't believe it. Anna. I can't.' Michelle was beginning to tremble.

'I'm so sorry,' Anna felt her lungs heave with the sobs that wanted to be let out. 'You must look for yourself. They're there.'

Michelle now seemed to be in shock. 'You mean Nicola? Are you sure it was her?' Anna waited. 'There must be another explanation. I know she's naughty but-'

Anna leaned forward. 'This is not Nicola's fault, Michelle,' she said. 'She is being exploited by a bunch of very nasty and dangerous men. They're not school kids.'

Michelle suddenly burst into tears. 'It's my fault! I haven't been watching them. I've been so busy and involved – ' A thought struck her. 'Were they from the Centre?'

'I don't know. They were just a bunch of men, maybe in their twenties, a couple older. I just don't know. But you know this can happen anywhere. Anyone.'

'You tried to tell me.'

'I had no idea *this* was going on, believe me.' Anna got up and went to sit by her. 'Michelle, I'm so sorry but the bruises aren't all that I saw.' Anna put her arm round her and felt the new shock ripple through her body.

Michelle was now trembling from head to foot. 'Go on.'

Anna put her head against Michelle's. 'She's been cutting herself.'

Anna called in sick to work and then texted Steve so he wouldn't worry to say she was simply tired and needed some time to work on something at home. She found jobs to occupy herself, taking Harry to the supermarket and tidying Faye's tumbled bedroom. But finally she had to just lie on her bed and think. In as many weeks she had been involved in two attempted rapes. The symmetry of her attack and Nicola's was hard not to notice. Strangers wanting to get sex through force. It was a bald statement of power. We do this because we want to and we can. Yes, Nicola had been foolish and reckless and to a lesser extent so had she. But this was not their fault. This was not even about lust, it seemed to be about some kind of revenge – there was contempt and hatred in it. No doubt some people would say men who did this had low self-esteem or had been brutalised and for some of them that may be true. But some of them were simply sadists and brutes, people who felt they were entitled. All of them needed to be stopped. What would happen now was up to Michelle and Nicola. But, Anna had privately decided, if Michelle didn't take action by contacting the police or social services or both, then she would. And tonight she would see how Faye was doing. She needed to say again how proud of her she was and check that she was ok.

She stretched her limbs and hoped to nap. But it was at that second that she remembered what she had seen last night and had almost forgotten. After first driving past the gang when she had turned the corner to come back round to grab Nicola she had seen a woman and a man talking half in shadow in an alley entrance. The man was young and tall and seemed to be demanding something of the woman. He was gesticulating with one hand and with the other was holding the woman's arm firmly in his grip. The woman was Afsoon.

# 12

Anna spent all the next day in the office trying to track down Cora. Gerald had given her as much information as he could but it was scanty and out of date. The surname he knew didn't seem to work and he had only a vague memory of what government department had sent her out to the dam construction site to look for disturbed native American artefacts. She tried Canadian museum staff, McGill alumnae lists and professional journals, their School of Anthropology and Archaeology. She couldn't access marriages or deaths on the government websites without dates. She looked up the dam website for historical data but there was nothing. Obviously, if no Native-American stuff had been found, Cora's presence would not have been recorded. If Cora had become well-known in her work then she would have been much easier to track but she could have gone to work for a university anywhere in the world, or indeed, any overseas employer. Anna wondered if the name Cora wasn't itself a short form or a nickname in which case it was almost impossible. She could be dead. Gerald had remembered the small town she had grown up in now almost swallowed up by the urban sprawl of Toronto. She had supposedly gone to marry a man in that city but there was no way of knowing who or if it ever happened.

In the late afternoon Anna phoned him. She checked whether she could speak freely and then told him she was having no success in tracing Kimi's mother. Would he be willing to have her put advertisements in local papers both print and online around Toronto giving Cora's name as he had known it and asking for her or anyone who knew of her to make contact?

'Who would you give as the contact person?' he asked, immediately wary.

'I would have to ask Ted if I could use Harts' as a contact. And my name.'

'I don't want anyone else to know about this, Anna, not even Ted. No-one.'

'No, I understand that. I think Ted would be fine if I just said that there was a distant branch of the family in Canada that you'd like to try to find. It happens all the time.' What Anna didn't say was that Ted wouldn't care if Gerald was a bigamist tracking down his six previous wives if it meant that the handsome fee got paid.

'OK then, but keep on with the other searches, too.'

'Now I've talked to you I think I'll post on *rootsweb* too. It's a kind of forum for exchange of information, if that's ok.'

'Of course.' Gerald was silent for a moment. 'Frances told me you'd met. You did well, she doesn't seem at all suspicious. In fact, she thinks she got her message over pretty forcefully and that you rolled over.'

'Good.' It was obvious that Gerald felt free to talk without restraint so she decided to ask something that had been bothering her. 'Mr Draycott, Gerald, why would you not just tell Kimi the story yourself? That way she would hear the true version. I found it very moving and I'm not even related to you.'

'I have thought of it, of course.' He hesitated. 'I love her very much but I don't understand her. She makes sudden radical decisions. She's a lot more vulnerable than she looks. She doesn't open up or share anything. When she was pregnant with Rhea I thought she was going crazy. Not in any dramatic way, I don't mean that, I mean she just seemed to turn inside and go, well, catatonic really. It was very frightening. She wouldn't get therapy although I offered it over and over and of course she wouldn't talk to any of us. You see I can't tell her the story without also telling her what Frances did. Even if I left out the part about what she's planning to do now it might tear Kimi apart. She's never been specially close to Frances but to discover that she's not even her mother, that she doesn't have full siblings, that Frances took her only because of a selfish power play – that we've been lying to her all her life, well, I don't know. I can't risk it. I can't take her surrogate mother away until I have a real mother to put in her place.' Anna was silent. Gerald sighed as though it was his last breath. 'I may be wrong but that's my judgement.'

'Ok. I'll go ahead, of course, but can I make a suggestion?' Gerald grunted. 'Write it down. Just like you told me and give it to your solicitor.'

'I see what you're saying and you're right. I will. You're going to keep on interviewing the rest of the family, aren't you? Keep up the cover?'

'Yes. Don't worry.' They hung up. Anna thought for a few minutes and then keyed in a number from her list. Afsoon answered immediately.

'I wondered if you could help me with something?' Anna asked. 'I'm afraid I'm being very cheeky. This is nothing to do with the project for Mr. Draycott so please feel free to say no.'

'Yes?'

'There's an exhibition on at the BMAG of Persian miniatures. I fell in love with them when I was working as a university librarian, we had some wonderful old books with illustrations painted on silk, but I know very little about them. Would you have time to meet me there and talk me through? I'll happily treat you to coffee and cake?'

Afsoon's voice sounded as though she was smiling. 'I would like that. I saw the exhibition advertised and was hoping to go anyway. It will be nice to have a companion.' They arranged the details and Anna sat back in her chair feeling both guilty and triumphant. Then she googled Wikipedia so that she wouldn't come across as a complete ignoramus. Lying was getting to be fun which was faintly worrying.

By the time she got home there was still some warmth in the day and everyone was outside. Harry was stretched on the lounger which was probably damp from a winter in the shed and George, Diane and Joan were clustered around a plastic picnic table perched on three rickety chairs. Anna wondered what it was like to be so organised and energetic that you actually cleaned things before you put them away for the season. Some people even sterilised their plant pots before the winter. She sighed. What did it matter? It was not like any of them were wearing white silk trousers or likely to be. The three grey heads were very close together and Diane seemed to be hooting. Again she had the sense of something going on.

She walked over to Harry and checked to see if he was awake. Only just. She bent and kissed his warm brow and he half-raised a hand to her and then let it flop back. She dragged a rusty folding chair out of the shed and over to the table. 'What are you lot plotting?' She kissed the two women and rumpled her dad's hair. 'Had some foreign power better watch out?'

The three of them glanced at each other and then George spoke. 'We must look like the three witches in Macbeth – all we need is a cauldron. Actually, there were plenty of male witches in Shakespeare's day. In fact-'

'George,' put in Diane covering his hand with hers, 'stick to the point, dear.' Anna had never heard Diane use a term of endearment with her father before and she was amused and pleased. Joan was looking down at the table and trying not to smile.

George looked startled for a moment at this new organising force in his life and then recovered. 'We have something to tell you, Annie.'

She decided to tease him a little. It would be wonderful if he and Diane married and she would be the first to throw the confetti. 'Don't tell me, Dad, you're running away to sea.' They all stared at her in astonishment. She put up her hands in surrender. 'Joke!'

'How did you know?'

'What!'

'Well,' Joan said, 'they're not running away, they are coming back.'

'You're going on a cruise?'

'Well, sort of.' George couldn't stop the eagerness in his voice. 'We've booked a container ship voyage – me and Diane! We're going to Suez on the MV Orinoco out of Felixstowe!'

'The cabin is massive!' Diane put in eagerly, 'it's got two rooms and an ensuite and we'll be up high in that tower thing! There's a lift! We're the only passengers!' And then they all talked at once and it was only when Faye came into the garden wondering why there was nothing to eat that they stood up and woke Harry.

Over fish and chips the whole plan was outlined and Anna had to admit it sounded like just the kind of adventure that George and Diane would find diverting. What she didn't ask was how they would cope with Harry with George gone. Faye was unimpressed but when Ellis arrived late (where had he been?) he was more intrigued asking George to find out if the officers still knew how to navigate by the stars or was everything computerised and what kind of cargo would be in the containers. He would get the movie of Captain Phillips on Netflix so they could be prepared for attack by pirates.

Anna went up the stairs behind Faye to the bedroom which was now 'Harry's room' – the one that had been hers too for over twenty years. Harry was outside sitting happily beside George and drawing maps with a stick in the grass. Faye had asked her for some jumble items for a sale at the Centre and she had suggested they look through the stuff together. It would give her an opportunity to see how Faye was doing. Faye had no problem at all letting it be known if she was angry for some reason but she wasn't always so obvious when it came to distress.

'Where shall we start?' They looked round the room lit softly by the evening sun and Anna suddenly wished she had not thought of this. She threw open the wardrobe doors and they both peered inside. Faye pounced on an emerald green sleeve and pulled the dress out.

'Mum? This is so cool!' It was a fifties style fitted dress in heavy satin which had come briefly back into vogue in the late eighties and Anna had been pushed into it to serve as a matron of honour to a friend. It was now retro-cool, she realised. What was it they said, just live long enough? It made her feel old.

'Start a pile. Here, let's use this chair.' Faye set to work like a mechanical grab and soon all Anna was doing was saying, 'Yes,' 'No,' 'What was I thinking?' After a while she moved the dressing table stool across to the chest of drawers and pulled open the second drawer down. This had been her own drawer for underwear, socks, nighties and so on. She had taken her best cotton panties, socks and tights to her own little single room together with some serviceable bras and other bits and pieces. What was left? It had been over two years since she'd really looked in this drawer. The exhausted old cotton knickers were heaped up like a particularly ominous cumulonimbus in shades of grey with writhing discoloured bras tangled among them. So much for washing whites together. Chuck them all out. She started to pull things out methodically. The winter tights could go in one pile, the sheer ones in another and those once in a blue moon items like her golfing gloves would just have to be stuffed back in somewhere. Then her fingers felt slippery lace. Slowly she extracted a flimsy black short nightie embroidered around the hem and across the bust with exquisite flowers and leaves. She stared at it.

'Mum, what's that?' Faye's hair had tumbled down out of its knot and was heaped down her back.

Anna looked at her daughter, skin flushed with the perfect bloom of youth, standing slim and tall. She held up the negligee by its spaghetti straps. 'They used to call these baby dolls.'

'Did dad buy it you?'

Anna stroked the petals of the black flowers. 'Do you remember at all that holiday we had camping in France? It was so hot I was always slathering you in sun-block – you must have been about five – it was the summer before I was pregnant with Ellis.'

'Yes! There was boy that sold ice-creams every morning on the beach and he shouted "Miko!" and one day you let me go and buy my own and I dropped it in the sand and he gave me another one.'

'Because you were bawling loud enough to clear the beach!' Anna smiled remembering the furious scarlet face. 'We went to a little town one day, I've forgotten the name, and there was a flea market going on so we strolled around it. We had no money in those days.' Like now, she thought but didn't say.

'You never got this from a car boot?'

'Yes. There was a stall with so-called antique clothing *'vieux vetements'*– just old rags mostly – but your dad bent over this big basket of undies, can you believe it, and drew this out. He made the woman on the stall laugh by insisting it was for him, not for me, and in the end he bargained her down and bought it. It's beautiful isn't it?' Her fingers didn't want to stop caressing the fine mesh and the silky flowers but finally she held it out to Faye. 'Put it on the Centre pile.'

'No, Mum. Don't you want to keep it?'

Anna's eyes filled with tears and she turned away to continue tidying so Faye couldn't see. 'I'll never wear it again, love. Someone else will be pleased with it.' There would never again be a time when Harry would slip his hands beneath it to cup her breasts and then lift it from her shoulders and lay it gently aside so that their bodies could press together with delicious heat. All sexual desire had left him when his illness took hold. For months, while he had grown increasingly cold and hostile to her in the grip of his delusion, she had felt as though her own thwarted passion was worse than useless – a fire that only produced ashes without warmth or comfort. Was it better or worse now? She couldn't bear to think about it.

Then she felt the pressure of Faye's arms round her shoulders and the weight of the tousled head against hers and it was impossible not to sob aloud. Faye didn't speak and Anna was grateful.

Later in the evening when Harry had gone to bed and the others were in the shed, Ellis came to find her where she was curled up with a book on the sofa. She had just wanted to get outside her own head and have a break from the tangle of worries and emotion. She was pleased for her dad, of course, God knew he deserved some fun, and the tenderness of her usually scoffing daughter had moved her – but it was the scene with Nicola that had stayed with her. One minute she had been asleep safe in bed and the next witnessing a horrific scene from a different world and having to deal with it. Faye had initially wanted to tell everyone and boast about their daring raid but it had only taken a couple of words from Anna for her to realise that even talking about it wasn't an option. Tash and Nicola. Then, the ongoing dramas of adolescent life not abating, it had been replaced by newer, less desperate alarms.

'Mum?' Ellis was getting so tall these days. He had passed her a year ago, shrimp that she was, but now he was up to his dad's shoulder. 'Can I ask you something?' He had been late from the tennis club and had not had the time or inclination to shower so his face shone greasily with dried sweat and his coppery hair was pasted in dark brown streaks to his forehead.

'Of course.' Anna put down her book. 'What's up, sweetie?'

Ellis seemed anxious and tense. 'Faye told me what happened. With Nicola.' Well, she couldn't ask Faye to keep it from the family but she had hoped she would. Apparently not. 'Why didn't you wake me? I could have helped.' Anna had not expected this. 'You were in danger and I could have been there with you.' He looked away. 'You didn't ask me.'

Anna didn't know what to say. It was true, it had never crossed her mind to wake Ellis and even if it had she wouldn't have done. Ellis was a child. 'It happened so fast, Ell. I didn't have time to think, I just ran out when Faye called.' He still wasn't looking at her.

'I can do stuff, you know. You can trust me. I'm not just a little kid.'

'Ell, I've lost count of the number of times you've helped me. You're brilliant with your dad and-'

'Don't do that, Mum. Don't condescend.' For once his mature vocabulary did not amuse her. He was spot on. 'Just remember I'm here when things happen, ok?'

'Yes Ellis. I'm sorry.'

She heard him tread slowly up the stairs and then the click of his closing bedroom door. Faye had probably gone to town on the girl power aspects of the Nicola incident but also Ellis had an intelligent imagination and he would have realised how dangerous the situation was. He was growing up and his self-esteem had been knocked. Another marker pointed out to her before she had noticed it for herself. She must pay more attention. It was impossible to go back to her book. She sighed deeply and picked up the tv guide hoping there was something on which would distract her. There was a gentle knock on the living room door and Joan's head popped round. 'Can I have a word?'

Anna gratefully made room on the sofa. 'Yes, please.' She wrenched her mind back to the grand scheme. 'It's very exciting about the trip isn't it? I'm so glad dad is doing something for himself for a change.'

Joan's neat little frame barely dented the cushions. 'Yes. But we forgot to mention something.' Anna nodded for her to explain. 'It will be during half-term so Faye and Ellis will be at home but your dad feels you might need some back-up so I would like to come and stay for that week if that would be ok with you.' Anna leaned forward and kissed Joan's rubbery cheek.

'That is so kind. I haven't had time to think it through. I can probably get time off and I'd sort of planned to spend as much time as possible doing things with the kids – as much as they'll let me anyway.' But to have another adult around whom Harry knew would be great. 'Can I let you know?' It was a tricky one. She would love to have Joan's company and an hour ago would have jumped at the offer but after what Ellis had said she needed to be careful.

'Well, the offer's there. I'll be off now – your dad's taking Diane home.'

Anna stood up and they hugged goodnight.

No sooner had she settled back on the sofa with a groan than the door-bell rang. It was Michelle. They went into the kitchen and Anna got down a bottle of wine. Michelle looked as if she hadn't slept for days.

'How's Nicola?'

'She's had the tests – pregnancy, STDs all that and she's clear, thank God. And no sign of drugs but I'm keeping watch on that. She's so shaken she even agreed to see a therapist so that's starting next week. I don't know the woman but I think she'll be ok from the brief word I had.'

'And how are you?'

'Stunned. In shock. I've given up my volunteer work and I've switched my flexihours so I can be home when Nicola gets back from school. She must have been frightened because she didn't even put up a fight when I told her.'

'Will she talk about it?'

Michelle sighed and picked at the cracker crumbs on the table. 'It's the usual. Good looking lad, older, made her feel special and grown up. She thought he was her boyfriend and then, whoops, along come his mates and the emotional blackmail – if you really loved me and all that. That's when the bruises happened. Then it escalated, of course. Three nights later, he told her to meet him, he was taking her to a party and then disappeared.'

'So how does she feel about him now?'

'Well, that's the only bright light on the horizon. She's not making excuses for him or saying she loves him - she hates him and she feels really humiliated as well. I mean, apart from the obvious she feels humiliated at being taken in. You know Nicola, it was always her pulling the stunts.'

Anna waited a moment and then asked quietly, 'Have you talked to the police?'

'They want names, descriptions, all that that she can't give of course – it all happened quickly and in the dark from what I can make out but they did seem to be taking it seriously. The media's been all over this kind of thing lately and there is the physical evidence.' Michelle paused and dropped her head into her hands. 'They gave me a pretty hard time.'

'I'm so sorry.'

Michelle raised her head. 'They want to talk to you.'

'Yes. I thought they would. Did Nicola have a name for the boy?'

'They call him Mojo. Sounds black doesn't it, but he isn't. Nicola says he's very good-looking and he's got some sort of accent. He's not a boy – older than that.' How much did she really see of the man Afsoon was with? It's so easy to blur things, to not remember accurately and the only thing she could rely on was that he was tall because he was a good head taller than Afsoon. 'Could you describe any of them?'

'It was a blur at the time and I was swinging the torch round to disorientate them so I can't really be sure of anything. I think most of them were late teens, maybe early twenties. A couple maybe older. Not much to go on.' Anna drained her glass. 'I've tried to remember the car but of course the headlights were on so it was hard to see.'

'You were very brave, Anna. I'm sorry I had a go at you before. Thank you for what you did.' Michelle looked so broken Anna went to her and put her arms round her shoulders.

'Don't blame yourself. We can't watch them all the time even if they'd let us.' Anna suddenly laughed. 'I've just remembered something that happened earlier. We just can't do right. Ellis had a go at me for being over-protective and treating him like a kid.'

## 13

As she showed Michelle out Anna realised that now she had to tell her dad what had happened and on cue his car turned into the drive and briefly pipped a greeting.  She left the door open and went back into the kitchen hovering between the wine rack and the kettle.

'Hot chocolate for me,' George said firmly and added. 'Now then, I think you'd better tell me what's been going on. It hasn't passed me by that you hardly slept last night and Nicola and Tash staying over wasn't planned, was it?'  So she told him.  He sat silently for a few moments.

'Why do they do it, Dad?' Anna asked knowing she sounded like a kid.  'What's the matter with them?'

George scratched his gorsey chin.  'Do you remember I said to you that I'd seen bruises in that pattern before?  The ones on your face?'

'Yes.'

'Your mother and I were part of that generation that's been labelled as free love and flower power and all that and it was true to an extent but there was a darker side.  In some set-ups it just meant that girls couldn't say no any more.'

'How do you mean?'

'I think it was very bad in some of the universities – the first-year girls, naïve and desperate for freedom, away from home for the first time, you know.  Wild parties.'  Anna thought of her own university experience a generation later.  She didn't remember too many wild parties – it had been bloody hard work and worry that there may not be enough jobs at the end of it and then she had met Harry and he and their friends were all the social life she wanted. 'But of course it happened in other groups too.  Girls just felt they had to go along with well, promiscuity, not to put too fine a point on it.  If they didn't they were told they were frigid and boring and inhibited bourgeiosie.  For a few young men and some who weren't so young, the lecturers and professors even, the attitude was that the girls were ripe for plucking and they were entitled to grab as much as they wanted.' George sighed.  'All done in the name of freedom from stifling convention. They said that the girls wanted it, enjoyed it, and I expect some of them did. The young women, especially the more sheltered ones just thought they had to go along with it whether they wanted to or not.  The term date rape hadn't been thought up but it happened all the time. It was usually the girl who paid the price, of course, in the end. For many girls it wasn't free love at all, it came at a high price. The boys often got off scott free.'

'But you weren't a student, Dad.'

'No, but when your mother and I set off on that trip to Katmandou there were a lot of others our age doing the same and most of them were drop-out students. We heard the stories and we saw how they lived. We'd put the camper van on a site one night and there were loads of tents around. It was just outside Lyons. We'd been driving for eighteen hours and we were shattered or we probably would have joined one of the parties but we just crashed. There was singing and then a few high-pitched cries but I fell asleep. In the morning, I'll never forget, a girl was sitting on the grass trying to get a fire going to cook something. She was so dirty you could see the streaks down her face where she'd cried at some point. Just a young girl, maybe 17? She had those marks on her face. When they all got up later I saw that she was the only girl in that tent. There were three men. They just sat round smoking weed while she cooked and cleaned up. That's how it often was with the hippie life. The women got the dirty end of the stick.'

'So what are you saying?'

'It's group think, isn't it? What they used to call peer pressure. I think men are more susceptible than women to it but I may be wrong. It just takes someone charismatic and selfish to be the leader and most others follow. Not all, but most, especially the weak and the cowards. Dominating sexually can make weak and empty men feel powerful.'

'But the man who attacked me was on his own.'

'Physically alone, yes, but what was going on in his head? What tribe was he feeling he was part of that would approve of what he was doing? What does he really think of women?' Anna didn't want to think too long about that.

George got up slowly and wagged his head from side to side like a dog trying to shake out a tick. 'I still feel very ashamed that I didn't do anything or say anything. That girl was so alone even if she was pretending to herself that it was all Life with a capital 'ell.'' He took his cup to the sink and rinsed it. 'I sometimes wonder how much things have changed in our enlightened brave new world.'

Anna was working on inputting different versions of Cora's name when Steve appeared at her desk with two polystyrene cups of coffee.

'You've been staring at that screen for hours,' he said, 'change your focal length immediately Mrs Ames!' Anna smiled and arched her back, lifting her legs under the desk. It was true, she was stiff and could see small flashes of light like shooting stars. 'Actually, I have news.'

'Really? Alice has aced the sandpit dash?' She sipped and set the cup down.

'Nope.' He drew his chair closer and she folded her arms to keep her hands out of harm's way. 'You know that climbing chap I told you about who had been in William Grant's regiment? I wasn't expecting to see him for another month or so but he phoned yesterday and was in Birmingham for a conference so he came round and met Alice. He wanted to talk about some new gear for the club. Nice guy, Alice had him eating out of her hand in about six seconds.' When Steve was this close she was always slightly scattered, slightly skittish as though her thoughts had been caught by a sudden breeze.

'Did he know William?'

'Yes. They weren't particularly buddies but he did remember him because he happened to be going out with one of the personnel officers at the time and she told him what had happened that made William leave. Shouldn't have done, of course, it was confidential.'

Anna forced herself to track the logic. 'Just a minute, back up. How did you get him talking about William?'

Steve laughed and tapped his nose comically. 'I had a cunning plan! I bought in a couple of bottles of Drakes and made sure I had one on the coffee table. Then I had a swig, disgusting stuff, and mentioned that it was a local firm and the family still owned it.'

'So he said, "As it happens I knew one of them-"'

'You've got it.'

'Sneaky.' Anna was impressed and relieved.

'You'd better believe it. File away for future reference!'

'So go on.'

'It turns out that Charlotte wanting to have a settled life with sprogs at home was just a cover story. She loved the army life. She would have happily sent whatever kids off to boarding school.'

'So?'

'There was an incident on William's last patrol. He was in charge of a small group, not even a platoon, only about five men. They went out at night but got separated and three came back but not William and his corporal. The major was new and jumpy so he wanted to get up a search for them even though there had been no insurgent action in that area for weeks. The others said, let it go for a couple of hours but he insisted. So he went out on foot with two men and they found William and the Corporal in a dry ditch, a wadi I think they call it.'

'Wounded?'

'No.'

'Asleep?'

'No.'

'So what?'

'In the act. In flagrante.'

'No!' Anna sat wide-eyed staring at Steve. 'So was he discharged for that? Is that forbidden in the army?'

Steve rubbed his cheeks. 'Not as such, but it's a tricky one isn't it? If the press got hold of it, etc. I think the major was as much shocked at him having it off with one of the ranks as the act itself. But of course it was hugely frowned on. I mean, they were supposed to be on patrol and people could have got killed looking for them let alone the potential sexual exploitation angle because of the difference in rank.' Steve ran his fingers through his hair so that it assumed its usual spikiness. 'Turned out they'd been at it for weeks.'

'Well, blow me down.' Anna noticed Steve's expression and burst out laughing herself. 'Sorry.' She thought about the time she'd spent with William at the factory and how fond of him the staff seemed to be and how much she herself had liked him. 'What a story. So, he's been found a job in the firm in the time-honoured way. He's a nice guy, actually.'

'Yes, Dave liked him. It was probably a moment of madness to take such a risk. There can't have been too many opportunities in the field camp so maybe that was why. His date said that Charlotte had been spitting fire and brimstone when they were told that a managed honourable discharge was on the cards.'

'I can imagine. I bet she put him through hell. She's her mother's daughter in some ways.' Anna thought for a moment. 'What happened to the corporal?'

'Don't know. Didn't ask. Does it matter?'

'No, I just wondered.'

After Steve had left Anna sat for some time thinking. So much of what she had observed now made sense. William's meek abdication of parental authority, Charlotte's barely disguised contempt for him. Did the family know the real reason for them leaving the army? Hard to say, but she suspected not. After all, William had fathered two sons and was a soldier on active service – why would there be any questioning of his sexuality? It wouldn't be in Charlotte's interests to tell them and have the children find out at some point. She needed William for all sorts of reasons that had nothing to do with affection. For one thing, if she ditched him her connection to army social life would be over. Anna shuddered inwardly thinking of the thousand ways Charlotte could humiliate him and make his life a misery. And of course he would stay for the boys. What else could he do? If he left Charlotte would have no reason to keep the secret to herself and he would probably never see them again. The family had the power and the money and, never mind the ethics of the situation, he knew it.

And then there was Dook. Was he the corporal? William had said they had served at the same time in the same regiment but she had no idea of his rank. He had certainly not seemed over-awed by William in the brief encounter that she had witnessed, but then, William was not a domineering figure. Some men took that for weakness and showed it. Certainly Dook hadn't exhibited any pleasure at William's appearance in his domain. William himself had been friendly but he was with everyone.

So much for the dull Draycott family, Anna suddenly thought, remembering her first impressions. Blimey. Everyone except Richard so far had a potent secret. Maybe she should have another go at the arrogant CEO apparent, Anna thought mischievously. She'd quite enjoy finding his weak spot. Stop it. Unprofessional and self-indulgent. She phoned him.

'Why?' he asked.

'You're the de facto head of the company,' Anna said ingratiatingly. 'You must be the one that keeps the family both informed and on board, so to speak. That's quite a skill. So often family firms fail because there is no strong leadership and factions develop.' Was that true? She'd just thought of it. 'It would be useful for the article to have your input.' She held her breath.

'Ok, then. But I'm very busy. I have to fly to Brussels on Tuesday. I could talk to you at the airport before the fight for a few minutes.'

Hoist on my own petard, thought Anna wryly. The airport was a thirty-minute drive. 'Right. Thanks! What time?'

'You'd need to meet me in the check-in area at 6.30 a.m.' Brilliant. Anna rang off and banged her forehead gently with the palm of her hand. And now she would have to think of some questions which meant doing a slew of research.

The police arrived just as she was getting ready to leave work for the day. There was a small waiting room just off Harts' impressive lobby and she showed them into that. It was clean, tidy and windowless with half a dozen modular chairs and a pentagonal coffee table.

'Would you like tea or coffee?' She was relieved when they shook their heads. One was a man in his fifties, she guessed, thick-set and heavily used. The other was a woman as sleek as a whippet. She told them what had happened on the night that Nicola had been grabbed. DS Griffiths asked a few questions about her account without taking notes. Then he settled back. The woman, DC Blake, spoke.

'So, to sum up Mrs Ames, you didn't get the number of the car and none of you took any photographs. You didn't call us at the time of the incident and you put all the girls and yourself into danger by not doing so.' Anna was shocked into silence. 'Not only,' Blake continued, 'did you not call us for assistance at the time, you did not report the incident.' Her radio barked something unintelligible. 'It was Nicola's mother who did that and not until the next evening.' They both looked hard at Anna. 'Why was that?' The skin across the bridge of the policewoman's nose was stretched so tight that it shone.

'My priority was rescuing Nicola. Then, when we got back I thought her mother ought to be the first to know.'

'So why didn't you take her straight home?'

Anna knew she couldn't explain. They were hostile with her because she had acted without them until all the drama was over. They had been side-lined. She didn't regret what she had done for a moment but they wouldn't ever understand.

'It was a complicated situation and I judged it at the time to be the best thing to do. If Nicola had been harmed I would have driven her straight to the police station.' Would she?

'But that would have been too late, wouldn't it? Why didn't you call us at the time of the alleged assault?'

Anna felt she was being bullied. Surely her actions were not the central issue here? 'I thought that the police may not get there quickly enough to prevent Nicola being harmed. She was on the ground already.' They both drew in their chins as if they were being worked by the same puppeteer. 'What will you do now?'

They stood up, bored. 'We've made a note of what you say happened. There's nothing else we can do given the lack of evidence. No actual crime took place, did it?' Anna bit her tongue. 'You don't have any names or addresses for these men or even any descriptions we can use. The ladies could have set the whole thing up. The girl is clearly sexually active but won't give us names so it's in her interests to have her mother believe they're making her do it against her will.'

'Nevertheless,' said Anna as calmly as she could, 'Nicola is a child and has been criminally sexually assaulted in the recent past.' Not a ripple. 'In other words, she has been raped.' Nothing. 'Any collusion on her part is irrelevant.' Meaningful glances full of contempt shared between the officers. Anna opened the door for them. She didn't trust herself to speak as she followed them out. Just Nicola's luck to get a couple like this on her case. Anna climbed the stairs quickly to her office and wrote a brief report so that she could quote what they had said verbatim should it be necessary. Then she went in search of Steve.

'Can I come round tonight after Alice is in bed? I just need to blow off steam.'

'Of course. I'll text you when she's nodded off. We're into endless repeats of The Tiger That Came to Tea at the moment. I came up with the brilliant idea of recording it so I could just put it on a loop but she didn't go for it for a moment. I could practically say every word without the book.'

'You're a hero. I'll bring a bottle and George is making his apple pie. I'll try to salvage a piece.'

'You've got me.'

## 14

Afsoon was waiting on the Art Museum steps. Rain was just beginning to glaze the granite and brick of Chamberlain Square as Anna ran down the waterfall of curving ledges towards her pulling her hood up. They dashed inside laughing.

'Coffee first?' They climbed the marble staircase and made for the Edwardian Tearooms. Afsoon was wearing her black slacks and grey sweater, the first outfit Anna had seen her in, and the coat she peeled off was a classic dun mac. Nevertheless, heads turned and elderly men looked over their wives' shoulders in yearning at her. Today she also had on a bright turquoise and coral silk scarf which seemed almost frivolous given her usual austere look. In fact, she seemed to be fizzing.

'We will have cake!' she announced, scanning the rows of buns and sponges on offer. 'I will buy *you* cake, Anna!'

When they were settled at a table Afsoon gazed around her and up at the decorative wrought iron balustrade while she stirred her coffee. Anna hoped she would not be asking any searching questions about the 'old books' that Anna had mentioned. She need not have worried. 'I like this building. It reminds me a little of museums in cities like Delhi and Kalcott.'

'The Victorian architecture?'

'Yes. All old cities have the architectural fingerprints of the empires which conquered them.'

'Did you like the travelling part of your job?' Anna asked, determined not to embark on anything controversial and spoil the budding relationship. She liked Afsoon and was intrigued by her. Surely she had not been the woman she had seen on the back streets of Deritend? After all, Anna had been in a state of high anxiety that night and had only recently woken from a deep sleep and it had been very dark.

'Yes, I did to begin. But after a few years you know it becomes airports and hotels. Everyone says this. I liked most the museums and meeting the curators. Sometimes I would meet one who knew my father and this was always a pleasure. You know, to talk of the people you love is a joy, is it not?' Anna remembered the comment Afsoon had made about Steve and blushed.

'How do your parents feel about you living so far away?'

'They are dead.' Afsoon's fork was elegantly poised for the next portion of cake but her buoyant expression had evaporated.

'I'm so sorry. They must have been quite young.'

'Not old. It was a plane crash. The sanctions. Our government bought US passenger planes and then when the sanctions came in they could not get the spare parts. There are many crashes.'

Anna felt herself needing to bring back the lightness into Afsoon's mood. 'Tell me about your father if you don't mind. What was his interest?'

Afsoon dug her fork into the cake and smiled. 'He was a wonderful man – a scholar of the Artaxerxes dynasty. But more than that a kind and generous father. I was a very spoiled little girl.' She put her fork loaded with cake down and folded her arms as though she had lost her appetite. 'When they died my life changed completely. I was just a girl. I was taken to live with an uncle in north-east Iran, near Khar Turan National Park. That part of the family was very different from ours. Very traditional. My uncle did not value me. I was a nuisance and a burden. He had to let me go to school because my parents had left money for it but he only wanted to marry me to someone of his choice and it was always fighting.'

'But you did get a university education. You must have been very determined.'

Afsoon's lips twisted. 'Very scared.' She stared into space for a while. 'I ran back to Tehran when I was fifteen and some friends of my parents took me in and made it possible for me to study. They felt sorry for me. My uncle never came looking for me and I have not seen him since. Those people that sheltered me, I owe them my life. They know I am safe and married now and they are pleased I am here.'

Anna touched her hand. 'I've made you sad with my questions and you were so happy when we met. I'm sorry.'

'No, no, don't be sorry. I have no friends and it's good to talk even if it is of unhappy things. I am here now and I have a very nice secret which I was thinking of when we met. It's why I was so smiley.' Anna grinned at the adolescent adjective which came so charmingly from this dignified woman's lips which now parted and finally took in a piece of cake.

'A nice secret?'

'Ah, a secret is not a secret if it is told!' Afsoon tapped Anna's hand playfully with her teaspoon. 'Come, we must go to see the miniatures and we will be teacher and student as you requested, will we not?' Anna, delighted that Afsoon's cheerful mood had returned, meekly followed her out.

It was when they were peering into the cabinet showing the court of Shah Abbas and Afsoon was explaining how the artists tried to keep a tension between realism and stylisation in their representation, when she froze mid-sentence. Anna glanced at her and then followed the direction of her gaze. In the arch which led to the next gallery, silhouetted by borrowed light, stood a tall man who was looking directly at them. For a second Anna had the surreal illusion that he had stepped off the document they had been immersed in. His confident stance, his dark hair and handsome features seemed momentarily to be from a different age, a totally different context. Then he was gone. Afsoon was trembling slightly beside her but her face showed no signs of fear – rather she seemed even more excited. She turned to Anna. 'I must go to find the Ladies toilet, but you stay here and I will return very soon.' Not waiting for a reply she was striding, almost running, up the gallery and turned left at the end through the arch. It was impossible not to follow.

They were slightly obscured by an angle in the next gallery but Anna could see them well enough. The man was bending his head to talk to Afsoon animatedly and frequently he touched her arm or her cheek with a tender, caressing movement. Her head was tilted up to him. After a moment she put her hand into the large tote she was carrying and pulled out an envelope. He took it quickly and stuffed it into his inside jacket pocket, glancing around. Anna held her breath but he had not noticed her. His expression was mischievous, not guilty. Then Afsoon stood on tiptoe to kiss him twice on the cheeks and Anna quickly retraced her steps to the cabinet. A nice secret, indeed. The man was gorgeous but surely she was not giving him money? Beautiful and cultured as she was, she would hardly need to pay for services, would she? What else could have been in that envelope?

In a moment Afsoon was back by her side linking her arm into Anna's and radiating joy from every pore. Anna felt let down. This must have been a set up so that Afsoon and her man could meet and that meant that she had been used – Afsoon had not seen her primarily, at least, as a friend, but rather as cover.

Walking through the city on her way home Anna decided to get Harry a treat and stepped into her favourite music store. She was still processing Afsoon's 'nice secret.' Richard was away frequently and they had no live-in staff. It would be easy for Afsoon to slip away from their remote house and no-one would suspect anything. As they had walked the galleries she had been playful and teasing and had particularly picked out the love scenes in the miniatures to explain to Anna.

She browsed the racks of records, pausing and smiling over some of the covers. They still had her dad's old record player at home and every now and then she and Harry had used to like to come here and browse the vinyls. She noticed the prices were steeper than the last time she had visited and was pleased because it meant that people were valuing them more. It also meant that she might be able to shift some of the carefully stacked LP's that they had accumulated over the years from jumble sales and charity shops and the money would come in very useful.

She picked up a single that she remembered from a Northern Soul night they'd been to in Wigan Casino when they were students. It was a bit scratched but it would be fun for them both to hear it again. She remembered Harry, having got himself on the outside of three pints of real ale, whirling about like a sycamore seed and hauling her, protesting, with him. The buttons down the back of the dress had suddenly popped all at the same time as he tried to slide her between his feet and she had had to run off to find her coat, furious with him. They had made up later with endless kisses on the back seat of the early morning coach back to Leeds and had fallen asleep propped up against each other.

'Can I help you?' She must have been standing there for minutes looking like a zombie.

'No, I'm fine. I'd like this one please.'

A local derby between Warwickshire and Worcestershire was on Five Live Sports Xtra in the kitchen while George pottered about assembling a casserole. She kissed him as he confided despondently, 'Three for fifty-eight – can you believe it?'

'Going to get changed and see Harry.'

'Ready in an hour.'

'OK.'

'Oh, Anna?' She paused with her hand on the kitchen doorknob. 'What's up with Ellis?'

'What do you mean?'

'If he wasn't so young I'd say he's in love.'

'You're kidding! He's eleven!'

George sliced into an aubergine with panache. 'Well, something's going on. One minute wild-eyed and secretive and the next gazing out of the window soulfully like the Lady of Shallot.' He tossed the cubes into a hot pan. 'And he hardly ever sees Mike now he's at the tennis club all the time.'

'Maybe we should go up there tomorrow after school. You, me and Harry. Surprise him.'

George laughed. 'That's what happens when you have a sleuth on flexitime for a mum!' He flipped the vegetables and nodded at her. 'Let's do it.'

Anna glumly accepted her punishment for her moment of inquisitiveness, malicious inquisitiveness, over Richard. It was horribly early, it was raining and the roads were jammed with people driving badly. Some cosmic algorithm must be responsible for this irritating feature of British life. She crawled along the A45 towards the airport glancing frequently at the clock on the dashboard and adding an hour since she hadn't got round to adjusting it for summertime.

He was in the queue for the Brussels flight. He saw her and pointed to a coffee bar tucked under the departure lounge escalator. Her spirits rose. A very strong coffee was definitely in order. She mimed to see if he wanted anything but he shook his head.

A security official was now interviewing him in the Business Class line and she halted her urge to get coffee for a few moments to observe him while he was occupied. How would you know that his dark blue suit was expensive, she mused? What was it? As he slid something out of his inner jacket pocket having stooped to put down his overnight bag, she found the answer. The clothing obeyed him, in fact, it was almost obsequious to him. Whatever movement he made the cut flattered. When he was still the suit immediately resumed the perfect shape for his body. She thought of Len. His army surplus greatcoat had a life of its own. It could never be accused of sycophancy. As Len moved it complained, protested, pulled, snagged, seams tore and if angry enough it rubbed him under the arms and at the back of the neck. It let him down in public by announcing its contempt for him - bagging, sagging and getting more dirty and creased than could be justified. Perhaps she should write an article on the personality disorders of clothing, Anna thought, and flog it to a Sunday supplement? She shook her head and smiled at her own whimsy. It was very early in the morning. Coffee.

She had only just sat down when Richard placed himself opposite to her and checked his watch. He wasted no time. 'So you've seen Kimi, I hear.' His agenda, then, not hers.

'Yes.' She tried very hard to pronounce the full stop after the monosyllable. It was wasted on him.

'And?'

'Richard, we've been over this. I work for your father within the remit he's given me.'

'But girls talk, don't they? They gossip and tell each other things they don't tell other people.'

She sipped her coffee to stop herself asking him if there wasn't a museum somewhere wanting to put him behind glass. 'Neither of us are girls, Richard,' was all she could allow herself to say. He grunted in disappointment. What an earth was he expecting? 'Actually, since you have raised this for the second time in as many meetings, I must say that I am puzzled as to why it has any interest for you?'

Richard's sharp face flushed. 'Of course it has interest! There's someone out there, isn't there, who has a very close connection with my family. Who knows what trouble he could make? I just can't take the risk.' Anna could not make sense of this.

'What risk? As I understand it he has never been any part of the family. He may not even know he is Rhea's father.'

Richard's mouth tightened in a way that reminded her of his mother. 'You wouldn't understand. What did you want to ask me, anyway?'

Anna produced one of her contrived questions. 'I've been reading interviews with other family business dynasties and it seems there is often a tension between generations over innovative versus traditional ways of doing things. Does Drakes experience this tension and if so how have you dealt with it?' She couldn't have got that out without a good four fluid ounces of stimulant at this time of the morning, she thought.

'Yes, that is a problem for many family enterprises.' He slid into automatic. 'When a CEO has been successful at maintaining and even growing the business he assumes that his is the only way to go and is resistant to new ideas and that is reinforced by the family hierarchy naturally.' He glanced at his watch again. This was familiar ground to him and his answer was slick. 'The upcoming generation may want to do things differently but lack the authority so there can be tension. We talk frequently at Drakes and we take small steps. Managing change is rarely successful if it's done drastically - unless things have got way out of hand. I would never allow that.'

'Of course your father is the current CEO,' Anna couldn't resist reminding him.

'Yes.' Richard hesitated. Anna remembered Charlotte's cryptic remark about there being no room for sentimentality. She took a gamble.

'There seem to be so many mergers of large companies happening currently,' she said as if simply thinking out loud. 'Cadbury's, of course, here in Birmingham, and now the pharmaceutical giants.' She did not look at him as she said this but gazed vaguely around.

'Why do you say that?' His nostrils had whitened and there was deep flush across his cheekbones that made his eyes glitter.

'Just wondering about your views on the wider business trends,' Anna said calmly. 'Any words of wisdom?'

Richard stood up. 'I have to go. I can't imagine why my father hired you. But,' he shook his finger near her face, 'I insist on reading this article before it is submitted for publication.'

Anna merely smiled and took another sip of coffee and he strode off. He knew he had no right to ask that, he was just posturing. But something had rattled him and she pondered it. Was there a merger in the offing or even a sell-out? In idle moments she had kept track of the stock market listings for Draycott's and over the weeks of this assignment she had seen them slip. Nothing dramatic, but the trend was down rather than up. The market was overcrowded for soft fizzy drinks and now people were looking at healthier options and in a tight economy less willing to waste money on nutritionally empty food and drink items.

And another possibility had come from this surprisingly fruitful encounter. Richard had displayed the irrational suspicion characteristic of paranoid thinking. Realistically, Rhea's father could be no threat to the business or the family even if he knew of his status and decided to make himself known. It might be very threatening to Kimi and Rhea personally but not to Richard. He had shown no affection for his sister so it didn't seem to be that he was concerned to protect her.

Anna got up and ordered another coffee, this time treating herself to a croissant, and sat down to think some more. There was something there, something she hadn't quite grasped. If she was right and Richard had a tendency to paranoia and the need for control how did that fit with the family dynamics as she understood them so far? Even if he didn't know the truth about William's army discharge his brother-in-law presented no threat. He was obviously under Charlotte's thumb and had quietly taken a post in the company which had no real power. Kimi seemed satisfied with her work on the financial side and had shown no interest at all that Anna could see in contesting Richard's position as heir apparent. She had never so much as mentioned her work to Anna – her passions were her daughter and her horses. She seemed to care for little else. Gerald himself was ready to step aside for Richard simply because he couldn't continue. She wondered if Richard or the rest of the children knew about Gerald's terminal illness. She must ask. Richard's wife, Afsoon, had no power at all and, on the surface, no support system of any kind. Perhaps he had engineered that. Perhaps part of her attraction was that she came without anyone or anything which could weaken his hold over her and her dependence on him. She could be completely dominated and do nothing about it. That may account for why he had waited to marry until he was in his forties. Where, among contemporary women, would he have found a woman with such class, beauty and intelligence together with a willingness to be subservient? An apparent willingness. The handsome man stroking Afsoon's cheek and kissing her tenderly in the gallery, Afsoon's natural habitat, popped up in Anna's inward eye. What would Richard make of his wife's 'nice secret'? Good luck to her, she thought, draining her cup and getting up to leave, he's a bully and a control freak.

So perhaps that was all it was, she concluded, walking between the politely retreating glass doors, maybe it's just the one part of his world that he can't control – the existence of the mysterious stranger who is Rhea's father. Or even simply that Kimi had dared to keep a secret.

## 15

By the time Anna, George and Harry got to the tennis club on Hawthorn Road, Ellis was on the court warming up. He had his back to them as they settled themselves in the specatators' benches. Harry was keenly attentive to everything and Anna became a little apprehensive. They never knew what fragments of memory could be stirred, as with the bike incident, and Harry had loved tennis although he'd not belonged to a club, just played on public courts with his friends. Anna pointed Ellis out to him, hoping to focus him on the present. 'That's me,' he said but smiled as he said it, and the boy was just how he would have looked at that age. Anna took his hand and stroked the long fingers.

      Then Rhea came on to the court. It was a few seconds before Anna recognised her. Her whites were immaculate, her hair disciplined into a knot under a peaked cap and when she hit her first practice serve there was a collective intake of breath. There was real power behind that stroke. Anna remembered the floppy, traily, frankly weird girl she had met and was astonished. Maybe Rhea chose that persona at home as a reaction to Kimi's muscular, over-protective presence. Maybe she had intuited that it would drive her mother frantic and give her some power. After all, much as Anna liked Kimi so far, she was a bit full-on, especially with her daughter.

      Now, the practice session over, the youngsters were being split into pairings for a game. The courts were limited and of necessity only three pairs at a time could play. Ellis had still not noticed them and had linked up with Rhea to sit on a bench at the front of the spectators' section waiting for their turn. Anna was rather amused to observe the two together. It was strange to see Ellis with a girl. Although he was two years younger than Rhea he was taller and even seated he was inches above her. She seemed to be doing all the talking. In fact, she seemed to be going on and on. Her hands gestured frequently and at one point she looked round as if in fear and Anna caught an expression of desperation in her eyes. Anna became more alert. Ellis was listening intently. Then she was called to play and walked quickly away wiping her eyes with a finger. Anna looked back to her son. Ellis had dropped his head in apparent dejection. What on earth was going on? Usually kids of their age joked and teased or maybe exchanged some comments about what was happening, but this conversation had been intense and emotional.

'Ow,' said Harry beside her.

'What?' She brought herself back to him. He was staring at her in bewilderment.

'Ow,' he repeated. She glanced down at their linked hands and saw that she had gripped his so tightly that she had hurt him.

She released his hand and stroked it quickly. 'Sorry, Harry. Sorry, darling.' George, on Harry's other side, suggested a cup of tea all round and rose to get it. By the time she looked back to the courts Ellis was playing against a talented blond boy whom she'd noticed before as one of the better players. Ellis won the first game which normally would have pleased her, but she had noted the aggression that he had put into his shots and wondered what was driving it. Could she talk to him about the conversation she'd witnessed? Maybe not that, but she could bring up Rhea's name surely? Tell him that she knew the girl, and knew her mother, and see what he said.

As she parked on the drive at home and Ellis sprang out and leaped up the steps to the front door, Faye burst out, rushed up to Anna and hissed in her ear, 'Tell him to wash! If you don't I will. He's disgusting! Bits of him are actually up my nose!' So Len must be here.

He was sitting in his usual toad-like pose on the frail garden bench and playing his flute. Anna put the kettle on and watched him fondly from the kitchen window while it boiled. She was proud of him. Without any help or encouragement except a desultory lesson or two on a tin whistle from an acquaintance of their mother's at the club where she had worked when he was a boy, Len had taught himself to play. He couldn't read music and didn't want to learn but he was pitch perfect and had an innate sense of musicality so that whatever tune took his fancy he would render delicately and faultlessly after only a few attempts. Sometimes he would play commercial jingles he'd taken to or film themes but today he was playing something he had learned from the James Galway CD George had given him for his birthday. *El Condor Pasa*. As Anna watched Harry appeared, attracted as always by the music. They rarely spoke. Harry lay down on the mildewed lounger and closed his eyes. Without her noticing, George had joined her at the window.

'Ellis is good isn't he?'

'Yes. I'm impressed.'

'Have you had a word?'

Anna turned to face him. 'Are you still worried, Dad?'

George stretched his neck and pursed his lips. 'Only a little. Not really worried, even. More puzzled. His light seems to have dimmed, if you know what I mean. He seemed to be having a very private conversation with that girl at the club.'

'Yes, I saw. Actually, I know her. She's Gerald Draycott's grand-daughter.'

'Small world,' said George in surprise.

'Not really. She goes to the Priory School which isn't far away and this is probably the best programme for junior players in the city. She's got a lot of promise herself.' Anna paused wondering how much to say. 'Actually, she is rather a strange girl and to be honest, Dad, I wasn't thrilled to see Ellis so caught up with her.'

George patted her on the shoulder. 'I know you'll handle it well,' he said. 'I'd have a word myself but it isn't the kind of conversation we have normally.'

'No, I've got it, Dad. I'll just let him have his shower. Are you ok to make dinner?'

'I picked up a couple of frozen pizzas from Sainsburys this morning and some garlic bread so I've only got to make salad. I'll get it sorted in half an hour or so. I hadn't reckoned on Len so maybe I'll bulk it out with that soup I made yesterday.'

'Not that Len needs bulking out but that sounds great.' George flicked his fingers at her and went out through the short passage to his shed. She mentally added another half hour on to his estimate and picked up the cup of tea she had made for Ellis to take upstairs.

'Hi - for you,' she said, taking two biscuits out of her pocket and putting them on his computer desk next to the mug.

'Thanks Mum but,' he picked up the mug carefully and moved it to his bedside table. Wasn't that supposed to be the other way round? She used her laptop as a tray quite frequently.

'Sorry. Hey, you did well today.'

'Mm. Thanks for coming. I didn't see you there till the end.'

'Our pleasure. Your dad really enjoyed it.' She paused while Ellis dunked his biscuit. 'I noticed the girl you were chatting to. She's very good isn't she? A really strong back-hand.'

Ellis swallowed and stared out of the window. 'She's amazing. She's so brave.'

Anna considered this. She noticed he did not ask 'which girl?' and seemed already to have her in mind. 'Brave?'

Ellis looked back at her as if remembering who she was and popped the rest of the biscuit in his mouth. 'Aggressive player, you know.'

'I've met her before,' Anna said. 'I know her mother, too.'

Ellis stopped chewing and stared at her. 'What?'

'I had to interview the mother as part of a work assignment. I went out to their farm. They have the most gorgeous horses.'

'What?' Ellis said again, his chin dropped forward. 'You *know* her?'

'Not very well. I've just run into Rhea a couple of times in passing.' She watched Ellis with surprise. He was completely disconcerted. It was as though she'd told him she'd seen a unicorn in the garden. Then, in a rapid shift, he blurted out that he'd forgotten to take Mike's textbook for chemistry that he'd borrowed and he'd have to go. He grabbed a book and was gone. She sat on the bed for a few moments trying to make sense of his reaction and not managing it.

Slowly she made her way to her own single bedroom and peeled off her work clothes. She was uneasy. It was unlike Ellis to be secretive, although she couldn't really even say he had been that. He was surely too young for romantic feelings. What she had observed of nascent sexual attraction in other kids had taken the form of play-fighting and insults, not the intense, almost adult concentration of his connection with Rhea. 'All this sex stuff is a bloody nuisance,' she told her reflection in the mirror sternly, 'what is the point of it? Nothing but trouble.' Then she remembered that tomorrow she had asked to consult Steve at work about the Cora search and her heart burgeoned with pleasure. She shook her head and groaned.

The office was a ferment of indignation and speculation. Anna, a little left out of the loop because of her unusual assignment, was quickly brought up to speed by Suzy. The big job they had been working on had blown up spectacularly when a clandestine trust fund had emerged to add to an already enormous inheritance. The problem was that the trust fund investments had turned out to have unsavoury links to organised crime which had been uncovered by a financial consultant whom Harts had hired. This meant that the whole cash cow was, as Suzy succinctly put it, botoxed. Probate could not be completed and Harts could not take its fee until the case had been investigated and that could take years. Most of the senior researchers had put in huge amounts of over-time and Ted was now trying to persuade them to wait for their money. She made for the sanctuary of Steve's office.

Steve closed his door behind her. 'I'm so glad you've got something for me to work on. It'll be great to have a real problem apart from all that,' he said tipping his head to the open-plan office. She quickly brought him up to date with her search for Cora, describing her as a distant cousin with whom Gerald wanted to get back in touch, rather than revealing the true facts.

'Have you searched the electoral register?'

'Wouldn't that take for ever?'

Steve swung his chair round and pulled a book down out of its cubbyhole and checked the index. He was pragmatic in the way he kept his research resources. Not everything had to be digitised. 'Here you go. Try this website – **canada411**. It's got the names and telephone numbers of everyone on the electoral register.' He pushed his fingers through his hair and then penitently tried to pat it down. Alice kept telling him off for his rooster coiffure. His bony, sculptured face was softened by the light from the screen and she couldn't help noticing the welt of sunburn on his neck from the weekend's climbing. Her fingers longed to smooth it. 'It would be great if she's on it but don't get too excited because she could have got married as you know. Hang on a sec.' He brought up a website and typed rapidly. 'Oh, drat, it seems Voisine is actually quite a common French-Canadian name. Oh well.' He turned to face Anna and smiled. Unbelievable to think that there had been a time that she would not have registered the staggering wattage of his smile.

'I'm trying some permutations of Cora and Voisine as far as spelling goes,' she said.

'Yeah.' There was a pause. 'These newspapers you're contacting – do they have online versions?'

'Yes.'

'Good.' There was no reason for her to stay but neither of them moved. 'How's Ellis liking the tennis?'

'Loves it. He's quite good.'

'Yes, I'm not surprised – he's got a good build for it and his hand-eye skills are great. I've noticed from the climbing. Watch out Andy Murray, eh?'

'Mm.' Anna wiggled her toes inside her shoes. 'Alice ok?'

'Mm. She's made an edict that we all call her Lisha like Faye does.'

'Ha.' It was becoming unbearable.

'Fancy a pub lunch?'

Steve almost leaped from his seat and within minutes they were out through the high green-glass atrium and striding down the red and black brick towpath. A light drizzle was drifting over them and making catspaws on the oily water of the canal. They passed his old apartment and it was impossible not to stop and look up at the huge curved window that was its most striking feature.

He glanced down at her, his eyes soft. 'Your hair's covered with tiny drops of water,' he murmured, touching the crown of her head lightly, 'You look like a nereid. I can just see you draped in a wisp of net curtain splashing around decoratively and luring poor yokels to their doom.'

Anna tried to smile. 'Do you miss it?' She asked neutrally glancing up at the apartment and trying not to think of what had happened between them in that room with the panoramic outlook. Steve said nothing and she thought he must be remembering the early days of living there when he and his wife Cathy were still together before the accident which had made him responsible for Alice and had caused the end of the marriage.

Steve wheeled round and knotted his hands helplessly behind his head. His eyes were dark blue and fierce and his face glistened with rain. 'I don't miss it, Anna! I miss you,' he said. 'I miss holding you, kissing you. I miss us!' Anna felt as though she was choking. 'I know nothing can happen, I know that. Harry is a fantastic guy and what he has is so unfair and me being like this is unfair on you but I can't help it, Anna!' He stopped and stared at her. 'You know when you were upset that night and you came to see me up there in the apartment and we were together for hours just holding each other and talking? Nothing happened but it was one of the best times of my life.  I never have had that connection with anyone else. I felt as though I had come home.'

'Steve-'

'Don't say anything.  I know there's nothing to say.  It's just that sometimes I think I'm going to explode with wanting you.  I thought it would be great to live near to you but it's worse.  It's so much worse!'

'I know.  I know.'  Anna could barely speak.

The next moment they were kissing passionately, hard and deep.  Then they stopped and stared, appalled, at each other.  'I'm not coming back to work,' Steve said, his voice almost sobbing.  'I'm going for a bloody run.  Tell them I'm not well.  Tell them anything.  I'm sorry Anna.'  A minute later he was out of sight.

Anna walked slowly back numb from the overload of sensation.  She had relied on Steve's self-control all these weeks without even realising it.  If he gave way how on earth could she hold out?  And then, it would all be over like an explosion that leaves only wreckage because neither of them would be able to stand the guilt of cheating on a good man who trusted them and who was dying neuron by neuron of a hideous disease.

Friday night's poetry session was uncomfortable.  For the first time since George had started these readings over two years ago, she felt tense and wrong-footed.  Normally Ashok came and Faye and Ellis and maybe a couple of George's poetry group friends or acquaintances passing through.  No effort was involved as people either read their own work or were given poems to read from some of the collections that George was constantly sent to review for the magazine he published.  No-one was expected to comment or critique, in fact, that would have been frowned on.  As far as Anna was concerned all she did was turn up and relax.  She enjoyed reading and hearing the others and if sometimes the poetry was less than brilliant so what?

But tonight's session would be different.  Faye had gone with Tasha to Steve's to babysit Alice and to revise, which meant they'd spend as long as they dared keeping Lisha up to play with, and Ellis was, as ever these days, at the tennis club.  Ashok was coming and, of course, Harry who no longer took part but seemed content to let it all wash over him.  But George was fond of Steve, his old campaign buddy over Briony's tragic situation, and had asked him to come.

Anna wished he hadn't after what had happened yesterday. His presence would be an ordeal – it would be impossible to relax and despite his air of vagueness her dad noticed everything.

'Is Joan coming?' she asked as she stacked the dinner dishes in the washer. Having Joan there would make it all right. She wouldn't feel so exposed. George was sorting through a pile of slim books and putting markers in here and there. He looked up in distress.

'I forgot to ask her. I know Diane can't come, there's a forum about endangered species or something she promised to be at but I forgot about Joan.'

Anna rapidly wiped her hands and pulled out her phone. 'I'll give her a ring, she's only fifteen minutes away.'

Joan replied in a whisper. 'Can't tonight. I'm in a U3A committee meeting. Sorry, Anna, can't chat, I should have switched off the phone.'

So half an hour later the five of them were there in George's shed either perched or sunk in an assortment of chairs whose best before date had expired decades earlier. Steve's presence changed the whole atmosphere. His animation, his energy, his sheer muscular vitality seemed to make the place throb uncomfortably. The shed was too small for him. George welcomed him warmly and handed him a book with three markers torn from newspaper sticking out. 'Have a look at those and see if there's one you like,' he suggested. 'You're all right reading one aren't you?'

'I'll give it my best shot.' He was friendly, smiling, willing to be a humble part of this group but it was impossible. Harry lay on a car seat, his eyelids already drooping. The sight of him wilting like an old man right next to Steve perched alertly on a bar stool set up something like anger in Anna. She knew it was irrational. She couldn't even understand why she felt it. Steve had done nothing wrong.

Ashok was unwrapping a chocolate orange. 'I nearly forgot to give you your vitamins!' he cried and tapped sharply before handing the foil package round.

'I'll just be a minute,' Anna said jumping up. 'Start without me.' They would assume she had gone to the bathroom but instead she leaned her back against the kitchen door and fought to control her emotions. One, two, three, four, she breathed. After a few minutes the trembling stopped and she opened the door quietly and went back to the shed.

They weren't reading poems. Steve and Ashok were in animated conversation and George looked nonplussed and side-lined. She had forgotten that Ashok, George's old friend and co-philosopher, was a computer scientist. When he and his wife had been kicked out of Uganda by Idi Amin in 1972 he had come to England hoping for a job in electronic engineering which was his profession then but finding no work offered to him and seeing that personal computers might become very big, he had started his own business. Now he was a modestly wealthy man but his joy was writing and reading poetry and when he and George had met at a local group they had bonded instantly and permanently. Anna couldn't remember a time when he had not been part of their lives. Now he and Steve were excitedly speaking some kind of strange language of which only the connectors and none of the nouns or verbs could be understood.

George tipped his head at them. 'And they say that poetry is obscure!' But Anna could see he was upset. He did so much for the family and this was his precious time.

'Right you two,' she said firmly, 'We'll have none of that filthy talk at my dad's literary soiree!' They laughed but they took the point and turned to George.

'Anna, would you like to start?' he said happily. 'I've just been sent a brilliant collection from Jenna Plewes. It's quite remarkably powerful – sensitive, strong and original.' He handed her a book with a torn receipt marking two poems. And she found that she was all right, that she could read and that the moment of panic had passed.

When the reading was over Steve had slipped away saying he needed to check on Alice since she had been snuffling earlier. George and Ashok stayed in the shed chatting as the session had been shorter than usual and she had taken Harry up to bed. These days he would even let her help him undress instead of insisting on George being there and she took a long time to bathe him with a flannel and prepare his toothbrush. When they were back in his bedroom and he was climbing rather awkwardly into bed she asked, 'Would you like me to stay with you for a bit, Harry?' She hadn't meant to ask it, the words had just overflowed out of her before she could stop them.

'What for?' he said, not unkindly.

'Just to keep you company, sweetheart.'

'I want to go to sleep now. There's no room for you.'

'Ok.' She had made slowly for the door and closed it quietly behind her. As she descended the stairs the front door crashed open and Faye and Tasha came in arguing hotly about Britain's Got Talent. They disappeared into the living room and the television noise came on. Anna stood still three steps from the bottom and considered the options. Too late to go out, too early to go to bed, too exposed in the kitchen, too noisy in the living room. There was no place left for her to go. She took the last few steps, picked up a cardigan from the coat rack and went out into the night.

When Harry had been in his wandering off phase last winter he sometimes went down the road to an old church where he could sit and listen to the organist practise. The priest there recognised him by sight and knew the situation. He'd been tactful and compassionate before and Anna found herself turning in at the lych gate and hoping he may be around. But it was Friday night and the church was locked against vandals. Anna found a bench and sat with her arms wrapped round herself, hunched and miserable.

Afsoon seemed to have no problem cheating on her husband. William and Gerald in their different ways had readily cheated on their wives and had only been stopped by circumstances. Were she and Steve being over-scrupulous? Would Harry know or even care if he did? There had been absolutely no sexual connection between them for nearly two years. *Nearly 2 years!* She snorted at herself. That was no time at all. If she had not met Steve she would have had no problem – it was him, the physical, warm, vital reality of him that was the problem. She might even have fallen for him if Harry had been healthy and their marriage sound. This was a new thought and she sat up abruptly to process it. Surely not? And yet several marriages she knew had come to grief when the couple were in their forties. Some disturbing ideas happened like, if not now, when? Is this all there is? How much longer to I have to put up with this? This/he/she is never going to change. And there was the never to be underestimated power of boredom and the consequent allure of a new, exciting romantic experience. Affairs didn't just happen in bad marriages, after all.

She shivered and rubbed her upper arms. It was a clear night and she tipped her head back to see what constellations she could identify. The air was too polluted in the city to see the Summer Triangle but she could make out, up near the zenith, Cygnus, the Swan. She squinted at it. More of a crooked cross than a swan, she thought. A memory came to her in full-colour and with sound and sensation and smells. It was the first day she and Harry had met, unromantically, in the queue for lunch in the student union. They had stayed talking for hours missing lectures and then, still talking, had gone out into the dark city streets and wandered, unseeing, around the city until they had found themselves on Woodhouse Moor among the winos and street people huddled on benches and they had lain down on the cold earth wrapped in each other's arms and gazed at the miracle of a starry sky looking down only on them. They had been fused in their cocoon of arms and lips and breath, at the centre of the universe.

Anna got up and went home.

Later, lying in her single bed and listening to a fox somewhere coughing, she thought about Steve's reading. The poem had been about an old man remembering his youth and the long walks he had taken over the Welsh hills never noticing time or hunger and Steve had read it in an unfussy way, his deep voice giving the words their due weight. It had been a good choice by George and at the end Steve had said how much he had liked it, surprise on the edge of his tone, and she could see by the way he turned the book in his hands that he had made a mental note of the author and the title. She tried to remember some of the lines. Wasn't there one about a meandering sheep track that went nowhere? And on that thought, she fell asleep.

## 16

Kimi's phone call was a surprise and a good one. She was inviting Anna and whomever else she wanted to bring to join her and Rhea and Kevin and two horses at the American Saddlebred Show at Moreton Morrell that Sunday. It had been weeks since the whole family had been out together and Anna raised it with them at dinner.

'There'll be loads of different breeds – beautiful horses – and it's in a lovely part of Warwickshire. We could take a picnic!'

Faye chewed her sausage and prodded a roast potato. 'Who's going?' Anna told her. Ellis looked up, startled, and almost choked on his food. 'So what happens?'

'I'm not sure. There'll be judging, you know. I suppose they ride the horses around and the judges pick the best ones.'

'Sounds like a riot. I suppose they'll be pooping all over the place?'

'Well – '

Faye licked her teeth. 'You need to get out more, Mum. I've got a feeling I'm going to be busy that day as epic as it sounds.' Anna made a face at her sarcasm.

George was wriggling in his seat and his eyebrows were hopping up and down. 'Dad?'

'It's just that Diane and I had planned to do some research on our trip. It's only a couple of weeks away and we want to look some stuff up and make lists. But of course we'll come if you want.' Ellis had tried to finish his sausage too quickly and was hiccupping. Faye banged him none too gently on his back.

Anna turned to Harry. 'Would you like to see some horses Harry?' Harry immediately got to his feet.

'Where? Where are they?'

'Not now, darling. On Sunday. We'll have a day out in the country. Ellis?'

'Yes, Mum, I want to come!' Realising he had sounded too eager, he added. 'I'd like to learn more about horses. I mean American Saddle-breds.'

'Right,' said Anna drily, 'we'll see if we can make up for that gap in your education. Just you and me and your dad, then.'

'What about Joan?'

'That's a good idea. I'll phone her after dinner. All right with you, Ellis?' He looked bewildered to be consulted.

'Oh, yup. Of course.' Anna tucked in her chin and tried not to smile. He did seem to have it bad as far as Rhea went for all he was only eleven.

Joan seemed rather subdued on the phone, her normally firm voice slightly hesitant and a little rough but she'd said yes, she would like to come and have a day out in the country and look at horses. There was something she wanted to talk to Anna about, nothing urgent.

Sunday started off gloomy but by the time they were in the car the sky was clear blue and only clumps of fair-weather clouds drifted about. Harry sat in the front with Anna as his long legs couldn't cope for more than a short time in the back seat. He had been momentarily alarmed by the fact that George wasn't part of the group but Anna had given him three CDs to choose from for the journey and the distraction was enough to break the mood. She glanced at him as Ellis clambered into the back wondering as she had done for some time whether he could still read, or, more accurately, whether his brain could still process the marks. He certainly hadn't picked up a book or a newspaper for ages. That time near Christmas when he had read a poem faultlessly at one of George's evenings was a very long time ago. She leaned towards him. 'Which one do you fancy?' He tugged open the glove compartment and took everything out item by item. A tyre pressure gauge, a notebook with a lump of chewing gum stuck to it, one glove, a torch, his Keruve GPS watch, not worn for weeks since he no longer wandered off on his own. It had been a godsend when he got lost, signalling his location on their receiver at home. Then he found the CD Anna had hidden.

'This one.' Anna heard Ellis groan.

'Right. Tom Waits it is then.'

They picked up Joan who was waiting outside her house with a cooler box. Twenty minutes later they turned off the M40 and were immediately in deep countryside. Anna asked everyone to look out for signs to the show, probably billboards or temporary notices on signposts but there was nothing. She imagined it would be something like the Three Counties Show and was hoping they'd beaten the main bulge of traffic and wouldn't have to queue too long to get in. In fact, they drove straight past the Warwickshire Agricultural College and were in pretty Moreton Morrell village before she realised they must have gone wrong. They turned back and drove slowly through the college gates and down the long drive with fields on either side to a collection of low brick buildings and a large covered arena. There had been not one notice and certainly no queue. They parked and got out. There were half a dozen other cars. It was so quiet. Between the visitors' car park and the larger park for horseboxes and trailers a couple of teenage girls were sauntering, one twirling a velvet riding hat in her hand. When Anna spoke to them they turned and pointed to the left of the arena. No-one was even taking money.

Then she heard a whinny and all of them looked at each other and smiled. Harry said, 'Hey ho Silver!' and Anna took his hand. They walked through a quadrangle of brick- edged beds filled with fennel and viburnum and other shrubs in a subtle palette of greens. 'This is nice,' said Joan, 'and there are the loos.' On the other side there was a covered outdoor area floored with peat and bark where an assortment of horses were being trotted round on leading reins. In the middle stood a grandmotherly-looking person paying close attention. Anna knew very little about horses but couldn't see any similarities between them and wondered what breed they were. She noticed with pleasure a snack van which was doing a brisk trade in bacon butties and wished they hadn't brought a picnic. Maybe later. Even now, at the hub of the activity, it was quiet. Various people stood around at the heads of horses. Anna and Harry looked around smiling at the beautiful animals.

'Hey! Mum! Watch out!' It was Ellis who'd been off in search of Rhea. Anna turned and saw a huge black animal towering above her. On its back was a tiny blonde woman dressed in black jacket and a flat black hat with a brim. The horse was enormous. Its foaming mouth was way above her head and on a level with Harry's. They both jumped back. The horse skittered past, sweating, its eyes rolling and its massive haunches pulsating. Swinging from between its back legs was a fully distended male member as long as a man's arm. Anna glanced at Ellis and they both snorted. Thank goodness Faye hadn't come. She had a clear and carrying voice. They watched it go both fascinated and alarmed. It was the size of a dray horse but that was where the resemblance ended. This horse was young, full of beans and only just under control, Anna thought. It had now stopped, raised its head and uttered a passionate whinny.

Despite themselves they were mesmerised. Most of the horses were as excited as teenagers clubbing.

'It's a Freisian. Isn't it a beautiful beast?' Kimi had found them.

'Yes. Is it safe?'

'Of course it is. Well, as safe as horses ever are. Come over here, I want to watch this.' They moved to the covered area and leaned on the wooden siding. The horses on leading reins were being lined up facing the judge. One, Anna thought, far outshone the others which frankly looked like riding school ponies to her. The good one, a gleaming chestnut with blonde streaks in its mane and tail, was standing proudly with its back legs stretched and it neck arched and head up to look at the clicking fingers of its handler. It did look as though it was about to pee but apart from that it was a pretty sight. The judge stepped forward and handed it a blue rosette. Kimi chuckled. 'I'm glad Paul's got something because I'm going to wipe him out in the three-gait.' Anna decided not to ask.

As they were turning away the horses, now all ranked with different coloured rosettes, were doing a final lap. Unaccountably the winning horse, which had behaved like a perfect gentleman up to this point, threw a tantrum rearing and bucking at the end of his rope. Unfortunately the judge had her back to this bad behaviour and was caught soundly in the rump by a kick. She fell forward slowly and silently. People rushed in.

'A bit ungrateful under the circumstances, 'Anna murmured.

'Well, that's horses. Do you want to come and see mine?' They turned away to cross the yard and Anna realised that Ellis had disappeared. Kimi looked across Anna and spoke to Harry and Joan. 'Hi, thanks for coming.' Joan grinned and Harry regarded her with interest.

'You're very good-looking,' he said. 'Can I kiss you?'

Kimi laughed. 'Maybe later. I want to show you my horses.' It was true, Kimi was looking particularly attractive. Formal riding clothes suited her, clinging as they did to her slim figure. Her hair, normally a mass of vibrating corkscrews, had been disciplined into a bun and a black bowler completed the image. But the main thing was that she was happy. Anna realised that she had never seen Kimi looking this relaxed. Normally she had a rather cynical, watchful air unless Rhea was around in which case she seemed on edge and anxious. They walked down between the rows of loose boxes. Joan insisted on greeting every horse that looked at her and Harry kept stopping and peering around at the unfamiliar sights. His face was animated and the air of vagueness which usually hung around him had dissipated. He was enjoying himself. Note to self, Anna thought - needs more stimulation. The familiar guilt gripped her heart. Harry never complained and rarely asked for anything and it was all too easy to put his needs last beyond basic care and safety. For the thousandth time she wished there was some sort of handbook for helping him and knew that there couldn't be.

They stopped in front of the last but one loosebox. There was Jesse snickering at Kimi and pushing his head through the U shaped grille. He seemed a bit over-excited Anna thought. Kevin was in there making some adjustments to the saddle. Anna smiled at him.

'Are you on soon?' Kimi nodded.

'Next event but one so we're going to walk him round a bit to get the ants out of his pants aren't we fella?' She stroked the long, trembling face. 'We had a good hour of exercise earlier on – there's great trails around here, so he shouldn't be too uppity.' Jesse did a little jig and tried to push Kevin into the side-wall with his punchball rear. Kevin silently pushed him back. Anna stared at the horse's rippling muscles, the dancing feet and the wild look in his eye and stepped back.

'See you later then? Looks like you'll need to concentrate.'

'We're in the covered arena – event 19. There's a place where you can watch. Wish us luck!'

Anna linked her arm with Harry's and went to find Joan who was chatting to a tortoiseshell cat. 'Shall we see Kimi's event and then picnic?'

'They're quite large, aren't they?' said Joan, side-stepping an approaching horse and rider.

'They're bloody huge,' said Anna. 'Have you ever ridden one?'

'No, but I once rode a camel across the Sahara for twenty miles.'

'Did you?' Anna looked at the pensioner with respect.

'I'd never do it again,' Joan said, wincing, 'It broke my bottom.' Before she could process this odd remark Anna had noticed Ellis and Rhea. They had not seen her, sitting as they were on a rail some way apart from the stables. Again there was that strange intensity between them and again it was only Rhea talking. As she watched the girl grabbed Ellis' hand and put it on her own chest. Ellis was nodding very seriously. There was nothing light or flirty or even particularly friendly about the way they were behaving. It was very odd. Then with her other hand Rhea reached into her jacket pocket and took out a folded piece of paper and stuffed it into Ellis' hoodie pocket. She released his hand and he dropped his head and nodded again. They both looked up and away as though some transaction had been accomplished and normal life might now go on. Ellis noticed their little group and waved, jumping down from the fence rail. Anna thought he looked relieved to see them. Rhea trailed after him, back into her usual droopy mode.

Anna filmed Kimi as she rode expertly round the large arena putting Jesse through his paces. He was a joy to watch. In the trot he lifted his knees so high he almost touched his own chest and his tail swept the ground gracefully. They were artists' horses, Anna thought, the ones who would be models for bronzes and oils. Kimi kept her hands and legs so still that it was hard to see how she was controlling him but he obediently changed pace every time they were instructed to do it. The horse that had won in the outdoor ring was there and did well but the combined beauty of Kimi and Jesse stood out in that magical way called star quality. They drew the eye and held it. Anna was looking forward to showing the clip to Diane that night. As she watched she thought again how strange it was that this young woman, knowing nothing of her real mother and how she and her father had met, had this deep passion for horses. A simple coincidence or something in the genes? Rhea didn't seem to have inherited it. She showed no interest in the horses all day but sat gloomily alone on a moulded plastic seat near the refreshment hutch working her phone.

By the time they left Harry was drowsy and he slept all the way home so Tom Waits was re-interred. Ellis was playing a game and Joan stared out of the window lost in her own thoughts. Anna remembered that she had said she wanted to talk about something. She caught her eye in the rear-view mirror and mimed a phone call, 'Talk later?' and Joan smiled wearily and nodded.

Outside the house was a dark grey Vauxhall with two men sitting inside it. Anna noted them as she turned into the drive. Ellis took Harry into the house as she went back to the road to find they had got out and one of them was holding something up for her to see. A jolt of adrenalin shot through her. Steve? Dad? Oh God, Faye? Quickly the man holding the badge stepped towards her.

'No one is hurt. There is no emergency.' The release of tension almost had her down. 'Can we have a word?'

She made them tea in the kitchen. Ellis had dropped his stuff and gone out to play football with Mike. Harry was asleep on the sofa in the living room. George and Diane were nowhere to be seen. They introduced themselves. Again, it was a Detective Sergeant accompanied by a Detective Constable but these two seemed different from the others. They were courteous; the cynical sneer so pronounced with Griffiths and Blake was missing from their eyes. Anna bided her time asking no questions.

'We want to talk to you about what happened the other night. The attempted gang rape.'

'Yes?' Anna tensed. 'I have already been interviewed.' The two men shifted uncomfortably.

'We've seen the notes of that interview.'

'Are you charging me with something?'

DS Iqbal looked startled and responded quickly, 'No, oh not at all. We're hoping you can help.' He glanced at the other man. 'I'd like to tell you this in confidence. There have been a series of gang rapes in Birmingham over the last five months – I'm sorry to say most of them were uninterrupted.' Anna froze. 'Usually that sort of thing is opportunistic – you know, some young men getting drunk and then stumbling upon a poor woman out alone.' She was beginning to feel rage build and quelled it. 'But there's been a pattern to these. It's almost as though they're organised.'

'Organised?'

'Nicola said that the young man she thought was her boyfriend was known as Mojo?'

'Yes.'

'She helped our identity team put together an image.' The younger man opened a slim briefcase and took out an A4 sized piece of card. He handed it to his boss with the blank side towards Anna. 'We were wondering if you might have seen this man on the night you rescued Nicola? She said he was not one of them but we wanted to check with you.' He held the paper in his hand and studied Anna. He had a clear brown complexion and cocoa coloured eyes, the skin maroon around the whites. He smiled and his face lifted and eased from its stern expression. She could imagine him as a family man. 'You were very brave, Mrs Ames, and so was your daughter and her friend. I don't think you have been fully commended for that.' As Anna felt a flush of relief and pleasure which she tried hard not to show, he turned the piece of card round so she could see the face. It was Afsoon's lover. She really had been there that night in that scary back street and so had he. She stared silently at the image of the man whom she had seen so clearly in the gallery at the BMAG.

'Who is it?' she asked but they were not to be put off.

'Did you see him?'

'He was not in the group around Nicola.' Why was she protecting Afsoon? Why didn't she just tell them? They watched her face and waited. 'I might have seen him recently in an art gallery in Birmingham but it might not have been him.' The constable got out his pad.

'Where and when, please?'

As they were leaving she asked again, 'Who is he?' and this time DS Iqbal answered.

'He goes by Mojo but his real name is Mohsen Amirmoez. We know he came into the country from Iran around eighteen months ago on a six-month tourist visa but he disappeared and Border Control have no record of him leaving.

'He's an asylum seeker?' Anna's thoughts were in turmoil.

'No. He's not seeking asylum. He has no reason to - he was not being persecuted in his own country. But it's true he does not want to go back. We've been in contact with the Iranian police. He skipped the country to avoid them. He is wanted for rape.' The detective sighed and met Anna's eyes. 'The girl was 13.'

'God.' They studied her face.

'You're sure he was not there that night?'

'It was very dark – there were no street lights.'

'Well,' the Inspector gave her a card, 'if you think of anything. Nicola may say something. Anything that can help.' Anna nodded and they left. She closed the door behind them and sank to the floor. She stretched her jaw and rubbed her face. None of this made sense. Afsoon was hardly a young girl for all her beauty. Surely she would not have anything to do with criminals like Mohsen even if he was from her home country. Could he be a relative whom she was protecting, a cousin maybe, and not her lover? But their touch had been so intimate and after seeing him she had been glowing.  Anna bit her index finger.  Had they come over together from Iran?  Had marrying Richard been a cynical cover?

What on earth was she going to do?  She stood up and walked slowly into the kitchen.  This man was a rapist and to take no action was not an option.  She could tell the police about Afsoon or she could tell Afsoon that the police wanted her lover and if she wouldn't deliver him, anonymously if necessary, Anna would.  Mrs Richard Draycott would be exposed and their friendship, if such it was, would be over.

Her phone jingled and she read the message from George saying he and Diane would be eating at her house.  She opened the freezer and pulled out a moussaka.  There would only be three of them as Faye was working so there should be enough.  She started to make a salad as the microwave whirred.  Five minutes later she dried her hands and rang Ellis but she didn't need to have done.  Hunger was always the best dinner gong with him.  He burst through the back door with Mike, both red-faced and sweaty and laughing.  It was good to see.  She shook her head free of the detectives' visit.

'Can Mike stay, Mum?'

'Of course.'  The meal would need bulking up as her dad would say.  'Do you like garlic bread, Mike?'

It was a relief to sit eating and chatting with the two boys.  Mike was relaxed around Harry having known Ellis' dad since infant school and, in the easy way of most boys, accepted that he might be a bit weird sometimes but so what, most adults were.  Harry seemed better, too, perhaps for the fresh air and stimulation of seeing the horses.  Mohsen Amirmoez was not her family's problem.  She would deal with it tactfully but firmly.

'Mum? Mike and me have got homework.  Can you stick my tennis whites in the wash?  Please?  Pretty please?'  He fluttered his eyelashes at her and Mike laughed.  She was so pleased to have him in this upbeat mood, her uncomplicated son back, that she agreed.  They were out of the back door before she could insist they cleared the dishes.  Harry picked up his plate to help and put it in the fridge.  She went to him and put her arms round his waist.

'Do you fancy watching a DVD, love?  Why don't you pick something and I'll come in as soon as I've sorted this lot out.'

In Ellis' room she pulled shirts, shorts and socks from his pungent laundry basket and stuffed them in the bag to take down.  Then she noticed his grey hoodie thrown on the bed.  She sat down beside it and felt in the pocket. The piece of paper Rhea had given him was there. For a moment she hesitated but then she opened it and read. Scrawled in black felt tip were the words:

*'Ellis, I'm writing this so if anything happens to me U can use it as proof. I know they R coming for me soon. I told you that they R watching the house and waiting to get me on my own. I'm carrying a knife, maybe you should 2 in case they've seen me with U. Do not betray me or abandon me!* <u>*They R watching us.*</u> *You are the only one I can trust. My life is in your hands.'*

Anna sat thinking. The adolescent style and melodramatic content could have been laughable in a more normal context but now, after the visit from the police, Anna felt dread seep into her gut. She had thought that Afsoon and Mohsen were nothing to do with her family but was something far darker than she had imagined going on around the Draycotts? Something that had put Nicola in jeopardy and now might threaten Ellis, her own son? She almost put the note back in the pocket but remembering Ellis' mood at dinner she thought he had maybe not read it. She pushed it deep into her own pocket. After all, it could easily have dropped out somewhere. As an extra precaution she took the hoodie with the rest of the wash. Not her fault if he didn't empty his pockets.

This was too much for her on her own. Secrecy and confidentiality be damned and be damned her turbulent feelings for Steve. He was the only one she could now turn to for advice and she was going to tell him everything. She needed help.

After watching The Shawshank Redemption for what felt like the hundredth time with Harry she took him up to bed and it was not until she was getting ready herself that she remembered she had promised to phone Joan. It was too late now. She emailed asking if she could go round for coffee the next morning as she'd be working from home. She also emailed Steve who was online and replied immediately that he had to be at the hospital with Alice all day on Monday for routine check-ups but would be free in the evening.

She thought that she would fall asleep in a moment but it was one of those nights where exhaustion turned to anxiety and stopped her from dropping off. Rhea was such a strange girl but maybe she had cause. Who knew what was going on in her life? Kimi rarely picked her up from the tennis club or school as she was old enough to catch the bus to Moor Street station and then the train to Lapworth to get home. She'd been doing it for years. But what if she didn't go straight home? What if, like Nicola, she had been drawn into a dangerous situation? Afsoon had said that Rhea sometimes came to her house to pet Beulah. Could Afsoon have taken the girl out for a meal or to a show and used that as cover for meeting Mohsen as it seemed she had done with Anna herself? In that case, he and Rhea might have met. Anna lurched over on to her stomach and groaned. Darker thoughts were crowding in but she pushed them away.

Then what to do about Ellis? She couldn't admit that she had been snooping, could she? Would he tell her anything if she tried to talk to him or would he clam up as he had done the other day and then be extra vigilant? He was a clever boy and would know how to keep secrets and it caused her physical pain that he might feel he had to. Should she talk to Kimi about her daughter but say what? That Rhea seemed rather anxious? Perhaps she should show her the note but if Kimi handled it badly that would only increase Rhea's feeling that she was under surveillance and could trust no-one.

## 17

Joan's email was in her inbox first thing in the morning and immediately Anna felt better knowing they would be having some time together.  She wouldn't tell Joan anything at this stage but she had proved through the Briony affair that not only could she be trusted but she could come up with some very good ideas when presented with problems.  As Anna drove over to Northfield she remembered first seeing her hanging out washing in the back garden of her small terraced house and not having the faintest idea that this neat little pensioner would connect her with high-profile people who would instigate an international media storm.  Joan's son Oliver living in New York had been key to the success of the campaign that got Briony released.  So had Steve and her dad, come to that.  Turning off the A38 into Hawkesley Mill Lane and then Mill Lane itself, Anna thought about what had happened to the rest of Joan's family.  A husband and son who had disappeared one calm summer evening off the coast of Devon and had never been found.  A meaningless, inexplicable tragedy.

As Anna parked on the road and walked to the front door she also remembered how tired Joan had looked after their day out.  What was it she wanted to say to Anna?  Was she ill?  At the thought Anna's heart chilled.  Joan was more of a mother to her than anyone had ever been, including her biological mother, but when the door opened Joan was smiling and putting out her arms for a hug.

It wasn't until they were seated at the kitchen table and the biscuit tin had been opened that Anna felt able to ask what she wanted to talk about.  Joan screwed up her eyes in her characteristic way and studied Anna's face.  'First, how are you coping, dear?  You've seemed a bit preoccupied just lately.  Is the job getting to you?'

Anna was so tempted to spill everything out that she found she had covered her mouth with her hand.  She removed it and tried to speak neutrally.  'It is a bit of an unusual situation and more complex than I'd imagined but I'm getting on with it.'  Understatement and discretion had never been her forte before working at Harts; now they had become second nature.  She wondered briefly if that was a good thing.  Then there was the ever-easier lying.  'I'm more concerned about you.  You seemed a bit knocked out on the way home yesterday – not your usual bright eyes and bushy tail at all.'

'I am nearly 70,' Joan protested. 'I can have an off day if I want one.'

'But you're ok?'

Joan hesitated and then smiled broadly. 'Fit as a flea. I just wondered if you'd decided whether I should come and stay while George is off on his awfully big adventure?'

'I would love you to come but there's a problem. There was a bit of a crisis with a friend of Faye's in the middle of the night a while back and I rushed off to help. It was fine. But Ellis felt side-lined. Why hadn't I woken him and so on. I think he's at an age where he wants very much to be taken seriously. He's drawn up a rota for when George is away so that Harry will never be alone and Faye's agreed to it because she wants me to let her go to a festival with Tash so she's after brownie points. Between them and me, of course, when I'm not at work we can cover it. It makes it easier that I'm working from home so much and can organise when I see people. But – I haven't said this to Ellis, it's very tight. I mean, it only takes Faye to have a memory lapse or me to be held up somewhere and it could be tricky. Harry can't be left any more. But I don't want to undermine him – you know, he's trying to be very responsible. Too grown-up really, I'm afraid.'

Joan moistened a forefinger and tidily prodded crumbs. 'Yes, I can understand that.' She seemed relieved rather than disappointed Anna noted with surprise. 'How about me as Plan B? If anything goes skewy I could step in? I can be at your house very quickly if necessary.'

'But I don't want you to put your life on hold.'

'I can keep my phone by me, I don't have to stop doing anything. I'd like to, Anna. I'd like to help if I'm needed.'

Anna covered her hand with her own. 'Joan, it helps just knowing you're here for me. You have no idea.'

Joan's hazel eyes suddenly shone with tears. 'I thought when you didn't say anything about me coming to stay that you didn't want me around.' In answer Anna jumped up and hugged her pulling her out of her chair but underneath their laughter at the clumsy grab she was alarmed. This was not the no-nonsense, self-contained woman Joan normally was.

Anna searched her face while she held her. 'Are you sure you're ok?'

Joan's chamois soft skin puckered into a teasing grin. 'I know you don't have enough to worry about Anna with your easy life but you're just going to have to look somewhere else for a project. I'm fine. See you at the sports centre Saturday as usual?'

'Holy crap,' said Steve. He stared at Anna for several moments. 'Why didn't you tell me before?'

'I didn't know who he was.'

'Not about *him* – about what happened that night! You could have been killed – stabbed – shot.' He seemed angry with her and she didn't like it.

'What would have been the point?'

'I could have come with you! Hell, Anna, I could have gone on my own and got the girls!' He was standing with his hands on his hips glaring at her.

Anna felt something in her head tighten. She said quietly, 'I handled it, Steve. I don't need a protector.' That sounded cold and defensive so she added, 'It would have been good to have you along but there wasn't time and who would have looked after Alice?'

'Promise me you will never put yourself in danger like that again!' He had grabbed her hands and was squeezing them. She pulled away.

'No, I can't promise you that. I'm sorry.'

Steve groaned and rubbed his face. 'OK, I was wrong to say that. Testosterone attack.'

She smiled at his frustration. 'So what should I do?' She took another sip of wine and breathed deeply. 'It seems to me that there are a couple of options. I can go to the police and spill. In that case Afsoon is up shit creek but for all I know she may belong there. Or I can go to her and get her to tell the police where Mohsen is – I know they'll tell me when they've got him if I ask. What do you think?'

'There is another option. I don't know if it will work or if I will be allowed to do it but I could see if he's on the Home Office list of persons of interest. There doesn't seem to be a terrorist connection but they track criminals too. They may know where he is, be watching him ready to pick him up when the time's right. He may be involved in something bigger and if the local police go in there it may be compromised.'

'Wouldn't they know? The police I mean?'

'Not necessarily. If he's a low-level player the security services may want to just keep him under surveillance until they can get the whole network.'

Anna chewed her fingers. 'Go on then.'

'I can't do it from here. That kind of stuff can only be done from a dedicated computer and that's at Harts.' Steve got up from his chair and began to pace the room.

Anna was thinking rapidly. 'How would it help, though?' Steve stopped and looked intently at her. 'Say he is implicated in something larger and the Home Office tell you to lay off him? Then I can't take any action can I? That would backfire on you and come to that, wouldn't they ask you how you know about him? This sort of thing is hardly your normal remit. As I understand it they come to you with stuff and you investigate, not the other way round.' Steve groaned and sat down. 'I know you're trying to help, but the more I think about it the more I don't want you to check on this man. What you find out could tie my hands and it might put more girls in danger.'

'I hate to admit it, but you're right,' Steve said helplessly. 'So what will you do?'

'If my hunch is right and this so-called Mojo is grooming or threatening Rhea into sex, money from her wealthy family, whatever, I don't believe that Afsoon knows about it. She seems fond of Rhea and she obviously adores Mohsen. I know it could all be front and deception but I just find it difficult to believe that she's a party to all this. I think that Rhea has confided in Ellis that she's frightened but daren't tell him everything. She's such a strange girl it's hard to know what she's thinking. I can sort of understand why she wouldn't confide in Kimi – her mum throws a wobbly if she won't eat a yoghurt. It's possible that she has been abused sexually and is terrified of it coming out and now she's being blackmailed but she may not want to reveal all that to Ellis.'

'You're going to see Afsoon, aren't you?'

'I think it's the only fair way to deal with this. I desperately want Ellis out from under this horrible stuff but I don't want innocent people to suffer.'

'What if Afsoon doesn't believe you? What if she refuses to do anything?'

'Then I will have no choice. I'll go to Iqbal myself and tell him everything.'

'What if she says she will deal with it and then doesn't?' They both were silent, thinking. 'Put a time limit on it. A short one. If you haven't heard from the police that he's been picked up in, let's say six days, you will act.' They stared at each other.

'Ok. That's what I'll do.' Anna stood up to go. 'Oh and another thing I've forgotten to tell you.'

Steve looked horrified. '*Another* thing?' She laughed.

'No, this is just domestic logistics. I'm driving my dad and Diane to Felixstowe the day after tomorrow to embark on this mad container ship escapade. He said they would go on the train until they found out it would take hours and three changes. I want to check it out anyway. Apparently it's sailing under a Moravian flag. The two of them are like kids off on a school trip.'

'Do you want me to take the day off and be with Harry?'

Anna noted the sensitivity of his phrasing. Not 'baby-sit' or 'look after' but 'be with.' She smiled at him and lightly touched his arm. 'No, it's ok, Faye has promised and she desperately needs to get some revision done so she'd be at home anyway.'

'I'll call round after work and bring Alice. We can fight it out on the tiddlywink battlefield.'

'Thank you Steve. Thanks for this evening too. My mind feels much clearer.'

Steve walked out with her to the door and opened it for her. 'Anna, I appreciate you coming to me. I want to be here for you,' he paused, 'when you want me.' She couldn't look at him but neither could she resist resting her head briefly against his shoulder. She went out into the night just as an imperious voice from upstairs demanded attention.

'Uncle Steve,' Alice wailed, 'I waked up and my bed is full of stories! And the Gruffalo weed in it…'

'Coming,' Steve called, grinning at Anna.

Anna walked the short distance down the road to her own house thinking that these days her bed was too often full of x-rated stories but she wasn't going to tell Steve that.

As it happened there was no time the next day to call Afsoon to arrange a meeting so it would have to wait until after the Felixstowe trip.

When she lurched downstairs at 6.30 and groped for the cafetiere she found it was warm. George was already up and zipping about like a dragon-fly. 'Tape-recorder,' he muttered, and trotted off to the shed. A minute later he was back to stare at Anna. 'Sun screen?'

'Shelf by the back door. Hat?' He trotted back wearing it, sun screen in hand. 'Dad? Haven't you made a list?'

'List!' he cried. 'That's what I started off looking for.' Anna sat down at the table and decided to rise above it. Diane would be on the ball she was sure and would be arriving very soon. The main packing was done and the cases in the hall. On her way to a shower Anna tapped on Faye's door and was met with deep silence. She opened it and went in.

'Sweetie?' Anna sat down on the bed and put a cup of tea on the cupboard beside it pushing aside her phone and a heap of scrunchies and pins. 'Wakey, wakey.'

'Oh God, go away.'

'Sorry, love, but we'll be leaving soon. Can you wake up a bit? You don't have to get up just yet – I just need you to be awake. I've brought you a cup of tea.'

A flushed face topped with a tangle of honey-coloured hair emerged in profile and a hand stretched out for the tea. 'Time?'

'It's nearly 7.00. We'll be off in half an hour.' She couldn't resist threading the tumble of hair through her fingers under the pretence of lifting it off Faye's face. She bent and kissed the top of her head. Faye grunted. 'You know where the emergency numbers are?'

'Mm. Don't stress.' Faye sipped and stared. 'Does dad need to be wearing his watch?'

'I don't think so, he hasn't gone off for ages but I'll leave it on the kitchen table. Just check on him fairly often, ok? There's loads of stuff recorded he can watch and if he wants to be outside just make sure it's at the back.' Anna paused and then added, 'Talk to him every now and then, darling, maybe even play the piano a bit. He might be a bit spooked with me and George not here.'

Faye raised her head. 'He's getting worse, isn't he?' When Anna looked away and didn't reply she went on, 'It's like he's fading out. Sometimes I can't remember what it was like to have a proper dad. Sorry.'

Anna fought the sob that threatened to rise in her throat and choke her. 'You could look at the photograph albums together maybe for a little while. You could help him to remember and -' she stopped.

'That would help me remember.'

'Yes, love.'

'Ok, Mum. I'm awake. Go and get in the shower and *drive carefully*!'

'Yes mam!' Anna did a mock salute. It wasn't just her son that was brave and Faye was growing up so quickly it still caught her by surprise. Only six months ago she would have been moaning and fighting not to have the responsibility of caring for her dad for one day. Now she didn't even negotiate a deal. It was good to have her by her side. 'Steve said he'd bring Alice round after work to play tiddlywinks with your dad. Is that ok?'

'Mm, 'course. Go!'

# 18

It took four hours to get to Felixstowe and then another ten minutes to negotiate the sprawling dockside. Anna felt as though they had gone into the land of Brobdignag. They were midgets among massive objects. Containers the size of bungalows towered in neat blocks to left and right as they drove slowly along looking for the wharf where MV Orinoco was docked. Huge cranes with pulley hawsers the thickness of a man's thigh slid their loads back and forth over their heads. The crane drivers were invisible from the ground and the few humans standing about in the distance seemed like peg dolls, tiny and forked. Then they turned a corner of the quay and saw the ship. Anna stopped the car.

'You don't have to do this, Dad. Don't do this!' She looked at George, sitting silently beside her. 'Seriously, you can back out. The money doesn't matter.'

George didn't even look at her. He couldn't take his eyes from the skyscraper in front of him. 'Oh,' he breathed, 'isn't she magnificent!' Anna turned to look at Diane in the back seat and was astonished to see her eyes gleaming with the same excitement. 'Why have you stopped? Drive on, drive on! We can stop by the gangplank like they told us.' So Anna drove on.

Within minutes of them getting out of the car two deckhands had run lightly down the gangplank and were holding out their hands for luggage and papers. The gangplank was at least four storeys high of any normal building. Anna stretched her neck and breathed deeply. George and Diane had almost forgotten she was there. 'Keep one hand always on the rail,' they told each other, having just been told that themselves. The young men grinned at the elderly couple so eager for an adventure. What were they, Philipino? Maybe Malay? They seemed kind and Anna beamed at them.

'Have fun!' she called, 'Be safe!' as they began to climb up but the hands that flapped back at her were saying 'go away' as much as 'goodbye' and she humbly went back to the car. When they reached the top she knew they would be going up the inside of the tower by lift to their cabin high above so she gave a last wave to the two small figures on the main deck waving back and got into the car to leave. Near the bow a gargantuan crane was loading yet another layer of boxes. It all looked horribly precarious. How could this block of flats possibly float? It defied belief.

Once she was out of sight of the ship she stopped again by a stack of containers that seemed not to be going anywhere at that particular moment.    Anything could happen.    She had read somewhere that sea travel was far more dangerous statistically than any other form of transport.    They would be going south across the Bay of Biscay and yes, the ship was huge, but things happen.    What about Joan's husband and son, taken by the sea with no explanation? What about the ferry disasters you were always hearing about when someone's carelessness caused massive loss of life?    George had told her that the ship was German owned and that the officers were from various countries but, thankfully for them, that English is the lingua franca of the seas.    Would they be kind to the old people or see them as a nuisance?    George and Diane were so excited, she couldn't bear to think of them being isolated or made uncomfortable.    Well, they had each other.    Hopefully they would call or email from La Havre. Until then she could only try not to worry.    She bent sideways and opened the glove compartment to look for a piece of gum.    All the emotion had made her thirsty.

In the passenger wing mirror she saw a sight so familiar that for a second she thought she must be imagining it.    A truck was approaching in the middle of the road and it bore the orange and green logo of Drake's soft drinks.    Then she remembered William telling her that they frequently drove containers to the port. She stared into the mirror and her eyes narrowed as she recognised not one but both of the men in the cab.    The truck passed her and she saw that there was a Maersk container loaded on the flatbed. Without considering what she was doing she started the car and pulled out to follow it.    At the gate the truck stopped and some paperwork was exchanged and then it pulled away to the left.    Anna had a quick word with the guard and then followed, letting a couple of passing cars get between her and the truck.    In fifteen minutes she was placed discreetly behind them on the main road west and she could take a breath and think about what she had seen.

In the cab, Dook was driving.    That was not a surprise since he was the depot manager although her impression had been that he left the roadwork to his team, but next to him in the passenger seat she had seen Mohsen Amirmoez.    The two men had been laughing and chatting.    They drove for an hour and a half and then pulled in to a service station.    Anna was trembling by the time she switched off her own car engine in the car park adjacent to the truck area.    She watched in the rear-view mirror as the two young men got out of the cab and stretched and then strolled towards the main building. She had to use the loo but she couldn't risk them seeing her. Both of them, Dook on the tour William gave her and Mohsen in the gallery, had seen her very clearly and would immediately recognise her.

She locked the car and followed at a distance of a hundred yards behind a family group yawning and pulling down their wrinkled clothes. When she came out of the toilet she glanced both ways and not seeing either of them walked quickly towards the exit. There was no time to get coffee, she couldn't risk being seen or being left behind. She didn't know whether they had stopped for a toilet break or for food. She put on her sunglasses and tried to stay with couples or groups and she was concentrating so hard on this that she almost missed noticing them waiting in the queue for a burger. It was a long queue. She got outside and ran to the car and drove as fast as she could to get fuel. Then she waited, hiding herself in an angle of the forecourt where she could see traffic taking the exit to the motorway. A thought struck her, that Iqbal should know about this and intercept them. She rummaged in her bag for her phone. It wasn't there. She knew exactly where it was – she had put it on charge in her bedroom last night but with the early start and getting Harry up she'd forgotten it.

In the hour and a half she had been following them so far Anna had been thinking very hard. What could connect these two men except the Draycott family? Dook and Mohsen didn't seem nervous or worried, quite the contrary. So whatever they were doing must be happening with the knowledge of the company, so did that mean one (or all) of the family? And there was another thing. Driving behind them Anna had had plenty of time to observe the container and had noted that it was not sealed as it must have been when it was at sea.

So, there was a perfectly innocent explanation. Or more-or-less innocent, hardly perfectly innocent. Afsoon's lover had got a job at the depot as a driver (possibly at her suggestion) and Dook happened to have taken a shine to him and asked him to go along on this trip to deliver a full box to the docks and pick up an empty one to re-fill from the depot. Mohsen could have forged papers to get the job or Dook may not be too fussy about such things. The loose panel on the container could just be carelessness about an empty box.

Then there was another possibility, not so innocent. Yes, the truck would go to the dock loaded with cartons of cans of Drake but the box they brought back may not be empty. Dook had been connected with the docks for years since he had worked for the firm and that would have been plenty of time to build up some shady contacts among the stevedores. Anna remembered something from one of the books George had read in preparation for their trip about container ships. The officers and even the crew very rarely knew what was in the boxes they were transporting (unless it was dangerous chemicals). Together with that, George had told her, only a tiny percentage of the crates were ever inspected by customs. What had he said? Two per cent she thought it was. So, if you wanted to bring stuff in illegally you would have a 50-1 chance of it never being discovered. If you added to that the huge profits to be made from smuggling right there was the incentive. Her mind had raced. Did Mojo have criminal contacts in Iran? Could she find out where this box had come from, what ship, what ports?

Sergeant Iqbal had said that there had been an outbreak of what he thought were organised gang rapes and he thought that most of the girls victimised had probably been trafficked. They had only discovered what was going on by cases like Nicola's where someone, either the victim or a witness had reported the crime. Nicola was unusual in that she was a local girl. That meant that they were almost certainly only hearing about a fraction of what was actually happening.

Anna sat up abruptly. The Drake lorry was turning into the fuel station and it stopped by a diesel pump. Dook opened the cab door and jumped down, a burger sticking out from his mouth while he wrestled with the fuel cap. Anna pulled her head back into shadow and watched him. He was a handsome man and he knew it. His walk had a slight swagger to it, a forward thrust of the pelvis that was on the edge of sexual aggression. She glanced at the cars being filled and noted that a pretty blonde woman had raised her sunglasses to stare at Dook. As he returned to the truck from paying he looked across at her as she smiled boldly at him and then he made a gesture that Anna had only seen before in American films. The woman immediately dropped her head and let her hair cover her face. It was not a flirtatious gesture – it showed contempt and hostility and the pretty blonde woman knew it. As the truck pulled away Anna followed thanking her lucky stars that her old VW had no remarkable features at all. She could have found half a dozen on any large car park. Nevertheless she held back until a towing caravan had come between her and the truck.

When she had told Steve last night about what had happened to Nicola she asked him about what Iqbal had meant when he talked about organised gang-rapes. How would that be possible without alerting the police? Steve had explained about 'black' websites. Any illegal activity websites including drugs, sex and money trading could be, with some expertise, hidden from mainstream users so that they became undetectable except by highly proficient analysts who would have to know they were there to look for them. Steve suspected that if there were web-organised gang-rapes happening then there would be an 'agent' of some kind who would be able to access the place, date and time information but who would not reveal the site to the 'customers' he procured. Once the website was set up then it could be used in an unlimited number of locations. All that would be needed would be a connection with a 'supplier' of girls and an agent or 'retailer' to attract customers and it would work like any other business. The supplier would set up the girl in a lonely place telling her some story to make her wait and then disappear and the retailer would drive 'the lads' to the location having collected cash from them and in the heat of the moment, vanish. Neither supplier nor retailer would be at the scene of the crime when it happened. The money would then be shared. There must be a third party organising it, though. There must be someone posting data on the website; place, time, date.

Anna felt cold and sick. What was in that container that was bouncing gently along an English country road ahead of her making for her own home town? Air-holes would be easy to drill and conceal and people could survive, however miserably, for a few days if they had food and water. Her hands gripped the steering wheel harder. What was she to do now? They were approaching a junction which could take her south and west towards Solihull or straight over to the city centre and home. She should go home but she couldn't. She indicated left. The totally innocent option still existed. She had no proof that anything untoward was going on but there was no harm in just observing.

As they became absorbed into the afternoon traffic toiling round the ring-road Anna wondered for the first time that day whether Faye was all right with Harry. Then she banged her hand smartly on the steering wheel. She had forgotten to put the Keruve watch on the kitchen table. It was still in the glove compartment. It didn't really matter, it was unlikely that Harry would wander off but she knew Faye would have felt more confident looking after him if he had been wearing it. Faye was right, though. Harry was fading away. There had been no emotional outbursts since the incident over the football Steve had told her about but then, there hadn't been much drama either. Everyone had adjusted a little maybe? Faye and Ellis were less confrontational these days certainly. Was that because each was caught up in her or his own world or was it that they sensed Harry's fragility and were walking on eggshells when he was near?

Anna felt the downward tug of sadness. Things should have been so different. Only a couple of years ago, before Harry became ill, he had been suggesting to her what they would do when both children had left home. 'You've got to see the Great Barrier Reef before you die,' he'd said. 'In fact, Australia would be a great place to spend a few months. I could take a year off school, a sabbatical, and we could tour round.' Anna had wrinkled up her face and listed, 'Spiders, snakes, sunstroke…' 'You'd love it! We could have the get-off-the-world years we never got to have when we were young.' Well, he was certainly drifting off the world now. All on his own without any companion, her long-limbed, copper-haired, green-eyed husband who had been so full of life, so connected with everything. She straightened her back and put her attention to the truck. It was signalling. She had expected it. They would have to take this route to get to the factory.

What would she do when they got close? There would be a fair amount of activity still going on around the plant in the factory but not the depot, it was mid-afternoon and the drivers would be still out. The trucks used a different access from the cars. Could she park in the visitors' bay and stroll over trying to stay hidden? Would it matter if they saw her? Well, it could. There was no reason for her to be by the lorry depot. She pulled back a little further and let more cars get between them as they approached the factory. Then, just as she was about to turn in, she noticed that on the other side of the depot was the social club. She went on past the goods delivery entrance and into the car park of the club. There were a few cars there already, probably club staff, so she parked on the far side of them away from the depot and waited. She could see into the yard and the main doors of the depot which always seemed to be slid back although they were probably locked at night. There was no-one in sight and she remembered William telling her that the work of the depot consisted of two shifts: 4.00 a.m. to 6.00 by which time all the trucks were loaded and on the road, and 4.00 p.m. until late when those that were coming back that day checked in. The lorry that Dook was driving had stopped outside the main door to the garage. He got out, but not Mohsen. He spent a minute or less in the dark of the garage out of sight and then reappeared, jumped in the cab and drove the container, not into the garage, but on and round the back of it.

This manoeuvre put them in clear view of her and she slid down a little in her seat. They both went quickly round to the back of the container and began unloading something. So she had been right, there was something being transported in the container which should have been empty. She squinted, trying to see more clearly. The crates they were unloading were large and obviously heavy. Even so, they moved quickly taking the crates from the container and then out of her sight between the depot and the truck. Each crate was about two metres long by a metre wide and just under a metre high. There must have been about a dozen of them. Afsoon leaped into Anna's mind. The connection was inescapable. She knew about valuable artefacts, art and antiques. Was she behind all this? She and her lover? She certainly had museum connections across the Middle East and into Asia. Had she manipulated the egocentric Richard into marrying her (he would be easily flattered) so she could hi-jack the company's transport resources when they had negotiated the collaboration of the depot manager who could be bribed. As Anna watched the two men unloaded a pile of cardboard cartons and shut the container firmly, locking down the fastenings. Dook jumped into the cab on the far side from Anna and began to reverse the truck.

Anna expected to see revealed what Mohsen was doing with the crates and cartons but there was no sign of any of them. They had vanished. There was only the back wall of the depot. As she was staring at it and trying to make sense of what she was looking at, Dook reappeared walking with a large plastic container. It was transparent and he was having a hard time carrying the weight. Water? He put down the flagon with his back to Anna, glanced around, and then opened a door which was so well camouflaged she had not seen it and slipped into the back of the depot with the water closing the door behind himself.

It was time to go. Anna's tyres squealed a little as she swerved back and out of the club car park. Now she was frightened. Artefacts and works of art did not need water. Neither did they need the air that the loose back panel of the container had let in. She drove deliberately a little slowly feeling vulnerable and thinking hard. Both men knew her and so did Afsoon. She couldn't put her own family at risk from a bungled police involvement. What should she do? She was hungry, thirsty and exhausted from the day. Decide not to decide just yet. Get home and have a shower and check on everyone and think about it later. As she knew from bitter experience rash moves were a specialty with her but she wasn't about to make one now. And then relief flooded her. She was not alone in this, she would talk to Steve.

Anna liked a full house but possibly not this full after the long day she'd had. It seemed that everyone had rallied round to help Faye with Harry but then peeled off to do whatever took their fancy. Faye, Tash and Alice were at the back end of the living room practising moves from a Pixie Lott video. They had cleared some space by stacking the battered old patio furniture in a precarious heap thus revealing how much the carpet needed shampooing.

Steve, Joan and Len were at the kitchen table working on Len's repertoire. The band (never called by its members by its embarrassing stage name The Bad Brothers) had been offered a set of gigs at local social clubs. Len even thought they might be playing at Drakes. There were several boxes of pizza, half a dozen beers and two laptops. Anna looked sharply at the greasy computers to check they hadn't borrowed hers. Steve was saying, 'Look this is a great track. Everyone loves this,' and Annie's Song rolled out tugging predictably at the gut. Len listened carefully as he chewed, wiped his mouth with the back of his hand, picked up the flute and rendered it almost perfectly. Steve and Joan clapped and whooped. She backed silently out and went to look for Harry.

He was not watching a DVD or a television programme and he was not in the bathroom. Anna glanced out of her bedroom window but couldn't see him in the garden. It was a cool day but he had gone out before without a coat. She tapped on his bedroom door but there was no answer and when she gently turned the handle and pushed it open she could see that the bed, although it was unmade, was empty. They had left so early that there had been no time for the whole getting up routine. The pleasure of being home began to fade and Anna's throat tightened. None of them was used to being in charge of Harry. Faye had obviously felt that a house full of people could be delegated to notice what was happening to him.

Anna quickly put her head into the children's bedrooms. Ellis was bent over his desk and scribbling furiously. He glanced back at her and nodded a greeting and then was back to his work. She ran down the stairs. There was only one more place to look. She greeted everyone in the kitchen but ignored their calls to stop and listen. 'Just need to go to the shed, back in a minute.'

At first she thought he wasn't there. It was beginning to get dark and there was no lamp switched on but then she heard a regular thump and in a moment Bobble was jumping up at her and barking. The old bus seat and the rocker were empty but in the corner behind George's desk chair there was a movement. She switched on the lamp. In its yellow light she saw her husband, curled up in a foetal position, sucking his thumb and moaning. He had been crying. His face was wet and dirty. He was holding, like a toddler with its blanket, George's Fair Isle cardigan, the one that always stayed on the back of the chair in case of a draught, too pilled and frayed to be allowed into the luggage for the ship. Anna slowly pulled the chair away and knelt beside him on the dusty boards. She took one hand in hers and stroked it, smiling and murmuring his name. As he began to focus on her and become calmer she let herself slide sideways so that she was sitting in a position where she could cradle his head and shoulders. He clutched at her, sobbing again, but it was with relief, not fear. She stroked the beloved face with the back of her hand over and over until he took a deep, trembling breath and quietened.

She should have foreseen this. Why did they ever think that he would cope with the double loss of George and herself? He couldn't understand what was happening and nor could they explain it. Faye simply wasn't experienced enough to know how to watch for signs of distress and distract him. No-one could blame her. Harry was normally so quiet around the place that they had forgotten him. It wasn't neglect, they just weren't attuned to be always thinking of where he was, what he was doing and how he was behaving. Being responsible for Harry was like having a toddler, albeit one with very low energy levels. The habit of checking on him every few minutes was one that she and George had developed but no-one else had. She had forgotten that. She had let him down by not preparing them properly. How many hours had he been like this? She felt hot guilt burn her face. She bent and kissed his hair, his forehead and his wet cheeks her own tears now mixing with his as they dried.

The shed door opened quietly. It was Steve. He took in the scene and dropped to his knees on the shed floor. 'Oh God, Anna, I'm so sorry.'

She looked across at him, strong and well, and swallowed the bitter words which rose up her throat. 'I don't know how long he's been here,' she said trying to make it sound like a genuine question.

Steve dropped his head, thinking, and then glanced at his watch. 'We played games until Len got here. He was fine. That must have been about an hour ago. We all went into the kitchen when the pizzas arrived and then Len started telling us about this gig they've got but they need new material. He must have gone out of the back door. I don't think he's been here long.'

'So he has eaten?' Anna was trying desperately not to sound accusatory. Steve couldn't be held responsible, it wasn't fair.

'Oh yes. He had three slices of pizza and a good dose of salad.' He ran his fingers through his hair so that it pointed up like a Mohican. 'Honestly Anna, I'm so sorry but I don't think he's been here long.' He smiled at Harry. 'I think I know what might have done it. Len was playing something and Joan said that was one of George's favourites and then we had a laugh about what they might be having for their dinner. You know ship's biscuits and all that.'

'Yes. That would be it.'

'So that wasn't more than fifteen minutes ago.'

'OK.' Anna became aware that Harry was wriggling in her arms and trying to break free. She had probably been gripping him rather tightly in her tiger-mum embrace. She let go and rolled up on to her feet. Harry unfolded himself and stood upright.

'Hello mate,' he said to Steve genially. 'Spurs against Newcastle?' It could be any game, there was no way he could remember what the schedule was, but the message was clear. Steve stepped forward, took his hand, and clapped him on the shoulder.

'You bet, Harry. Just let me see what the little monster's doing and we'll go back to mine and watch the football channel.

Ok?' He turned to Anna. 'Ok?' As they made for the door Anna took Steve's hand and raised it to her lips. It was an apology whether he knew it or not. 'We'll pop back in an hour or so, and I'll take Alice home to put her to bed. Would that work?' Anna nodded. Yes, that would work.

Back in the kitchen Joan had plated up Anna's pizza and arranged a pretty bowl of salad to go with it. A large glass of red wine stood beside it on the table and a folded napkin, too. The mess was cleared away and the table top was clean and shining. Anna had to stop herself from whimpering in gratitude. 'Chocolate trifle for afters,' Joan said pointing at the bowl on the side and giving Len a warning look. 'Len and I are leaving now, I'll give him a lift to his bus. Ok?'

'Thank you,' Anna said in what sounded like a seven-year old voice. 'Do you want to hear about the ship?'

'Not just now, dear. It will wait.' Joan slipped on her coat and prodded Len so that he took his eyes off Anna's trifle and heaved himself to his feet. As always a faint smell of week-old wet laundry clung to him.

'I can just play you that Annie's Song.'

'Not tonight Len. She's done in. Come on.' And, amazingly, little grey-haired Joan shepherded the huge bulk of him out at an impressive rate of knots.

Anna heard the front door close and stared at the plate of food and the glass of wine and burst into tears.

## 19

At ten o'clock the next morning she phoned Afsoon. She'd been giving the meeting some thought. Not at Afsoon's house, obviously, and not in the city, but there had to be a pretext that she could use on the phone. Compton Verney. The beautiful Warwickshire stately home that was now an art museum was tastefully modified and elegance itself. It was totally Afsoon. It sat in grounds designed by Capability Brown so they could wander by the lake after strolling the galleries and then Anna could bring up the subject of Mohsen Amirmoez. There hadn't been a chance to talk to Steve but she had woken up feeling clear about what she must do.

'I will be bringing my husband, too. He's got dementia but he can cope with this and he'd enjoy the pictures and the fresh air. It's such a lovely day.' Cunningly making it look spontaneous, Anna tutted at herself. Afsoon asked a question Anna had not anticipated.

'How much is the entrance ticket, please?'

'Er, I'm not sure. I haven't been for a while.' There was a pause.

'I know a beautiful walk I could show you around the lakes at Earlswood. Maybe that would be pleasant in this fine weather?' Anna remembered the envelope Afsoon had handed to her lover. Then she remembered the supermarket sweater.

'Fine. That will be lovely. It will do us all good.' The arrangements were made. Anna laid her phone down on the table and stared at it. She could imagine that Richard would not be generous with an allowance for his wife. He was the sort of man who wouldn't want to give up control or give her the means to free herself of him should she so choose. As long as they were married he would keep a very tight rein. He'd probably insisted on a pre-nuptial agreement. So was Afsoon squirreling away small amounts of money here and there? If Richard gave her an allowance, as he must do since she had no other source of income, she could buy the cheapest clothes knowing he would not know the difference and give what she saved to Mohsen? She was so beautiful that she could wear any cheap garment and look stunning. So poor Afsoon, caught between two unscrupulous and cold men. Anna shook her head. She was allowing herself to go too far in her speculation. It was entirely possible that Afsoon was implicated in whatever was going on at the depot, horrible though that thought was.

Harry had, of course, forgotten the previous day's trauma and was happy to be in the car by her side. From the CD player came the groaning chants of Tom Waits accompanied at intervals by a groaning, equally incomprehensible, chant from Harry. Despite the seriousness of the task ahead Anna couldn't stop herself grinning. The identity of the present prime minister had vanished from Harry's world well over a year ago, he hadn't known what day of the week it was for months and had now forgotten what broccoli was called and how to operate the television remote. But – he never forgot that the Tom Waits CD was in the glove compartment of her car. It could have been worse, she reflected, he might have fixated on the Ring Cycle in which case she would have had to sell the car.

Bobble lay on the back seat slobbering on his blanket in the excitement of the moment. He was growing very fast just as she'd feared. Glancing at him in the rear-view mirror Anna thought about Ellis. He still took the dog for walks and fussed about in the garden with him but he was different. George was right. Every now and then a dark mood would come over the boy and he would want to be alone, often sitting for an hour or more on the mouldy green bench in the garden, texting or just staring. Bobble seemed to sense his mood and would creep close to him and settle on one of his trainers loyally. She had to talk to him. She couldn't just let this drift. Something was wrong and it had to do with Rhea. Why hadn't he confided in Anna? He always had before. Probably Rhea had ordered him not to. Was the girl in serious trouble or was she just a fantasist? Could there be some horrific connection with the contents of those crates and a dark street in Deritend? But surely Dook or Mohsen would not involve one of Gerald Draycott's grandchildren? Unless. Anna resolutely pushed the thought away. She was in danger of becoming a bit of a fantasist herself.

Afsoon was waiting for them dressed in her jeans and grey T shirt. A navy sweater was draped stylishly around her shoulders. Other women could spend thousands of pounds, thought Anna, and not look anywhere near as good. She was smiling radiantly and stepped forward to take Harry's hand as soon as they got out of the car. She was one of those people to whom the tact and empathy of good manners come naturally, it seemed. Or was she just skilled at being charming when she wanted to be? Harry's eyes brightened and he wrapped Afsoon in his arms, ignoring the proffered hand. Anna had not realised before his illness how susceptible her husband was to a pretty woman. He had kept that well hidden.

'Sorry!' Anna muttered.

'No that's fine. How are you Harry?' He stared at her in frank admiration.

'Ok, let's go,' said Anna. 'Is this the path?' Bobble on his lead led the way and they formed a small procession across the planked footpath until it opened out into a wood beside the lake and they strolled easily alongside each other. Afsoon seemed so carefree, so relaxed that Anna couldn't believe that what she knew about her could be true. And yet, it must be. What other explanation could there be? She linked her arm with Anna's and leaned down a little to her in a confiding way that Anna couldn't help finding endearing.

'I think I am ready now to tell you my nice secret,' she said, her eyes glowing. 'You are my friend are you not?' Anna stared at the ground not knowing how to respond. Afsoon squeezed her arm. 'Yes, you are, of course. Do you want to hear?' Harry had lagged a little behind them throwing sticks for Bobble and they stopped to let him catch up. Afsoon almost pulled Anna round to face her. 'Do you?'

'Yes. Yes, of course, if you think you should tell me. If you're sure.' Anna tried to decide how she would be expected to respond to Afsoon's admission of a lover. Cosy glee? Girlish excitement? Womanly solidarity? Oh, bloody hell, there is no right way to respond to someone telling you that they are having an affair. Did Afsoon think that western culture was so degenerate that such news would be considered a bit of a laugh? Afsoon did not seem either so trivial or so naïve and yet her manner was bubbly and teasing.

Afsoon lifted Anna's chin with one finger playfully so that she could not avoid meeting her gaze. 'Haven't you guessed? I'm pregnant.' All the fragments of Anna's thoughts whirled briefly and blew away. A chill calm followed. Whose baby was this? Afsoon frowned. 'Why are you not congratulating me? Why are you so serious, Anna?'

Anna glanced round to see where Harry was. He and Bobble were sitting by the lake, their game of sticks over, watching a group of children learning to sail in tiny dinghies. 'Let's sit down,' Anna said quietly. 'Of course I'm happy that a new life is starting but there is something I have to talk to you about. You will feel that this is none of my business but I'm afraid it is because it has affected my family.' Afsoon sat on the grass, her arms embracing her knees, a short distance away. She looked, for the first time since Anna had met her, afraid. She stared at Anna, her eyes huge.

'Tell me then.'

'A little while ago the sister of a friend of my daughter's was the victim of an attempted gang rape.' Afsoon frowned and she seemed about to speak. Anna raised her hand a little to stop her and went on. 'She is fifteen. She thought she had a boyfriend who loved her but he was just grooming her and then set her up to be attacked.' Anna paused and took a deep breath. 'My daughter phoned me and together we rescued the girl from the men. The incident happened in Deritend in the early hours of the morning. I can give you the date.' Afsoon looked puzzled. 'When I drove round the corner from where the attack was about to happen that night I saw you with a man.' Afsoon raised her hand to her mouth. 'Then, in the Birmingham Art Gallery I saw him again. You went to him and you seemed intimate.' Anna watched Afsoon's face. Now, she noted with surprise, it had a soft look.

'I can explain.'

'I haven't finished, Afsoon.'

'No, but I can explain. That man you saw both times, his name is Mohsen.' She leaned forward and took Anna's hands. 'Can I trust you? I want to tell you the truth.'

'The truth?'

'Yes. He is my son. Mohsen is my son.' The distant sounds of the children shouting on the water and the sight of strands of hair blowing across Afsoon's flawless smiling face imprinted on Anna's mind. She was speechless. 'I told you that when I was only fifteen I made the journey back to Tehran and those friends of my parents helped me? I did not tell you that I was pregnant. The old man whom my uncle wanted me to marry forced me to have sex. They did it so I would have to marry him. But as soon as I knew I was pregnant I left on that terrible journey and I never told them. I escaped. Thank God.'

'Does Richard know?'

Afsoon looked beseechingly at Anna. 'No. He would never have married me if he had. This is a bad thing, I know, but I had to do it. Mohsen and I came to the UK on a six-month visa. He was not doing well in Iran and I hoped we would have a chance to start a new life here.' Anna thought about what DS Iqbal had told her. She supposed the phrase 'not doing well' could be used to cover the rape of a child if only by a mother blinded by love. Every single thing Afsoon was saying was shocking her and she struggled to assimilate the revelations.

'Mohsen is here illegally.'

Afsoon clutched at Anna's hands. 'Yes, this is the problem. He must be secret for now but he cannot work so I must give him money. Sometimes he gets a little work on the market but not enough. I find him a place to stay but it is just a small room. I must give him every penny I can.'

'He's not working at Drakes?'

Afsoon looked astonished. 'Working for Richard's company? No, of course not, how could he?' She looked at Anna quizzically as though she may have not fully understood what she had been saying. 'He has no papers.' Anna was silent, thinking about how to go on. 'But you see, now it will soon be ok. I will be able to tell Richard about him.'

'Will you? Why?'

'Because I am having Richard's child! It is all he wanted. He is fond of me in his own way, which is a rather cold way, but I always knew that he wanted me only so I could have children for him.' Anna remembered Kimi's snide remark about her being Richard's brood mare.

'And you didn't mind?'

'Mind?' Afsoon exhaled sharply with amazement. 'Why should I mind? If I have a child for Richard he will not care so much about Mohsen. I could tell him some story so he would not know he was already here and I could have them meet and then maybe Mohsen would live with us and Richard would adopt him so he would be legal and I would be so happy.'

Anna briefly mulled over the ethics of this scenario. It seemed that Afsoon was as self-serving as Richard in her own way and love had nothing to do with the marriage for either party. She had seduced him in order to provide a legal identity and a home for her son. But Afsoon was dreaming. Richard would mind very much that he had been lied to and that his wife and the mother of his child had an adult male son whom he was expected to welcome into the dynasty he hoped to rule. Fat chance. When he discovered what kind of a man Mohsen was, he would be even more furious. He was no fool. He would put two and two together in the amount of time needed to call his lawyer.

But there was a far more important issue that Anna had to raise now. She looked into Afsoon's radiant face and sighed. 'There's something else, I'm afraid.' She was sure now that Afsoon had no idea what her son had been up to. Anna only had a small idea herself and that was enough to give her nightmares.

'Something else?' Afsoon's smile faded. 'Oh, Anna, please don't tell Richard, please.'

'It's not about that. Well, not directly. But it is about your son.'

'What do you mean?'

'I told you that the sister of my daughter's friend was groomed by a man she thought was her boyfriend?'

'Yes, that's horrible. I have read of such things. But a girl should not be allowed to be out on her own. That would never happen in our country.'

'Well, be that as it may, she did form a relationship with this man that she met indirectly through some voluntary work her mother did and then he persuaded her to see him at times when they could be alone. One thing led to another. She was a naïve girl thinking to begin with that she was having an exciting romance with a handsome man but instead found herself manipulated into having sex with strangers. She was wrong but she's a child and her mother thought she was safe. The fault lay with the older man who seduced her and then set her up to be finally gang raped for money.'

Afsoon seemed unsure of what to say. 'That is a terrible story. I am sorry for the girl. Is she safe now?'

'Yes. She has got medical help and is having counselling and believe me, her mother and sister will never let her out of their sight for years.'

'I don't understand why you are telling me this bad story, Anna.'

'The girl and her mother went to the police and reported what had happened. They made an image of the man she described who had groomed her.' Anna paused.

'Yes?'

'It was Mohsen, your son.'

Afsoon leaped to her feet. 'No, it was not. Of course it was not! How can you say such a thing? Mohsen is an honourable man. Those pictures could be anyone!'

'The police made enquiries among their informants on the streets. Several of them independently identified the man in the picture as Mojo – well known to be a pimp and a drug dealer.'

'You see! Mojo! That's not him – there are many people who look dark like this. Foreigners all look the same to you!'

Anna had no choice but to go on steadily. 'One of the informants was from Iraq. He is an asylum-seeker but he is here legally hoping for refugee status. He had met Mojo and they had talked a few times and he told the police that the man's real name was Mohsen Amirmoez.'

'No! You cannot believe what an Iraqi says! This is a fraud, Anna! This is a - set-up. How can you not see that!' Afsoon's eyes were wild with fear.

'The police had not mentioned the name. They couldn't because they didn't know it but when this man told them they contacted the Iranian police.'

Afsoon sank back down on the grass. Harry was calling to the children and waving while Bobble barked. Anna glanced at him and noticed that the sailing instructor was shepherding the children to the opposite bank. She would soon need to go and get him but she couldn't stop now.

'They sent a photograph of Mohsen to the Birmingham police and told them that he was wanted in Iran for the rape of a girl but had left the country before they could arrest him.'

Afsoon rocked herself back and forth in anguish. 'No, no, he did not do that. It was a lie the family made up. I had to get him away. It was a lie, Anna.'

'I'm sorry, Afsoon, I would give anything to believe you but I don't. Your son is a dangerous man and the police are looking for him.' Afsoon rocked and wailed.

Harry was now standing and calling quite loudly to the children. The sight of them must have triggered the protective instinct of a teacher who had been responsible for scores of field trips. Anna stood up. 'I have to get Harry. But there's something I must ask you.' Afsoon was now lying on the ground and sobbing. 'Stay there, I'll be back.' Anna's heart was already pounding with tension but she ran as fast as she could the thirty yards to the bank.

Bobble liked this new game and raced towards her barking wildly. She slowed as she approached Harry and forced a smile to her lips. 'Darling? Are you having fun?' She glanced to where the children were clustered against the far side in their dinghies, the instructor standing fiercely behind them staring across the water. 'Shall we go and see Afsoon now? That beautiful one you like? Come on.' She turned him away, linked an arm in his and began to walk back. As soon as the children were out of sight he forgot them. By the time they reached Afsoon the woman had calmed herself and was standing tall. In fact, she was icy.

'I thought we were friends,' she said to Anna, ignoring Harry.

'This has nothing to do with us, Afsoon. This is about doing the right thing.'

'We could go out on a - um,' said Harry beaming at Afsoon. 'Dinner and a movie?' Despite the seriousness of the situation with Afsoon, Anna was momentarily distracted by her husband's out-of-character remark. A *movie*? What randomly activated neuron was responsible for *that*?

Afsoon narrowed her eyes. 'The right thing?'

'Queen Nefertiti,' Harry exclaimed triumphantly, 'that's who you are!'

'You must tell the police where Mohsen is or tell him to give himself up.'

Afsoon's look could have turned a jelly to stone. 'Never.' She began to walk away.

Anna raised her voice a little. 'If you don't, I will have to tell them about you and that you know where he is and then the whole family might find out. Afsoon, please, do it, tell them or tell him.'

The tall woman turned back and regarded Anna with a mixture of contempt and astonishment. 'You are all wrong about him and I will never betray him!'

'Don't go,' said Harry. 'Don't be angry.'

'Then I must tell them,' Anna said slowly. Afsoon stood stock still for what seemed like minutes while Anna waited and Bobble brought a stick hopefully. Harry looked from one woman to the other in bewilderment. Finally Afsoon seemed to come to a decision and her defiant posture slackened.

'All right then, Anna. I know these things you are saying are not true but if the police are looking for my son then we must sort out the accusations.  I will tell him to give himself up to them.'  Her face seemed to have sunk in on itself and for the first time Anna could see that she was older than she appeared.  It was horrible to push this further but she had to.

'Six days, Afsoon.  If the police have not told me that he has given himself up in six days I will have to tell them all I know and then they'll come to you.'

Afsoon nodded curtly and turned to stride off across the plank bridge towards her car.  Anna's legs almost gave way.  She put a hand out to Harry who was looking upset.  'Why were you rude to that woman?'  Harry demanded.  'You should go and say sorry.'

Anna looked up at his indignant face.  Impossible to explain. She took his arm and smiled at him.  'Do you fancy a beer?' she asked, 'because I bloody do.'

'Beer and chips!' said Harry happily.

'You've never said a truer word, my sweetheart. Come on.'

## 20

When they got home the house was quiet and Harry tottered into the living room, exhausted. She knew he would sleep now for an hour or so. She sat down at the kitchen table and pulled her laptop to her. The packed email inbox was yelling at her. She scrolled down noting with a sinking heart all the things she had to do and then stopped at an email from Ted. She hadn't been into the office for over a week. She glanced at the date. Thank goodness it was sent only this morning. He wrote in his idiosyncratic faux illiterate style, a mix of phone text and can't-be-bothered:

*Thort we shud catch up. Re draycott. Come in asap.*

She replied that she would be in the next morning and give him a report. She wondered briefly what, of all that she now knew about the Draycotts, she could tell him. Very, very little. There was a quick message from her dad from Le Havre sent, it seemed, from a wifi café and all seemed well although he said they hadn't actually slept for more than an hour. No explanation. By the time Faye had come roaring in slamming doors, she had dealt with what she could, closed down her personal email and opened her work one.

She scrolled slowly down erasing the flurry of administrative group messages and pausing only briefly to check the social ones on the staff intranet. Nothing she felt like getting involved with. Life seemed rather too serious for that at the moment. She went back to the main list and continued down. Suddenly, her heart jumped. There was one from the Canadian search forum re. Cora Voisine. She opened it.

*Dear Mrs Ames,*
*I am contacting you at your agency because I may be able to help you with information about Cora Voisine. Please give me more details about why you are searching for her. I have googled your agency and it seems bona fide but I would like to know more about your interest in her. I'm sure you understand my caution.*

*Regards,*
*Marie Fourier*

What a sensible letter, Anna thought. She would have written in much the same way herself in response to the request she had posted.

It would be great to be able to give Gerald some information. Within seconds she had the scene in her head. A reunion between the dying lover and the teary-eyed object of his devotion (mother of Kimi) and a general rosy glow. Anna grunted at herself. Hadn't she had much the same image of her meeting with her own mother? And look how that had turned out. Quickly she replied with a message about how her client had met Cora in Canada thirty-two years ago at the Wanapitei River dam build and would like to know if she would be willing to talk to or even see him? He was now seriously ill and so the matter had some urgency and was important to him as he had been very fond of Ms Voisine. Her client's name was Gerald and he would meet any expenses if Cora would be willing to travel to meet him. Anna felt she had no need to give the full name. If Marie was in contact with Cora the information about the dam and the first name should be enough. Marie wasn't the only one needing to be cautious.

Faye slid into the kitchen and drooped herself over a chair. 'My head is so full,' she moaned, 'that if I move it's going to slop all over the floor.'

'Need help revising?' Anna closed the laptop and sat back.

'No, I have to stop. Right now I know way too much about everything.'

'Cup of tea?'

'That Len of yours has eaten all our biscuits. When I came in yesterday when you were out he actually was stuffing some in his pockets! Speak to him!' Faye tore off her scrunchie and shook her head so that a heap of chestnut curls sprang around her shoulders. Anna put the kettle on, went to the pan cupboard and emerged waving a pack of Belgium chocolate chip cookies. 'Yeah! Thanks Mum – you're a star.'

'And now I have to find a new hiding place. Have you seen Ellis?'

'Nope. Happy to report.'

'Faye!'

'Well, he's such a wuss these days. He's all moody and adolescent. I told him it's a really bad look when you're only eleven. He'd better get over whatever it is before he goes up to Year 8 in September or they'll crucify him.' Anna put two mugs on the table and sat down.

'What's the matter with him? Do you know?'

'Attention seeking - duh.' Anna mulled over the psychodynamic theory of projection and let a moment pass.

'So he's said nothing to you?'

Faye dipped her cookie into her tea. 'You're joking. I can't even get him to have a half way decent fight with me. I told him yesterday that he looked like a big girl's blouse in his tennis whites and he just looked sad. So boring.'

'I think he's having a hard time, Faye, just go easy on him would you? A bit of sisterly affection wouldn't go amiss.'

Faye sat up and regarded her mother with bright eyes. 'Ok. Can I take him to bowling with my mates?' She quickly rolled her hair back up into the scrunchie and picked her phone out of her hip pocket. 'Tonight?' Obediently, Anna went for her purse. Out-manoeuvred again.


Anna greeted the hoots and teasing with equanimity as she made her way through the open plan office to her desk. 'Where's your tan?' 'Shall we show you where your desk is?' and so on. She lifted one hand and waved her index finger in circles, smiling beatifically like the Queen. Suzy was by her side in moments.

'I am so glad to see you! There is absolutely no-one here I can talk to.'

Anna swivelled her seat and began picking through her mail while Suzy perched on the corner of her desk. 'What's up?'

'I think Rob's going off me.' What a relief. An episode from the soap opera that was Suze's life would be so diverting. 'I suggested we go for a romantic weekend in Paris and he said he couldn't afford it! Do you think he's seeing someone else?'

'Maybe he can't afford it.'

'No. There's something going on – I know it. And after I spent a whole hundred pounds on fucking lingerie.'

Anna laughed up at her. 'I presume that's the word used as an adjective and not an expletive?' They both hooted. 'Have you offered to pay for both of you?'

'No! I'm not doing that. He suggested it – but now says he's had to pay the garage for that prang he had and is skint – but that's the thin end of the wedge isn't it? Shelling out for my own romantic weekend?'

'Couldn't you think of it as empowering? You know how men used to pay for everything and then they got to call the shots.'

There was nothing of interest in the pile of mail and Anna leaned sideways and dropped it all in the nearest paper recycling box. Suzy brightened.

'Hey, that would be fun. I could totally humiliate him by ordering food for him in restaurants and telling him what to wear and then just talking about myself for hours.' Anna's office phone rang. She listened and replaced the receiver.

'Honestly, I've only been in the building five minutes and Ted's on at me.'

Suze slid off the desk and grimaced sympathetically. 'Let's have a drink one night, ok?'

'Definitely.'

'Anna?' Suzy seemed unusually hesitant and Anna paid attention.

'Yes?'

'You always look fantastic of course in your own charming little Hindu goddess fashion...'

'Spit it out.'

'Are you all right?'

'What do you mean?'

'You look, I don't know, tense, wired, uptight. I'm sorry. You just look as though you're having a hard time.'

Anna dropped her head. 'I am a bit. I can't talk to you about it, Suze, or I would but it will soon be over I think. All I can say is I'm worried about Ellis and I'm worried about some stuff that's going on and I don't know how I'm going to sort it out. But I will.' The next thing she knew Suzy's arms were round her and a swift kiss had been delivered to her cheek. The waft of delicate perfume and the affectionate embrace almost brought Anna to tears. She hadn't realised how wound up she had become, how much in need of touch, of comfort. She saw Suze move quickly away and glanced at the door. Ted was tapping his watch. She stood up and followed him to his office.

She wasn't in there for long. She had cobbled together some interview material from Richard, some comments from Frances and a lot of Gerald's family history stories. Ted let her talk and then raised his eyebrows. 'So what else have you been doing? Has the Canadian relative made contact yet?' So she could tell him that, too, and hoped that would hold him for the time being. He wanted her to talk. The bloodhound instinct that made him such a good researcher was telling him there was a lot more to this project than met the eye. When he had commended Anna's discretion it had not occurred to him that he would be on the wrong side of that. Like all good detectives he was nosy and he wanted the inside scoop. Both of them knew that the way things were set up he couldn't actually come out and ask her for it. But after an uneasy silence he dismissed her. She walked down the hall to Steve's office. He was perched, as ever, in front of his bank of screens, typing furiously. She opened the door and then tapped on it.

'Bad time?'

He whirled his chair round. 'No, not at all. I could do with looking at something else for a while. Sorry. Didn't mean that the way it sounded.' She pulled up the spare chair and sat down by him. 'Are you ok?' She nodded. 'Heard from your dad?' She nodded again. He glanced at the open door and lowered his voice. 'Have you set up to meet Afsoon?'

'I've seen her. I took Harry yesterday and we met at the Earlswood Lakes.'

'And?'

'Mohsen is her son.'

'No!'

'She's fiercely protective of him and thinks she's the one supporting him in his illegal status by what she can save from her dress allowance.' Then she told him everything that had been said. When she had finished he swung gently from side to side on his swivel chair, staring at the floor.

'I think you've done everything right, Anna. It can't have been easy when she kept saying that you were her friend.'

'No, it wasn't. I felt like crap.' Steve's eyes were soft as he looked at her. If they had been alone he would have taken her hand. As it was they sat in silence for a few moments. 'There's something else, Steve.'

'You're going to have to stop doing this to me, Anna. Just when I think it's safe to relax you say something like that.' He was grinning now but she knew he was paying attention. He just wanted to put her at her ease as far as possible. She knew that what Suze had said was right and even though Steve hadn't actually come out with it, he was reading the signs of stress in her face and manner too.

'I saw a Drake lorry at Felixstowe after I'd dropped dad and Diane off. Dook was driving it, you know, the depot manager who might or might not have been William's lover from the army?' Steve was beginning to frown in concentration. 'Well, never mind that. His passenger was Mohsen.'

'Do they know each other then?'

'Well, they obviously do. They seemed very matey. So I followed the truck back. It had a container box on it which of course it would, but when they got back to the depot they didn't drive it into the garage they went round the back and unloaded some crates. There was no-one about – it was between their drivers' shifts. The crates were about twice the size of coffins and quite sturdy.' Steve was listening intently. 'When the truck pulled away I saw there was a door in the back of the garage so they must have taken the stuff inside.'

Steve whistled softly. 'What do you think? Weapons? Not cigarettes because that would be cardboard cartons. Booze?'

Anna lifted her face to his and looked into his eyes. 'Dook went into the depot and came back with a huge plastic container of water and took it inside.' She saw the horror and the comprehension arrive simultaneously in Steve's eyes.

'This is a police matter, Anna. You need to tell them.'

'I just have to do one more thing Steve. There really could be an innocent explanation. To be sure I have to go to that depot and see what's inside.' Steve was silent for a moment.

'I'm coming with you. I can be your cover story. If Dook's there you can introduce me and ask if he's got a job going. I'm your brother just out of jail so he won't want me but it will do. If he isn't there we can tell anyone who is that we're looking for him and have a mosey round. I'll come in your car but we need to go back to my house first and pick up a couple of things.'

Anna regarded him with admiration. 'You just thought all that up?'

Steve tapped his head. 'Smarter than the average bear. I've got a sustificut to prove it.' She was grateful and it made sense. 'I think we should go now.' Steve looked at his watch. 'The depot should be pretty quiet at this time of the day.'

And so it was. The doors to the garage were wide open as usual. One truck was in the yard and a mechanic's legs poked out from underneath. They walked past slowly and were ignored. Steve suggested they go inside first. There were a couple of trucks parked but no-one in the office. Anna immediately looked to the back of the space and saw that there was nothing there. It was completely bare. Just as she had feared. Steve glanced around and took out of his pocket a laser tape measure. He leaned against the office-end wall and switched the torch-like gadget on. A red spot appeared on the far wall and Steve scribbled down a reading on the back of his hand.

Then they went outside and strolled to the back of the garage trying to look natural. Anna pointed out the door. It was not padlocked, it was a Yale lock, unusual in an industrial complex but much less obvious. The brass of the lock had been painted the same colour as the aluminium siding. Again Steve glanced round and across at the social club checking carefully that no-one was watching. Then he took from his coat pocket a stethoscope. Anna turned away from him, scanning from side to side in case anyone appeared. They were not visible from the factory but they were visible from the club. He listened for what seemed like an age. There could be no believable explanation for what they were doing except the truth. Anna itched to go to the corner of the building and check that there was no-one approaching but if she did that she would not be able to mask Steve from the view of the club. It took all her self-control not to tell him to hurry up. Then he stood up straight and put the instrument back in his pocket. His expression was blank.

'Anna, can you pick those wildflowers?' She looked where he was pointing at some rosebay willowherb growing out of a crack in the old concrete pad.

'Why?'

'I'm going to walk back up to the other end of the building. I need a fixed point to sight for the measurement. Stand exactly parallel with the back wall, do you see where the plants are? Just take your time looking at them and then pick them and keep yourself in profile to me. Do you understand? Don't look at me. Just get the flowers and bring them with you. Give me about thirty seconds before you start picking them.' She nodded.

She drove for a couple of miles until a pub came into view and then pulled in to the car park. The rosebay willowherb was already wilting on the back seat. Steve had been silent but she knew it was because he wanted to wait until they were away and safe before he said anything. They stayed in the car – it was more secure to talk in there. 'Ok,' said Steve, 'these are the facts. The outside of the garage is two metres longer than the inside. There's no evidence of fresh paint on the inside or the outside, even the paint on the Yale lock is chipped by a key so this concealed space has been there a while. Several years, I'd say. It must measure two metres by about thirty. I didn't measure across but it doesn't matter. That's quite a space in there.'

Anna could wait no longer. 'Did you hear anything?'

Steve looked sick. His eyes were very dark when he faced her. 'Yes. I heard noises. No speech but noises that sounded like something shuffling and breathing. I could hear breathing, Anna.'

'God.'

'Yes. Do you want me to come with you to the police?' She thought for a moment.

'Thanks but no. If you don't mind I'll pretend I used the equipment and made the measurements. I'm getting this horrible feeling that we've found just a corner of a very nasty web and we don't know who's involved. I think it would be better if you stay incognito. Do you know what I mean?' Steve agreed and gave her the laser tape measure showing her how to use it. She wrote down in her notepad the lengths he had recorded on his hand. Then he passed over the stethoscope and she folded that into her tote.

'I can understand the measure, Steve, for your mountaineering, but how come you have a stethoscope?'

'It's from when Alice used to get ill – you know when she was between operations. I needed to be able to detect the slightest change in her lungs and heart. They trained me how to use it.'

Anna raised her hand and put it lightly against Steve's cheek. He placed his hand on top of hers. 'I'm glad you're on my side,' she said quietly.

'Always.' Steve glanced out of the window. 'Well, we're here now, fancy a coffee before you drive me back to work?'

'Just let me phone Joan to check Harry's all right. He should be because she's taking him to Diane's animal refuge to see a St Bernard they've got in. They're taking Bobble back for a look at his old haunt too.' Five minutes later they pushed open the door on to red tiles and wooden tables and a big smile from behind the bar. Just what was needed.

Anna sat on the moulded plastic chair in the waiting room at the central police station and felt peaceful for the first time for weeks. It would all be out of her hands soon. That's what we pay our taxes for, she thought, so that when these difficult and dangerous things happen we can just hand them over to the experts and walk away.

There was only Ellis and possibly Rhea to try to understand. She felt now that her earlier fears about the girl had been over-wrought. It was true that the children of wealthy families were always at risk from kidnapping but that sort of thing didn't happen here, did it? Kimi couldn't be more protective but she let Rhea use public transport in the city on a daily basis. All the kids from her private school did and some of them must come from very well-off families, too. The buses were full of them at certain times of day. She glanced at her watch. The duty officer had gone away fifteen minutes ago to look for DS Iqbal.

The door opened and Anna saw with a sinking heart that it was DS Griffiths approaching her. He saw her and just looked tired. He nodded for her to follow him and they went into a small interview room.

'I'm waiting for DS Iqbal,' Anna said.

Griffiths settled himself heavily on the chair opposite. 'He's on another case. It's not like the telly you know, love, when everyone gets a personal detective at their beck and call.'

'Please don't call me 'love', my name is Mrs Ames,' Anna said. 'I have something serious to tell you.'

'Do you.'

Anna told him what she had observed from Felixstowe to the Drake depot and the results of her investigation today. Of Mohsen, she only said that the man with Dook appeared to be the same one as the suspect in the gang-rape incident. DI Griffiths rubbed his eyes.

'Do you get off on this?' he said. 'Little Miss Marple?'

'I find that remark offensive. Will you take this report seriously or shall I wait for DS Iqbal?'

'If I see him I'll tell him what you said,' Griffiths said standing up. Anna remained seated.

'I haven't seen you take a single note. What will you tell him?'

'That the woman who couldn't be bothered to call the police out to a possible major crime incident now wants us to go and search a garage on private land belonging to a very important local businessman because she *thinks* there's something nasty going on.' He squinted at her. 'Correct?' Anna did not reply. 'You make me sick, you self-important career women. You run to us fast enough when you get yourselves into messes, don't you?'

Anna stood up. 'You are being unprofessional and I will be lodging a complaint.'

DS Griffiths grinned and looked around the bare room. 'Why? What did I say? Your word against mine, my lady. Now if you would be so kind as to excuse me from your fantasy life I have real work to do.'

## 21

Anna drove home realising that she had played this wrong. DS Iqbal had given her his mobile number probably to avoid this very thing happening. She would phone him when she got home. She felt very tired and flat. What could she do about that pitch dark corridor two metres by thirty in which there were God knows how many terrified people? Only the police could do anything. Were people injured? Dying? Why had Steve only heard breathing? Maybe their mouths were taped or they were drugged or more likely they had been told they could not make a sound. She pushed the horrifying images away. She thought about what Steve had said about dark websites and the organised gang-rapes. If Mohsen was the 'supplier' did he work with Dook to provide the poor girls? Perhaps Nicola had only been a standby in between deliveries from Felixstowe.

At home Harry and Joan were still out and she could make her calls in peace. Iqbal's voicemail told her he would call her back and she gave her number again. She could do no more. She also needed to speak to Gerald about the email from Marie Fourier. So far there had been no reply to her recent contact. Gerald answered immediately and was excited that there had been progress. She had not seen him for a couple of weeks and he sounded weaker, she thought. 'How are you feeling?'

'Oh, not great, you know. Can't be helped.' He paused. 'Something's come up and it's the last thing I want. I was just about to call you but I wanted to wait for office hours.'

'That doesn't matter, Gerald, you can call me any time, you know that. Do you want to tell me now? ' She prayed silently that he would not. She was tired but he sounded pretty done in himself and she liked him. He was a good man who, for all his wealth, had very rarely put his own needs first and now couldn't even die in peace.

'It's quickly told, Anna, thank you. It's Frances. She's saying she wants to have a big family meeting to discuss what will happen to the firm when I die.'

'Nice.'

'Yes, it is isn't it?' Gerald managed a dry chuckle. 'But the thing is, I wouldn't even mind that, it has to be sorted out although Richard will naturally take over. No, she wants to use it as a platform for the big reveal.'

'The big reveal?'

'She wants to tell everyone, including Kimi, who Kimi is. And more than that, who she, Frances is, that she is the one who owns the company, not me. I mean, of course, the majority share. She wants them all to know that Kimi will be effectively disinherited apart from what I've left her in my will.'

'Oh dear.'

'Yup.'

'Why is she doing this?' She heard Gerald's laboured breath.

'To punish me, of course, and Kimi. I thought she would leave it until after I'd died, but no, that isn't quite fun enough. She wants to watch me suffer. I hadn't realised how bitter she is.'

'Not to say cruel.'

'Mm.'

'There is one way you could take the wind from her sails, Gerald. You must have thought of it.' He sighed.

'Yes. You suggested it before. And you were right. I'm not going to have Kimi put up on the scaffold like that. I'll ask her to come and see me at the flat in town and we can have a proper talk. She'll be shocked and probably hate me but at least that way she won't be served up on toast for Frances' pleasure. As long as Kimi's all right I can cope with anything Frances throws out. In fact, Kimi may decide not to come to the meeting. After all, why should she? That really would take the wind out of the Gorgon's sails! And if I get to have a proper talk with Kimi I can give her some suggestions too about career choices. She's very able but she needs to get some qualifications.'

Anna felt a hot tide of affection run through her for his practical unselfishness. 'You can also tell her how much you loved her mother and love her, too.' Anna could hear the intake of breath at the other end of the phone. 'Do it soon, Gerald. It's not for me to advise you but I feel sure that's the right thing.'

After the call ended she got up and walked to the dresser with its decades of family clutter. Stuck behind a mug holding a dusty peacock feather was one of her favourite photos of Faye dressed as Superman for her eighth birthday. Then there was one of Ellis' school photos, still in its cardboard mount. How old would he have been? His head seemed too big for his neck and he had a front tooth missing. Six? In a clip-frame was one of her with George. The professional photo of her with her degree certificate was framed somewhere in what was now Harry's bedroom but the one she really liked was this snapshot. Harry had taken it. She was making a daft face at him in her cap and gown and George was sticking his fingers up behind her head. Her dad looked so young. His hair was dark and thick with long sideburns and he was wearing the only tie he owned – a ridiculous elongated diamond shape. He would have been younger then than she was now. All those years on his own quietly putting his daughter first - but now he had Diane. 'Dad,' she whispered. 'Be safe. Come home, safe.'

Then there was the photo of her and Harry stuck behind a wooden tub full of paperclips, drawing pins and a pair of dice. The emulsion was peeling off and the colours were faded. She picked it up. It was taken by George on the day they had moved into this house. They had been in equal parts both ecstatic to have their own home and terrified about the responsibility of paying the mortgage. Now she was on her own and even more worried about paying the bills. But how happy they had been. Ellis hadn't yet been born and Faye was just a baby. She thought of Gerald trudging home to his manor house with a cold and vengeful woman waiting for him. Who would mourn him? Richard couldn't wait to step into his father's shoes and Charlotte seemed indifferent to him. Kimi herself was hardly affectionate from the little Anna had seen. She put the photograph back in its place.

Her phone jumped about on the hard surface of the kitchen table. It was DS Iqbal. 'Got your message. Can I help?' So Griffiths had not even bothered to speak to him. Anna told him what she had seen and done. There was a pause.

'Are you sure it was Mohsen with the Drake's driver?'

'Yes, I am. I saw him quite clearly when they went into the service station and again later. I couldn't phone you because I'd left it at home on charge.'

'DS Griffiths mentioned something this afternoon. Just a quick word. He thought there was nothing to it.' Another pause. Anna pondered the reason for his hesitation, but he was younger than DS Griffiths and probably junior. Even if he thought it was worth investigating, her telling Griffiths would have made it hard for him to do anything because it might seem as though he was going over the older officer's head. She wished she had thought of all this earlier. She waited, miserably, for Iqbal to bow out.

'I'll tell you what I'll do, if I can, Anna. I know someone in the helicopter patrol unit. He has a heat-seeking device on board –

you know – to look for perps hiding in the woods, missing kids, that sort of thing.'

'Yes.' Anna's heart expanded and she took a deep breath.

'He's in the Solihull sector. I'll see if he can go low over the depot and maybe something will show up. If it does we can go in. If it doesn't I don't know what I can do. It is possible that there are trafficked people there, I'm not saying that it's not, but they could have been moved quickly on. It's been nearly six hours since you were there, right?'

'Yes, but there would be drivers around until about 10.00 tonight. The trucks start coming back in to re-load around 4.00.'

'Even so. They could have already been picked up.'

'Yes, I suppose so.' Anna was silent for a moment. 'Thank you, though. There could be something really bad happening.'

DS Iqbal sighed. 'I'm afraid there is always something really bad happening. Sometimes I wonder what is the matter with us. Anyway, I must go. I'll do my best Anna.'

'Will you let me know? Either way?'

'If we raid the place I'll need to interview you. Otherwise I'd rather not contact you. Please use my mobile if anything else happens. It gets – er – complicated otherwise.'

'I think I've learned that lesson. Thank you again.'

It was so strange to be Friday and no poetry session to relax into. Soon Faye and Ellis would be in for their dinner and it would be just the four of them unless Joan could be persuaded to stay. Where was Harry? Anna scrolled down her phone for Joan's number but then heard the front door open and they were both there. Harry looked worn out and stumbled into the front room. Joan followed Anna into the kitchen looking worried.

'I'm sorry, dear, I think I've overtired him. I didn't realise he was so –' she paused.

'Low in stamina?' Anna said, putting on the kettle.

'Well, yes. It's hard to remember that when he's still a young man. Well, to me he is.'

'I know.' They sat down at the table and sipped the hot tea.

'He liked seeing the animals though. The St Bernard is just adorable. How can people be cruel to helpless creatures?' DS Iqbal had asked the same question only minutes before.

'Perhaps that's the point. They can't fight back so maybe some people behave badly because they know they can.' Anna wished she had not given up the cookies so easily to Faye. Were there any of George's Kitkats left in his stash? She got up to check the cupboard. One. She broke it in half and gave Joan a slightly melted bar.

'Mm. Thank you, dear. I've been meaning to say, I had a chat with Briony the other day. Usually she just waves and smiles, you know, always in a dash, but we had quite a talk.' Briony Clark. So many images crashed into Anna's head at her name that she had to shut them down.

'How is she?'

'Looking for a crusade.'

'What?'

'The criminology is going well, I think. She didn't say so but I think she's getting very good marks in her assignments, but now she wants to specialise, she wants to find a cause to invest all her energy in. I think they have to focus on something specific in their second year in September. You know, a sort of area of specialty.'

'Not women's prisons then?'

'No. Probably had enough of that and in any case, ours are so much better.'

So Briony wanted a crusade, a cause to fight for. How about trafficked girls confined in a metal box on a container ship for days and then crated for God knows how many hours and then shut up in the black hole of Drakes' depot here in decent old England, land of the good British values, Anna wondered grimly. And what a treat they had in store when they were finally released in Shangri-La. Slave labour at best, prostitution and gang-rape at worst. Lovely.

'Can you stay for dinner, Joan? It's only spag bol but there's plenty.'

Joan stood up and shook her numb bottom. 'No thanks. I'll be off. Now about tomorrow, I'll come to the pool to meet you and Harry but I won't go in – I've got a bit of a chest.'

'Don't come then! Look after yourself. I thought you were looking a bit peaky before.'

'Are you sure?'

'Of course. We'll be fine. Then I've got the whole weekend with nothing planned. It will be so great just to chill. I might even make a start on the weeding.' Joan raised her eyebrows at her. 'Or not.'

The family were finishing off a lemon tart when Steve knocked at the door. Faye let him in on her way upstairs. She was packing for the first festival of the season that Michelle had promised to take her and Tasha and Nicola to near Evesham for the weekend. These days Michelle was being a very, very hands-on mum. Since Steve had brought the huge treat of Alice to live near them Faye had dropped her antagonism and sometimes even spoke to him. 'Come to see Ellis,' he said to her. She was already at the top of the stairs.

Harry was always delighted to see him. It was a ritual that no-one commented on any more that when Steve was in the kitchen Harry would bring him gifts. He had started it the previous Christmas – no-one knew why. On this occasion as soon as Steve was seated Harry brought him Bobble's rubber bone. It was disgusting – slimy with slobber and stuck all over with dust and hairs. Bobble ran to Steve and looked hopeful. Without pausing in what he was saying Steve stood up, went to the back door and threw it for the dog wiping his hand on his trousers.

'So it's more of a walk than a climb. We'll start at Hartington and then go north to the High Peak Trail, spend the night under canvas somewhere and then do another fifteen or so the next day. Might get some scrambles in on the way. John's wife is going to meet us with the people carrier and bring us back down to our cars Sunday afternoon. Do you fancy it?'

Ellis looked glum. 'Can't.' He glanced around a bit desperately, Anna thought. 'There's trials tomorrow at the tennis club and I really should go.'

Steve touched his shoulder. 'That's ok. Another time.'

'What about Alice?'

'I'm dropping her off with mum and dad in Ambergate on the way up and then I'll pick her up coming home.' Harry put an apple into his hand. 'Thanks mate.'

'Well, have a great time. You deserve a break and some fresh air.' Anna stood up to see him out. Ellis flapped a hand and went out to the back garden and Harry wandered off into the living room.

'Thanks for the email,' Steve said at the front door. 'Let me know what the police find out, ok?'

'How?' Anna smiled at him.

'Oh, right. I'll be out of phone range. Well, I'll give you a ring as soon as I've got a signal.' He looked down at Anna in the soft way that caused the familiar tantalising knot of pleasure and frustration. 'Take it easy yourself Anna. You need a break, too.' Then he was gone and there was that clench in her stomach that always followed a parting from him.

Harry was dozing on the sofa. She was glad he didn't want to watch television, she just wanted to be quiet. She sat down beside him, drew up her legs and lifted his arm to be round her shoulders. He murmured but didn't fully wake. She lay stroking his hand, trying to think about good things - normal, cheerful things. Ellis so invested in his tennis. Faye out with her friends. Nicola having innocent fun like a kid should. George and Diane off on their awfully big adventure. When she realised she was picturing them in the iconic Titanic pose at the bow of the ship, she grunted softly in amusement. Leonardo di Caprio in a cardigan and Kate Winslet in an oversized green sweatshirt and granny glasses. The windows were open and a robin was calling a trill. She closed her eyes.

## 22

Saturday was a blowy day with energetic squalls followed by a flash of sun and blue skies. Anna stood in the garden, rake in hand, peering up at the activity. In a break in the rain like now she could see layer upon layer, high and higher in the atmosphere as the clouds changed from fluffy clumps to chalky scrawls. The wind was whipping each flock along and she noted a massive black cumulonimbus fast approaching. She had raked a pile of dead plants and leaves and now she didn't know what to do with it. It was too much for the compost heap so she would probably have to bag it up and take it to the tip.

That used to be Harry's job. Now Harry was being pestered by Bobble to play. Sometimes Harry was up for it and would throw the ball again and again but today he didn't seem to even notice the dog down on its knees begging him for some action. He seemed to have withdrawn a little further but he could just be tired after the swim. Anna sighed, glanced at the cloud darkening the garden, put the rake into the tool shed and latched the door. After this morning's swim Harry had had a hard time climbing up the short ladder out of the pool and she and the attendant had had to help. They had already cut back on his time in the water to fifteen minutes and it seemed that another two or three minutes would have to go. The last thing she wanted was for Harry to run out of energy while he was still in the water.

'Come on, sweetie, let's go in, it's going to rain. Bobble! Come here, boy.'

It was seven o'clock on Saturday evening. The casserole Anna had made earlier was almost ready and the smell made her hungry. She wondered if Ellis was home and called up the stairs but there was no answer. He hadn't wanted his parents to go to the trials – no families allowed it seemed which probably made a lot of sense. She didn't expect to hear from Faye at the festival unless she fell out with everyone and wanted picking up which was not going to happen. She decided to phone Joan later and see how she was. She pulled some green beans from the vegetable drawer, washed them and started to slice them into a steamer. Her phone rang. It was Kimi.

'Hi Anna, how are you?'

'Fine. Well, a bit achey, I've been trying to tame the garden.'

'Good for you. I'm ashamed to say I just pay someone.'

'Sounds perfect to me.' There was a pause. Kimi had never before made a purely social call so Anna waited to see what she wanted.

'I'm just phoning to see when Rhea will be ready to come home.'

'I'm sorry? She isn't here. She must still be at the Club. I didn't know Ellis was planning to bring her back here but dinner's almost ready and there's plenty for everyone.' There was a different quality to this pause and Kimi's voice was much sharper.

'No, she said she was spending the day with Ellis at your house. The Club isn't open today – they're doing it up for the spring tournament.' Anna looked quickly round the kitchen to see if there was a note for her from Ellis in any of the usual places. No. There was no message on her phone, she knew that.

'Just a minute, Kimi, I'm running up to his room.' She bounded up the stairs and flung open his bedroom door. Everything was in order as always with Ellis so she could see immediately that there was nothing different except a piece of paper resting on his laptop. She picked it up. It said, "Sorry, Mum. XXX." Her legs gave way and she groped for the bed.

'Is that it? Is that all it says?' Kimi's voice was trembling – with rage or fear Anna wasn't sure. 'Rhea hasn't answered her phone all day – she told me she wouldn't so not to call. Have you spoken to Ellis?'

'No, I thought he would be in the trials like he said. I'm going to hang up and try him now.'

'Wait!' Kimi shouted immediately. 'I'm coming over. Tell me your address – I couldn't get it out of Rhea. Oh hell, Anna, what the fuck are they doing?'

Of course there was no answer from Ellis' phone. Anna forced herself to check his cupboards and drawers. She couldn't see anything much missing – maybe a sweater, some socks? It was hard to tell. Then she opened the top cupboard where Ellis kept his camping equipment and saw that his back-pack and sleeping bag were gone. A smell of burning brought her to her senses and she ran downstairs to snatch the beans from the stove and plunge the pan into cold water. She turned off the oven. Harry wandered in, disturbed by the sound of running feet and the smell of burned food. Anna's thoughts were racing but he still had to eat so she ladled the casserole meat and vegetables out on to a cold plate for him. She placed a glass of water by his side and sat down opposite opening her laptop. There was nothing in the email inbox from Ellis.

'Where are they?' Harry asked as he loaded another forkful.

Where indeed. Anna suddenly realised that her entire support system had disappeared. She was alone with Harry. Her whole body wanted to run out of the door and look for Ellis and Rhea but what about Harry? He was already sleepy – there was no way she could take him with her to scour the streets, it would be so distressing to him that it would be cruel and she would never be able to leave him in the car if she had to go on foot. She checked her phone again, tried Ellis again, left a text message and a voicemail. It had been twenty minutes since Kimi's call so she should be here shortly. Just in case, Anna tried Steve's phone. No connection. She called the tennis club but got a recorded message. She sprang up from the table where Harry was slowly finishing his food and strode into the front room to look out of the window. Nothing, and it was getting dark. The rain was relentless now.

Ellis. Her kind, clever, soft-hearted boy was out there somewhere with that nutcase of a girl. Who knew what she was involved with? Out there was Mohsen, and Dook and countless others. A horrible thought came to her. Was Rhea lined up for the same treatment as Nicola? They may not even know that she was Draycott's grand-daughter but, her thoughts were racing now, if they did, what possibilities for blackmail and extortion there were! Ellis was just a kid but that wouldn't stop him trying to save her. Shit! Shit! Why hadn't Kimi checked with her about the arrangement? But it was no use being angry with her, that wouldn't help anything and if the kids were determined to go off then they would have thought of some other plan anyway.

Headlights shot into view and were then quickly dimmed. Anna ran to the front door and down the drive ignoring the driving rain. 'Have you heard anything?'

'Have you?'

They dashed into the house. Quickly, they decided to phone the police. Not 999. Anna dialled Iqbal's mobile and he answered almost immediately. He was on duty, it seemed. She explained what had happened and who Rhea was. She didn't need to spell it out –

he grasped the implications at once and told her he would organise an APB for mobile units and notify transport police to monitor railway stations in Birmingham and London since that was the destination of choice for most teenage runaways. 'Normally, we'd have to leave it longer before we take action but this is a special case because of the context. Do they have money?' Anna had her phone on speakerphone so glanced at Kimi who shook her head.

'Not much,' we think.

'OK, I'll notify the motorway police to check service stations in case they're hitch-hiking. Have you called the hospitals?'

'No, but we can. We'll do that.'

'I'll get someone on to checking St Basil's here and Centrepoint in London. It's doubtful they will have got anywhere like that yet but we can alert them.'

'What should we do?'

'Stay at home. They may come back. In fact, it's the most likely scenario. When kids get cold and hungry and run out of money and it's getting dark, they tend to go home unless that's what they're running away from, of course.'

When the call had ended Kimi got busy on her phone contacting all the Birmingham hospitals. Anna paced the kitchen thinking. She didn't believe they were going to stroll in through the door. Ellis was not an impulsive child and, more than that, he would know she would be frantic and wouldn't be so thoughtless as to put her through that unnecessarily. So, he must have a good reason for not telling her that he was going and where he was. The only reason she could think of was that Rhea would have convinced him that to do so would put them in danger. Or greater danger. In that case, she must have feared what Anna (and her mother) would do if they knew what the two had planned.

Anna stopped pacing and stared out of the kitchen window into the dark and the rain. She thought back to Rhea's strange note to Ellis. Was *she* being blackmailed? Certainly, if they were planning to meet and in some way pay off a blackmailer, Anna and Kimi would attempt to stop it. A strange thought that a young teenager would have done something to be blackmailed about. Then Anna had another worrying thought. She had been puzzled by Richard's almost obsessive focus on the identity of Rhea's father. Was something going on there? Did he worry about exactly this scenario, that Rhea would be in some way the victim of extortion if her father discovered the family's wealth? Why else would Ellis agree to this desperate move if he wasn't convinced that Anna would involve the police or some other authority and Rhea had persuaded him that that would result in worse danger, perhaps even danger to Anna and Kimi themselves. Her heart was pounding now. She remembered how hurt he had been when she had not woken him to help with Nicola's rescue. He had promised then that he could be relied upon – that he was brave and resourceful enough to be of real help. Of course he wouldn't do anything that might put his mother in danger. Damn!

Kimi had finished her calls with no result. They hadn't expected any. A hospital would have contacted them in case of accident or illness.

Anna told Kimi what she had been thinking but the woman shook her head. 'No, it wouldn't be that.' She looked squarely at Anna. 'Trust me, it wouldn't be.'

'Has Rhea talked about anything she was worried about?'

'You're joking. Rhea doesn't tell me anything. She's always been secretive even when she was a child, when there was no reason to be. I've worried about it but it's just her. Some people are private people.' Anna made no comment. 'She's not shown any interest in boys, either, although she's still young for that. I think one of the reasons she likes Ellis is that he's bright and switched on but not into that kind of thing yet.' Anna was only half listening while she came to a decision.

'Kimi I have to tell you something and I think you're going to be very angry with me.' Kimi threw back her hair and stared at Anna. 'That day at the horse show I saw Ellis stuff a note into his pocket which Rhea had given him. Later, I found it when I was looking for something else. I've no idea whether he read it or not. I should have told you but I thought it was just a fantasy.'

Kimi's eyes were boring into Anna's face. 'Where is it?' Anna pulled open a drawer in the dresser and took out the sealed brown envelope she had put it in. She tore open the envelope and read the note. Kimi exploded. 'You stupid woman!' Kimi yelled, 'Why the fuck didn't you show me this? Who are you to decide what's a fantasy or not? I'm her mother! What were you thinking?' Anna had been thinking of Ellis and only Ellis. That was the truth.

'I'm sorry. I should have done.'

'This changes everything, Anna. I'm going out there to look for her – I'm not sitting here waiting for the police to see if they feel like taking this seriously. You're going to answer for this, Anna. I could have protected her if I'd known. If anything happens to her you'll have me to deal with!' Kimi was blazing with rage and fear.

'Where will you go?' But Kimi was already out of the room and a second later the front door slammed. Anna sank into a chair and dropped her head in her hands. Kimi was right, of course she should have shown her the note. And she had let things drift with Ellis instead of making him open up to her and now both children were out there in God only knew what horrific situation. It was torture to do nothing and yet what could she do? Harry could not be left alone and Joan wasn't well. Her phone rang and she snatched it up. Len.

'Hey Sis.'

'Len, thank God.'

'What?' He was startled.

'I need you here right away. Ellis has gone off somewhere with a friend who is in trouble. I need to go and look for them and dad's still away. Can you come to be with Harry and hold the fort, be here in case Ell comes back or calls on the landline? You're the only one I've got Len.' She realised that she was shamelessly grovelling to him but she didn't care. Whatever it took.

'What about that gobby daughter of yours?'

'She's away and in any case she's still a kid. I need an adult here. This could get very serious. I might need to be out all night.' She didn't need to fake a sob. 'Please, Len, get a taxi and come now.'

'I've got no money.' She could hear that the normally laconic tone of Len's voice had changed and become brisker, almost excited.

'I'll pay when you get here and I'll get Harry into bed. No, wait, I may be upstairs – I'll leave money by the front door and it will be unlocked. Do it now, Len, please.'

She put a £20 note under the phone by the door and went into the living room as calmly as she could. Harry was drooping she saw with relief. 'Come on, love, time for bed.' He didn't protest as they climbed the stairs and went into his bedroom and she forced herself to be cheerful and unrushed as he slowly removed each shoe and sock. He didn't like to be helped with this part of the routine. She wondered if they could give the teeth cleaning a miss and when he had his sleeping shorts and T shirt on she turned back his bedclothes to entice him in. He looked towards his bedroom door as if puzzled by a change in the order of things but then climbed in and rolled over. She covered him up and turned the dimmer switch on his lamp right down. She bent over and kissed him and, smelling the familiar scent of his skin, was suddenly overcome with tears. 'I'm sorry, Harry,' she whispered, 'I've been careless and now our boy is in danger. I'm so sorry.'

She left the room closing the door quietly and went downstairs in a blur. But all the time, through the fear and self-recrimination, she was thinking – a clear, rational part of her brain was chugging away. No point in just setting out into the night like Kimi. She needed a plan. Where do people go, where do kids go, at night? Suddenly she remembered the words of the priest from the church down the road. Months ago when she had been talking to him about Harry, trying to understand the random tragedy of his illness, he had told her about how the churches were involved with rough sleepers, street people, offering them a safe bed for the night. He might be able to give her some kind of direction. She sat down at the kitchen table and googled the church. There was a mobile number for the priest – Andrew Dunster. She phoned it. He answered after four rings and she quickly reminded him of their conversation.

'Yes, of course I remember you. How is Harry? Has he gone missing again?'

'No. He's safe. It's my son. I'm very afraid that he is trying to be a white knight to a friend who could be in a very, very dangerous situation. I need to know where to go in the city to look for them. Where do kids go? Where do night people go?'

Andrew was immediately business-like. 'I can take you to some people who might be able to help. There's the Salvation Army, the Birmingham City Mission and the Street Pastors – they're all out at night and they're the best source of information and help. Do you want me to pick you up now?'

'No. I have to wait a few minutes for my brother to come and look after Harry but in any case I need to have my own car because I've no idea how this will develop. Can I meet you somewhere?'

'Do you know the Bullring – the open market?' Anna said she did. 'I'll meet you on the corner by St. Martin's. The Salvation Army will be there setting up hot food and drinks and I'll phone the other organisations when you get there so you can talk to them. Then we can figure out a plan. Ok?'

'Andrew, thank you so much. I didn't know where to turn.'

'See you in a few minutes.'

The front door opened and Len grabbed the note from the table and disappeared. When he came back they both went into the kitchen. Anna explained the situation and her plans in a few words.

'Blimey,' Len said, impressed, 'it's like the telly.'

'Well, let's hope the scriptwriters make it a happy ending, eh?' She stood up and pulled on her waterproof. 'There's some casserole left, you can microwave it, and oh, just eat anything you can find, and Len, please don't go to sleep. Leave the light on in the hall and in here and in the living room. There's plenty of DVDs if there's nothing on tv and can you keep the landline phone by you? You've got my number and-' She became aware that he was talking over her.

'You've forgot, haven't you?'

'What?' She stared up at his benignly grinning face but inside she was screaming at him to let her go, leave, look for Ellis.

'That night when the owl came in and Harry broke your arm and you passed out?'

'What? Yes, of course I remember!'

'I managed all right then didn't I?' She grabbed him but her arms only went half way round so he patted the top of her head. 'You go and do what you have to. I'll be here.'

## 23

It was nine o'clock on a Saturday night and the streets of Birmingham were anything but quiet. Anna turned into Edgbaston Street and pulled off the road on to the pavement by the church. It was illegal but she didn't care. The priest was there talking to a Salvation Army officer under a huge umbrella. As she approached they turned to look at her and smiled.

'I'll let my team know,' the officer said. 'It's early yet so I'll have time to have a word. Do you have a picture?' Anna scrabbled in her bag for the one she had grabbed from the top of the piano on the way out. It was the most recent school photo. The officer studied it carefully. She told him about Rhea and gave a description of the girl trying not to make her sound too eccentric. He wrote Anna's number down carefully in a small notebook. The rain thudded into the pavement and rattled the awnings on the market stalls. Already Anna's jeans were wet from the knees down. Was Ellis out of doors in this?

'I've talked to the team leader of the Street Pastors, Anna,' Andrew said when she'd finished. 'Here's his number – he's expecting to hear from you. They won't be out on duty for half an hour or so, so it's a good time to get to talk to him too.'

'Thank you. Thank you both.' The officer walked away taking the umbrella with him and Anna turned to Andrew but he was waiting to speak to her. He was squinting through the rain driving into his face.

'I'm very sorry, Anna, but I have to go. When you called I was with an elderly parishioner and his wife. She's probably not going to last the night and I promised I would be there with her at the end. Do you need me to find someone to be with you?'

'No. You've been so helpful - I appreciate this so much.'

He smiled and touched her shoulder and was off, snapping up the hood of his raincoat and walking quickly towards his car. She tucked herself under the porch door to the church and phoned the Street Pastor team leader giving him descriptions and her number and then looked around wondering where to go next. In the other direction from the market there was a flight of steps going up the hill towards the shopping mall. She glanced at her watch. The mall may still be open, she didn't know when it closed, and that might be just the place for kids to go. If someone was trying to arrange a meeting he (or she) would have to pick a place that kids would know and could get to on public transport. The Bullring Shopping Centre would be the perfect place. Having met the kids they could then be taken anywhere, Anna realised, but it was a place to start.

She pulled down her hood over her hair and began to climb the slick stone steps but then found there were legs and feet in her way so she had to push it back so she could see. A group of men were barring her way. They were holding cans of beer and a couple had cigarettes between their fingers. Their clothes were creased and dirty and most were unshaved – street people, she assumed, waiting for the free food that would be handed out by the Army. She assessed them rapidly. They didn't look dangerous, they looked like a nuisance.

'Excuse me,' she said firmly.

'Why, what have you done?' one of them leered at her. The others laughed. She tried to look good-humoured about it. Getting angry would fuel the joke.

'Very funny. But I am in a bit of a hurry so if you gentlemen don't mind?' They hooted and laughed.

The leerer hadn't finished yet. 'What are you doing all on your own, darling? Bit of late night shopping for naughty knickers at Ann Summers?' Some of the men did not laugh at this and began to move aside looking embarrassed. One of them muttered at the leerer to leave her alone. A different man stepped forward.

'You look like that other one. Not clubbing dressed like that.' The leerer turned away, sucking on his can of beer, losing interest.

Anna studied this man's face. He seemed ok. 'What do you mean? What other one?'

He hunched his shoulders against the rain and peered at her. 'There was a lady here a bit ago. She were wearing a posh coat like you, she were in pieces. Looking for her daughter she said.'

'Yes,' said Anna, 'I think I know her. Where did she go?' To her surprise the men seemed to deflate as a group and began to move away including the one who had just spoken. Anna reached out and touched his sleeve. 'Which direction?' He didn't meet her eyes but jerked his head away from the mall to the other side of the church. The men had now moved well away from her and were drifting towards the market. One held back. He was older than the others and looked as though he had been living rough for many years.

'Missus?' Anna nodded and waited for him to speak again. The rain drilled into his unprotected skull. His skin was deeply folded into the bones of his face so that the stubble stood out in uneven brindled patches of bristle. When he spoke she could see that several teeth were missing and those that remained were brown with rot. His clothes were sodden but he seemed not to notice or cower away from the rain like the others. He stood straight and the eyes that met hers were clear grey and steady in their gaze. 'Your friend. She went off with a chap a woman shouldn't go off with. He said he'd take her to her girl but he will na'. We all know him but he's not one of us.' Anna felt the rain run down her throat and under her clothes in a cold stream. She began to shiver.

'Where would he take her?'

'Back of the markets in all likelihood. Don't go there on yer own.' He held her eyes and then turned and walked away up the hill to the mall flicking his cigarette end away from him.

Anna stood for a moment in the rain but then turned back to the market and began to walk towards it. The Salvation Army was setting out tureens and tall flasks next to plastic bags full of baps and piles of paper plates under the dripping awnings of the stalls. Knots of people were standing about waiting for it all to be ready. There was laughter and some bantering between the officers and the homeless men and women and a generally good-natured and relaxed atmosphere. Several dogs were standing about, some lively and wagging their tails, others cowed and wary. Anna wove her way through the stalls and began to stride more briskly towards Moat Lane parking garage. She had no idea where to go except vaguely in that direction and was beginning to think this was a stupid idea. The car park itself was closed but then, as she walked past, she saw set back away from the road in a concrete alcove under the entrance ramp a couple of men and a sack of something on the ground. She stared at them, trying to assess the situation. One of the men kicked the bundle and it moaned. Anna froze and then moved forward.

'What's going on?' she said loudly, hoping her voice was not trembling. It was hard to see in the dark corner and she didn't want to go in any further.

'Fuck off.'

'I'm a Salvation Army volunteer,' she lied, hardly able to hear her own voice for the pounding of her heart. 'Would you men like to come and get yourself something to eat?' One of them sprang out of the shadow at her. His head was shaven and his skin burned a livid orange in the street light.

'Fuck off, bitch,' he spat at her. She glanced at the other one. He seemed to have shrunk back into the shadows. The bundle on the floor was whimpering. Suddenly, the red tide of fear vanished and her brain cleared. She was in survival mode. Anna knew she couldn't show fear but neither could she be provocative. She couldn't outfight these men so she would just have to try to outwit them.

She sharpened up her vowels. 'I think I should inform you we're filming a documentary at the moment with a team from the BBC and you might want to know that you're on close-up from the Outside Broadcast telephoto Steadicam.' She had no idea what that meant, if anything – she was desperately stringing words together. 'Look, you can see it up on the church café roof.' The rain was pouring down. The man glanced at where she'd pointed for one second and then dashed off running down the street towards Digbeth, dog-legging as he went. Anna was knocked to the floor by the second man racing out of the shadow and away. She staggered to her feet and rushed to the heap on the floor.

Kimi was moaning. Anna gently turned her so that she could see the damage. She was a horrific sight. Her face was a pulp of blood and muck. Her nose was streaming with a thick red flow which had soaked her shirt and torn bra. Her jeans and panties were round her ankles, filthy and stinking of urine. Male urine. She made a strangled sound and Anna realised that under the mess on her face a gag was biting into her cheeks. Anna couldn't undo the knot it was so tight so she dropped to her knees and gnawed at the slimy fabric, tearing at the shreds as they gave way until she could work the last string loose and out of Kimi's mouth. Her teeth were coated with metallic-tasting jelly. She refused to allow herself to vomit. Then Anna saw that the coat had been pulled down off Kimi's shoulders and the arms tied behind her. This was not the first attack these men had colluded in - it was as efficient as it was brutal. Anna looked back to Kimi's face. The eyes were swollen and full of blood and a patch of raw flesh near her temple showed where a handful of hair had been wrenched from her head.

Anna gently removed Kimi's shoes and pulled off the soaked, reeking jeans and underwear. She would keep them. Then she took her own coat off, oblivious of the cold. It had stopped raining and a chill wind had sprung up. She put Kimi's shoes back on murmuring reassurance all the time.

'Can you stand?' Kimi groaned but, clinging to Anna and almost pulling her over, she made it up on to her feet. She was at least six inches taller. Anna pulled Kimi's coat up and zipped it to cover her bare chest and then wrapped her own coat round her naked legs. With one arm round Kimi's waist and holding the jacket up with her other hand, the soiled clothes clenched under one elbow, Anna encouraged her forward, a step at a time. They turned painfully like a single wounded creature towards the cheerful lights of the market stalls. After a hundred slow yards a man came running towards them.

'Do you need help?' A woman in uniform was close behind.

'Yes,' sobbed Anna, 'we need help. Please. We need help.'

The hospital waiting room was packed. Saturday night in A&E. The police rape team had arrived and were processing Kimi after she had been given a light sedative for shock. Anna had told the two female officers she was keeping the panties and only giving them the jeans. 'Just in case any evidence goes missing,' she said fiercely. They had studied her quietly. Then the older one had suggested that an orderly could put the panties in a plastic bag and Anna could watch her stow it in a hospital safe inaccessible to the police. Anna thought hard. 'I want your names,' she said, 'and I want the name of the orderly.' They nodded slowly and backed away. A moment later a scared looking girl came offering an open ziplock bag and Anna dropped the panties in it. She got up stiffly and followed her to the office, watched her lock the bag away, and then went to the bathroom. She washed her face and hands six times before she could stop and then she turned into the toilet cubicle and was violently sick.

When she got back to the emergency ward Kimi was in a bed and still looked terrible. She grabbed Anna's hand as soon as she got close enough. 'Rhea.'

'I know. Are you all right if I go?'

'Yes. Go.'

In the hospital lobby Anna phoned for a taxi to take her back to her car. She knew she shouldn't be driving, she was trembling from head to foot, but there was no other option. Within fifteen minutes she was back at the car; parts of the city were now in full cry with horns blaring and police sirens and shouting and laughter, other parts silent and deserted. She got into the car and then got out again. There was a sticker on the windshield telling her that she was illegally parked and would be fined accordingly. She tore it off and stuffed it in the glove compartment. In the taxi she had checked her phone and now she rang Len. He sounded wide awake - she glanced at her watch. It was only 11.30. No one had phoned.

She began to pull away and into the one-way system and checked her petrol gauge. That was ok. She turned the heating on full realising that she had left her coat with Kimi. She had absolutely no idea where to go. After a couple of miles of driving she pulled over into a convenience store parking lot and stopped. She felt drained and desperate. Where were they? For the hundredth time she tried her son's phone. She waited for the recording but instead heard his real voice. For a second she couldn't believe it. 'Ellis? Is that you? Where are you? Are you all right?'

'Mum. I'm so sorry.' His voice was thin and scared.

'Never mind that, sweetheart, where are you? Is Rhea with you?'

'Yes. But Mum. There's something wrong with her.' He took a deep breath and almost cried, 'Can you come?'

'I'm in the car – just tell me where you are.'

'I don't know, Mum. We got on a bus and went as far as we could on our passes and then we walked for ages and now I don't know where we are.' Anna was thinking desperately.

'What number bus?'

'I've just thought of something.' His voice sounded stronger. 'Mum? I've got an app on my phone that when you take a photo it records where the photo is taken, like it's linked to a GPS. Hang up and I'll take a photo and then I can tell you.'

'Have you got credit?'

'Enough. Hang up now, Mum.'

In the seconds she was waiting Anna grabbed the Atlas and Street A-Z and had found a pencil. Her phone shrilled again. This time Ellis sounded better. They were in a bus shelter opposite a pub called The Jockey. He gave her the data and she programmed the satnav. They were about eight miles away in a heavily built up area and she reckoned it would take her fifteen to twenty minutes.  She made it in twelve.

Ellis was sitting tensely bent forward at one end of the bus shelter bench and Rhea was at the other.  The girl had her chin thrust forward and was staring into space, her feet tapping manically. Anna parked in the bus bay and leaped out of the car.  Ellis ran to her and she grabbed him and held him tight.  'Are you all right Ell? Did anyone hurt you?'

'No Mum,' he said in a muffled voice near her ear, 'I'm ok, honestly.  But there's something wrong with Rhea.'  They both turned and looked at the girl who had not moved.  'I'm sorry, Mum, I thought-'

'Never mind that now.  Just get in the car, Ell, and I'll get Rhea.  Sit in the front.'  Anna walked slowly to the girl, smiling. 'Hi, Rhea.  How are you doing?'

Rhea swivelled her gaze and fixed it on Anna.  'Come near me and I'll bloody cut you,' she said.  Anna could see a blade sticking out from the girl's coat sleeve.  Her eyes were rimmed with black mascara that had run in the rain making a mad mask.  She was trembling from head to foot.

Anna continued to smile.  'Do you remember me?  I'm Ellis' mum, Mrs Ames.  Your mum and I are friends.'  Rhea's eyes seemed not to be seeing her although she was looking directly at Anna.  'I've been watching you play tennis.  You're very good.'  It was very cold now and Anna was starting to shiver despite her efforts not to.

'Everybody's always watching me!  Go away!  Leave me alone!'  In her agitation the knife clattered on to the asphalt and Anna grabbed it.  'I'll kill you, you witch!'  Rhea sprang up and stood shaking in front of Anna.  Anna took a step forward and wrapped the girl in her arms.  As strong as Rhea was she was pinned and couldn't get free.  She screamed and bit and kicked but finally she broke into tears and wilted.  Anna half-dragged, half-carried her to the back seat of the car and strapped her in.  She was weeping but had stopped struggling.

'Look at me, Rhea.'  She wouldn't. ' I'm your friend and I'm taking you to a safe place, ok?  Ellis is here, too.  We're taking you where you'll be safe.'  Anna waited for a response but the girl was in her own world.  'Just rest now.'  She got in the driving seat.

'Ell,' she whispered. 'Keep an eye on her. If she makes a move tell me and I'll stop the car.'

'Yes Mum.' Anna switched the ignition on and pulled away from the bay. She turned round in the car park of The Jockey and began the journey back.

'Has she taken anything that you know of Ellis? Pills?' She was still whispering and keeping Rhea's face in the rear-view mirror. The girl seemed to have gone into some kind of trance.

'No.' There was silence but it was a certain kind of silence. Anna glanced quickly at her son.

'Ellis tell me if there's anything I need to know. You won't be betraying her, you'll be helping her.'

'She smokes. Skunk. I think it's really strong.'

'Have *you*?' Anna had stopped whispering in her anxiety.

'No! I hate that stuff. I tried to get her not to but I'm just a kid and she wouldn't listen.'

'Has she smoked today?' He nodded.

For the rest of the journey Anna was silent until they were stopped at a traffic light and nearly at their destination. Then she turned to Ellis and got his attention. 'I'm taking her to hospital. She needs to have proper medical attention.' Anna didn't want to tell Ellis about Kimi. She didn't ever want to tell him if she could help it but she certainly wasn't going to tell him tonight.

The A&E receptionist raised her eyebrows when she saw Anna return with two kids in tow. Anna asked Ellis to sit down and she put an arm round Rhea who now seemed to be in a dream. Her eyes were rolling in her head and her mouth was hanging open. She was leaning on Anna for support. Anna fixed the receptionist with a meaningful look. 'I need a psychiatric nurse or doctor. This is an emergency. I'm not a medical professional but I think this girl, who is thirteen, is in drug-induced psychosis and she needs help now.' The receptionist glanced at Rhea, looked again, and then nodded. She picked up her phone.

Ellis' eyes were round with astonishment. It was now after midnight and A&E was in full swing. To his left was a stab wound wrapped in a bloody tea-towel on a heavily muscled and tattooed arm. 'All right, son?' the arm's owner enquired genially. Ellis blinked. Opposite was a heavy set young man in a rugby football shirt covered with vomit and snoring loudly. One leg was swollen from the knee to the ankle. Then, mercifully, a doctor and a nurse came through the swing doors and, at a nod from the receptionist, approached Anna. The doctor crouched and spoke gently to Rhea who immediately spat at him.

'Can I have a word?' said Anna.

Within half an hour the girl had been admitted, Kimi's nurse informed, and Anna and Ellis could go home. Anna knew she should have gone to see Kimi herself but she was spent and she didn't want Ellis knowing what had happened. Len had been phoned and put in the picture and so had DS Iqbal to whom Anna gave the fuller version of the night's events. She silently thanked whatever benevolent gods there were that he had been on duty that night. Bad things happen all the time, but, as her dad had reminded her, there are also angels. On the drive home she thought about Andrew even now sitting by the side of a dying woman, the honourable homeless man with the clear eyes, the Salvation Army cheerily doling out the milk of human kindness and the Street Pastors who at this moment would be helping drunken girls into safe taxis and giving flipflops to those who had lost or broken their high heels and were staggering among broken glass on the street. Or they would be crouched on the pavement comforting someone whose life had gone wrong, wracked by guilt, rejection or remorse. Angels everywhere.

Ellis was wide-eyed and silent in the passenger seat. Her gut clenched with the thought of what could have happened to him. But it hadn't. Tomorrow they would talk.

# 24

When they got home she sent him upstairs to wash his face and hands and get into his pyjamas while she made comfort food: a big pile of hot buttered toast with lashings of honey and hot chocolate for him and tea for her. Neither of them had eaten for ages. Len was sleeping in George's room. She sat down on her son's bed with the tray. He was wearing his Despicable Me outfit.

'Ell,' she said finishing a mouth-full of hot deliciousness.

'Mm.'

'You probably saved Rhea's life today. I hope you realize that.'

'How d'you mean?' he said thickly through his toast, 'I was an idiot.'

'If she'd gone off on her own anything could have happened. Deep down she must have known she was safe with you and when she was past being able to help herself, you got help for her. Not only that, you worked out how that app on your phone could be used so I could find you. That was quick thinking kiddo.'

He put his plate and mug back on the tray and shimmied down the bed. 'You were brill, Mum.'

'Let's face it,' said Anna, standing up and watching his eyelids flutter into sleep, 'we're both pretty damn hot.' She waited a moment but he was asleep. She switched off the bedside lamp and crept out on to the landing shutting the door softly behind her. Len's snores came resonantly and soothingly through George's door. On the landing her smile faded.

It was late but it had to be done. Anna picked up her phone off the kitchen table and scrolled to the number. It rang four, five times and Anna dropped her forehead into her hand and rested it there. She would have to keep trying. But then it connected. Gerald's voice was sleepy and startled.

'I'm so sorry to wake you, Gerald, but there's something you need to know.' Ten minutes later she put the phone back down. He would go into the hospital immediately having Jimmy, his driver, take him and check on both his daughter and his grand-daughter. She wondered if he would arrange to have Rhea transferred to some private facility – she was going to need prolonged help. Anna suspected that she had an underlying psychological condition which had been inflamed by the skunk smoking. That on its own should not have produced such an alarming paranoid outburst, unless it had been mixed with some toxic rubbish which was possible. Where had she got it from? Easy enough to get hold of, she supposed. From the odd hints Kimi had dropped it seemed as though Rhea had become increasingly bizarre for some time. As for Kimi, it was hard to know at this stage how seriously injured she was. There had been so much blood. Anna shook her head to try to clear it of horrific images. No chance. She would go and visit tomorrow if the poor woman was still hospitalised.

She put the mugs and plates in the dishwasher and turned off the kitchen light. It was a weary climb up the stairs and once in her own room she slumped on the bed. Hell, why not have the whole family go to sleep without cleaning its teeth? She felt too exhausted for such niceties. But the moment she turned off the light and lay down she was wide awake. She turned the lamp back on and lay on her back staring at the ceiling. From deep within her came an avalanche of tears and she wept for many minutes until her body ached and her stomach was clenched in a painful knot. What was that phrase a nurse had used once when she had stubbed her toe and her whole foot had bruised? Indirect violence. Yes.

She got up and tiptoed out of her room, across the landing and into Harry's room, the one that had been their oasis of comfort for so many years. She eased his door open and looked inside. The dimmed light showed him sprawled across the big bed, his long limbs taking up every corner but he was deeply asleep. She left the door ajar and went back to her own bedroom, pulled the duvet off her single bed and tucked the pillow under her arm and then crept back. She made a nest for herself on the floor beside Harry. When she was finally still she didn't allow herself to think, to remember, to feel, but only to listen to the familiar, so much missed sound of his regular night-breathing and eventually she slept too.

But not for long. The nightmare was back but this time she was in pitch darkness in a box and someone was in there with her trying to smother her with a hand clamped over her screaming mouth. That small part of the brain that is always conscious, like a nightwatchman, was trying to get her to wake up. She struggled to do it, do anything to wake herself up, and finally she did and burst the surface of her dream into consciousness. She was soaked with sweat and panting. Her heart was banging like a mad drummer in her chest. She became aware of a sound in the room. Then she realised that Harry was beside her on the floor. He was crooning something and stroking her hair.

'No monsters,' he said. 'all the scary things gone away.' It was what he used to say to the children when they had nightmares. He spoke clearly, like his old self. She lay on the crumpled duvet on the hard floor and let the moment happen. He gazed at her kindly for a minute or so and then climbed back into his bed and went back to sleep. The unexpected miraculous act of love seeped into her muscles and nerves and she slept.


She was loading the washing machine and Ellis was reading an email from George out loud when Gerald phoned. Could he come to her house? Kimi was being discharged and wanted to see her. 'Just a minute.' She put the phone against her chest and asked Ellis what his plans were for the day or did he want to just chill? He looked amazed at the suggestion.

'Mike and me and his dad are going to watch the league semi-final. Mike's on the bench as reserve. Dad's coming. I told you last week, Mum. We're going round in a minute.'

'Great.' She walked out into the hall. 'OK, Gerald, that will be fine. Kimi remembers my address, doesn't she? Oh, right. I'll give you the postcode for Jimmy, have you got a pen?'

Len had pushed off home after the massive fry-up she had made him as a thank you so she had the house to herself. After the call she thought about tidying up and looking for any vestige of hostess food that might be around and then decided to carry on loading the washing machine instead. It was hardly going to be a normal social occasion and she suspected that neither Gerald nor Kimi gave a stuff about how tidy her house was and what little snacks might be on offer. Better to do something useful and washing seemed about the most useful thing to do. There were quite a lot of things she would like to wash clean but she had to make do with clothes.

Half an hour later a sleek white Lexus drew up outside, began to turn politely into her drive and then backed out again and parked on the street. George's car and hers left no space. She opened the front door and went down to help Gerald with Kimi. Glancing at Gerald's face, Anna was shocked at how ill he looked. He was deteriorating very quickly and this was the last thing he needed. Kimi leaned heavily on Anna's shoulder to take the weight from her father but she was wearing fresh clothes and seemed calm. A thick white pad covered her nose and her left hand and fore-arm were in plaster in a sling. Jimmy stayed with the car.

In the living room Kimi sank into the armchair and Gerald sat near her on the sofa. Anna brought coffee, served them and sat down herself. Gerald glanced at Kimi who blinked permission and turned to her. 'Broken ribs, two, I'm afraid, and a fractured wrist. They're pretty sure that she won't have any permanent damage to her eyes, her sight seems normal, but her nose was broken.'

'I never liked it anyway.' Kimi sounded as though she had a heavy cold. Shit, thought Anna, I hope we're not going to do the brave little lady performance. That would only make things worse. No need to dwell on bad stuff but it needs to be acknowledged as she knew only too well herself. 'But I hurt like hell.' Anna smiled, relieved at the usual Kimi forthrightness.

Gerald went on as if he had not been interrupted. He seemed to need to give Anna a report – she certainly hadn't asked for one. She was so glad that Ellis was not here to see Kimi's swollen, multi-coloured face. 'One tooth loosened but they think her dentist can save it. A lot of bruising-'

'Dad,' Kimi interrupted nasally. 'You don't have to do this.' Gerald stopped talking and looked desperately out of the window. 'Anna, they've taken stuff off to be tested, you know, and they'll get back to me. I think the police already know who one of the guys is, he seems notorious but no-one's ever agreed to testify. They asked me if I would be willing to go through with a charge. Try to sodding stop me, I said.'

Anna looked carefully at Kimi's composed expression. 'You are very calm about this. I don't think I would be.'

Kimi was quiet for a few seconds and then said, 'This isn't the first time. It's happened before.' Anna was so surprised she could think of nothing to say. Gerald was jolted out of his vicarious pain, too. They both stared at her. Kimi went on steadily. 'They call it date rape now, don't they? Some such thing. But it wasn't really. It was freshers week at uni and someone in my hall of residence wanted to go to a party and she didn't want to go alone. We all got very drunk and I passed out on a pile of coats on a bed. When I woke up I felt sore – you know – and I went to the loo and well, realised what had happened. I'd never done it before. I tried to forget about it. I wasn't bashed about like this, but then – '

'Rhea,' Gerald said.

'Yes.' Kimi looked at him placidly as though it was a relief to finally tell her secret. 'I could have had an abortion but I didn't want to because I wanted an excuse to leave uni. After that night I felt scared all the time, to tell you the truth. I always thought I could look after myself, that I was a toughie, but it proved I couldn't, that I was vulnerable, pathetic, a victim. I hated it.'

Anna wanted to jump in and contradict her but she intuited that wasn't what was needed. Kimi was re-living her feelings then, not now. Nevertheless, surely this second rape would make her feel even more vulnerable?

'I'm sorry you felt you couldn't tell us,' Gerald said, the pallor in his face reflecting the misery in his voice.

'Well, you were so busy with the company and away a lot and mum, well, I'm sorry Dad, but I just didn't have the guts to tell her. She's always been disappointed in me – I've always felt that she cared more for the others than me.' Gerald's eyes flickered at Anna. 'I couldn't stand her disapproval. It was easier to just not say anything. Charlie and Richard were too busy with their own lives to take much notice at the time. I think they might even have been relieved that I wanted to keep it all quiet and not lumber them with some hopeless bloke as Rhea's father.'

'Do you know who it was?'

Kimi started to laugh until she realised it hurt and stopped. 'No. I have no idea. It's funny really because I think Richard's beginning to think I'm keeping it secret to spring something on him but the truth is I literally have no idea who Rhea's father is. She's practically an immaculate conception.'

Anna was curious. 'Has she ever asked?'

'She did once when she was seven and she'd noticed other kids had dads. I told her that he was a sperm donor and I had no idea who he was. I said I'd wanted her so much I'd given up on uni to have her.' Anna was shocked in a different way and she could tell Gerald was, too. But what would have been the right thing to tell a child or even an adult about such a conception? She remembered her dad saying that it was the girls usually that paid a high price for casual sex. If it was non-consensual like this then the cost soared. There was silence for a few moments. Anna took another sip of coffee and frowned.

'You're wondering why I'm not a gibbering wreck, aren't you?' Kimi asked her, guessing correctly. Anna nodded. 'I'm not an overwhelmed kid any more. As soon as I realised what was happening, that they weren't taking me to Rhea, that they didn't have a clue where Rhea was and didn't care, that it was me they wanted, I fought like hell but I soon knew I wouldn't get away from two of them. So, I decided, you know, in my head, all right you bastards but this time I'll get you back. This time you're going to pay. I managed to bite one of them while he was gagging me so that wasn't all my blood on my face and on the gag. When I clawed at them, they tied my arms back but I knew I had some tissue under my fingernails. All the time it was happening and through all the pain and nausea I was thinking, if you don't kill me, I'm going to get you and you're going to remember me for the rest of your sad lives, you fuckers.'

'Blimey,' said Anna.

'Because now I'm not a frightened little teenager. Now I've learned to tame powerful horses and raise a child and stand up for myself and I'm strong and I despise men like that far more than I'm frightened of them.' She paused and thought. 'There's another thing, too.' She looked at Anna. 'Last time no-one came for me. No-one was looking out for me. This time there was you.'

'Well -' Anna started to say.

'No. You could have run away and got help. That's what most people would have done, or just run away. You made them leave me alone. You rescued me, Anna, there's no other way to put it *and* you kept evidence so I can get my revenge. I couldn't stop them doing what they did, like I couldn't stop the first one, but I can stop them ever doing it again and your help is part of that. I don't feel like a victim, Anna, I feel like a bloody avenging angel! Each photo the police took, each swab, each x-ray, I thought Gotcha!'

The sight of Kimi, hair springing from her head in quivering coils and a huge white plaster over her nose, two purple swollen eyes and deep welts across both cheeks talking the talk in no uncertain manner was almost comical. But it was brave and it made psychological sense. Anna stood up. She had remembered something Gerald needed to do and now was as good a time as any.

'I'm going to go and hang out the washing,' she said. 'I may be gone some time. Your dad has something he's been wanting to talk to you about, Kimi.' Gerald glanced up at her, his pale face calm, and nodded. She closed the door softly behind her. As she walked into the kitchen she allowed herself to feel a small welling up of satisfaction. Ellis was safe and so was Rhea, now getting the attention she needed. Kimi had thanked her for standing up to the thugs and Gerald was making the connection he had been longing to make for years but didn't think he had the right. She had made Afsoon a fair offer and it wasn't her fault if Anna was forced to tell the police everything she knew when the six days were up.

Anna met Steve for lunch at the Café Rouge in Brindley Place. He had texted her on Sunday night that he and Alice were safely home and she had her hands full dealing with Faye's graphic account of festival camping and piles of muddy gear. Normality had never felt so good. Faye even said she should go away more often as Anna seemed much more laid-back than she usually was. If only she knew. This was the calm after the storm. She postponed her talk with Ellis – he seemed not to want to discuss the strange goings on with Rhea and she respected that. Far from Kimi being angry with her dad about her own origins she was positively chipper. She had whispered in Anna's ear before leaving, 'So glad I'm not related to that cold bitch. Keep up the search and let me know!' She was, of course, flooded with novocaine and adrenalin. Soon, she would have to deal with whatever was going on with Rhea which would be tough. Kimi would need all her fighting spirit to help her daughter.

It was so good to see Steve as he swept in that Anna almost jumped up and hugged him. His skin was still glowing with wind and weather from the two-day walk and his eyes glittered blue and bright. 'Hey up,' he said, sitting down, 'Want a drink?'

'I *want* a gallon of red wine but I'll have half a lager, thanks.' He laughed and went to the bar. She shamelessly let her eyes roam over his wide, square shoulders and back and down his strong legs. What an extraordinary thing sex is, she thought. With someone you care for it's the best feeling in the world but when it's forced, it's the worst.

'How was your walk?' she asked when he had sat down with their drinks and a menu.

'Great on Saturday afternoon but then it got a bit squally and we pitched the tents. By the time we got back from the pub it was torrential rain. Sunday was nice, although parts of the Pennine Way can get really boggy, surprisingly enough since it's so high up.' She listened to him chat on, her chin on one hand, not wanting him to stop.    Their food arrived.

'So, how about you?' he said finally.  'Quiet weekend?'

'Mm. Not so much.'

He swallowed a mouthful and screwed up his face.  'Let me guess. You've got something to tell me.'   So she told him.   He became increasingly concerned.

'Are you all right, Anna?'  He picked up her hand and held it in his own warm one.  'Tell me the truth.'

'I think so.'   It felt so good to have his hand around hers that she let it lie.

'Ellis?'

'Yes. Yes, I think he is.'

Steve was quiet for a few moments.  'Anna, can I ask you something?'

'If it's do I want the chocolate hazelnut cheesecake for pud, yes.'  He smiled and raised a hand to the waitress.

'It's just that I don't understand how women can like books and films that have men being violent to them.  What is that about? Do women really *want* to be beaten and controlled?  I know *you* wouldn't but why would any woman want that?'

Anna thought for a moment.  'Years ago, Faye was very into casualty make-up, you know, what they do for tv and film dramas - wounds and black eyes and scars and bloody noses, all that.  You can buy the stuff from a company in London.  We gave a pirate party for her tenth birthday because all her friends wanted to have slit wrists and clotted blood in their eyebrows, the works, and they squealed with joy when I made them up.  The more realistic the better. I even used bits of black thread to stick on to make it look as though they had stitches.  They loved it.'

'I can see Faye getting into the drama of that and probably little boys would like it too, but they were just kids and it was like dressing up.'

'Yes, that's exactly what it was.  Play-acting.  But one little girl who came wouldn't take part.   She backed away, I mean, literally backed away when she saw the others even though they were clearly playing and having fun.  I asked her if she wanted to be made up.  I tried to make a joke of it, like, can I do you a black eye? She was horrified, Steve.  It didn't take me long to cotton on and I took her into the kitchen for a cake and told her I had some other make-up and I could do a butterfly face painting if she would like. The girl was Tasha, now Faye's best friend. She had seen the real thing. She had seen her dad slam her mum up against the wall and give her a real black eye and real cuts in her eyebrow from his punches and worse. One time in front of the children he'd thrown her down and kicked her belly because she was pregnant. She lost the baby, of course. She'd heard her dad swearing and Michelle screaming with fear and crying with pain. It wasn't exciting or fun to Tasha because she knew the horror of real violence.'

Steve thought for a moment. 'So what you're saying is that these women that like reading that stuff have no idea what real violence feels like and if they did the last thing they would want to read about would be sexual sadism?'

'That's my theory anyway.' Anna laughed. 'Also, the men in those made-up stories are always rich, handsome, adoring and ask permission before they do anything. Hardly real life.' The cheesecake arrived and Anna said yes, she would like an extra dollop of cream. Surely, apart from anything else, last weekend had burned up a few calories.

'I almost daren't ask you this,' Steve said, 'but is there any news on the depot?'

'No. I forgot about it until this morning and then I texted DS Iqbal rather than phone him in case he was asleep or something. I can't keep running to him. No word yet but I think there would have been if they'd found anything.'

Steve looked worried. 'I definitely heard breathing, Anna.'

'I've been thinking about that. Could it have been a guard dog? Assuming there was contraband of some kind in there, they may have put in a dog to put off any intruders. One dog may not be enough for the heat sensors to pick up. I don't know.'

'It's possible.' He leaned over and scooped a lump of cheesecake with his finger.

'Hey!' She tapped him smartly on the knuckle with her spoon. 'But it's been four days now since I saw Afsoon. I gave her six to dob Mohsen in or get him to do it himself. I can't imagine what she's going through. And she's pregnant.' Steve suddenly burst out laughing. 'What?'

'Do you remember being a bit miffed about this assignment for Ted and how boring it would be?'

She scraped the plate and licked her spoon. 'Well, we all know I'm never wrong.'

## 25

On the way home she called in on Joan. It was a while before the door was opened and when she saw Joan's face her smile faded. 'What's the matter? You don't look too good. Can I come in?'

The living room was cluttered with the stuff of illness. Boxes of tissues, over-the-counter shrink-wrapped tablets, an overflowing waste bin and a small forest of glasses, mugs and plates. Joan herself was bundled into a pale blue fleece dressing gown with splashes of what looked like cocoa down the front. Her little feet were stuffed into Tigger slippers.

'Have you seen the doctor?' Anna demanded, more fiercely than she had meant.

'Tried to. Can't get an appointment until next week.'

'Rubbish. Give me the number.' But when she phoned, the reception clerk repeated that it was not possible to see a doctor unless Joan came in at 7.00 a.m. the next day before the phone lines opened and booked one of the emergency slots. 'How is she supposed to get in for that?' Anna demanded. 'She's too ill to drive!' The receptionist apologised and hung up. 'Madness.'

'I'm all right,' Joan whispered.

'I can hear your chest rattling from here, of course you're not all right!' Anna rang NHS Direct. After twenty minutes of questions, many of which Joan had to answer, breathing with difficulty, they were told that since Joan's GP surgery was still open there was nothing they could do. At that moment the doorbell rang and Anna went. It was Briony Clark, Joan's neighbour. She looked startled to see Anna.

'Mrs Ames. Anna. What are you doing here?'

'Joan and I are friends - we got to know each other after your mother died. Anyway, that doesn't matter now. The doctor won't see her and I don't know what to try next. She's got a chest infection by the sounds of it. I could take her to A&E but we'd be there hours and I don't think she's well enough.' Briony went past Anna into the living room and looked at Joan.

'You're worse than this morning. Fuck this. Have you got your car here?' This to Anna who nodded. 'Right, let's wrap you up and get you some antibiotics.' She spoke to Anna again. 'You drive and I'll go in the back with her. When we get there I'll go in and sort them out.' She took off her own coat which was a rather nice black wool one, Anna noticed, and wrapped Joan in it. They shuffled out and Anna jumped into the driving seat. At the doctor's practice Briony strode in and returned a moment later for Joan with a wheelchair. They disappeared. Ten minutes later they were back and Joan was stuffed into the passenger seat. Briony reached over and turned up the heating, waved the prescription at Anna and vanished into the chemist next door. Joan and Anna, now side by side and about the same petite size, looked at each other with pursed lips and raised eyebrows.

'She's a bit of a force of nature, isn't she?' Joan whispered hoarsely. They giggled.

'Right,' said Briony, getting into the back and snapping her safety belt on. 'Let's get you home and in bed, Joan.' No one argued.

Later, when Joan was tucked up with a hot water bottle and they had cleared away the mess in the living room, they sat down with a cup of tea. 'I'll check on her later,' Briony said, 'and I'm off tomorrow, no lectures, so I can come in a few times and see if she needs anything.'

'How's it going, the criminology?'

'Good but maybe not quite what I want. I may take a law degree or go into a fast-track career with the police after I've graduated. Are you working on anything?'

Anna thought carefully. She couldn't reveal too much but Briony's intellect and drive could be harnessed very usefully, maybe. 'It's not my case as such but peripherally I've stumbled across a nasty criminal activity that I didn't know existed. I think the police are still trying to get on top of it.'

Briony was hooked. 'What is it?'

'Well, it seems that there may be a so-called dark internet website that sets up gang rapes and they think there's a cell operating in Birmingham.'

'Ugh. How does that work?'

'Not completely sure but the theory is that there's a restricted access control site with encrypted software which the people involved, the criminals I mean, can get into and another one, more open but where you need special browsers, which 'interested parties' can access.' Anna frowned in concentration. 'The restricted one gets data from the guy who is going to set up a girl – where and when – and passes that on to another person who will recruit and organise the male participants.' Briony grimaced. 'Then the more open one is for men who want to take part, the customers, to leave a mobile phone number or something. Probably one of those £1 pay-as-you-go phones, not their usual one obviously, so there'd be nothing to track.'

'Where do they get the women?'

'I'm afraid it usually is girls – quite young ones. Sometimes it's opportunistic but usually it seems either to be a kid that's been groomed into believing she has a cool boyfriend or –'

'Trafficked girls.'

'Probably.'

Briony sipped her tea and dropped her chin, thinking. She had looked self-possessed and elegant when Anna had met her at Birmingham airport for the first time a few months ago, despite her terrible experience in America, but now she looked even more impressive. Her naturally pale blonde hair was cut in a shoulder length bob and fell obediently forward in a disciplined waterfall when she dropped her head. Her large blue eyes, previously unmade up, now had a subtle edging of grey kohl and mascara which gave her a stylish yet authoritative look. No wonder the doctor had rolled over. She had not changed the natural pallor of her skin but now it seemed to gleam slightly. Probably some expensive cosmetic with minerals and reflectors or something but it worked. After a few moments she looked at Anna quizzically. Anna braced herself.

'I'd like to be involved with this but I don't know how. The police won't let me in, I'm sure, and my IT skills and equipment aren't high-tech enough for this sort of thing.'

'You could use the strengths you do have.' Anna tried not to sound as though she'd thought all this through in the last five minutes.

'Like what?'

'You have a university department at your fingertips. You have research skills and channels of research available to you. Some of your lecturers may be able to help. What you could do which the police don't have time to is see what's going on elsewhere. When something like this springs up like a toxic mushroom, my guess is it's already been proved profitable somewhere else. Some other police departments may be battling with this. There may be international or even global networks but this is a very new area and so far it's been mostly drug sales that have been monitored, well, that and black market fiscal trading. The police and the border control people are swamped with stuff at street level. You could look at a more macro level - you know, pull back and see if there are matrices emerging – networks of criminal behaviour in this activity.'

Briony's eyes were shining. 'Yes. I could do that. I would love to do that!'

Anna felt slightly guilty – she may have oversold the idea which was only in her head after all. 'Of course this may be a purely local phenomenon. There may be no dark websites - there might not be networks.'

Briony sprang up. 'Don't worry about Joan, I'll keep an eye on her, but I'm going home now to work out how this might be set up as a research project. Thanks Anna.' She stopped at the door, remembering her manners. 'Nice to see you again.'

'You too.' Anna waited until the front door had closed and then walked up the stairs to Joan's bedroom. She was not asleep but was comfortable and listening to Radio 4. 'All right?'

'I daren't not be!' Joan joked. 'No, I'm fine. I will be after the antibiotics take hold. You girls have really come to the rescue.'

'Call me a girl more often and I'll rescue you again,' Anna said. 'Have you got your phone by the bed?'

'Yes. Don't you start. Go home and leave me in peace.' Anna kissed the clammy forehead and left.

She was at the office when Richard called on her work extension number. He demanded that she go immediately to his office to meet him. She resented his tone and told him, with as much politeness as she could muster, that she was not his employee. In a quieter voice he said that he urgently needed to see her and that he would very much appreciate her making it a priority. If it was more convenient he could come to her or meet at a place of her choosing. The dramatic climb-down impressed Anna and intrigued her. He really wanted to talk or to find something out. She decided that it would suit her better to see him at the factory after all. It would give her an excuse to wander around the depot maybe and take another look. She said she could see him that afternoon at 2.00 thinking that the depot should be deserted then and he agreed.

What could he want to see her about? Had Gerald, or Kimi herself, decided to reveal the truth about Rhea's paternity? Why should they?  It wasn't the sort of family where people confided their personal vulnerabilities – quite the opposite from what she had seen. On a different level, maybe he had discovered her involvement with Kimi's rape and Rhea's hospitalisation.  Did he think she might go to the press, surely not, or put it in the putative article she was supposed to be writing about successful family businesses?  That sounded more like it.  She opened her email account but there was nothing from Marie Fourier.  Should she contact her again?  It had only been a few days since the last contact she reminded herself, it had just felt as though it was much longer.  Anna glanced at the date. Her dad and Diane would be back in a few days and it would be nice to plan a welcome home party.

Faye and Ellis being on school holidays and sharing a daily routine where one of them would be with Harry and the other could have free time had turned out surprisingly well.  The incident on the day of the Felixstowe trip had not been repeated.  If it was their turn to be with Harry, they stayed with Harry.  Their cooperation had surprised and pleased Anna.  Next September Faye would be at university and Ellis would be in Year 8.  It shouldn't be a problem for him as Mike and most of his other friends would be going up, too, since it was the local comprehensive.  The cohort of friends had made the transition to big school go pretty well.

It would be a problem for her. Ellis was growing so fast. She had glanced at the cost of the uniform and sportswear and shuddered. There was no way he would still be able to wear his Year 7 clothes. All non-essential house-maintenance jobs had been shelved and that meant that the boiler and the gas fire had not been serviced and no-one had cleaned the gutters which Harry used to do regularly.  When the cars needed their MOTs at the end of last year she and George had told the mechanic just to fix what was needed to pass and not do a general service and since they had been going to the same garage for years he had agreed.  But he had warned that the VW would need new tyres very soon and that would be upwards of £200. Anna just couldn't see a way out of it.  She couldn't work at a second job because she was needed at home.  George couldn't be expected to be on duty 24-7 when he was 70.  This Draycott job had given her a lot of flexibility but it would soon be coming to an end.  In fact, she was surprised that Frances hadn't nixed it already now that Gerald was so ill.  Perhaps she'd forgotten about it.  And another thing, she suspected that Faye going to university would cost quite a bit even if she did take out the full student loan and work a few hours each week. She groaned and covered her face with her hands.

'Come on, it may never happen.' Suzy set down two paper cups of coffee and pulled up a spare chair. 'What's up?'

'Money. Well, lack of it.'

'You're as bad as Rob.' Suze shared a flat with her sister and had quite a nice inheritance from an aunt besides her family being well-off. Anna thought she had probably never had to worry seriously about money in her life.

'How's that going? Paris?'

'It went. It was last weekend. Disaster.' Suze threw back her thick hair and exhaled loudly.

'Tell me.' Anna reflected on how comforting other people's troubles were when you were feeling fragile. She didn't think she could have stood it if Suze had had a magical, wonderful time. She tutted disapproval at herself.

'Well, you know my French isn't brilliant, ok you don't, but it isn't. It turns out his is non-existent so he followed me round like a lame lap dog terrified of being abandoned and not able to find his way home. I had to do it all. It was such a strain. When I went before it was with Ralph who's really fluent and all I had to do was look gorgeous and shop and be grateful. It never occurred to me that I'd have to be in charge. He practically wanted me to take him to the loo.'

Anna opened her drawer and took out a chocolate biscuit bar. She offered half to Suze. 'So were there any, er, compensations?'

'No! There weren't! He was even stupid enough to get a stomach bug. If that isn't a turn-off I don't know what is. Puke and diarrhoea are hardly aphrodisiacs.'

Anna choked on her biscuit. 'Stop! Too much information!'

'Anyway, I've come over to ask you, to beg you, to have lunch with me. I'll pay.'

'What have you seen?'

'I don't normally go to Harvey Nicks in the Mailbox as you know, but yesterday I happened to be wandering through-'

'Surely not.'

'Yes, and there was this kimono thing. They're all the rage, but I can't decide if the colours suit me – they're not my usual ones but I need something stunning for my cousin's wedding rehearsal. I can't let the bride upstage me. Please, please come and advise me.'

She added another encouragement. 'You might see something for yourself!'

Anna scoffed at that but glanced at her watch. 'I can if we go now but not any later because I need to be in Solihull at 2.00.'

'Fab! I'll get my jacket. See you in two.'

## 26

Anna had no time to check out the depot before the appointment as the traffic out of town had been especially turgid. Richard had again come down to meet her in the lobby and they went up in the lift together. In his spartan office he seemed suddenly nervous, quite unlike his normal thrusting persona. 'Drink?' he offered, indicating the mini-bar. She shook her head. 'Coffee, tea?' Again, she smiled a refusal. Finally he pulled a chair over and sat next to her.

'I have to tell you, this isn't about work. I mean, about the Company. You're the only person I could think of to turn to but you must understand that what I'm telling you is in strict confidence.' He gave her a sharp look.

Anna felt her hackles rise but controlled herself. 'It's the nature of my profession to respect confidences, Mr Draycott,' she said. 'It's also my personal ethic not to gossip.'

'Good. Of course.' He paused. 'It's my wife. It's Afsoon.' Anna re-balanced her thoughts and reined herself in. 'You met her once, I think.'

'I met her several times.' He was not interested in that.

'Mrs Ames, Anna, I don't know what to do. She's gone, she's disappeared.'

Instantly, Anna had the sickening sensation of tumblers falling into place in her brain. Damn. Why hadn't she and Steve considered this possibility? She bought herself some thinking time. 'How do you mean? Did you have a disagreement?'

'No. We never do. She's the perfect wife in that way, she never confronts me.' Anna tried very hard to remain impassive. 'She just wasn't there when I got back from my convention in Brussels on Saturday night.'

'Are her things missing?'

'When I checked her wardrobes I noticed she'd left behind the most expensive dresses, oddly, the ones I bought her.' He thought a bit more. 'She left her furs, too. They were extremely costly – Russian sable and mink.' His mind was running on the same lines, she supposed, when he added, 'But her good jewellery has gone.' Anna remembered the large diamond ring on Afsoon's finger. If her other jewellery was up to that standard she could live on it for some time. She needed to phone DS Iqbal urgently.

'What do you want me to do, Richard? This sounds like a job for the police.'

He frowned. 'I don't want to involve them. She doesn't have her own bank account or I would have checked it - she had no access to mine.' He looked into Anna's face. 'Do you think there is another man?'

Of course there is another man, Anna thought, her son, Mohsen Amirmoez. 'I don't know what I can do, Richard. She is an adult and entitled to leave if she wishes. I assume she has not tried to contact you.'

'No.' For a moment Anna almost felt sorry for him. The down side of being in control of everyone is just this kind of unexpected move from someone you thought was docile. He would never have anticipated it. Afsoon had outsmarted him and not only him. She stood up.

'I'm sorry. This looks like a personal matter and I don't think I can help. But if you suspect any kind of criminality you should go to the police.'

'Do you know any private detectives?'

'No. I'm sure you can find one easily enough though. I have to go, Richard. I wish you luck.' He hardly noticed as she left.

She ran to her car pulling out her phone as she went. As soon as she was inside she called DS Iqbal. It went to voicemail. She banged her hand on the steering wheel and a man passing by glanced at the noise. She, caught by his look, looked back. It was Kevin. She wound down the window, it would be rude to ignore him.

'Hi Kevin, how are you?' It was an effort to sound normal.

He stood silently for a while and then mumbled, 'Had to bring some stuff for Miss Draycott.'

'Right.' His eyes were on the ground and his face was flushed with embarrassment at having to make conversation. She decided to spare him further social challenge. 'See you, then. Bye.' He walked off to his battered white van parked down the far end of the yard and she wound the window back up.

She couldn't drive to the police station again, that hadn't exactly worked out last time and she couldn't face another meeting with DS Griffiths. In any case, part of her knew with a cold certainty what the detective would tell her, if he knew. The horse had bolted. Mohsen had disappeared, too. Giving Afsoon six days was supposed to have been a courtesy but instead it had provided a chance for her to organise their escape. With enough money, and the engagement ring alone would have been plenty, a forged passport could have been bought and two airline tickets to a destination unknown. They would not return to Iran where he was wanted but they could be anywhere else in the world. The police would not track her since she was doing nothing wrong, and would be unlikely to track him. The time, effort and money involved simply wouldn't be forthcoming for a crime he was only loosely in the frame for. There was no hard evidence of his involvement in the organised gang-rapes or even in Nicola's attack. They wouldn't follow him just for his illegal residence status. They would be relieved he had gone and was off their patch.

She turned the key in the ignition and drove thoughtfully away. The full implications of her action in alerting Afsoon to Mohsen's situation were rapidly becoming clear. Because of her decision a sexual predator was free and would almost certainly continue his activity in whatever corner of the world they settled. As she crawled along in the late afternoon traffic back into the centre, she tried to work out why she had done it? Why had she given Afsoon (and Mohsen) this chance to escape? Pity for Afsoon? Had she been seduced by the woman's apparent affection for her and claims of friendship? How misguided that was. She should have told Iqbal everything she knew as soon as he gave her the information from the Iranian police.

A worse thought struck her. If her phone call to him only moments ago had connected, he would have realised that she knew Afsoon, Mohsen's mother, and had been deliberately with-holding that information. She would have had to tell him that she had, in effect, warned Afsoon that the police were looking for her son.

Although it was the last thing she had intended, she had obstructed the police in their duty and aided and abetted a suspected felon. She felt as though ice was running in her veins. She pulled over at a greasy spoon café and ordered tea. For an hour or more she sat staring out of the window thinking. It didn't get any better. Only the day before yesterday she had been smugly congratulating herself on how well she had negotiated turbulent events. Fool. She had been flip and jaunty with Steve on the strength of it. Today she had had a nice girly lunch with Suze as though everything was fine. What had she said to Ellis? 'We're both pretty damn hot.' How self-deluded could she be? How could she not have seen the possibility that should have been staring her in the face that both Afsoon and her son would make their plans to run the minute they knew the police were on to him? Afsoon probably still didn't believe that Mohsen had done anything wrong, she was blind to his crimes, but she would do anything to protect him. Now Richard would never know his child – had Afsoon even told him she was pregnant? And it was all her fault.

Since only Steve knew that she was aware of the connection it was very unlikely that it would come out. She would not be charged herself. Nevertheless she would know for the rest of her life that her thoughtlessness had let Mohsen escape the law so that he would be free to carry on terrorising girls. Her phone rang. She saw it was DS Iqbal and almost cancelled the call. Instead she let it ring three times, took a deep breath, and answered it.

'Just checking you all got home safely on Saturday night?' he said. 'I got your text about your son and his friend.'

'Yes.' Her heart slowed. Discreet of him not to mention either name on the phone. 'Thanks. Did you hear about the woman who was raped near to Moat Lane Car Park?'

'I did.' He paused. 'I believe there was a connection with the missing girl?'

'Yes, her mother. She'll be ok though. She will definitely press charges. Do you know if there's been an identification?'

'The rape unit will be talking to her.'

'Of course. Could I ask if there was any result from the helicopter search over Drake's depot?'

'No, it was negative. Nothing in there.' He paused. 'Mrs Ames? I need to ask you something?'

'Anna, please. Of course.'

'You seem to be involved in a spate of criminal events just lately potentially or actually involving violence towards women. In the case of your daughter's friend's sister and the woman at Moat Lane the victims were known to you. The girl who went missing is that victim's daughter. Is there a connection you need to tell me about – some information you could give us?' He couldn't know anything but his experience and policeman's intuition were putting up red flags.

Anna looked at the ring of wet tea on the grey plastic top of her table and dropped her paper napkin on to it. It would do no good to confess; Afsoon and Mohsen were long gone and she had no hard evidence of his involvement, anyway. The situation with Kimi was a separate attack with no links to the organised gang she was sure. 'No, I don't think so. Just coincidence.' Now she had lied to add to everything else. Iqbal waited. She forced herself to be silent, not to babble verbiage that could incriminate her.

'There is something I can tell you,' Iqbal said. 'The suspect who may have been Nicola's abuser, Mohsen Amirmoez?'

'Yes?'

'He's disappeared. Completely vanished. My theory is he got a tip-off we were looking for him. I've put out alerts but he's almost certainly left the country. Would you have any ideas on that, Mrs Ames?'

'Perhaps he heard that you were questioning people who knew him?' Anna's voice was flat and she felt sick.

'Perhaps. Well, try to stay out of dangerous places yourself, all right? Bye.'

So, she was not just a fool, she was a self-serving liar too.

At home Faye was waiting for her. 'Mum! I need to go to work! Where were you? I phoned you loads of times -' She was pulling on her coat and twitching up her knot of hair, furious.

'Sorry, I was driving,' Anna said dully. 'Do you want me to call them? Explain it wasn't your fault?'

'Like they'd believe you!' Faye was pushing past her.

'Do you want me to take you? I could get your dad and drive you over?'

Faye stopped in her tracks and calmed down immediately. 'Would you?' They roused Harry from his reverie on the sofa and encouraged him into the front passenger seat. Anna set off again into the late afternoon traffic. It was almost a relief to do this minor penance and Faye was delivered in time for her shift. She turned the car round and set off back home. She had no desire to see Steve – what had happened had not been his fault, it was her decision, but she just couldn't bear to tell him the outcome yet.

All evening she went through the usual mundane tasks, cooking for the three of them, paying some bills that couldn't be left and doing the most urgent ironing. At nine o'clock she phoned Joan who was feeling much better and sounding it, too. She did her best to make her own voice cheerful. At nine-thirty Harry was ready for bed and she took him up, letting him slowly peel off a slipper and then a sock and then do the same on the other side. Eventually he was ready to get into bed and she turned back the covers while he climbed in. For a moment she lay down beside him on top of the duvet holding his hand but he soon became irritated by her taking up room on his bed and gave a little kick with one leg. She rolled off and stood up. His rejection of her, slight and inconsequential as it was, resonated with her self-disgust.

By 11.00 Ellis was asleep and the house was quiet. She looked for an email from her father but there wasn't one. She sat gloomily at the kitchen table for a while and then went up to bed but it was no use. She read until her eyes were burning and gritty, heard Faye come in and go to bed, and it was still only 1.00. She went downstairs and made a cup of tea and watched tv until a faint light showed outside the window. Another day. She switched off the television, climbed the stairs to her own room and lay wide awake until it was time to get up.

Steve phoned as she was making a shopping list for the welcome home party. He had insisted on making the long round trip to pick George and Diane up from Felixstowe so that she didn't have to. What a relief that she didn't have to go into work and face people, but this flexible time was coming to an end. She was trying to put together a phoney article, supposedly for submission to Forbes, just to cover Gerald and satisfy Ted, or at least, keep him at bay, but it was impossible to work on that today.

'Everything's ok, we've just stopped at a service station to have a break and get a drink but I wanted a word about tonight.'

'Yes?'

'They seem exhausted, Anna, and I think a party would be too much. Diane isn't even planning on coming to yours, she wants me to drop her off at her house. She said she can't wait to get into her own bed. Your dad just keeps dropping off to sleep in the back. Do you think it would be a good idea to put it off a day or two?'

Anna pushed the list away from her. 'Yes, that sounds like the best thing. I'll let Ashok and Joan know – oh and Len.'

'See you later then. I'll be back in time to get Alice from nursery so Faye won't have to be around.'

'Thanks Steve.' So there was nothing to do. Nothing that she could summon the energy to do anyway. Harry was in the living room on the sofa staring out of the big window at the rain. She had put on a CD for him of Billy Holliday's melancholy songs. They seemed to fit the mood. She went and sat beside him and stared with him. The minutes passed and eventually her eyelids closed.

Harry's hunger woke her and she stumbled into the kitchen to make them a sandwich. There was a text on her phone from Kimi asking her to call. She did. Rhea was now in a secure young people's psychiatric unit undergoing evaluation. Kimi sounded subdued and resentful. 'It's just normal teenage stuff, all that weird behaviour, isn't it? I think they're pathologising her.' Anna didn't agree but hadn't the heart or the self-confidence to say so at this point.

'Is she talking to you?'

'Well, not really, but then she never did, did she?'

'How's your father?'

'Really worried about her and about me. I've told him there's no need.' She sounded dismissive and Anna wondered whether Kimi had taken on board how seriously ill he was.

'He loves you very much, Kimi.'

'I know, I know. But he seems to feel he has to protect me. I don't bloody need protecting – it's annoying. I don't give a fuck about Frances' threat to cut me off. I've got a little surprise up my sleeve for her. I'm definitely going to that meeting.'

Anna was startled out of her dullness. 'Are you? Why?'

'You'll see. Dad says you have to come – I think he wants moral support. He likes you.'

'In that case I will. Any news on the DNA tests?'

'It's too soon. Another couple of days, but they say they've talked to people on the street and they're keeping covert surveillance on one of them until the test results. They've got his DNA on file so they can see if there's a match. There's never been anyone willing to testify before. I expect they thought I was just some poor street woman who they could intimidate.'

'Well, they got that wrong.'

An hour later a text from George alerted Anna that he and Steve were about to arrive. Diane had been dropped off as requested at her own house. Anna put the kettle on and rushed upstairs to change the sheets on her dad's bed. Len had used them so he would definitely need fresh ones. She opened the window in the bedroom and then ran out into the garden and picked an armful of mock orange to put on his chest of drawers. Faye was summoned from her room and Ellis arrived at the front door in his tennis whites just as Steve's Yeti drove up. Anna got Harry to stop shuffling placemats in the kitchen and join the welcome party at the door, so there was a posse of smiling faces to greet her dad.

He stepped stiffly from the car, straightened up, and waved happily at them. Steve got his case and followed him up the path. George looked both healthily tanned and completely worn out. They almost pulled him up the steps to hug him and exclaim on his sea-dog weatherbeaten looks. He laughed and patted Anna on the head and hugged the children and they made it eventually into the kitchen where a large chocolate cake was waiting for him. Anna had thought of it at the last moment and the cake was barely cool before it was iced but looked wonderful with the little pirate flag Faye had made with a cartoon of George's face between the crossbones. He seemed rather overwhelmed.

'Sit down, Dad, the tea's almost ready.'

'This is all very nice. Anything happened while I've been away?'

Anna, Steve and Ellis all looked vaguely in different directions. 'No,' said Faye, 'nothing – it's been really boring except for the festival – that was mega. And I've got weeks before the exams are over! My head feels like it's going to explode.' George patted her hand.

'Happy birthday to you, happy birthday to you,' sang Harry to George looking at the cake, so Anna cut it and Ellis poured the tea. They were just settling down to a second piece and ready to hear all about it when George stood up, a little shakily.

'This has been a very nice welcome,' he said, 'but if you'll excuse me I think a nap would be in order. Tales of the sea another time, right?' Steve leaped into the hall and lugged the suitcase up to George's bedroom and George followed slowly, one step at a time hanging on to the bannister. On the landing he took Steve's arm and croaked, 'Ask Anna not to wake me up for dinner, Steve, I just want to sleep, ok?' Steve nodded.

## 27

It wasn't until dinner had been cleared away later with no sign of George re-appearing that Anna had a few minutes to herself. It was so good to have her dad back in the house even though he was dead to the world. She herself had gone beyond exhaustion to a kind of dull torpor. Her brain was on a hamster wheel of self-recrimination; the remorse over letting Mohsen escape only giving way to worry over her behaviour with the police. DS Griffiths had been right in one way. She was quick enough to call the police for help when she needed them, to rescue Kimi and then to look for Ellis and Rhea, but when she could have been the one to help them she had disastrously compromised their investigation and then lied about it. There was nothing she could do about it either. If she now confessed to Iqbal what would happen? He would be an ally lost, not just suspicious as he was now, and she could be charged with a criminal offence. That would mean that her job would be seriously put at risk, integrity and honesty being two of the probate researchers most valuable tools, and in the worst case scenario she could go to prison. In either case what would the family live on? She reflected grimly that honesty had a price she was not willing to pay much as she despised herself for it.

She dragged herself up and rooted among the bits and pieces in the stationery drawer finally finding an L.S.Lowry card with its matching envelope. She sat down again and wrote a note to Andrew Dunster thanking him and telling him what had happened with Rhea and Ellis. She wanted him to know his help had been worth more than a quick phone call.

Bobble, who had been taking a nap after all the excitement of tidying up cake spills, suddenly sprang from his basket barking and then ran into the hall. Ellis was teaching him to retrieve things and he did exactly that, running back into the kitchen to proudly present Anna with a dented and damp envelope. She tried to take it from him but his brain switched to tug of war game and he wouldn't release it until she remembered to order 'Give!' at which point he released it reluctantly. 'Good boy.' Anna patted his head and tried to read what was on the mauled paper. She could make out her name so she lifted the flap and pulled out a note written on printer paper. In block capitals was type-written:

AS YOU SEE WE KNOW WHERE YOU LIVE.  MIND YOUR OWN BUSINESS AND BACK OFF OR YOU WILL REGRET IT AND SO WILL YOUR FAMILY.  YOU HAVE MADE ONE SERIOUS MISTAKE.  DON'T MAKE ANY MORE.  WE WILL PROTECT OUR INTERESTS.

She ran to the front door and down the drive but there was no activity on the road either way so she went back into the kitchen. She studied the note, her brain racing.  It was not crude or illiterate or even angry.  It was clear and cold and ruthless.  But who would have sent it?

Her first thought was that thug lit up by the orange street light who had Kimi's blood on his hands.  He had got a good look at her and could have followed her to the hospital and then back home but it seemed unlikely.  The CPS was not relying on her evidence, after all, although she would be asked to give it in court she expected.  Far more damaging evidence would come from Kimi herself and the forensic team.  Had Kimi had a note like this?  She would have to check.

What about the attack on Nicola?  Had there been another person in the vicinity she had not seen?  Had someone observed her intervene, coolly noted her car registration, and tracked her down? But why?  She had not been able to identify any of the men and boys involved and no-one could know that she had glimpsed Afsoon and Mohsen hidden round the corner.  And why now?  Did it have something to do with Mohsen's disappearance?  Perhaps the gang didn't know that he had left the country.

She inhaled sharply.  *She* didn't know it.  She had just assumed that he and Afsoon had left because it would be the logical thing to do.  Iqbal had assumed it, too.  They may still be here.  This note could be from Mohsen himself, in hiding but still running his part of the operation.  Or, Afsoon could have left on her valid passport to prepare papers and a place of safety for him but he could have stayed in the UK - in Birmingham.  Afsoon.  Her stomach clenched. Afsoon knew she had seen him on the night of the attack on Nicola and knew Anna had recognised him at the art gallery and had seen the information on him the police had.  Afsoon could be the one that tied up all the pieces and had delivered Anna to her son. Anna remembered the cold look on Afsoon's face before she nodded and turned away in that sun striped wood by the lake. She would do it. Look what she had already done for him.

The thought that Mohsen was still here and watching her had two effects on Anna. One was pure fear that set her heart pounding; the other was anger and the anger drove out the grey self-recrimination that had engulfed her. How dare that arrogant, sadistic young man threaten her and her family? But quickly came the realisation that she was powerless. Again, this was all speculation, only the note was real. Someone, or rather some people, were feeling threatened by something she had done, and were warning her to stop doing it or else. That was all she knew for sure.

The thought of going to the police crossed her mind so rapidly that it left no trace. She had burned her boats there. But she needed to talk to someone and share this if only so that if anything did happen to her, there would be this. It would be, of course, untraceable. Computer paper is ubiquitous and a computer printer does not have idiosyncrasies like an old typewriter would have done. She was quite sure that there would be no fingerprints or any other DNA on it – the writer would have made sure of that. The envelope had not been sealed so there was no chance it had been licked and in any case, Bobble's slobber was all over it. She couldn't bother Steve tonight, he would be tired out from the long drive, but she could see him tomorrow at work. All of a sudden she needed the security and support of the office environment as well as Steve. But it wouldn't be fair to ask George to take over Harry the minute he got home. He had not emerged from his room for dinner and when she had checked he had been snoring.

Anna wrote a note to Faye, who was doing a late shift, asking her to be awake ready to take over when she left for work around 11.00. That would mean that while Faye slept in Anna could get Harry up, a job which she had never asked the children to do, make sure he had breakfast, check on how her dad was doing, and then she would be free to go to Harts, see Steve and concentrate on trying to make some sense of this bloody note. She dropped it into a plastic sleeve that she found crumpled in the back of the stationery drawer and put it out of sight in her briefcase. She placed the note to Faye on her pillow.

When she got into bed she fell instantly asleep and mercifully dreamed no dreams.

The next morning Anna was clearing away the breakfast dishes when Kimi rang. She was blisteringly furious. 'Those shits at the CPS keep on at me whether I'll testify! I've told them a million times, and the police that I will. Are they trying to protect these bastards? What the fuck's going on?' Anna let her rant on and waited for a pause.

'Kimi, I hate to suggest this, but do they know who you are?'

'What? Of course they do.'

'No, I mean, do they know that you are the daughter of Gerald Draycott of Drakes Enterprises?'

'What difference would that make?'

'I think it might make quite a lot, sadly. Would your dad mind if you told them that?'

'No, of course not. Ok, I'll get back to you.' And she had gone. Anna would have to ask about whether she, too, had received an anonymous letter another time.

Ted was in the lobby at Harts chatting with Josie, the receptionist. Anna was hoping to slip by but Ted was not the kind of boss who allowed that sort of thing.

'Morning Anna. How's it going?'

'Just finishing the first draft,' she lied.

'Let me see it as soon as you've knocked it into shape, ok?' He stared at her speculatively. 'So, you'll be free to start work on other cases soon, won't you?' No definite time period had been set for this project but Anna knew she couldn't spin it out much longer. A straightforward article on Drake family dynamics and business success would have taken her under two weeks for both the interviews and the writing but the events that had actually occurred in connection with this story had meant that she had already been preoccupied for much longer and it wasn't over yet.

'Gerald wants me to go to an important family meeting in a couple of days,' she said truthfully. 'I should be able to wrap things up soon after that.' Ted grunted. There wasn't a lot he could say given the financial benefit to the company of Gerald Draycott's fee but he hated not being in control and in the know.

Anna went up the green plate glass stairs to the main office and to her own desk. She could see that Steve had someone in with him so she would have to wait. Suzy glanced up at her, waved, and then went back to her phone conversation so Anna turned on her computer and opened her emails. Kimi only had her work email address and had sent this half an hour ago. Anna checked her phone and noted four missed calls from her. She had put it on silent while she was dealing with Harry and then forgotten to switch the ringtone back on. Kimi was incandescent.

You were right! The minute they knew about dad and Drakes they were fucking fawning on me! Couldn't believe it! Then the police got in on it and phoned me and thanked me for being so cooperative and they were sure the guys would be picked up today and held until the DNA results are in tomorrow!!! Ugh! What chance some woman without backing eh? No wonder so few go through with charges. I'm so mad I could kick every one of them from here to next week!'

Anna phoned. 'Please don't kick anyone, Kimi,' she told the voicemail, 'they aren't all like that, I'm sure. Well, I hope.' She hung up. She stood up and peered across at Steve's office and saw with relief that he was now alone.

But it was hopeless. She no sooner started to tell him what had happened than someone would come in. After three attempts she gave up and asked if she could go round that evening after dinner. He put his spread fingers up to his face in a comic scared kid pose. 'Please don't say you have something to tell me!'

She groaned. 'Brace yourself, buster. I have something to tell you.'

Steve pretended to stab himself in the chest and fell to the floor just as Ted appeared looking disapproving.

She felt as though she was carrying around a box of explosives which she had hoped to offload on to Steve, or at least share it, unfair as that was. Now, she had to keep it to herself for hours more. She spent the afternoon at the computer knocking together some kind of an article which helped to calm her nerves. She found that she dropped effortlessly into the kind of knowing, rather snide journalistic style that she particularly detested and that she was, in effect, writing a pastiche if not a downright parody. Ted would sniff that out in a second. She selected all and deleted. At least she could try to be honest in her style even if the article itself was completely phoney.

When she got home George was pottering about in the kitchen. He had the washer and dryer fully occupied and was sorting through a pile of pamphlets and scraps of paper on the kitchen table.

Harry was helpfully putting those he had discarded in size order. George looked much happier than he had the day before.

'I've got dinner sorted, love, it's slow-cooking so you don't have to worry about that.'

'Dad, you've only just got home – I didn't expect you to resume full active service straight away. Where's Faye?'

'I told her to buzz off. Harry and I are fine.' He looked up from his papers. 'It's so good to be home.' She went to him and gave him a proper hug.

'It's so good you're back. Was it a big adventure like you hoped?' He patted her back.

'It was very interesting, you know, the tugs and the docks and the stevedores and, well, it's amazing really how they move those huge things around so easily. We really enjoyed watching the pilot boat come zooming out to drop him off in a couple of seconds and then away. My goodness they have to be nimble! The captain and crew were very kind and we did get to explore a couple of the ports.' She pulled away and grinned at him.

'I can feel a massive BUT gathering momentum, Dad!'

He groaned and threw his head back. 'We couldn't sleep! We hardly got a wink of sleep! You can't imagine how noisy those ships are with the engines vibrating and no dampening in the living quarters so everything juddered and shook and squeaked and banged. The nearest thing to it I can remember was when I had that MRI scan of my head last year when they thought I had a screw loose.' Anna smiled, remembering he had had the scan for a potential audio nerve tumour. 'Like being in a metal dustbin and someone hitting it repeatedly with a hammer. I feel as though I've spent six days in an MRI scanner! It was as bad for Diane – and, of course, when the ship's at sea which ours was most of the time the engines are going day and night. I could even hear them last night!'

'Come off it, Dad, you were so fast asleep you couldn't have heard a bomb explode.'

'It gets into your body, the beat of the engines,' he wailed. 'I kept surfacing last night to go to the loo and each time I thought I was still on the ship! And when I put my head on the pillow I could hear the thump, thump, thump.'

'Oh dear. I'm sorry. So you must *not* go down to the seas again, to the lonely sea and the sky, eh?'

'Masefield didn't go on a container ship the size of the Empire State Building, did he? I imagine one of his tall sailing ships would have been quite a lot quieter.' He stopped sorting out his souvenirs and put the kettle on, popped open the tin of teabags and pottered over to the fridge to get the milk. The sight of him with his hair sticking out like a half-blown dandelion and his cardigan done up at the wrong buttons made Anna feel so much better. 'But the captain let us go into the chartroom and that was very interesting. And I sat up with the watch one night, a chap from Denmark, the first mate Piet, and we made up doggerel verse together – that was good.' He finished making three cups of tea and set them down on the table. 'There's a lot of very little at sea when you're a passenger, we found. A bird landing on deck was quite an event.' Then he produced the remains of the chocolate cake and put that out too. 'Before our gannets get home.' Finally he settled himself and picked up his mug. 'Now then, Anna, what's been going on with you? You looked as though you'd lost a shilling and found sixpence yesterday when I got back.' Not so tired he hadn't noticed his daughter's badly disguised misery.

'It's a long story, Dad, and one I don't come well out of, I'm afraid.'

'I'm listening.' So she told him. He was her first and best confidante and it was a relief to let it all out. She did not tell him about the note. That was too new and too worrying – she would tell Steve, though, when she saw him later. 'So, I've been feeling awful about how stupid I was and now it's my fault that that horrible man is free and I think the police suspect that I know more than I've said, which I do, and DS Iqbal is very suspicious of me when he's been nothing but helpful.' She pushed her plate of cake away. 'It's a mess but there's nothing I can do.'

George was quiet for a moment and then he picked up one of her hands and held it. 'So let me get this right. You gave Afsoon a chance to do the right thing about Mohsen because you took pity on her, you probably saved Kimi's life at considerable risk to your own and you rescued Ellis and got the proper medical treatment for Rhea. Is any of that untrue?'

'No, but – '

'The only thing you did wrong was to trust someone else to do the right thing. I can completely understand why Afsoon made the choice she did, but that's not the point. You can't control what other people do. You gave her the moral choice – he is her son and perhaps she had that right. Now, think about what would have happened if you had told DS Iqbal what you knew when he showed you that photo from the Iranian police. She would, of course, have been questioned. Her husband would have wanted to know why and she would have had to tell him. Their marriage would have been over because a man like you say he is would never trust her again. She would not have told the police where Mohsen was, she would have defended him to her death, so they wouldn't have got him. The end result would have been the same.'

'So he wouldn't have been arrested either way?'

'Of course not. The police had already tried talking to people who knew him but none of them gave out his whereabouts, did they? Too frightened I imagine, he sounds like a nasty piece of work. They were too afraid and his mother was too besotted to grass on him.' He rubbed his beard around in circles, scratching under his chin. 'So give it up, Anna. Give up this self-laceration. You've been brave and resourceful and it's pointless. Anyway, you've got quite enough to deal with sorting out your real nightmares without adding to the burden.'

'My what?'

'I'm not that deaf my dear, and my room is the closest to yours. Ever since that time on the canal bank – that night – you've been crying out and weeping most nights. I don't know if you remember the dreams but even if you don't, they take their toll.'

Harry looked up and stared at Anna in concern. 'Monsters,' he said.

Anna reached across the table for their hands. 'How can I be scared with my brave champions to look out for me?' she smiled.

'You might also consider a bit of therapy,' said George seriously, getting up to check on dinner and start laying the table.

## 28

The really great thing about having George home and Steve within walking distance was that on nights like this she could crack open a bottle of vino and get thoroughly stuck in. She arrived at his front door with a bottle of red in one hand and white in the other.

'Oh, right, it's like that is it?' he said opening the door wide for her to come in.

'Please tell me Alice is asleep.'

'Alice is asleep.' She fell into one of Steve's deep armchairs and let her head loll back.

Steve returned from the kitchen with two glasses half full of white wine. 'I'm not giving you any more until I know what the latest crisis is and then, if it's anything like the others, I may drink both bottles.' Anna smiled and then became serious.

'Afsoon and Mohsen have disappeared.'

Steve took a sip of his wine. 'I can't say I'm surprised.'

'What?'

'It didn't occur to me when we were discussing what to do but when I was on the walk the situation kind of unknotted in my head and I thought that she may refuse to give him up and then her course would be obvious.'

'Ok, then. There's something else.' Steve caught the seriousness in her voice and didn't make a joke of it. He nodded for her to continue and she could tell he had switched to full concentration mode. She took the note out of her pocket and handed it to him. 'This got pushed through our door this morning.'

He glanced up at her and then back to the note. 'Do you have any idea who might have sent it?'

'I've been thinking about it all day. It's possible that Mohsen didn't leave. I assumed he had when Afsoon disappeared and the police told me he'd gone but he may not have done. Or, there may have been another person who I didn't see that night who was involved in the attack on Nicola. It could even have been one of the group who got my car registration and traced me.' She tipped the glass to her lips and winced at the acidity of the wine she had hastily grabbed from the bargain bin.

'Let's think about who knows who.' Steve's forehead was deeply creased and eyes had become dark. 'Mohsen knows who you are if we assume Afsoon has told him. Mohsen knows Dook.'

'Dook knows me,' Anna broke in. 'Remember William introduced us at the depot.'

'Following the theory that these may be organised gang-rapes and that they may be run through some dark internet website -' Anna could see he was pursuing a line of thought and didn't interrupt. '-Maybe Dook learned coding in the army – he was involved in logistics wasn't he? Maybe he's the computer guy, the central control.'

'But surely he wouldn't want to be known? Isn't the whole point that these people, the three, don't know each other? He and Mohsen clearly know each other pretty well.'

'Hm, well, you'd think so.' Steve's hair was now sticking up in a castellated ridge. Neither of them was drinking the wine Anna had so looked forward to. 'Just a minute. There's another possibility. What if there is no website? What if it's just two men working together without any need for a forum for organising events?'

'You mean just Dook and Mohsen working together?'

'It could be. Probably Mohsen gets the girls somehow and maybe Dook arranges the men?'

'How could he do that, though, without a contact site?'

'Dook was in the army. He may have got to know a few rotten apples in there and kept contact. There are bases all around the Midlands and it wouldn't be hard for military on passes to come from further afield.'

Anna's stomach churned. 'You mean like a paedophile network.'

'Yes.' Steve looked at her steadily. 'Well, this *is* potentially a paedophile network.'

'But wouldn't that be really risky? For Dook, I mean. So many people would know who he was – any one of them for any reason could shop him.' Steve stood up and paced the room. The lamplight threw soft shadows around the walls as he passed each luminous globe but Anna couldn't stop seeing in her mind's eye the dark streets only a few miles from this cosy room and maybe a scared girl waiting in the gloom for her 'boyfriend'.

'Let's just take that paedophile parallel. How did they get away with it for so long? Well-known men got away with it for years, decades. There were key contact people who gave them access, however unwillingly, and they did it because they were scared. Scared of being hurt or more often scared that some nasty secret of their own might come out. In two words, intimidation and blackmail. Dook could control a small handful of men that way and they would be the visible faces, not him.' Steve had stopped pacing and now was standing stock still. 'He would have had the chance to find out quite a bit about other soldiers in the close confines of army life. And not just the men, of course, he could have watched the officers and got some dirt on some of them.'

Anna was horrified. 'Not William, surely. He's such a nice man.'

'But he does have a family and a lot to lose, doesn't he? He fits the profile. And look at the contacts he's got not just in the military but in local sport and even in Drakes itself. You told me once that people go to him with their troubles. Flip that over and there's another link in the chain of potential blackmail.'

Anna stood up, too. 'Do you know what, Steve, I don't want to talk about this anymore. It's making me feel sick.'

Steve stepped towards her and put his arms round her shoulders. 'These are only hypotheses, Anna, we're just exploring. None of it is real at this point.'

'So what do we do?' She rested her head against his shoulder and the smooth, fragrant wool of his sweater felt like a caress.

He kissed the top of her head briefly. 'There isn't anything we can do right now. Let's think this through and come up with some other scenarios. But you need to be careful, Anna. Don't go out into any more deserted backstreets or along lonely canal paths or anything will you?' She knew he didn't know anything, he was just trying to make a joke by putting forward situations he assumed she would never in a million years subject herself to. Her face, hidden by his warm, comforting embrace didn't smile. It was all she could do not to howl.

When she let herself back in to her house it seemed as if everyone was in bed but in the kitchen the light was still on and Faye was sitting at the table frowning at her laptop.

'All right?'

'Not really.' Faye gave a huge sigh and slumped in her chair.

'What's up?' Anna patted her daughter's dejected back on the way to the kettle.

'You know the three unis I've got offers from?'

Anna knew only too well. Two of them were far away, one in Northumberland and one in Wales and Faye would have to pay accommodation costs, or rather, she would have to. The one in Birmingham would be much cheaper as Faye could live at home but it seemed unfair to limit the girl's choices. When Anna had gone to university George had made it possible for her to go wherever she wanted. Times had changed.

'I'm looking at all the courses I'd do in the first and second years for Business.'

'Yes?' Anna sat down beside her and Bobble leaned against her leg. She pulled his ears gently. He was already twice the size he had been when they got him and so was his food bill but there was something about the look in his eyes that made him impossible to resist. She massaged his head. He thumped his tail.

'Mum?' Faye's face turned to her, forehead wrinkled with anguish. 'I don't know whether I want to go.'

'Sweetheart, you're just fed up with all the revising you've been doing. You'll feel differently when it's the autumn and everyone's going off to an exciting life with new friends and much more independence.'

'Mm. But it's more of the same isn't it?' Faye shook her hair down and ran her fingers through it. Anna picked up the scrunchie from the floor before Bobble ate it. 'I know there would be fun stuff but you do have to sit in lectures and write essays and have exams and things, don't you?'

'Well, yes, that is pretty much the deal with universities.'

'I just don't know whether I want to.' Anna thought for a moment or two. Some of Faye's friends were in a highly emotional state at the thought of leaving each other, leaving home and the exciting prospect of new experiences and no parental monitoring of their wilder excesses. Was Faye getting cold feet? She gave the appearance of total self-confidence but she wouldn't be the first young person to secretly dread the challenge of university life. Anna remembered how Kimi had felt about being a freshman but, of course, she had had a terrible experience. Tash wasn't going to university. She wanted to have a gap year before she did. Michelle couldn't afford for the girl to go travelling round the world and wouldn't have allowed it, probably, these days, but Tash had found a job working as a classroom assistant at a school for pupils with special needs. It was a sensible decision because she could see whether she really liked the work before committing to full-time training for it.

'Are you thinking of a gap year, like Tash?'

Faye lifted her hair off her neck and pulled two strands forward from each side to trap under her nose and upper lip like a handlebar moustache. 'Not really,' she lisped. 'She's always known what she wants to do. I'm only doing this business thing because I'm getting good marks on my A level.'

Anna was concerned. 'I didn't know that, Faye. I thought you were really interested. You know that meerkat mugger head-hugger thing.'

'Well, that was fun but it was the product design part that was fun, not all the other stuff – you know the business plan and marketing and all that.'

'So what are you thinking?'

Faye looked at Anna shyly from under her eyelashes and released her moustache. This was such an unusual expression for her daughter to have that Anna was quite startled. Faye had the full range of hostile, demanding, challenging and generally intimidating expressions but this look was a new one. 'Don't be mad at me.'

'Why should I be mad at you?' Anna was growing more concerned by the second. What with one thing and another if Faye now announced she was pregnant, her mother might very well disappear in a puff of smoke and never be seen again. 'Talk to me, darling.'

'You know Mecklins?'

'What?'

'Mecklins. The toy company. You know.'

'No?'

'They're world famous, Mum! Honestly!' Anna got up and went for the half bottle of wine in the door rack of the fridge. She poured herself a glass. She had, after all, only had half a glass at Steve's and the world was not making much sense and it was past midnight. Needless to say Faye looked as fresh as a daisy and was now regarding her with her usual measure of exasperation. 'They're out near Lichfield so they're not far away if I had a car. I've only got a month to my test.'

'I think I might have missed something?' Anna sat down again at the table and drank deeply.

Faye looked puzzled. 'Keep up, Mum! Read between the lines here! They've got apprenticeships, duh. You've got to have A levels in something like art or design or textiles or something like that which I have sort of. But in any case I've got that meerkat thingy. It's a proper career structure. And they pay you, Mum.'

'Just a minute. Are you thinking of this because you think we can't afford university?'

'*Can't* you?' Faye looked shocked and disapproving as though her mother had revealed an unsuspected penchant for bankruptcy.

'Yes, of course we can.'

'Well then, why would you say that?'

Anna had the feeling that things were getting off track. 'Faye, are you asking me if it would be a good idea for you to try for an apprenticeship at Mecklins instead of going to uni?'

'That's what I just said.' Faye tapped at her laptop and turned it to face her mother. 'Read about it. I'm going to bed.'

So Anna sat up for another hour researching the idea and it was not a bad one. It sounded like an excellent apprenticeship with transferable skills to other companies if necessary. It was true Faye was more artistic than interested in business for all her manipulation of the family budget. She had never really been academic like Ellis. Faye obviously planned to go on living at home and Tash would still be around at least for a year for company. She tried to push down the feeling of relief for this possible financial boon because she knew Faye and it was perfectly possible that tomorrow she might want to study abroad or something even more exotic and expensive.

She climbed the stairs slowly trying to keep mulling over Faye's idea so that no scary monsters could make their entrance before she had a chance to fall asleep.

## 29

For once Anna had given some thought to her appearance. After all, an invitation to a board meeting at Drakes didn't drop into your lap every day and she felt she may need at the very least to appear competent. Suzy always yelled at her if she wore black to work but she felt this occasion called for it so she selected the neat suit which she had last worn many months ago for her first meeting with Briony in Chicago. She pushed away the thought of how disastrously wrong that had gone and zipped up the skirt to find that it was loose on her. She swung it round. It was very loose. Feeling as puzzled as the incredible shrinking man who found his trousers were too short, she put on the jacket and discovered that she could pull that away from herself by at least four inches. It was too late to find anything else so she took the jacket off, found an ivory draped top to go under it, tugged the jacket back on and slipped her feet into the only pair of spiky heeled shoes she possessed. They felt weird but she reassured herself that she wouldn't have to do much walking. She fastened her best gold rope chain round her neck and tottered into Harry's room to look in the one long mirror in the house. Her dark hair was sticking out around her head in a becoming artful disarray, she thought, smirking at herself. A few pounds less suited her. She had even improved herself to the extent of a rose tinted lipstick and rubbed a little dash of it into each cheek as instructed by Suze on countless occasions.

Ellis appeared behind her in the glass, grinning. 'You know, Mum, if you were tall and blonde and didn't have any wrinkles, you'd look half way decent.'

She was early at Drakes and decided that before she changed her driving shoes for the spikes she'd have another swift look round the back of the depot. No one seemed to be about. She glanced in the huge garage, noted that the office door was closed and walked towards the back. It was an overcast day and cool for May, it would be just her luck that a sudden shower would turn her chic appearance into something very much more wet hen. She glanced up at the clouds but they were a gloomy undecided grey pall. Just a quick look. She hurried around the corner and stopped abruptly. There was a white van by the door in the back wall. She noticed the cracked back left light cover and the number plate. She couldn't remember all the numbers but she remembered the letters. A game that she had played with the children creating mnemonics to recall random numbers or letters had stuck with her so that she had the habit of doing it almost automatically. HMG – Horses My Game. It was Kevin's van.

'Looking for someone, Mrs Ames?' She turned to see Dook glaring at her in an unmistakeably hostile way. 'It's private back here – not for visitors. What are you doing here?' His Geordie lilt did not make his words any warmer.

She stared up at his narrowed pale eyes and immaculate slicked back hair and thought rapidly. 'I nearly ran over a cat coming up the drive,' she said, 'and it ran this way. I was just checking it was all right.'

'There's nae cat,' he said without looking round. Like a reptile he seemed not to need to blink.

'Ok, maybe it ran the other way.' He was silent, studying her. 'I'd better get on, anyway, Mr Draycott is expecting me for a meeting.'

As she moved to step round him he touched her shoulder lightly to halt her and bent his head. For a crazy moment she thought he was going to kiss her. 'Your daughter's a looker,' he said softly in her ear, 'You should watch out for her.'

'My daughter!'

Dook was already striding away and before she could gather herself he was behind the wheel of a red pick-up squealing out of the yard. Anna stood very still rigid with fear. It was him – he was the one who had sent the note. Somehow he knew that she was suspicious of that door at the back of the depot but how could he know? She turned quickly and saw the Social Club and as she watched Kevin came out of the side entrance. He must be a hundred yards away but she could see him clearly and anyone there would have been able to see her and Steve that day. It was the obvious place for the drivers to go when they had finished their shifts. But why was Kevin there? Another errand for Kimi? He was walking towards her across the car park.

'Anna!' It was William calling her and smiling. 'Are you lost? We're about to begin and I saw your car arrive from my office window so I knew you were here.' She forced herself to smile back and walk quickly towards him. Dook, Kevin, William – all in the same place at the same time and all watching her. There was no time to think.

The spiky heels stayed forgotten in the car as William and Anna rode up in the lift to the boardroom. 'Dad said you'd be here,' he said chummily, 'and I must say I was delighted. They're dull old things, these meetings, and we might get through a bit quicker with an observer. You'll stop us all rambling on.'

'Will everyone be there?' Anna asked just for something to say to cover her racing thoughts.

William considered, his pleasant rosy face rumpling in thought. 'I think so – well, except for Afsoon, she's off in London visiting galleries.' Not told the family then, Anna noted. 'Charlie's up there already and Richard and Kimi and Gerald have only got to come from their offices.'

The lift had stopped at the top floor and the doors were sliding back. 'And Mrs Draycott Senior?'

'Frances? Oh, she'll be there – I saw the Rollo in her space when I came to look for you.'

He pushed open the door to the board-room and ushered her in. It was another dull Drake space. The large table looked unfashionable enough to have been put in in the 1950's – no glass, chrome and black leather here. Frances was dressed in her signature pearl grey which exactly matched her hair and had a silk scarf in cobalt blue figured with tiny chains in silver draped elegantly across her shoulders. She was sitting in the chair next to the CEO's which remained empty at the head of the table and was admonishing Charlotte who was looking bored and restless and checking her phone.

'Put that away and turn it off, darling,' Frances said and then, hearing the door, turned and saw Anna and William. 'Mrs Ames. This is a surprise. I wasn't aware you would be here.' Waves of frigidity rippled towards Anna who was moving to a chair in a corner away from the main table.

'Mr Draycott invited me,' she said simply and sat down.

Frances regarded her suspiciously. 'I cannot imagine why. You do understand that if any confidential matters come up you will be asked to leave?'

Anna smiled politely without nodding. She needed a few moments to gather herself before the meeting began and hoped she would now be left alone. William waved a coffee cup at her from the things laid out on a linen-covered side table but she shook her head. She couldn't trust herself to hold a cup and saucer without it clattering and slopping. Dook's hot breath on her hair and the smell from him of engine oil and some musky scent together with the whispered threat were all she could think of. Faye. Oh God. The thought of him watching her daughter, hiding and tracking her, maybe even waiting for her to come out of work late at night made her almost faint with fear. The minute this meeting was over she would phone Faye and tell her that from now on she would be picking her up from work. Never mind that the restaurant paid for a taxi when she was on late shift. But what about other times? Faye was not a child and she was often out and about with her friends hopping on and off buses, shopping, going to the cinema. How easy would it be for Dook or one of his gang to follow her to the cinema and then wait until she went to the loo and was on her own or -

'Sorry to keep you all waiting,' Gerald said, coming in to the room behind Kimi. 'Richard's just coming. Hello Anna. Glad you could make it.'

'I don't know why -' Frances began. Richard came in and sat on the other side of the CEO chair. Kimi smiled at Anna briefly but her face was still showing some colour from the bruising. The dressing on her nose had gone.

'So I'll just get a coffee and then we'll get started.' He looked so thin and pale that Anna's heart lurched for him. He had aged twenty years in the last few weeks. He moved and looked like an old man. No-one even offered to get him his coffee. All these people, all well provided for by his efforts and not one of them leaped up to help him, not even Kimi. She was checking papers in a file which she then placed on the table. Anna saw that he was feeling giddy and was steadying himself against the table and without thinking she was at his side.

'Can I help?' She took his elbow and with the other hand picked up his coffee cup and saucer. Then he was seated and she moved away. The faces round the table regarded her with curiosity.

'Well, well, Mrs Ames, what have we here?' Frances said snidely. 'Gerald's got a little friend.' Anna did not rise to the bait.

'Oh, do let's get on with it,' Charlotte snapped. 'I've got a million things to do.'

Gerald cleared his throat. 'This is not a formal meeting and there will be no minutes taken, which is why Anthea is not here, but some things need to be sorted out in this family.'

'We all know the score,' Charlotte said, 'I don't know what we're doing this for. Why are you putting yourself through it, Dad?'

'We don't all know the score as you put it Charlotte. That's why,' Gerald said rather abruptly. Richard turned his whole body in his chair and looked enquiringly at his father, his face flushing slightly with suspicion. 'You know that I'm ill and I think you realise that I haven't got very long. I'm sorry not to be able to see my grandsons and grand-daughter grow up but these things happen. People get ill and die and it's very rarely on the date they would have picked.' Everyone except Frances looked down at the table.

'Bad luck, Gerald,' muttered William kindly. Anna glanced at him. At least someone was showing some compassion, or was this William in automatic nice guy mode? Her phone vibrated in her pocket and she glanced at the screen. It was Ted. Rather than interrupt with an apology she left the room quietly and a few moments later returned trying to disguise her feelings.

'Anyway, the meeting is to sort out a few things as I said,' Gerald was saying. 'The first thing is who will take over the running of the company.' Charlotte looked puzzled and William raised his head in enquiry. Only Kimi continued to keep her eyes lowered. Frances had a slight smile and her eyes gleamed. Like a leading actor waiting eagerly in the wings to come on, Anna thought. Richard's flush deepened. Gerald turned to him. 'I know you are expecting to take over as CEO, Richard, but the fact is that decision is out of my hands. For many years now, over thirty in fact, I have held no shares in this company and I have no power to say who will take over.'

'What?' Richard's face drained of colour. So he had not been in Frances' confidence.

'But we only have a minority stake even all put together!' said Charlotte. 'If you don't have the majority share, who does?'

It was Frances' moment. She rose to her feet like a salmon cresting a waterfall. 'I do!'

'Mother?'

'But dad inherited the company, not you,' Charlotte said.

'Your father betrayed the trust placed in him so I took over,' Frances said, her voice sharp with bitterness and triumph. 'He agreed to it and we made it legal.' She took a deep breath and turned towards Kimi but Richard interrupted her.

'But I'll still take over when dad dies, won't I?' His callousness was breathtaking.

Frances looked shrewd. 'Yes, probably, but it would be on the same basis.'

'You mean you would still own everything and I would work for you?'

'You'd still have your shares. That's more than your father had.'

Richard's jaw was as tight as a steel trap. 'I have plans for the business, Mother,' he said tersely.

'Yes, we do!' broke in Charlotte. 'We've worked it all out. You can't just suddenly come out with all this after thirty years!'

Frances slammed her open hand down on the table. 'You think I don't know what you two have been plotting? You couldn't wait for your father to die could you, so you could sell out to Loeman's? What a nice nest egg that would have been and to hell with the Company!'

Richard was getting angry. 'It's the right time, for Christ's sake! We need this merger or we'll go under.'

'Rubbish,' Frances hissed at him. 'You and your sister were carving out a nice little deal for yourselves from it, weren't you?' Now Charlotte, Richard and Frances were all on their feet, furious and almost beyond coherent speech.

Into the pause came Kimi's calm voice. 'To say nothing about a profitable little bit of insider trading which may be of some interest to the FCA.' Richard spun round to glare at her. Charlotte turned to her brother and looked as though she would punch him.

'You've done what?'

'Yes,' Kimi went on, 'quite a nice little wodge of Loeman's shares in Afsoon's name. I expect you thought the merger would be announced in, say, a couple of months and their shares would rocket, wouldn't they? You didn't give dad long to die, did you, Richard?'

'You never cut me in!' Charlotte had turned beetroot and was spitting flecks of saliva across the table. 'You bastard!'

'How dare you!' Richard yelled at Kimi. 'How dare you accuse me of that!'

Kimi calmly took a small stack of photocopies out of the file in front of her and passed them round. 'You should have used your personal bank account, you know. Embezzling the firm to pay for shares in your wife's name was hardly going to pass me by.'

Anna was almost as shocked as the others. So if Afsoon had taken these shares with her she would be a wealthy woman, merger or not. Would Richard have let her actually hold them, though? Unlikely. Nevertheless, even if he still had the documents he would need to broker them into his own name and without the consent or even presence of his wife that was extremely unlikely. No wonder he had been so agitated by Afsoon's disappearance and had not wanted to involve the police. A turn up for the books indeed. Clever old Kimi. So that was what she had meant by a surprise for Frances.

Frances had turned from crimson to white. 'You embezzled this Company? Your own family Company?'

'I would have re-invested, obviously-'

'You,' Frances went on, 'stole from *me* – your own mother!'

'Well, I didn't know-'

'And you!' Frances turned to Kimi, all restraint or reason gone. 'You back-stabbing little whore! This company has fed and clothed you and bought you your precious horses and put up with your bastard child when you're nothing but a bastard yourself and this is what you do to repay us! Well, I'm not going to protect you and your father for one minute longer!' But Kimi only smiled at her and Gerald raised himself awkwardly to his feet.

'Not to steal your thunder, Frances, but I'd rather explain this part myself.' He looked at Kimi and smiled and Anna was glad to see that the young woman smiled warmly back at him. 'I recently told Kimi the truth about her parentage so you don't need to.' Frances slumped into her seat while Richard and Charlotte glanced at each other in bewilderment, their anger forgotten for a moment.

'What do you mean, Dad?' asked Richard.

'Kimi is my daughter but not your mother's. Her mother was a beautiful, talented and smart Canadian woman with whom I spent the happiest time of my life.' Frances flared her nostrils and looked put out. This was not panning out the way she had planned. 'She asked me to bring up Kimi as my own and your mother agreed as long as I gave up my ownership of Drakes to her.' Far from experiencing the sweetness of revenge, Frances now found herself put in rather a mercenary light and was being gazed at by her own children, who were already mad with her, with expressions ranging from disapproval to contempt. She lashed out.

'The truth is your father had a sordid affair with a little Canadian Indian who dumped her kid on me to raise.' She turned to Kimi and almost spat at her, 'I got stuck with you and much joy have I had of it! You've always been a thorn in my side.'

Kimi regarded her coolly. 'Well, that's a relief. I would have kicked myself if I'd made your life pleasant since you have never shown me anything but coldness and disdain.'

Frances leaped up again. 'You bitch! You brought shame to this family and never so much as a word of gratitude or apology. Your mother's daughter! And even she didn't want you!'

Unnoticed by everyone except Anna the door had been opened and closed quietly a moment before and a tall young woman with a cascade of black curly hair was standing by it. She now stepped forward. 'Oh yes, she did.' Six pairs of eyes swivelled to the back of the room.

'Good afternoon. My name is Marie Fourier and I am Cora Voisine's daughter. Your mother's daughter, Kimi, your half-sister, and I'm here to tell you that our mother loved you and thought of you until the day she died.' Kimi had staggered to her feet all composure gone, her hands to her mouth. She made an inarticulate moaning sound. Gerald, with all the speed he could muster stumbled towards the young woman and took both of her hands in his.

'You are the image of your mother. It's like she's here.' Tears stood in his eyes and his entire body trembled with emotion. No one in the room could have doubted that Cora had been the love of his life. 'But is she really dead?'

'Five years ago, I'm sorry to say.' Marie now had an arm around Gerald and as Anna pushed her own chair forward she lowered him into it. Kimi was still standing staring at her, hands across her mouth, and had not moved a muscle. Marie knelt beside Gerald's chair, her fine profile etched against his dark suit. 'I always knew about Kimi, about her 'secret' daughter, and she always knew where Kimi was.'

'Why didn't she come for me?' Kimi's voice sounded like a child's, thin and high with anguish.

Marie unfolded herself and rose to her full height. She was a little taller than Kimi. She wore a simple linen outfit of cream and white and against it her skin glowed golden and rose. For a moment Anna pictured the young engineer standing with his back to the shining river watching a woman like this ride bare back out of the wooded mountain side and into the rising sun. It would never be forgotten. No wonder he was smitten for life. Marie walked towards Kimi and held out her hands. Kimi didn't respond. She seemed frozen.

'She was a free spirit – and free spirits often don't age well, I'm afraid, and they don't usually manage to hang on to many material possessions. None of her relationships lasted and some of them left her bitter. We were often very poor and we moved constantly. We were her only children and if she loved anyone beside herself it was us. Don't misunderstand me, she was an amazing woman but not a conventional one.'

'I could have met her!' Kimi wailed again.

'She knew you would be safe as long as Gerald was alive and that he could give you a much better life than she could. She trusted him.' Marie turned to Anna. 'It was when you said that Gerald was very ill that I decided I must come. I must make myself known to Kimi in case she needed me.' She turned back to Kimi. 'In case *you* need me. Please say you do because I have wanted to meet you all my life – to have my very own sister not just in my head but right here where I can see and touch you.'

Kimi sobbed and made a step forward as though she was learning to walk for the first time and in a second Marie had enfolded her in her arms and was holding her as though she would never let her go.

After a pause of a few moments the rest of the Draycott family, upset and too overwhelmed to continue, left the room and Anna followed them closing the door softly on Gerald and the sisters. On the way down the stairs (impossible to be stuck in a lift with any of them) William caught up with her. 'Not quite your average board meeting,' he joked drily. 'Nature red in tooth and claw more like.'

'Hm,' said Anna, trying to outpace him.

'Just a minute.' He stopped her with one gentle hand on her arm. 'You're crying. It'll be all right, you know – you needn't worry for them, they always survive.'

She looked up at his concerned face. 'I'm not crying for them,' she said, 'I'm crying for me. I would have given anything for my mother to love me so much or even at all.' He took a large white handkerchief out of his pocket and handed it to her wordlessly. She blew into it.

'Families, eh?' he said.    'Fancy a bracing snifter in my office?'

'No thanks,' said Anna, 'there's a bottle of red with my name on it waiting for me at home.'

'Go to it,' said William.  'Drown 'em.  That's what I do.'

## 30

It was hard to believe that it was only four o'clock when she got home. It felt as though she had been away for days. She walked in, spiky heels dangling from one hand, and found Ashok making tea in the kitchen.

'Anna! Want a cup?'

'I suppose so, thanks.' She sat down. 'I was planning to consume at least a gallon of wine but it's possibly a tad early for that.'

'Bad day?' Ashok placed the mug beside her and went back to wipe down the counter top. She always knew when he'd been because the kitchen had a smoothed down, all's-right-with-the-world feeling instead of the rather rackety debris her own family left. There were blue irises, probably from his wife's allotment, in a vase on the windowsill and when he produced biscuits they were arranged in a circle on a little plate. It was very comforting and Anna jumped up and hugged him.

' Thanks. Just a bit much.'

'Your dad's out in the shed. We're collating the second volume of *More*. Thank goodness we didn't say it would be monthly. What did we say?' He mused and pursed his lips. 'Oh yes, "an occasional magazine" I think we called it.'

'That's what the Cloud Appreciation Society call theirs,' Anna told him. 'It's nicely undemanding on everyone. How's Rani?'

Ashok picked up the two mugs for George and himself and smiled fondly. 'That woman will be the death of me,' he said, winking at Anna. 'I get no peace. You don't mind if I take these out do you? If I leave it too long we'll both have forgotten what we were supposed to have been doing.'

Anna sat and drank her tea. She had absolutely no idea what to do. She had already texted Faye who had texted back acknowledging the lift. She would have a word with her later in the car – well, more than a word, but what could she tell her? Watch out for nasty men? Don't feel you can walk down the street without being afraid? Make sure you're never out alone? She didn't want to give those kinds of messages to make a victim of the girl and in any case Faye believed herself to be invincible, like all healthy young things, and would take not a blind bit of notice. Anna finished her tea and rinsed out the cup.

Upstairs she hung up her suit and put the ivory top in the laundry basket. The shoes, unworn, were put back in their own box. She pulled out a flannel shirt of Harry's and her jeans and trainers and when she had changed wandered into Ellis' room and stared out of the back window down the garden. Harry was enjoying the break in the clouds and was lying on the recliner while Bobble chased a squirrel. It cheered her up a little just to watch the dog playing. He was almost always smiling and seemed dizzy with delight at every new thing. His tail even now, in full play-hunting mode, was twitching back and forth like a metronome on 6/8 time. She could see from the way that Harry's head was turned that he was enjoying the spectacle too. It was almost time for his next check-up. She sighed. What was the point, really? It was just a matter of time. They monitored his vital signs and tinkered with his meds and kept careful track of any changes she or George reported but all the time, every moment, his poor brain was dissolving. They only went to help with the consultant's research as requested and Harry didn't protest. Not yet, anyway. She had not lost him to divorce or death but still he was going away, fading out, blurring. She shook herself in annoyance. Self-pity at this point? She needed her wits to be at their sharpest to try to figure out what on earth was going on and stop it before anyone else got hurt.

She sat down at Ellis' desk in front of the window superstitiously hoping that his braininess might be contagious. She was almost sure now that the note came from Dook or one of his associates. The cool threat it contained had the same feel as his words to her. No anger or bluster just a very scary business-like efficiency. How do you get someone to stop doing something? If you've got nothing on them to blackmail them you try to frighten them and if they can't be frightened personally you threaten the people they love. You could write on the back of an envelope the rules for intimidation – they were very simple and had worked for centuries, probably millennia. All you needed was the muscle to back up the threats and Dook almost certainly had that. He would not be so confident if he was acting alone. So who else?

Mohsen could still be around and she must not forget that possibility. He was young, strong and criminally inclined. William? It just seemed incredible that such a nice man would be involved but that was nonsense – it could all be a front. Or, William could be being blackmailed into things he would never normally do, as Steve had suggested. Dook might have photographs of him with male prostitutes or even famous people whom he would want to protect if they had not yet come out. On the other hand, Dook may have nothing personal to do with William at all – she must not forget that connection was just in her mind from the subtle hints of body language when she had seen them together and the link with the army.

Who else? Kevin. She had now seen Kevin twice at Drakes which in itself would be unremarkable except for the fact that his van was parked round the back of the depot by the door to the concealed storage space. But – he could have parked it there to take a short cut through the chain-link fence to the Social Club car park to get a drink or a sandwich. The fence was down in several places probably as a result of the lorry drivers doing just that. Again, Kevin seemed an unlikely suspect. He was so quiet as to appear almost sub-normal, never raising his eyes in conversation and living in that little wood in an odd lonely corner of a field. For all she actually knew, Kevin and Dook had never even met each other.

The other possibility, of course, was the old X factor. Not talent as in the television show but the unknown. The unknown unknown as Donald Rumsfeld had put it. Was there an unknown unknown? A group or an organisation of which Dook was a part but no-one else she knew of? It was so easy to construct a scenario using only the fragments observed or suspected but that could be completely blown apart by new information. But if so, why would Dook take the trouble to threaten her? If it had been Dook. She felt as though she was grabbing at wisps of cloud that dissolved on touch.

Looking at it all another way, what reason did she have to believe that *anything* wrong was going on? Well, there was the note. That was, ironically, the most concrete thing. Then there was Dook's threat today. Also Mohsen had been identified by Nicola as her boyfriend and had pimped her out and Mohsen and Dook definitely knew each other. Apart from that there was only that concealed space at the back of the depot and that could have an innocent explanation. The crates may have contained nothing more than engine spares imported for the trucks and kept locked away against theft.

'Mum?' Ellis broke her thoughts.

'Oh, sorry, love, I was hoping being in here I would imbibe your scintillating brainwaves.'

'Ha. Is it working?'

'Not really.' She got up. 'I need to get the dinner on. Had a good day?' His face was coated with sweat and the remains of a choc ice. He was pulling his tennis whites out of his sports bag and pushing off his trainers without undoing the laces. 'Ellis!'

'What? You do it.' Which was true. 'Oh, Mum, Steve texted me today to see if I want to go to the sports centre tomorrow. They've got a climbing competition on late afternoon and he'll take me after work. Can I?'

'What about Alice?'

'Her gran and granddad are here visiting so they'll pick her up and feed her.'

'Of course, I forgot.' Anna's heart sank a little as she realised she would not be able to talk things over with Steve that evening. 'Yes, that's great. I'll be working from home tomorrow anyway – there's an article I've got to finish.' There was the noise of feet pounding on the stairs.

'*That's* where you are!' accused Faye appearing in the doorway as though Anna had been found in a crack cocaine den. 'I was looking for you everywhere!'

'She seeks refuge in the cerebral zones of my boudoir,' said Ellis.

'Freak. Mum, I heard back from Mecklins. They texted me for an interview. Will you take me?'

'When?'

'They gave me a couple of dates but the first is tomorrow morning at 11.30.' Faye wrapped her long arms round her pint-sized mother and unleashed suffocating kisses equally balanced between affection and aggression. 'Please? Please, Mum, I never ask you for anything-'

'Can't breathe - ' Anna snorted. 'Yes! Of course I will. Just let me ask this - '

'Cool, Mum! You're the best!' She was gone.

'And as for that article that will have to write itself tomorrow,' Ellis began.

'I'll do it in the car while I'm waiting for her.'

George called up the stairs, 'Anna? Is it me for dinner?' She leaped up.

'No Dad, it's me. You just relax. I'm on it.'

Faye certainly cleaned up well. Anna felt quite shabby as she clutched the steering wheel beside this vision of poise and style in the passenger seat.

'Suit?'

'Tasha's mum.'

'Shoes?'

'Market. £5.' Faye comically fluttered her eyelashes at Anna. 'And make-up by yours truly with a little help from my darling mother.'

'I didn't do anything.'

'No but you very sweetly lent me your new lipstick.'

'Nice of me. I hope you put it back.' She glanced again from the road to her daughter as they stopped at the lights. 'You look really lovely Faye.' The girl had brushed her hair so that copper points of light shone from it and she had tucked it up into a large bun ring but not so tightly that it lost its curl. Chestnut tendrils had been teased loose around her nape and ears and the mass of hair perched at her crown made her slender neck look even more delicate. She had plucked a few stray hairs from her eyebrows and applied mascara thickly to her lashes but had held back from anything more. The soft rose pink of Anna's lipstick perfectly complemented her creamy skin and chocolate eyes. Dook's words, popping up suddenly, shocked her out of her trance of maternal admiration. 'Your daughter's a looker,' he had said.

'Faye, there's something I need to talk to you about.'

Faye's newly shaped brows drew together. 'Can't it wait, Mum, I'm doing my mindfulness.'

'What?'

'Dad and Ashok trained me last night so I don't have nerves for the interview. I need some quiet and peaceful vibes. Tell me on the way home.' So Faye sat serenely, eyes closed, inhaling and exhaling steadily while Anna drove and pondered. She had decided to tell Faye that there were some unpleasant people threatening Harts' employees and she should be particularly vigilant and not go anywhere on her own for a little while. Would Faye take any notice? Probably it would go in one ear and out of the other but sometimes she did pick up that Anna was being serious. Actually, it was all she could do. She couldn't be with her twenty-four hours a day.

When they drew up in Mecklins' visitor car park Anna looked around impressed. This was her favourite kind of architecture where an old building has been tastefully modernised and given new life. It was what she liked about the Harts offices. The factory, which must have been Victorian, had been preserved in its red brick ornamented splendour with the name carved in stone on an arch over the main entrance, but all the windows had been replaced with large panes set in black aluminium frames. Along the frontage were huge stone tubs placed in squares filled with large pebbles and over-flowing with a red, pink and flame flowers.

'Good luck, darling!' Faye gave her the briefest of air kisses so as not to mar the perfection of her lips and strode off elegantly with her black portfolio in one hand and a tote in the other containing a sample of her work. Anna noticed that there wasn't even a hint of a wobble on those towering heels. Had the girls been practising? A surge of murderous rage burned up inside her. If anyone dared to hurt her girl -   But what could she do? The answer was obvious. Stop snooping. That's more or less what Dook had said. Back off, mind your own business. But another voice niggled at her that to do nothing could be just as dangerous. As the note had said, they knew where she lived. If she showed fear, what other pressures could be put on her in the future? Blackmail and intimidation – that was how they seized and kept control. Those words of Steve's bounced around her thoughts. It would be so much better if they, whoever they were, could be stopped.

Two young people came out of the main entrance laughing and pushing each other playfully. As they had driven in, Anna had noticed that this small town had some attractive coffee shops and a thriving market spilling down several streets in the pedestrianized centre. She could see Faye fitting in well here. Before Anna's anxious thoughts could return her phone rang. No name came up on the LED screen.

'Yes?' she said cautiously.

'Mrs Ames? Anna? It's Briony Clark. I hope you don't mind but I got Joan to give me your number.'

Anna relaxed. 'No, that's fine. How are you?'

'I think I'm on to something. You were right –this dark internet website is operating in Leeds, Manchester and London as well as Birmingham it seems.'

'My goodness.' She had had to keep reminding herself that this whole thing was just a theory of Steve's. It seemed he had been horribly correct. 'Are there several or just one central site?'

'Not sure yet, but London has a couple of dedicated IT experts who they've taken off the drugs investigations because there's been a spate of gang rapes and the MO seems to be the same in each case. They have just managed to infiltrate the users' site. You know, where the would-be rapists go to find out when and where, so things are happening.' Briony sounded both excited and horrified. 'Manchester is just logging the attacks so far and noting the similarities but Leeds are like Birmingham, they're setting up units based on the London model although it's hard to say whether that will reach them before the sites are taken down. Apparently they change the name on the control site frequently.'

Anna stared unseeingly at the pleasant façade of Mecklins toy factory. 'What's your guess about how long this has been going on?'

'Not long. I can't find any records of this kind of an almost industrialised operation before about six months ago. It's set up to have lots of security shields. Often the girls don't speak English and the men setting her up call each other by code names which are changed every time. In each case the targeted girl is alone and the rapists have been told where to find her. It's all arranged electronically so the perpetrators can hide behind any identity they choose, or none.'

'Ugh. How did you get all this so quickly?'

'I've got a brilliant lecturer who specialises in cyber-crime and he has great contacts with various police forces because he's helped them out with stuff in the past so they're happy to co-operate over this new thing.' Anna thought of Steve and how his skills were called on by government agencies. 'He thinks I should make this the subject of my thesis and I'm more than happy to. It's horrible and it's got to be stopped.'

'Ok. Keep in touch, Briony.'

'Will do.'

Anna put her phone in her pocket and tapped gently on the steering wheel. If this was happening in London, it would be likely that the central organising website would be there although not necessarily. It could be on a mountain top in Scotland if wi-fi was accessible. It could be anywhere – even in another country. She was pleased that Briony had got hold of this for several reasons: one was that she wouldn't let go, she was a Rottweiler when roused as Anna knew from past history; another was that Anna now felt that she had an ally, potentially a hard-headed partner. Whatever it was that Dook was mixed up in, whether it was this gang-rape nightmare or something else, she would need as many allies as she could muster. She realised that the decision had been made. She was not going to let things lie. Bad things happen when good people do nothing. She knew enough to know that bad things were happening.

Mecklins' huge front doors slid open again and Faye walked out. Anna searched her face but it was expressionless. She made her way to the car coolly, got in and slammed the door shut. Only then did she turn to Anna with an ear-splitting scream of joy. 'They want me! They loved my stuff – they think the Meerkat Mugger Head Hugger may be commercial! I'm so excited I could burst! Wait, wait, I've got to tell Tash – drive, Mum, drive – Tash, I've got it! How brilliant is that? We've got to go out tonight! Wait, I'm tweeting it-'

So Anna drove away, smiling like an idiot. And it wasn't all relief about not having to find university fees. There is nothing like the excitement of finding your own passion, the place where you fit. Of course university wouldn't have been right for Faye. She would have gone through with it probably but with only half her heart and brain.

They were turning off the ring road when Anna's phone rang. She fished it out, glanced at the name, and handed it to Faye who was still foaming with excitement. 'It's Pops. Tell him your news.' Five minutes of gabble later Faye handed back the phone and passed on the message that George was taking Harry over to Diane's animal sanctuary for the day to help out with some spring cleaning and wouldn't be back for dinner.

'Drop me off at Tash's, Mum, would you? We've got to organise a night out.' Anna drove on into the city only half listening to Faye's chatter. As she parked outside Michelle's house she waited for a gap in the flow.

'Faye, I need to tell you something. There's been some threats to Harts' staff just lately and everyone is warning their families to just keep a look-out and not go anywhere on their own and –'

'Right, got it, chill.' Faye jumped out of the car and ran on her four-inch heels up the path to Tash's house. A second later the door opened and she vanished inside.

It was quiet at home and Anna set about making some lunch thoughtfully. She ought to write that silly article, that cover story. It would have to be done for Ted. It would have to at the very least *exist* to justify her time off work. Gerald would back her up, she was sure – after all, it was his idea. Just as she opened her mouth to take the first bite of a cheese sandwich her phone rang again. It was Len.

'So when's the thing? You know for your dad?'

'Er.'

'You said you'd have a welcome home, then you said not yet, so when is it?'

'Oh. I haven't arranged anything yet, Len. Sorry.'

'What about dinner this Sunday? You could do a special one.'

Anna bit back a sarcastic response. 'Ok. Good idea. We've got something else to celebrate as well. Faye's got an apprenticeship at a toy factory not far away.' There was a disapproving pause.

'You mean she's not going away?'

'Yes. Good isn't it?'

Len grunted. 'I think George likes roast beef, doesn't he? With roast potatoes and all the trimmings? That would be really nice.' Anna smiled.

'What do you think dad might like for pud?'

'You can get one of those sticky toffee puddings and some ice-cream, that would be best.'

She went back to her sandwich. It was strange to eat something at home without feeling the pressure of Bobble's adoring body against her leg – they must have taken him with them. Anna sighed, feeling both tired and tense. She could go for a walk, she could write the article, she couldn't think clearly any more. She was just going round and round in circles. Then she realised that no-one would be at home for more than a few minutes all day. Once more the enigma of Kevin's compound, as she was now calling it, came to mind. Was he involved with all this or not? She couldn't go looking for Mohsen, even if he was still in the country, she wouldn't know where to start, and she couldn't go back to Drakes after that confrontation with Dook. But, maybe she could just stroll past that caravan in the woods. After all, Kevin knew she and Kimi were friends and it was Kimi's land after all. If she bumped into him she could say she was thinking about keeping a horse of her own there and was checking out the land for rides. She was really getting very good at all this lying.

## 31

As she drove south she realised she would have to park by the pub
and go up the canal path – she couldn't very well leave her car in
Kimi's yard without asking and she didn't want to disturb the
reunion between the sisters for such a trivial reason. The thought
disturbed her - that path was not a happy place for her. But, the sun
was shining, it was early afternoon, there would be many people
around and maybe going there would lay some ghosts to rest.

When she drew in to the pub car park by the bridge it was
over half full. She crawled down to the end nearest the canal and
tucked the VW under a tree feeling a little guilty about taking up a
customer's space. Maybe she'd call in for a coffee and a little
something on the way back. The sunny canal bank was sparkling
and fresh with summer foliage flicking in the breeze and there was
still Herb Robert and Queen Anne's Lace visible among the
encroaching nettles. A canal boat chugged by with waving adults at
the back and a bored child at the front. Anna smiled and waved
back. The sky was a brilliant dome of blue and she wondered idly
why Homer described it as coppery in The Odyssey. But then he
described the sea as wine-dark as well. Was colour as subjective as
other kinds of sensory experience? It would be interesting to know
if the ancient Greeks had actually seen colour differently like people
with colour blindness do. How could that be known? She let herself
enjoy the shine of the grass as it bent in the breeze and the prettiness
of the purple vetch by the waterside.

She halted at the five-barred gate but only for a moment. She
had her cover story and knowing the owner now meant she didn't
have to be so careful about the warning notice.

A rutted track, now hard and dusty, curved up the field
towards the copse. It seemed a bit bold to just walk up it so she
climbed through a break in the hedge to approach the caravan from
an oblique angle so it would appear she had merely stumbled across
it. At this time of day Kevin should be at work, in any case. As she
got closer she saw that the enclosure was larger than she had
imagined. She slid behind a hawthorn bush to have a good look
through a gap in the fence. On one side was a low run of brick-built
pens. The caravan was set at a right-angle to these and on the
opposite side to the pens was a newly built wooden shed about the
size of a single garage. Heaped around was the clutter of stacked

wood, buckets, some tarpaulins and an old fridge. The pens looked as though they might have been built many years ago for pigs but were dilapidated and partly covered with corrugated iron weighted down with bricks. They had an unusual feature. From the back to the front where each wooden gate was bolted, every pen had a covering of the kind of mesh you get in chain-link fences. This was pegged down to the ground with hooked metal spikes at uneven intervals, probably where a soft spot could be found in the broken concrete of the yard. Was Kevin keeping birds in there? Maybe breeding peacocks or something similar for sale.

Electric cables ran from behind the caravan to the pens and to the wooden shed so she assumed the generator must be back there. There was a low hum from something but otherwise the place was silent. The only way in and out was through a solid high wooden gate which would open on to the track which led to the canal-side. Otherwise the whole compound was encircled by barbed wire wound through an assortment of fence panels, more corrugated iron, and old doors. Kevin must have the dog with him for which she was very grateful. She would have had to move away fast if it had started barking at her. There was no point in trying to get in and she was just about to give it up when she heard the sound of a vehicle coming up the track. Quickly she dropped back down trying for better concealment but in a position where she would still be able to observe most of the compound.

The gates swung open and Kevin's white van trundled in. He and another man got out and at the sight of him Anna felt a chill. He had a look of Kevin but was taller and more thick-set. Had it been him on the tow-path that night? Neither man spoke but, as though this had happened many times before, Kevin unlocked the padlocks on the pen gates and the other man backed the van up, parked and opened the back doors. Kevin then walked over to the caravan door and rapped on it once. He went back to the van and was hidden from Anna's view for a moment. The caravan door opened and a person came out. Anna had full view of her, if it really was a woman.

When she had been a librarian Anna and her colleagues had pored over a book from their medical collection which was due to be re-cycled because it was so out of date. In it were medical conditions which have not been seen in England for decades. The woman she was looking at on the steps of Kevin's caravan had sparse, coarse black hair hanging down in an unkempt rope. Her skin was open-pored and a dull putty grey and her neck and body were fat and slack and covered with layers of misshapen clothing. But the most striking features were her eyes. They were so prominent that they were almost out of their sockets on her cheeks and circled with purplish rings of flesh. In one hand she held a large plastic container of water like the one Anna had seen at the depot. She stumbled down the steps with it. Behind her came a brown dog. It was some kind of terrier cross, bunchy with muscles and its tail went between its legs when it saw Kevin. It slunk under the caravan. The woman was trying to lug the container across to the pens but it was too heavy for her and she stumbled, slopping the water on to the ground. Kevin took two strides across to her and hit her on the side of the head with such ferocity and speed that Anna almost cried out. If she had have done, her voice would have been the only sound.

Watching the scene in the yard was eerily like watching a silent film. No-one spoke. The dog did not bark. The woman did not cry out and was now painfully pushing herself up off the dirt. Kevin and the other man ignored her and started to unload the same kind of heavy crate Anna had seen Dook and Mohsen store in the back of the depot. Kevin backed into a pen bent over to get under the mesh and the other man followed holding up the other end of the crate. Then the man left and Anna could hear screws being undone and then Kevin left, moving quickly and closing the pen gate behind him and bolting it. The woman, who had gone back to the caravan, now reappeared with a freshly filled container and walked slowly down the caravan steps and across to the pens. Anna could hardly bear to look at her such was the pathos of her situation. Did she even know she was ill? Did she know that a simple medication would return her to health? How long had she been like this? It could be years for the condition to have become so desperate. And still, as the men worked moving one crate after another and the woman made repeated trips to bring water, there was no sound except the small noises of boots on grit and a bolt being pulled. A walker a few yards away would have no idea that there was anybody here. When she had finished bringing the water the woman stood watching, her arms hanging loosely by her side like a zombie awaiting command. A blackbird suddenly trilled in the bush where Anna was hiding and it rang out so loud that she jumped.

Now the men were on to another part of the process. Kevin went back to the first pen with a long pole in his hand. On the end of the pole was a spike. He unbolted the gate again and eased it open, the pole pointing into the pen. He jabbed repeatedly with it and then darted in followed by the other man. In seconds they hurried back out carrying the empty crate. The gate was secured and they moved on to the next pen.

Anna's thighs were burning as she crouched under the hawthorn. She dared not move in case one of her feet was on a twig. The silence of the whole operation unfolding in front of her was more terrifying than chatter or even curses. What had come out of those crates? Creatures that needed water and air but made no noise. Suddenly there was a sound. A phone was bleeping in the wooden shed. Still the dog didn't bark. Anna looked to see where it was and could only make out a snout poking from the darkness of the space under the caravan. Kevin immediately strode across to the shed, took out a different set of keys from his pocket and let himself in. The other man lit a cigarette and stared at the pens. In a few moments Kevin was back and without a word they finished their task. The crates were loaded back into the van and the other man got into the passenger seat. Kevin unlocked the big gates they had come in by but did not open them. He strode back to the woman and pointed at the caravan. She hobbled up the steps and went in. Then he whistled briefly, once, and the dog appeared crawling to him and fawning with terror, the whites of its eyes stark against the filthy concrete. He climbed up the steps and locked the caravan door and then made a quick movement to the dog which instantly positioned itself on the top step and crouched into submission never taking its eyes off Kevin.

Anna saw with sickening understanding that the dog, a poor prisoner itself, was not guarding the compound, it was guarding the woman. Kevin opened the gates, got into the van and drove through them. She heard the engine idling as he locked them from the outside and then they drove away. She fell forward on to her knees and gave a huge shuddering exhalation of breath. From the canal bank came the sound of voices and laughter and a plane from Birmingham Airport cruised lazily overhead, flashing silver in the sunlight. She forced herself to get up slowly and breathe calmly. Now that she was standing she could see something moving in the nearest pen but she didn't want to stay in that place a second longer. She ran back down the field and through the hedge and it was only when she was over the gate and on the path and could see a little family group approaching with two children on starter bikes that she allowed herself to breathe normally.

Poor woman, oh God, poor woman. The police needed to be told and if they didn't act she would tell Social Services, the RSPCA, anyone, anyone who could help. In a corner of a Warwickshire field there was an internment camp for a single prisoner, a slave, where atrocities were being committed. She had never been so horrified in her life as she was by this sustained, deliberate cruelty. How long had this been going on? Surely Kevin's family in the village didn't know about this? Kimi certainly didn't. She had told Anna she had never been down there and she had had the farm for over ten years. It was impossible to guess the woman's age, as sick as she was. Was she Kevin's wife? Was she his sister? Was she a kidnap victim? How on earth had this been allowed to go on?

One thing was sure. Quiet Kevin was not shy, he was a bully and worse, a sadist. The flush on his face when she saw him at Drakes the first time had not been shyness, it had been anger. If the man with him had been her attacker that night on the towpath she had had a very lucky escape. In her horror at what she had seen Anna barely considered what creatures might have been transferred to the pig pens. She strode into the pub car park and pulled her keys out of her jeans pocket. She was so angry and upset she didn't know who she would phone first. She pressed the fob to centrally unlock the car.

Instantly there was a hand across her mouth and her arms were wrenched behind her back. That smell. Tobacco and manure and engine oil. Then they were both on her and had pushed her into the back, ramming her down in the well between the seats. She found that her wrists had been taped. The car engine started and she struggled to get up until a blow to the top of her head forced her back down. She did not lose consciousness but lay very still knowing the next blow would be harder. Her heart was pounding so hard it felt as though it would burst from her chest. The car was driven fast and then took two sharp turns and braked. The passenger door was flung open and then the back one. The man appeared with a roll of duct tape and a Stanley knife in his hand. Within seconds he taped her mouth and then, throwing her around like a straw bale, he taped her ankles together. Then he pushed her back down.

'Stupid bitch,' Kevin said from the front. 'Serve you right.' He started the engine. 'You was warned but you couldn't leave it, could you?'

'Didn't think we seen you, did you?' The other man added. 'I bet them nettles stung your bum.' He spoke to Kevin. 'What we going to do with her?' Kevin started the car and backed up. 'She's seen, hasn't she? We can't let her go.'

'Shurrup a bit. I'm taking her back to the depot. We can lose the car at Brian's. He can crush it for us.'

'Are you telling Charlie?'

'Shut the fuck up. Let me think.' Kevin must have made a U turn because Anna was squeezed one way and then another. 'I'm going back for the van. I don't want to get stranded at bloody Drakes. You can drive this.'

'Ok.'

'Just leave her alone, we haven't got time for games, ok? And don't talk to her 'cos you're such a stupid fucker you'll blow it worse.' Again there were two turns and then a swift braking. 'Follow me and don't lose me, all right? We need to get there together. If that smarmy bastard's there I'll deal with him. Don't do anything – just follow me. We'll dump the car after. Let me do the talking if he's there.' The car bounced as Kevin left the driving seat and the other man moved across.

She could hear him pop open the glove compartment and rifle around. Then, unbelievably, there was Tom Waits filling the car. After a moment the man put the car into gear and drove off and after another moment he released the CD and flung it out of the window.

Down in the well of the back seat Anna's shoulder sockets were beginning to scream with pain. They had pulled back her arms too tight. But she had to think. Who was Charlie? Who was the 'smarmy' one? Could it be William – he had an upper-class accent? But is that what they meant? The man driving obeyed Kevin and did not speak. After a couple of minutes Radio 2 came on with Steve Wright's afternoon show. Anna had read books where a kidnap victim was able to tell the police how many turns to the right or left had been taken so the route could be retraced. There was no way she could do it. In any case, she knew where they were going. She was going into that black hole at the back of the depot. She wondered what the time was and whether there would be drivers about. She had left the house at about 2.30. That couldn't have been more than an hour ago and drivers didn't start arriving until 4.00. Anna's phone was in her back pocket and it now rang with the Woody Woodpecker song that Faye had loaded. Within seconds, the car had swung to the left and stopped. The front and back doors were opened in quick succession and the man reached in and tore the phone away from her so roughly that the stitching on the denim pocket tore. Then he was back in the driver seat and they were off, faster than before, presumably to catch up with Kevin.

In grabbing the phone he had jammed her head down painfully against the tubular steel of the front passenger seat where it was bolted to the floor. She tried to wriggle away from the pressure but he yelled, 'Stay still, bitch!'

Through all that had happened in the last fifteen minutes Anna felt a sense of unreality as though this was happening to someone else, or in a dream. It had been so swift, so unexpected, and the whole scene at the caravan enclosure had been so surreal that she realised she was in shock. Her brain and emotions simply couldn't process rationally what was happening. The man was switching radio stations.

'And another great day to take the kids out to the park!' the DJ was chirping. 'But don't forget our competition! Who has the silliest laugh in *your* family? Send it in to the show and you could win a night out at the Glee Club for four – and now, it's everyone's favourite Dolly Parton and Jolene.' The driver began singing along.

Anna forced herself to think. Surely they weren't planning to kill her – whatever the things were in the pens, presumably illegal and smuggled in from Felixstowe, it wouldn't be worth life-sentences in prison which killing her would bring. If they got caught. She could understand why they might want to get rid of her car, now covered with their DNA, but why not torch it? Crushing it seemed an odd choice unless that made more sense in a built-up area like south Birmingham. Her head was now ringing with pain as the movement of the car continually banged the steel support against her temples. Her arms had gone numb. Think. Think. There would be no-one at home to miss her. They all had their plans and probably Faye, coming home to get changed, wouldn't even check to see if she was there. Why should she? Ellis would come in from tennis to get ready to go climbing with Steve but again, why would he worry if she wasn't around? She could have gone to the shops or anything.

Anna realised with a sinking heart that no-one would be home until late in the evening. No-one would miss her for hours. Her phone went again and this time the driver threw it out of the window. She was relieved. That's what she had hoped he would do. She didn't want Kevin getting hold of all the numbers of the people she loved best in the world.

There was only one course of action she could take. She should be as submissive as possible. Any action or resistance on her part would bring violence. This is how it must feel, she thought, for that woman, that embodiment of misery cowering back at the caravan, for every single hour but much, much worse. With herself, desperate though she was, submission was a reasoned tactic in the hope of surviving an hour of terror. With that poor enslaved woman it was a way of staying alive through years of violation.

She breathed in through her nose and then out again since her mouth was taped. For a second she thought of Faye 'doing' her mindfulness. Lovely Faye, young and thrilled to be succeeding at what she enjoyed doing. This helped. Anna made herself think about what Faye might now be doing; going through clothes, making more calls, trying to decide how to celebrate, laughing and chatting with Tasha and no doubt speculating on the quality of young male apprentices at Mecklins. The car screeched on two wheels round a corner and Anna was thrown harder against the back of the seat. Now her head was forced under the seat. If a heavy person got in to the car her skull could be crushed. Think of Ellis. Ellis would be finishing the last few games of the afternoon before coming home. She saw him in her mind's eye, thin and gangly, the bright copper patch of hair bouncing on his head as he slammed the ball across the net. She sobbed involuntarily. Think of her dad. George, looking over his glasses at them all on poetry night, beaming with pleasure and anticipation, his quick glance selecting the right person for the right reading while Ashok pulled out of his pocket their 'vitamins' for the night.

Anna could see a half empty packet of tissues among the dust and crumbs on the floor and a leather glove she had looked everywhere for last winter. Her left knee was pressed at an unnatural angle against the hump in the seat well and the muscles and ligaments up her thigh and into her groin were feeling as though they were on fire. Harry, think of Harry. She sobbed again, unable to stop herself. Think of Steve. God.

Then the car was bouncing and she realised they must be on rough ground. Please God Kevin had not changed his mind and decided to get rid of her and the car in some staged accident. Surely they weren't that far gone? They were smugglers not murderers, weren't they?

The engine stopped. The driver got out and all was quiet for a few moments. Then the back door was pulled open and the two men dragged Anna out, banging her head again on the sill of the door. They were at the back of the depot and frightened as Anna was, she felt a moment of relief. She was becoming dizzy and it was difficult to focus her eyes but it was clear that they were going to carry her into the concealed space at the back of the depot through the door with the Yale lock.

'At least he's not here,' the man said.

'Shut up. We need to get this fucking car out of the yard before anyone comes.'

They dumped her on the floor and ran out, the door closing quietly behind them and the lock clicking shut. For a few moments she lay still, listening. She heard the van start up and then her own car's engine and in less than a minute there was silence. They had gone. At first it seemed as though she was in pitch darkness but as her eyes got used to it she saw that there was some light coming from a badly fitting frame round the door and, higher up, through small holes in the siding. Bad as it was, it could have been worse. They had not blindfolded her or hurt her beyond rough handling. She knew that her shoulder may be dislocated but it didn't hurt now and there was nothing she could do about it except try not to move too much. She had a headache to end all headaches but she didn't think she was bleeding. What time would it be? Nearly 4.00 o'clock. It would be at least four hours, probably, before anyone missed her. Then, overcome with pain and shock, she slipped out of consciousness.

When she came to she could hear the sound of lorry engines and then changes in the sounds as they manoeuvred into the depot and parked in their bays. There were voices, too, calling, and some laughter but no distinct words. Anna wondered what the material was at the back of where she was. If it was thin aluminium sheeting, she might be able to bang on it with her feet and be heard. She tried to move and a searing pain ripped down her body. Then she realised. If she did make a noise, it would be Dook who would come, not one of the drivers. She may be better off not attracting attention.

She lay still for a long time noticing that the little amount of light coming into her space was now dimming. Would Steve think to come here once he realised that she was missing? He might. But what could he do on his own? He could hardly break down the door on the chance that she was there and not out at the pub gossiping with Michelle about Faye's new job. They would try to phone her to see where she was. But people routinely don't answer their phones or leave them somewhere. Would it worry them that she wasn't at home and didn't answer her phone or would they just shrug and decide to go for fish and chips? The noise outside was dying down now, she realised. Eventually there was silence.

A musty, rank smell came from dim shapes in the prison she was in. Whatever creatures had been kept here must have urinated and defecated and the mess had not been cleaned out. She felt pressure in her own bladder. Her earlier mood of determined optimism was slipping away as the light faded. She allowed herself to realise that Kevin was possibly not going to let her go. She had not only seen him but he believed that she had seen whatever it was that he was warehousing. It could not be innocent, or even low-level criminal activity or he would have pretended he had not seen her, let her leave, and got rid of whatever it was fast. It had to be serious for him to wait for her and capture her and then get rid of her property, her car. If it was serious, then she was in trouble. After all, something had to happen to her.

A terrible thought struck her. What if they got Faye or Ellis to force her to be silent? Or, what if they took them just for revenge? Could it be that this smuggling stuff was only the tip of the ice-berg? A side-line? What if Kevin was involved with the network, part of the criminal organisation that Dook and Mohsen might be involved in? She thought about that new shed with the electric cable running to it. Was Kevin the third man? If so, he couldn't let her go, she would bring attention to the very thing he had taken so much trouble to hide. But surely, taking her was worse? Why wouldn't he have pretended not to see her and got rid of the creatures and any gear that might incriminate him? Her head ached and her whole body was sore.

A scraping noise set her heart racing. A key was turning in the lock. By now it was completely dark outside but in the glow of light from the Social Club Anna made out a silhouette in the open door.

A dark shape came towards her and then made itself shorter and fatter. 'Oh dear, dear, Mrs Ames. What a state you're in.' It was Dook crouching beside her. 'What are we going to do with you?' He took a torch out of his pocket and moved it slowly over her. She looked beyond him and saw that the door was still open but it was hopeless. She couldn't move let alone run with her ankles taped. Dook sat back on his haunches seeming to be thinking. The torch stayed on Anna. Was he gauging how frightened she was and how easy it would be to destroy her? She made no move and forced her eyes to stay steadily locked on his.

Anna's train of thought ground on to its conclusion. For reasons she only partly understood, she had had it. Ever since that evening on the tow-path she had been afraid – the steel cable tightening in her head had rarely eased. Her fears for herself, for Faye, for Ellis, even for Rhea had wound her up so tight that it was as if she had not taken a proper breath for weeks. Seeing what had been done to Nicola, to Kimi, to that poor woman in the caravan, she had been suffused with rage and fear in every particle of her mind and body. Under the ordinary doings of everyday life she had been carrying a heart constricted with barbed wire.

Now, as they gazed at each other in silence, moment after moment, the cable released and a profound peace came unexpectedly over Anna. Her thoughts stilled. She saw her fate in his large grey eyes which shone eerily in the uplight from his torch. There was no anger or violence in his expression but there was recognition of an inevitability. She was going to die. She didn't want to and Dook didn't want to kill her but he could see no other way. He saw that she had understood that. They regarded each other solemnly like lovers who knew they would have to part. She thought of Harry and Faye and Ellis. She thought of her dad and Steve. They all seemed small and far away. She blessed them silently.

He leaned forward and tore off the duct tape covering her mouth, instantly replacing it with his own hand. 'There's no-one here but if you cry out I'll punch your head in, understand, hinny?' he said softly. She nodded calmly and he released her. Again, he studied her, keeping the torch on her face. 'You shouldna' have been snooping. That mad fucker Kevin shouldna' have snatched you. But you did, and he did, so -' Dook stopped.

Then into the pause came a loud rattling noise very close by. It startled both of them. Dook froze. It went on for a minute and then stopped. Then another shape filled up the doorway. A much larger one than Dook.

'Anyone there?' it said.

Anna couldn't believe her ears. Before Dook could do or say anything she yelled as loudly as she could, 'Len! Len! It's me, Anna. Help me!' Immediately, Dook killed the light but Len had seen her and he lurched forward towards her.

'What you doing here? What's going on?' He knelt beside her.

'Watch out, Len, there's a man – ' but she saw Dook slip out of the door and away as silent as a shadow.

Len had understandably not fully grasped the situation and took the default position that he was somehow to blame. 'I was only having a whizz,' he said, sounding scared. 'Came out of the gig to cool down a bit and then I saw the light.'

'Len,' Anna said as calmly as she could, 'do you think you could get this tape off me very, very gently?'

At that moment an enormous din broke out in the yard and Len ran to the doorway. Lights beamed up in different directions and the sound of squealing brakes and shouts could be heard. 'Hey, Anna, you should see this! It's Steve! He's got that bloke and he's punching him! Woah!' Len danced from one foot to the other and made swinging movements with his own arms.

'Len, 'Anna moaned, 'could you just-'

A police siren blared, screamed and cut out. 'The police are here! Steve's got him down on the floor, he's kicking the crap out of him! Oh no, now the police have got Steve – they're pulling him off -' An ambulance siren wailed its two notes.

'Len,' Anna whispered, 'please-' And then she fainted.

# 32

When she opened her eyes there was a round chocolate face filling her vision. 'You 'wake m'dear? You just rest easy. You in hospital safe an' sound.'

'My shoulder.' Anna noticed with surprise and disapproval that she was croaking and tried to clear her throat.

'All set back. One side was out an' it will be sore but no damage done.'

'Thank you.'

'Anywhere else you hurt, darlin'?' The nurse was holding her hand and stroking it in a very soothing way. Anna tried to remember.

'My head. My head got banged about. I don't think it's bleeding.'

With great tenderness the nurse lifted strands of hair and turned Anna's head gently from one side to the other until it had all been checked. 'Some bruising, a little cut, too. I'll just fix that for you.' In a moment the cut was washed and antiseptic applied. It didn't even sting. 'Now, I'll have a word with the doctor and you may have to get your head examined.'

Anna managed a weak laugh. 'Should have been done years ago.'

The nurse snorted. 'Oh, an' your husband waiting to see you, darlin' Shall I tell him he can come in?' Harry? What? How could he have made his way to the hospital? Were all the family there?

But it was Steve who slipped in the door and stood staring at her, his eyes blazing. 'Anna!'

'Steve, what's been happening? How did you know where I was?'

He came to the bed and pulled up a chair to be as close to her as possible. He picked up her hand and held it between his two large warm ones. They were trembling slightly. 'Anna, are you ok?'

'Well, actually I feel rather nice, I feel -' And then Steve was kissing her, softly and tenderly on her lips, her eyes, her brow, kissing and kissing her and it was lovely. She couldn't have made him stop if her life depended on it. Then the tears welled up and he was kissing those and crying himself and half-lying on the bed holding her.

'I was going mad,' he said, 'I thought they'd hurt you, I would have killed them.' He looked so passionately at her that her brain stopped working and her whole body filled with the noise of her bounding heart. 'I love you, Anna, I love you so much. I can wait for ever as long as I can be with you, but I can't go on living without you.' His face was so close to hers he had gone out of focus – a blur of blue and brown and pink. He stroked her hair and her cheek. Anna closed her eyes and smiled.

After a few moments he drew away and sat back down on the chair and held her hand. 'How did you know where I was?' she asked again. Then she remembered. 'Oh God, Steve, there's a poor woman in Kevin's caravan, you've got to do something quickly! Tell the police!'

But he continued to sit and stroke her hand. 'We know all about it. We've been there.'

'How could you have done?'

'What we don't understand is how you managed to persuade Kevin's brother Darren to wear the Keruve watch. That's how we got them.' Steve smiled at her confused face. 'Let me start at the beginning. When I went to get Ellis for the climb he was a bit concerned because he'd tried to get hold of you to see if you wanted to come to the sports centre and your phone was ringing but no pick up.'

'Yes, because -'

'Let me just finish this bit. So then he remembered that the GPS Keruve watch was in the glove compartment of your car so he turned on the receiver and it was tracking movements. At first it seemed to be at Drakes, which made sense, you could be in a meeting there, but just as we were about to turn it off, we saw it go to a location which we discovered was a breaker's yard which was weird.'

'They crushed the car, but -'

'So, we kept watching and it went out to the country and seemed to end up in the middle of a field. That's when we decided there was something wrong. I made Ellis stay at home to be the contact person and I drove as near as I could along the tow-path to that location. But when I got out and walked close to it I could see it was some kind of camp or something and there was no sign of you or the car but there were men so I crept back to my car and phoned DS Iqbal, remember you gave me his number, and said you had received a threatening letter and now you and your car had disappeared.' Steve ran his spare hand across his face and through his hair. 'To be honest, Anna, I thought they might have crushed you with the car. I was desperate, but it seemed more likely they had brought you to Kevin's place so I got the police because I knew I couldn't tackle them on my own and get you away safely if you were there.' He exhaled. 'Also, I knew the police would have a hard time finding this place without me to guide them.' She could see that even remembering the anxiety he had felt had darkened his eyes.

'Does Ellis know I'm ok?'

'He was brilliant. A real hero – he liaised with everyone. Yes, he knows you're ok and the rest of the family do, they're on their way here now.'

'I was there, Steve, I was watching when they were unloading something. I didn't realise they'd seen me. They probably saw my car under the tree by the pub and looked out for me. When I went back to the car they grabbed me and tied me up. What was in those pens? What had they been smuggling?'

'Reptiles. Couple of caimen, some lizards, an iguana, turtles. Poor things, the RSPCA will be picking them up.'

'That's why -'

'Yes, that's why the heat-seeker in the helicopter didn't pick them up.'

'They're cold blooded. Of course. But the breathing you heard? Surely you couldn't have heard an alligator breathe?'

'No, it was Mohsen that was in there hiding from us. Kevin refused to use his name till the police forced him - called him 'that smarmy one' and you can see there might be a tad of resentment, Mojo being handsome, young and a magnet for girls, evil though he is. He'd gone in to feed the animals and then we came along so he just kept very still but of course he had to breathe. He didn't know I had a stethoscope, that I could hear him.'

Anna thought for a moment. 'But why would they kidnap me and crush my car just for some reptile smuggling? I mean, it's bad, of course, but they could have let me leave and then moved the animals on. It seems like a huge over-reaction.'

Steve shifted and became more animated. 'It wasn't you seeing the animals that Kevin was worried about, although Darren was. No. Kevin didn't want his smuggling discovered but he has a far worse secret that even his brother wasn't in on.'

'The shed.'

'Yes. It was amazing, Anna. The police showed me the computers he has in there.'

She remembered Dook's soft words. 'He made a mistake. Kevin. Dook told me but I didn't understand. He didn't need to take me, he could have ignored me and then quickly cleared the site. But once he had grabbed me, then Dook had no choice but to get rid of me.'

Steve shook his head from side to side. 'I can't think about that. While I was waiting outside to come in and see you, I got a call from Iqbal. Their guy has cracked the coding and exposed the dark website Kevin was operating. He hadn't the training to set it up, but Dook had from his army days. Kevin just did what Dook told him. Not just in Birmingham but in London, too. Probably there are copy-cat sites up north.' They sat silently for a moment thinking of the misery generated by these men. 'Oh, and they think some girls may have been brought in the same way the reptiles were. One of the uniformed officers found some human hair stuck in nails along the back wall of where you were. They're bringing in sniffer dogs for drugs, too.'

'God.'

'Yes. Imagine that. Being in a container for hours and hours and then that black hole and worse at the end of it.'

'All in hopes of a better life.'

'Yes.'

Anna sat up ignoring her headache. 'What about the woman? The one with chronic hypothyroidism? I saw Kevin hit her, Steve, she's being treated like a slave. No, she *is* a slave. Kimi didn't know she was there, she thought Kevin lived alone. Who is she? Is she alright?'

'Darren started gabbling as soon as he realised that Kevin had been up to something really bad in the shed. He couldn't tell us enough to try to get a lighter sentence for himself. It seems that she is Kevin's wife but he told the family that she'd gone away, left him, and they believed him, of course. What woman would want to live in a caravan in a field for years? Especially with him. He swore Darren to secrecy because he said that she was round the bend and would be locked up in a 'looney bin', to use his expression, if Darren told.'

'But that's not true. You can cure hypothyroidism.'

'I know, but I think it suited Kevin to tell both her and Darren that story.' Steve's forehead creased. 'It's not going to be a quick fix with her, I'm afraid. She's extremely traumatised and she's internalised everything negative that Kevin has told her about herself, but she is being helped by Women's Aid – they're getting her medical treatment, too.' He brightened a little. 'And that poor terrified dog has gone to Safe n Sound.'

'Oh, great. If Diane can't bring it back to happiness and health, no-one can.'

They both sat back and sighed. 'Blimey,' Anna said at last, 'What a do.'

'But we still don't know how you got Darren to wear that watch. If he hadn't put it on the whole thing wouldn't have come out. We might not have found you in time. It doesn't bear thinking about - it makes my stomach flip over. How did you do it?'

Anna was puzzled, thinking back to that painful car ride. She remembered when Darren took over the driving of her car from Kevin in the pub car park. She couldn't see anything with her face pressed into the carpet in the back seat well. Then she burst out laughing. It hurt but it felt good.

'I didn't. Tom Waits did.'

'What?'

'Darren was looking in the glove compartment while he waited for Kevin to drive off – I could hear him. He found a Tom Waits CD but he must have also found the watch. It looks expensive, doesn't it? He must have put it on his wrist. I had no idea.' She laughed again. 'We're going to have to find another CD for Harry to listen to. Darren chucked Tom out of the window after playing him for about thirty seconds!'

'Well,' said Steve after a pause. 'He's not all bad then.'

The door opened and a throng of loved faces appeared.


The next morning Anna slept late and breakfasted on her own. It was a perfect summer's day and George had flung open the kitchen windows. Two rectangles of yellow light lay across the pitted oak table. On the counter top was a sunlit heap of elderflowers, heavy headed on their slender stalks, waiting for George to turn them into cordial. Anna poured herself another mug of strong coffee and sat back with it cradled in her hands.

She realised that for the first time for weeks she had slept well. It had only been a month or so since Darren had felled her on the tow-path. So much had happened and she needed to get some kind of perspective on it. About the Draycott family she had very mixed feelings. Would they have been able to get along if the financial stakes had not been so high for them? There would have been no incentive for Frances to stay in a marriage with a man she cared nothing for, nor Charlotte for that matter to stay with William only to humiliate him. It was money that kept them welded into a dysfunctional stranglehold. If Gerald had not been forced to take on the family company perhaps he would have been much happier as an engineer. Cora wouldn't have married him but he could have been happy with someone else, maybe. Each person in the family, it seemed, was dominated by the need to control or was the victim of it. Even Richard was only following in his mother's narcissistic footsteps when he chose a partner who would, he had hoped, keep up appearances and enhance his status rather than love him. He couldn't have known that the beautiful object that was Afsoon cared little for money but would be willing to sacrifice *him* in a heartbeat for her venal son. Even Kimi had been blind to her daughter's problems believing that habitual indulgence could be a substitute for love. So many people in cages, no matter how gilded.

And then there were the cages that were not gilded. Greed could produce even more evil than wealth. Thelma, Kevin's wife, was now in a residential home being nursed back to physical health at least. She had been turning into a cretin in the proper sense of the word. Anna's heart constricted with the memory of that woman's suffering. She would go and see her. Maybe Michelle would come, too; it was she who had taught Anna about the horrible dynamics of domestic abuse, and maybe over the weeks and months they would be able to convince Thelma that she was of value, that Kevin's worldview was not everyone's, that she could love and be loved.

For women being abused by the ones they love the insults, mental and physical, bleed into the soul. They drain self-confidence and joy away and leave bewilderment and fear. In Thelma's case, add to that no money of her own, no family to support her, nowhere else to go and a debilitating illness. Fat, mad and bad he would have told her she was. Like the vicious net of exploitation and abuse falling on those frightened, hopeful girls who had the tragic misfortune to encounter the likes of Dook and Mohsen, the methods of intimidation and control in relationships are simple, too, thought Anna. Humiliation, shame, isolation and dependency enforced through common domestic terror.

Harry wandered into the kitchen from the garden and sat down at the table. Anna put out her hand but he just looked at it. 'Are you all right, love?' He frowned at her. She drew her hand back.

'Can't find my desk,' Harry said. 'Have you seen it?'

'Do you want to do some writing?'

Harry shook his head in annoyance. 'No. I need it to take things.'

Anna thought for a moment about what he had been doing. 'A wheelbarrow?'

Harry's brow cleared. 'Yes. I want a wheelbarrow.' She got up and put out her hand again.

'Let's go and see if it's in the shed.' Harry stood, towering over her, and took her hand like a child. Anna felt again the love and passion of Steve's kisses and stood, stricken, by her husband. A whirlpool of feeling engulfed her. Rage and distress at what Harry was going through, longing for the marriage that had dissolved and would never come again and a visceral desire for Steve. Impulsively, she stepped towards Harry and circled his waist with her arm. Was there anything left? Any memory trace of the countless embraces they had shared? Harry stood quietly neither rejecting her nor responding. After a moment she stepped away and smiled up at him. 'Let's go and help George, shall we?'

It was while she was in the garden that Kimi phoned. Gerald had been taken into hospital and was asking to see her. 'Marie and I are here, too,' said Kimi. 'Marie would like to meet you properly instead of at the Drake zoo.'

## 33

Gerald was in a private room tucked away from the main ward. He was hooked up to a drip, presumably to control pain, but looked serene despite his frailty. She smiled at him and he managed a hand waggle back. Marie stood up as she entered the room and stepped forward with her hand outstretched. 'I want to thank you, Anna, for finding me!' Under her breath she added, 'Before it's too late.'

'I'm so glad you came,' Anna said, 'so glad you took the initiative and didn't wait.'

Kimi unfolded herself from her seat and joined them, hugging Anna. 'Are you all right? I know about what happened at the farm. I'm still trying to get my head round it.'

'Yes, I feel the same. How's Rhea?'

'Massive attachment to her cute therapist. They say it's not a problem and she seems calmer and more, well, normal I suppose. The main thing is, she's happy there.'

'Good.'

'Dad wants to have a word so we'll go and get coffee. See you in a bit.' They went out together already conversing, the bouncing manes of dark and fair hair almost touching. Anna moved to the side of the bed where Gerald could see her more easily and pulled up a chair.

'How are you, Gerald?'

He took her hand. 'Worse in my body, better in my soul.' He grinned. 'That's probably the best way round when you're dying.'

'Marie seems lovely.'

He rested his head back on the pillow with satisfaction. 'You noticed how well they got on, her and Kimi?' Anna nodded. 'She's a vet, you know, Marie. Amazing. Specialises in horses. Incredible.' He thought for a moment. 'I'm sorry that Rhea is going through difficulties but now Kimi will have some support – she won't be dealing with it alone.'

'Have the rest of the family been in to see you?' To her surprise Gerald almost hiccupped laughing.

'Oh yes, they come. They want to know when I'll pop my clogs I expect. But when more than one or two of them are here they just bicker with each other. Do you know, I don't even care who takes over the business. What does it matter? It's so great to close my eyes and ignore them. I almost enjoy it. I have had one surprise though.'

'Mm?'

'Yes. William comes quite often. Not with the others but frequently in the evening when I'm feeling at my lowest. He seemed to know when to come. We never had much to do with each other before but he just comes and reads the paper to me or chats about sport or some funny thing that's happened. It's comforting. I appreciate it.' He looked out of the window and was silent for a moment. 'It's surprising who's there for you at the end, and who isn't.' Anna felt tears well up behind her eyes but quelled them.

'Yes, he's a good man.'

'Anyway, I wanted to see you just to see you, of course, I've grown fond of you Anna and you've been very helpful to me, but there is something else.' He felt under the pillow and produced a folded piece of paper. It was a cheque. Anna stiffened. 'I want you to have this.' She took it from him and unfolded it. It was cheque for £20,000.

She handed it back. 'That's generous of you, Gerald, and I'm happy that you feel I helped you because I am fond of you, too, but I cannot and quite frankly, don't want to, accept the money. It's against professional practice and I personally would feel uncomfortable about it.'

Gerald smiled at her, his skin already waxy she noticed sadly. 'I knew you'd say that. I talked to Ted and he said it's fine by him but he also told me a little more about your circumstances.' Did he, indeed. Anna felt irritation rise within her but tried not to show it. 'Money can cause all kinds of problems, Anna, but it can also help. This is not for you, I knew you wouldn't accept it for yourself, it's for Harry – when the time comes.' To her astonishment Anna instantly burst into tears. Gerald patted her hand. 'There will come a time, quite soon maybe, when your father will not be able to manage on his own, but with some help bought in you'll be able to keep Harry at home for as long as possible. Maybe to the end. Let me do that for you, Anna. You've helped to make my end-time as good as it can be. Let me do the same for Harry.'

Anna dropped her head on to Gerald's bed and wept silently for some minutes while he laid his hand on her hair like a blessing. She hadn't fully realised how deeply she had been worrying about exactly this. All other money worries were nothing compared with it. What would they do when Harry needed more help than George could give and their budget was stretched to its limit? When she had stopped crying she dried her eyes, took the cheque and kissed Gerald on the cheek. He was tired and she stood up to go as Kimi and Marie came back.

At the door she stopped for a moment and smiled at him. 'Goodbye Gerald,' she said, 'Don't forget your sextant.'

For reasons Anna could not fathom, Faye and Ellis had decided to take charge of the delayed 'welcome home' Sunday dinner. It wasn't that they were, individually, incapable of cooking, it was the idea of them working as a team that was alarming. Moreover, they had insisted that everyone go out and not return until 1.00. Len was ordered to appear at that hour, too.

So they piled into Steve's car and went off to pick up Joan. She got in the back, wedged beside Alice, and Bobble excitedly stood on them with his sharp claws and slobbered in their faces. His tail beat a tattoo on the neck-rest of the driving seat. They drove to Safe 'n Sound. Diane would bring George back in her own car so the return trip would be calmer. Harry was in the front with Steve. He opened the glove compartment and began shuffling things around. Steve winked at Anna in the rear-view mirror. Then Harry took everything out and laid it on the floor by his feet. Steve switched on the radio and punched in Radio 3 but it was something by Phillip Glass and Harry became agitated. Steve switched to Radio 2 and the golden tones of Ray Charles filled the car so Harry relaxed and sat back.

It was good to be at the animal sanctuary on this glorious morning. Good to be away from traffic and the city. The field next to the farm was thick with dandelions and daisies and Alice immediately ran to it and scrambled over the fence. She was becoming adventurous. No-one seeing her now would recognise the fragile creature Anna had met lying so still on her hospital bed. Anna looked quickly round the paddock while Steve re-parked. There was a Shetland pony in the far corner but it was showing no interest in Alice and in any case was well used to being petted by children. To be on the safe side Anna climbed the fence, too, and hovered behind Alice as she picked the bright yellow flowers.

'Sit there!' Alice ordered. Anna sat. 'Make me train.'

'Chain,' Anna corrected smiling and started piercing the first dandelion stem with her fingernail. 'And what's the magic word?'

Alice looked mulish but when Anna stopped what she was doing and raised her eyebrows, said, 'Pees.'

'Good girl.' As she was working, Anna glanced back to the building and saw that the group had sat down at a wooden picnic table by the office door and Diane was lurching out with a tray of mugs and a battered tin. She waved a mug at Anna. 'Here you are, darling.' Anna showed Alice the crown she had made and then placed it on her head. 'Shall we show the others?' She stood up. Alice nodded and set off across the field so fast that Anna had to run to catch up with her and swing her over the fence.

'So you see,' George was saying as they approached, 'each ship has its own feel, its own personality. The crew become fond of certain ships but don't want to sail on others. It seems irrational but it isn't. We felt it, didn't we, that our ship was a kindly one?' Diane nodded, indulging George's whimsy.

'Despite keeping you awake night after night?'

'We would have got used to it eventually. It wasn't her fault.'

Steve's phone went and he got up and moved away a few paces. Anna kept an eye on him and noticed that he was listening intently and then seemed shocked. He finished the call, glanced at Anna, and sat down again at the table so it was not anything he felt able to share with the group. After they had chatted for a while Harry got up to stretch his legs and Alice, bored by all the talking, skipped off to look around. Steve immediately stood up and went after her.

'How are you doing, dear?' Diane asked Anna. 'We heard what happened. You were very brave.'

'I was very lucky,' Anna said.

'You can't believe it, can you?' said Joan. 'We know such things go on but it comes as a shock when it's happening where you live and people you know are caught up in it.'

'How is that poor dog?' Anna asked.

'I'll show you in a minute. He's still terrified, of course. That yard and the caravan were all he knew I expect so now, from his point of view, he doesn't even have that. It will take a while for him to trust anyone but he's stopped trembling and he's eating well and we'll just have to hope for the best. We'll never let him be homed out. He'll stay here and maybe in time he can join the other dogs.'

'The strange thing is,' Anna said, 'that Kevin was really great with the horses. They loved him. They would snicker when he came near and rub their noses against his shoulder.'

'Mm. People aren't easy to understand, are they? Give me animals any day, present company excepted, of course,' Diane laughed. She stood up stiffly and straightened her back. 'I just need to sort some things out before we come over to yours.'

'I'll help,' said Joan.

Anna stood, too, and tested her shoulder by rolling it back. It was still sore. She strolled round the side of the building following the direction that Harry and Alice had taken to the small barn where hay and straw were stored. The sight that met her eyes made her smile.

A few loosened bales of hay had spilled on to the floor and Harry was asleep on them. He was lying full length on his back with his ankles crossed and his arms folded and a smile of pure contentment on his face. Anna had almost forgotten how curly and luxurious his eyelashes were. Faye's lashes. Alice was frowning with concentration on her task. Her fine silver hair lifted and blew out around her head and her little dungarees were brown with dust on the knees. She had dismantled her crown and was placing the flowers on Harry laying one carefully down and then, for a second, scrutinising the effect before she placed the next one. He had several in his hair and a couple set between his fingers. Anna sensed a movement and saw Steve to her right in the shadows, grinning. He lifted his phone briefly to indicate he had taken a photo.

But Anna didn't want to have a photograph. She wanted to let this image sink into her memory so deep that she would never need one. Harry appeared as he had been when he was well and strong – long and lean, his hair gleaming chestnut in the sun, his handsome, intelligent face composed and at peace as the shadows from little Alice's efforts flickered over him. The dandelions studded his body with bright yellow as though he lay on a bier. His interlaced fingers were so familiar to her that she almost couldn't bear it. She could nearly believe he would wake and laugh at the joke he had been playing on them for so long and she would see again the bright gleam of mischief in his green eyes and feel him stoop to lift her and pull her into his arms laughing at her amazement. She stood still struggling to contain her emotions. Die now, she willed him fiercely, die now like this.

Alice looked up at her and waved a small arm. 'More flows, Anna,' she ordered, 'get more flows.'

Anna blinked and smiled. 'Alice, you need to say please if you want someone to help you.'

Alice waggled her fingers in admonishment. 'Not Alice. Lisha. Pees, pees, pees, Anna.' Anna was glad of an excuse to turn away and have something to do. As she stooped to pick more dandelions, Steve was beside her.

'All right?'

'Yes, of course. Alice is having fun, isn't she?' She didn't want to share that moment even with Steve. The urgency and clarity of her wish had shocked her. 'Was your call from anyone to do with Kevin and all that?'

'Yes, it was. It was Iqbal. You're not going to believe this, Anna. You know that police officer you didn't like who gave you a hard time over not calling the police for Nicola?'

'Griffiths, yes. Why?'

'He's one of them. He's one of the network. There are others too.'

'What, an organiser?'

'No, not that. A rape would be planned when he was the duty officer and if a call for help came in he would just, well, not hurry to respond. Sometimes he would not hurry for an hour. He'd get his cut if he managed it. They were beginning to see a pattern at the station so they weren't surprised when his name came up.'

Anna remembered something from when Kevin and Darren had been talking. 'Is his first name Charles or Charlie?'

'Yes!' Steve looked amazed. 'How could you know that?'

'It's one of my superpowers,' said Anna.

## 34

Half an hour later they were on their way back to Anna's house. 'Don't come home yet!' Faye had wailed on the phone, but they were all getting hungry. 'We may need a Plan B,' Anna told Steve.

They were not allowed in the kitchen but told firmly to stay in the living room. Len arrived and joined them, complaining. For twenty minutes or so they chatted about recent sensational events and congratulated Len yet again on his fortuitous choice of urinal that night at the depot but then conversation faltered. It was now 2.30 and there were seven hungry people becoming more and more depressed and rebellious. Alice blurted out that her stomach hurt and Steve came to a decision. 'Come on, love, let's go home and get a sandwich.' He swooped her up. A frisson of envy swept the room.

'Need any help?' Joan offered hopefully.

'What have you got?' Len asked.

Shouting came from the kitchen followed by a crash and yelling. Steve looked round at everyone. 'All right, let's do this. In two's, and there and back as quick as possible, ok? I've got cheese, tomato, don't eat the ham that's for Alice's tea, and peanut butter. Oldest and youngest first, ok? Sorry, Anna.' George and Diane shot off behind Steve and Alice.

'I haven't even had my breakfast,' groaned Len. 'It's not fair. That daughter of yours, Sis, is a pain in the bum.' Anna noted that he had had a shower and washed his hair in preparation for the feast so it was understandable that he would be feeling put out.

'You mean your niece?'

'Half-niece.'

'Just a minute!' Joan sat bolt upright and grabbed her bag. She unclasped it and delved inside. 'I thought so! Here, let's share this.' One quarter of a double Twix didn't go far but it was most welcome. Joan hid the wrapper. George and Diane appeared, breathless. Diane had hiccups. They motioned Anna and Joan to go with Harry but Anna told Len to go. 'Your need is greater than mine,' she said, 'but I'm only doing this because you saved my life. We're even after this!' Len's bulky form and Joan's tiny one disappeared down the drive at speed. Harry could not be persuaded to go. 'What's going on in the kitchen?' George asked after he'd got his breath back. 'How are they doing?'

'I had a quick look but they weren't there. Will you look, Dad?'

George returned a minute later. 'They're both there and they say it will only be a couple of minutes. We'll have to make up a tale about the others being down at Steve's.'

'You can do that now you're an old sea-dog.'

Thirty minutes later Diane and Harry were asleep in front of a DVD and Len and Joan had returned. 'Go on, then,' Len said. 'He's made you a cheese and pickle sandwich.'

At 4.10 they were all back in the living room and Alice had joined the sleepers. Anna was doing a crossword puzzle with Joan and wondering whether the insurance company would pay out for a car being hi-jacked and crushed and Len was telling Steve about how he should tackle men like Dook in future. Faye threw open the living room door, a radiant smile on her face. 'Dinner is served,' she announced.

They all staggered to their feet except Alice who was allowed to sleep on since it was almost her tea-time and took their places at the kitchen table. Faye placed a large casserole dish in the middle and said, 'We decided to be more innovative than just having the same old roast beef.' Len groaned. 'This is an original blend of what was it?' She turned to Ellis.

'Specialities de cuisine from around the world.'

'That's it. Served with–'

'Pommes de terre grown in our very own English garden.'

'I hope you tied the sack back up properly,' said George.

Brown goo with chunks in it was ladled out on to each plate. Everyone reluctantly picked up their knives and forks. 'What happened to the roast beef?' said Len.

'Don't ask.' Faye tossed back a tendril. 'You'll love this. It's our own recipe.'

Anna gingerly picked out a lump and put it in her mouth. Everyone else was doing the same and looking thoughtful. Harry was eating steadily with no apparent ill effects. Bobble waited anxiously to be noticed like a boy at his first game.

'So let me get this right,' George said finally. 'You've emptied every tin in the cupboard into the saucepan except, I hope to goodness, Bobble's food and put in a generous dash of most of the spices we possess.'

'Possibly,' said Ellis. 'But it's a bold taste, isn't it? What Masterchef would call courageous, I think.'

'I'm getting baked beans with a hint of aloo sag and possibly an aftertaste of spam,' Joan said.

'Hm,' said Steve, 'The diced gherkins are an idiosyncratic touch but yes, I think that works in the mouth.'

'I think I'd rather have had roast beef,' said Len, 'and don't tell me you've stuffed up the sticky toffee pudding. If you have, I'm leaving.'

Faye regarded him good-naturedly. 'Tempting though that is, the sticky toffee pudding as requested will be cooked to perfection in what, Ellis?'

'Three minutes,' said Ellis reading the package and opening the microwave door. They high-fived each other as the appliance whirred.

After dinner was cleared away and everyone except the family had gone home, George and Anna went for a short walk with Bobble to the park. The evening was as glorious as the day had been and they turned their faces up to a salmon and purple striped sky. They strolled to the bench by the playground and sat down. Bobble was allowed off his lead and ran happily round in circles, sniffing.

'Are you all right, Annie-get-your-gun?' George asked. 'You've had a bit of a time, haven't you, what with one thing and another.'

She leaned back on the seat and took a deep breath. 'I'm still a bit churned up,' she admitted, 'but it's ok. Actually, Dad, I had a moment when I was a prisoner that I really thought I was going to die. I don't mean I was frightened that I would. I thought it was a certainty. But it was calm. In a way it was peaceful. Hard to explain but it's given me a kind of new base-line if you know what I mean?'

'A new sense of perspective?'

'Mm. It was a feeling almost of relief. That death was nothing to be afraid of.'

'I think I understand.' They were quiet for a moment.

'It's good that the man on the tow-path turned out to be Darren.'

'Why?'

'Mainly I know now who it was, you know, the unknown monster is usually worse, but also, well, he's not a monster, he's just sort of sad. I'm not making excuses for him but the police said his dad was horrible to the boys – you know, taking it out on them for being a waste of space himself. I'm more upset by Kevin's coldness and cruelty. And Frances. It was so calculated. I feel sorry for Gerald being punished all those years.'

George picked up her hand and held it. 'You've not just been at the sticky end of all this, you've been one of the angels,' he said. 'I'm proud of you, love.'

They sat silently on the bench watching the sun dip over the horizon and the sky turn to flame and gold. Bobble gave up his game and came to sit by them. Every now and then groups and families made their way home in the dusk along the path talking quietly. Eventually they got up, George clipped on Bobble's lead, and they turned for home.

'Just one more thing, and if I'm intruding, I'm sorry,' George said. 'I know how much you love Harry, Anna, but that doesn't mean that you can't love Steve, too.'

Anna should have known that he had been observing everything. 'I don't know, Dad. I just don't know.' She linked her arm with his as they walked along the familiar street.

When they turned into their drive they could see the lamps were lit in the living room and hear a dull deep beat of music from Faye's bedroom. They stopped and savoured the moment before opening the door and ushering each other in.

## Thanks

I am grateful to the Alice Paul House in Cincinnati for the work it does and the comradeship of the staff and residents I worked with there, despite it revealing to me a world of domestic terrorism I had only dimly glimpsed before. Catharine Stevens has been a very knowledgeable resource for genealogical research which I appreciate greatly. Her breadth of expertise is truly impressive. Any idiocies in this area are my own. I am also deeply grateful to Terry Quinn and others who read the manuscripts and who gave helpful feedback. My sons, John and Daniel, have been, as always, interested and encouraging which keeps me keeping on.

Geraldine Wall was born in the UK but lived for many years in the USA where she moved with her family. She worked in a refuge for abused women and taught in colleges there and also in the Cayman Islands before moving back to Birmingham where she now lives.

Email: geraldine.wall@blueyonder.co.uk

42713710R00174

Printed in Poland
by Amazon Fulfillment
Poland Sp. z o.o., Wrocław